OF THE BLACK WING

TRISTAN GRAY

Previous versions of the stories within this book have been published separately, online, in 2021, 2023 and 2024. This full collection contains revised editions of all six stories.

First published in print and online in 2024 by Tristan Gray

1

Copyright © Tristan Gray, 2024

The right of Tristan Gray to be identified as the author of this work has been asserted by him/them in accordance with the Copyright, Designs and Patents Act 1988

ISBN 978-1-80-517891-0

Typeset in EB Garamond

Printed and bound in the UK by Clays Ltd

CONTRIBUTORS

Author – Tristan Gray
Cover artist – Syd Mills
Cover designer – Morag Hannah
Development editors – Margaret Kingsbury and April Jones (Salt and Sage Books)
Scots editor and proofreader – Gillian Hamnett (Dark Sky Pages)
Gaelic editor – Mara Livingstone-McPhail
Beta reader and proofreader – Matthew King

CONTENTS

CONTRIBUTORS	v
MAP OF THE SEANN ÀITE	ix
THE WORLD OF THE SEANN ÀITE	xi
WHISPERS TO A CROW	1
NAMES OF THE DEAD	35
A GIFT OF THE SEA	75
THE WOVEN THREAD	117
EYES OF GOLD	173
THE RED RAVEN	229
ACKNOWLEDGEMENTS	285
LANGUAGE NOTES AND GLOSSARY	287
ABOUT THE AUTHOR	293

THE WORLD OF THE SEANN ÀITE
The characters, locations, languages, peoples and beliefs depicted in these stories

Ahar: Raiding captain from the far south with a love of languages and tall tales.
Àirde Sgreamhail: The screaming cliffs. Have claimed many sailors in their time.
Álfar: Sjøfolk word for fey or elves.
Alwealda: the God the Àrdish.
An Taibhse Ùine: The Ghost of Time.
Annis: Àrdish raider in the employ of Eònan.
Aodann Òir: A golden face. Tied to the strands of fate; grants wishes to be freed.
Àrdish: Southern peoples rapidly settling across The Seann Àite with their language.
Artrí: A mythical warrior king of the south.
Baobhan Sìth: Fey who charm people to feed on their blood.
Beinn Mathan: Bear Mountain.
Brianan: Experienced Fili in the employ of Eònan.
Caer: 'Fortress' in one of the southern tongues.
Caerdrich: An ancient blade with a will of their own.
Caitlin: Old remnant of the Sciathán Dubh.
Cànan: Language of the people of The Seann Àite.
Canmarr: One of the Àrdish/ Daoine kingdoms of The Seann Àite.
Caoineag: A weeping spirit who speaks the names of the dead to herald their passing.
Ceasg: An ancient and powerful fey ruler of the sea.
Cernos: An old Daoine god of forests.
Cirein-cròin: A gigantic sea beast famed for feasting upon whales.
Cuthac the Seer: An old Daoine god of prophesy.
Dallahan Sea: A small sea scattered with islands off the coast of The Seann Àite.
Dìleas: Fiadh's horse.

Daoine: The people of The Seann Àite.
Daoine Sìth: The fey people of The Seann Àite.
Dun Caraich: An Àrdish/ Daoine fortress town.
Einherjar: An immortal army of the dead in Sjøfolk myth.
Eirian Cleddyf Llachar: The bright blade. Southern warrior god of the Daoine.
Elisedd: Lover of Eirian Cleddyf Llachar.
Eònan: The Daoine Rìgh of Ghav Rhien.
Fáidh bhean: Prophetess.
Fèinne: A Daoine warband.
Fearann Eeile: The realm of the Daoine gods.
Fey: Beings of magic who once shared the world with humanity.
Fiadh: The Crow, remnant of the Sciathán Dubh.
Fili: Keepers of tales, lore, and poetry of the Daoine culture.
Filidhean: Plural of fili.
Formori: Ancient giants who battled the Daoine gods.
Gaes: A sacred oath or pact.
Ghav Rhien: Daoine island town off the coast of The Seann Àite.
Giant's Fall: A great staircase carved into the side of Beinn Mathan.
Glaistig: Fey who tend to the crops and nature around humanity.
Hengist: Sjøfolk raider in the employ of Ahar.
High Chalice: Citadel of the religion of Alwealda in The Seann Àite.
Horn of the Deeps: Ancient relic of a far-flung culture.
Housecarl: Person guard of lords of the Sjøfolk and Àrdish.
Jarl Vestamr: Sjøfolk lord who has conquered many of the isles.
Kempe Fell: Daoine port town on the coast of The Seann Àite.
Kobold-kin: Sjøfolk term for an Aodann Òir. Creatures of the earth.
Làmfada: Long of arm. Southern god of light of the Daoine.
Lance of the Dawn: Powerful spear wielded by the Tyra of the Sgiath Athar.
Lot: Mysterious god who schemed against those of the Daoine and Sjøfolk.
Merrow: Creatures of the sea who lure sailors to their deaths with song.
Norns: Sjøfolk keepers of fate.
Oeric: Foreman in The Three Willows.

Othair: The father of the gods of the Sjøfolk.
Red Queen of the Eilean Fitheach: The Queen of the Raven Isle.
Rìgh: Daoine title for a lord.
Rìaghan: Goddess of fate of the Daoine.
Rian: Àrdish boy picked up by Ahar's raiders.
Sæunn: Sjøfolk ruler of Kempe Fell installed by Jarl Vestamr.
Samhuinn: Daoine festival marking the beginning of winter.
Sciathán Dubh: 'The black wing'. Order of fey in service to The Rìaghan.
Seanadh: festival of the old gods
The Seann Àite: 'The old place'. Homeland of the Daoine.
Seiðr: A ritualistic magic of the Sjøfolk.
Sgiath Athar: Mythical order of warriors in service to Othair.
Sìd: Fey mounds of the Daoine Sìth. Portals to Fearann Eeile.
Sjøfolk: Sea peoples who have conquered the coast of The Seann Àite.
Sjøtunge: Language of the Sjøfolk.
Signe Grímsdóttir: Previous Sjøfolk ruler of Kempe Fell.
Skysted: Northern island fortress of the Sjøfolk.
Svana: Sjøfolk first hand in service to Ahar.
Tech Duinn: House of the dark one. Afterlife of the Daoine.
The Three Willows: Àrdish settler village within The Seann Àite.
Tur Eumor: Ruins that were once the home of the Sciathán Dubh.
Tur Pailt: Daoine trading town on the coast of The Seann Àite.
Tyra of the Sgiath Athar: Fearsome legendary warrior of Othair.
Völva: Sjøfolk practitioners of Seidr.
Wærmund: Àrdish priest of Alwealda in Three Willows.

A note to the reader

Many of the words above, and some of those contained in this book, are either directly taken from, or have been inspired by, Scots and Gaelic. Throughout these stories, you may find sections that are tricky to understand. Some of the dialogue is written in Scots – a language spoken across much of Scotland.

I introduced Scots and Gaelic into my writing because it was important to me to recognise the culture that has inspired so much of the mythology and worlds of these stories. Scots is experiencing a revival in Scotland, and playing my small part to support that feels like a fitting acknowledgement of its role in my work.

The Scots dialogue has been crafted by Scots language consultant, Gillian Hamnett. It's a mixture of Scots words – with largely standardised spellings – and English words, so that the dialogue is accessible to all readers. Many of the Scots words will appear similar to their English counterparts and are spelled with phonetic reference to the accent they represent. You might notice that some words, which otherwise appear with Scots' spellings, appear in English instead. This is to convey emphasis or switches in register used by characters, depending on the context they are speaking in, and to whom they are speaking.

A glossary has been provided by Gillian for translation of all the non-standard English words, to further assist with this. Her work on this book has been invaluable, and without it the words of characters like Annis, Oeric, Hengist and Rian simply would not exist.

I encourage you to learn as you read.

CALL OF THE BLACK WING

WHISPERS TO A CROW

A lonely light shone in the darkness, a single candle-lit lantern swinging from the tavern's door through the fog. A single beaten path led to its door, far from the well-travelled road. This was no place for travellers. There was no stable to shelter her steed, nor a sign to announce some alliterative name that waifs would remember and pass on to their fellows in other taverns along the way.

But this *was* the place. She paused and unfurled the message that had stayed clenched in her fist for so many miles, a crude diagram and a cruder attempt at spelling out a name not in the tongue of the message's author: Wærmund. This place, a final refuge for those who had lost their home, too far for any but the desperate to travel to, where only an empty purse could make the journey worthwhile.

She dismounted and knotted Dìleas' reins around the sturdiest post of the dilapidated fence. With her cloak pulled close against the bite of the night's wind, she walked to the door and gave it a push. The wood lurched free of her palm to slam open, the wind coursing through to sweep up the curses and grumbles of nearby patrons.

She hauled the door shut with squeals of complaint from its hinges, but it had been closed barely a moment before the eyes of the room had moved on. To cards, to coins, to mead and beer. Anything but the black-clad newcomer who'd brought in the autumn chill.

A pall had fallen upon this place. No laughter between comrades in from the fields. No brazen bets and sordid tales ringing between the rafters. Two dozen men sat in silence boded well for no one.

There was one who caught her attention, however. A coin turned over in one palm, the other's fingers drumming away the time. Someone waiting for something in a room of many waiting for nothing.

His eyes were on her when she sat across from him, the coin abruptly halting its journey across his knuckles. His stare quickly ran along her blades, the longsword across her back and the hilts of knives strapped to her side.

The few about him muttered and whispered to one another as they fixed eyes upon her. One made the sign of their god across his chest, but the man before her shushed them. "Enough, it's ma coin, it's ma business whit Ah dae wi it," he snapped at them. "Youse do wi yours how ye choose."

"The Craw?" he said to her, turning and looking her up and down with a barely concealed sneer. "Ye dinnae look lik whit Ah expected frae a Craw."

"What did you expect?" Her Àrdish was learned from old books rather than the tongue of the north, but she spoke it well enough.

He shrugged. "Ah dinnae ken. Big black eyes, mebbe some feathers pokin oot frae yer tunic. A necklace o beaked skulls aboot yer neck? No just a wee lass wi eerie eyes, that's fur sure."

It wasn't exactly the cry for help she had been expecting, but nor did it drip with the open contempt she was so used to in the south.

"You called for a Crow, and you promised some coin. I'm afraid you'll be waiting for another to sweep in on feathered wings," she said, her hands joined at the thumb in a weak imitation. "So how about you explain to this Crow what kind of creature you have at hand, now?" The words came with a smile dimpling her cheeks.

The smile was not reciprocated. The contempt was there, sure enough, clear on the faces of the men turning their backs about him.

"No yin, but mony, Craw. Ye can hear them in the nicht, the bayin ae a score ae hounds, a monster sent by the deevil ready tae snatch us awa." His eyes dropped now; it was easier to speak to a stranger if you pretended it was something else. The hand not preoccupied with the coin was now held tight around the wooden pendant hanging from his neck, his knuckles white.

He continued, "It aw stertit wi the eve ae summer. It wis jist yin, first. Ye ken how it goes, Craw. A wee yin faws intae some pairt they cannae be found, a parent hushes up a mishap, tries tae hinder gossip ae an ailing that cuid spread. But then anither, an anither."

"Ye lose a few yins. Happens, no township goes withoot a few bairns lost wi the changing ae the seasons. But no a dozen. No in yin summer wi no track or trail ae the lost."

She felt a chill then, the weight that hung over the tavern starting to manifest with every detail spoken. There were no smiles now.

His hands were wrapped over one another now, sequestering the coin away from her gaze. There was a mark on one finger, a divot where the flesh had been compressed by a band wrapped around it for many years. He had lost someone too, this foreman, though it would have been many winters ago.

"Oor priest telt us no tae fret, that a guid harvest wid come if we prayed an cleansed oorselves, that some ae us had sinned an The Lord Most High had led the pure awa. Then more went missin. Some ae us stopped listenin in time, Lord save their souls. They accused the faither ae lyin tae them, something tae dae wi his servant."

His words came fiercer now, the words spat forth. "A veil ae sorrow fell oan the Willows. Too mony gone, too mony angry. He left us, he stopped answerin the howls ae grief at his door, the bastart! He aye promised us the harvest, but the harvest fell soor. The rot claimed it, it claimed some ae ma men, tae. We left him in his place ae faith surrounded by nocht but death."

"This isn't your town?" she said, hands flat between them.

"It's naebody's toon. Jist a place between places."

A place between places for a Crow with no place to go. It has a poetry to it, she thought.

"You mentioned there were accusations about the priest's servant," she said, hands open. "Why? Seems an unlikely target for the grief of lost children."

The response came with a sneer. "She wisnae richt, that yin. Arrivin withoot warnin wi the winter snaws, no wi yin ae us. She didnae speak wi us, didnae share oor food or in oor services. She seemed no tae pray or tak the bread, strange fur a priest's servant, ye ken? She wisnae richt, wisnae ae the faith. It wisnae richt fur a priest tae keep such company."

"You believe he was breaking his vows?"

"Ah believe he'd been led astray. Ah cast nae judgement oan a servant ae the Lord."

He might believe that, even if the gods saw through it.

One of his companions tapped him on the shoulder and leaned in to whisper into his ear. She threaded her fingers together on the table. This kind of thing wasn't new to Fiadh. Especially down here in the Lowlands; a town would deliberate when help didn't come from a lord or temple, and settle on hiring a Crow. But they didn't want to do it, it was never their first resort, and the moment they came to discuss whatever magics plagued them, real or imagined, some had second thoughts.

Every single time they began this frantic aggressive whispering to one another, discussing the wisdom of having 'one of them' about when they had enough trouble already. She caught the foreman's name, Oeric, and discerned some disagreement over pointing a Crow towards a temple.

Fiadh wished they'd gotten this discussion over and done with before she sat just across from them.

The second farmer glanced up to see her eyes still on them and snapped, "whit's that Craw? Huv ye got the hearin ae a hoolet an aw?"

"Well, no, but you are barely two yards from my head, so speak your words to me directly. If you do not trust me to get the job done, then do not put out a sign for a Crow. Give me your task, or tell me to go, your choice. But if I'm staying, I'm going to need to know what happened to your priest, and his name."

She waited as they flitted their eyes back and forth from her to one another, but their foreman did not leave the silence long before speaking.

"Faither Wærmund." She stilled her face at the name. He was the one, though it would be best that they did not know she recognised the name. "Still boarded up in the temple, for aw Ah ken. Surroonded by nocht but the rot. Me an ma lads are here ti the month's end. The Ealdorman at Dun Caraich husnae deigned tae bless us wi his ain; the Faither's ain folk up in the High Chalice willnae answer, sae we're left tae pit notice oot fur a Craw. Pray that this is ower afore Seanadh twa morrows hence, afore the slaugh taks whit's left frae us."

"Slaugh?" The restless dead who legends told would flock from the west in the winter months to steal away those who might leave a path for them open. The Seanadh was a festival of the old gods meant to keep them at bay; it seems the priest wasn't particularly good at the job he was appointed for.

The man grumbled into his drink. "Aye, Ah'm a follower ae the Lord, it's true, but ye dinnae go messin wi auld powers oan their festival days. It's asking fur trouble. We mak oor offerings as it bodes us weel."

This wasn't much to go on, apart from misbegotten fears about rituals they didn't understand and scare stories about undead hosts and questing beasts. Missing children, rot in the crop, a mysterious new stranger in the temple? Could it be a witch? Some kind of carrier of wasting spirits?

"Your Seanadh, where do you make your offerings?"

The man grunted and twisted his face in surprise, while one of his companions turned and almost spat his words across the table.

"Whit business is it ae yours, witch? An you here oan behalf ae the Order, an aw? Come tae dig oot petty heracies an prey upon good men an add the chains ae the High Chalice tae oor hurt?"

"Shut it!" The foreman's hand slammed down loud enough that people across the tavern jumped in their seats, the clap leaving a silence hanging as the two men glared at one another barely a foot apart.

"Your Seanadh, where is it?"

He grumbled as he turned back to her, the mutterings on other tables returning. "The auld wood, whit's left ae it. The Order cut a path through tae the Chalice but there's still a pairt fur the auld gods deep within it, far frae the pilgrimage road. But we paid oor dues, we gave whit's been asked ae us even efter the Order's temple wis built. That's oor way. We paid oor way."

Maybe they did. But for this village, at least, it seemed additional payment had been claimed.

He continued, mumbling down into the tankard clasped in both hands. "Ma grandfaither used tae say that the payment wis fur oor patron. The fox ae the Willows, he cawed it. It kept a watch ower us, an in return, we kept its Willows. Long gone noo, those trees. Fell alang wi the orchard wi the path frae the Sooth."

The Order and the road had been here for years. Why would the keepers of the wood abandon this township to such an intrusion by child-snatching creatures now?

He didn't leave her to her thoughts for long, looking up and meeting her eyes directly for the first time. "Whit's yer name, Craw?" He said, leaning in a little. "No that Ah'd miss yon eyes ae yours if ye returned. Ye'll be back, right? Afore the coming ae the Seanadh?"

She was careful not to let the question settle as her eyes rested on the coin she couldn't see but knew was clasped in his hands.

"My name is Fiadh. Where is your township?"

"It's the Three Willows, mebbe a nicht's ride tae the north if ye came by saddle." He paused for a moment, looking at her more intently than before, "Dae they aw look like ye, Fiadh? Aw the Craws? Dae they aw huv yon silvered eyes?"

She stood then, turning from his gaze, "They do, Oeric. Don't spend that coin, I'll return for it when the deed is done."

***

The stonework was finely crafted, beautiful, even, in its own way. Kneeling figures carved in solemn rows gazed adoringly at the figure at the head of the archway. Or, at least, where the figure should have stood. The keystone of the arch had been ripped free and torn through the shattered remnants of the door below it. She could still pick out the pieces, arms raised aloft here, sunbeams radiating outwards there.

No mere farmhand or priest is strong enough for such destruction. Even if the men of the Willows are the superstitious kind to take their anger out on stone. "Still boarded up", they had claimed back in the tavern. Whatever had torn its way through had done so long after the villagers had departed. Alone, in this still village, only strange in its emptiness and silence under the cutting wind, this temple had been disturbed.

The grass around the entrance had been tended meticulously as if every blade had been trimmed to the perfect length to flatter the temple that stood within it. The bushes were the same, kept shapely in a way that seemed almost vain for such a structure.

She stepped across the boundary, flinching as she always did to enter the hallowed places of another, and cast her gaze about the shadowed hall.

The arched interior was held aloft by wooden pillars, small, like the township that it had served. Its roof was timber, not thatch, and supported by walls of stone. The faithful had worked hard to build this place, an effort that had not prevented whatever creature had smashed aside the benches in its entrance.

The wooden benches had been scattered, the hall itself a mess of shattered woodwork, splinters and spans littered and piled high against the walls. She had seen this kind of destruction before, in too many places. Places of faith dashed by the fury of those who took insult at the proud symbols at their door or, as was so often the case in this borderland between the old and the new, had themselves been laid low and driven out by the very people who erected these stones.

Her home had been one of these places, once.

She could smell it, too, now, snapping her from her reflections. Not the stench of some beast, but the unmistakable sickening sweetness of the recently deceased. She turned with care to look upon what she knew to already be there.

The corpse sat at the altar, still propped up in the ornate seat behind it, overshadowed by the great forked beams of the Lord's symbol. The light of the hall's sole opening into the sky lit him in a ghostly pale glow, enhanced by the gleam of a knife thrust through his hand into the resin-varnished altar below, still gripping a roll of parchment.

She could feel the blade at her back grow chill, as if the dead priest caused it to draw the scant heat from the air around them. Long silent, Caerdrich sensed something here and she had learned to keep their council. Such warnings from the sword had led her to escape from more than one monster in the dark.

Fiadh's eyes narrowed against the bright contrast of the hall as she stepped lightly towards the altar. She raised a sleeve across her face as she stepped up to the level of the altar and closer to the slowly deteriorating body sat against it.

Caerdrich did not speak false; they never did. This priest was far too pale for even a man killed after weeks shut away in this hall.

He was pale as ash. No veins protruded from the wrists that extended beneath decorated red robes of the priesthood of Alwealda, the God of those farmhands in the tavern and the southern kingdoms. His head lolled back, exposing a neck that had been torn at as if bitten by a dog or ... Baobhan Sìth, perhaps? She had one answer to this mystery. Perhaps it was her kin who took this man, fed upon him, seduced him, and made him their puppet. The men of the village had run from it, leaving it to take their young. Perhaps they believed their coin could relieve their guilt.

It was a tempting theory but a false one. They had indeed abandoned this place, but not in a wild escape from any kind of fearsome beast. It was of no interest to farmers to lead a Crow into a trap, nor to hide from her the tell-tale signs of a bloodthirsty fey preying upon a township.

Nor would such a creature leave the corpse of its prey so peaceful, its hand pinned against parchment. They cared nothing for identification when they were done feeding, nor would they celebrate their success with such wrathful destruction of a temple that held no meaning to them on their departure.

Something more was going on here, something Caerdrich could see but she could not, not yet.

The knife had pierced the hand but there was no blood upon the altar; the priest had been drained of his blood before the blade had struck. Why? What possible purpose could it hold? What possible object of rage did he cling to?

Her hands moved with the utmost care, holding his grip in place as she drew the blade free, slowly, deliberately, to avoid doing damage to the roll between his fingers.

The fingers prised apart, she opened the roll to something she had not expected: a mess of lines scrawled back and forth across the paper – less a careful last message and more the scrambled thoughts of a broken mind. The last lines were in an unintelligible hand, devolving into a black line stabbed across the page.

> *"The Lord claims his due, and I have given it. I have given every breath to his mission in this forsaken place.*
> *He speaks to me in a different voice now, from beyond the veil. He guides me with a new purpose so I might give myself fully to his mission here. It may stain me, it may tarnish my name in the annals that will tell of this time, but it is in his name and his alone that I must work.*
> *His whispers once came from beyond the veil, but they guide my every step, now. They come to me in my dreams and from the shadows around me.*
> *He whispers, and I listen."*

That last line sent a chill down Fiadh's spine. She had heard people speak like that before. Not in a temple like this, not among the people of the south, but even in a different tongue the meaning was the same.

Whispers in the dark.

The whispering god had spoken to him, she could feel it, the sharp taste of his words still lingered in the air. This priest had been led astray – a man who had wandered from the path and been called to another by kind words and promises.

Lot had taken his soul long before another took his life.

But she was not here for a lost man's soul.

Fiadh ran her eyes across the altar, turning the sheets over one by one, looking for anything that might leave hints as to the nature of the creature who had come to this town and tore it from its normality – anything that was written in her tongue or that of the villagers of the Three Willows, not the opaque religious script of the Àrdish. A note by the priest to his order, perhaps. Notes to himself about his companions, or even better, discussing the children who had vanished under his eye.

The symbol of the High Chalice was everywhere, the Lord's symbol encircled in the crimson wax of their seal. There was another scrawled into the corners of the paper, however. A variant, the circle instead crowned by the forked symbol in the shape of a two-headed key. The very same from the paper that had guided her here. His name, Wærmund, was signed in the corner each time. He met his end before she could draw his secrets from him.

The whispers did not come at random. She had heard them herself, once. In a hall not dissimilar to this, a hallowed place of stone soon to be drawn to destruction by Lot's tempting words.

Caerdrich had sensed it. There was more to this place than simply another temple built on the ruins of a people long departed.

She began scanning the floor around her feet, crouching close to it, hand brushing back and forth just above the surface, frantic now. This was no longer about the coin of a village foreman.

There! Marks of the creature's footfall. But there was no sign of the long print of a woman, instead only the circular marks of something entirely different.

"Pawprints", she said aloud, her eyes following the steps up and away from the altar. "In dust?" This holy man must have been at his seat for a long while before the creature killed him. Perhaps long enough that he was here when the townsfolk came knocking at his door, and yet he did not answer.

So, it was not one of the blood-drinkers after all. She might escape the stain of association with the death of another man of faith, yet.

She grimaced at the thought. Too many saw the Baobhan Sìth, with their rumoured power to take raven forms, and the Crows, as two sides of the same coin. Where deaths came at the hand of the blood-drinkers then violence against those Crows who remained surely followed.

The prints ran away from the altar, accompanied by a scattering of crimson drops, whether from the priest or the fey creature it was hard to tell. Fiadh followed them away and down, towards the corner of the room where a smear ran across the wall and floor. What has been done here? Had the priest become the unwitting servant of a demon in his own temple? Deceived by the whispers as to its true nature?

She followed the prints, clear circles in the dust. But when they came to the rear of the temple, they were different. No longer a line of pawprints in the dust, but a swathe of prints and scuffs. All before a back door closed flush against the timber walls, lined in iron trim and crisscrossed with further support within the grey metal.

"The children's feet. They were alive," she said, whispered words lost into the howls of wind beyond the walls.

Fiadh sighed and sat back on her heels. It was one thing to go back to the inn with news that whatever creature that had plagued the town was gone together with their mislead priest, quite another to come with the news that so were their children. They'd lost so much already. Should they return here they might walk straight back into the embrace of the whispers which had already led astray one more prepared than they astray.

Selfishly, there was also unlikely to be any thanks for the messenger of that news. Including the reward promised for ridding this town of its rot.

Caerdrich's chill pricked at the hairs on the back of her neck. It was a warning, she knew. There was yet more to this place, somewhere.

"What can you see, blade?" She said, her gaze running over every feature of the temple around her, searching for anything that might reveal a deeper truth.

Fiadh crouched and brushed at the slats of wood forming the floor, following the edges of the scuffs and trails of crimson. There was a split here, where the slats had been cut short in a neat line. There was a section that had been splintered, too, and fragments of rusty nails remained where something had been torn free: A handle, and a handle meant that this was intended to be lifted.

Following the dead at the beckoning of a sword was not the intended ending of a small job to banish some imagined monster from a temple. But her task here was not yet done.

Her fingers failed to find purchase on the edges of the split boards. They were finely crafted, clearly the product of a great deal of investment by the local townsfolk. This may have been a longhouse once, the hall of some small laird or shrine to the old gods before the Order travelled north into their lands.

There was no access possible without a handle. This was no task for sgeanan or sword. Unfortunately, this obstacle could not be tackled with subtlety.

Fiadh stood and released her cloak, placing it carefully to one side as she glanced about the hall, looking for something heavy, with weight and leverage, a stand perhaps or ... there! A tall metal candle stand leant against the pews. Of northern make, it seemed unusual for a place of prayer but there were few who could match the handiwork of the Sjøfolk with iron. It would be a shame to damage such ornate handiwork for such a menial task, but needs must.

Her woollen surcoat and braces of blades were folded over her cloak, leaving bare arms free for the task at hand. The scabbard holding Caerdrich was shifted to remain hung over her shoulder away from her waist where it might hamper her swing. The cold air of the hall pricked at her skin, and she felt a shiver run across her shoulders. No matter, it would soon be a welcome relief.

The base of the stand struck home to splinters but little more. It rose and fell as Fiadh settled into a rhythm, bringing it overhead in a long sweep to her right, left hand gripping fast at the base of the candle's holder. The wood shuddered, then cracked, each blow tearing further into the beams. One beam began to break away, then another, breaking off and tumbling down into the void beneath. As the third snapped and fell she halted the swings, placing the battered and dented stand to one side.

Her breaths came heavy, their misty clouds swept up with the steam rising from her shoulders. The sweat already ran cold against her skin, the first chills of the coming winter clinging to her closely and stripping away the heat of her labour.

Crouching once more, she gripped the edge of her new opening in the floor and pulled hard. It came up easily enough, a door half as tall as a man rising up on quiet hinges and falling back along the rear wall. Below her, now, a series of stone steps far older than the woodwork around it stretched down to a paved floor below.

Fiadh sighed, swinging Caerdrich's scabbard from her shoulder and into her hands. Nothing good ever came from underground. Things hidden from view beneath the earth were only worth placing there so they could do no harm.

The air drifting from the opening was stale, carrying nothing stronger than moisture and rot. Rot with the distinct tang of iron.

She took the first stairs carefully, the soft steps of her boots drowned out by the wind's howl about the walls. Her left hand wrapped about Caerdrich's hilt, a momentary shift in grip giving her the comfort of the easy movement of the well-oiled blade.

Nothing greeted her progress, and there was little of note in the dank corridor that ran below the rear of the temple. The rough stone of the steps was matched by its walls and the paved floor beneath, protrusions of moss and weed clearly left untended for months, if not years.

Two doors were embedded in the wall running beneath the main hall of the temple, near-identical slabs of roughly hewn wood held in place by cords of iron crisscrossing their fronts in a mirror of the one above them. Twin bolts ran their width, but both lay unsealed. One had been firmly hauled closed; the other hung open. From that doorway ran the streak of blood that stained the temple above.

It was quieter beneath the floor, the shriek of the wind dampened by the descent. The quiet was unnerving. It always was in places that should otherwise be walked by so many, but it gave some comfort that there would not be any beast or man waiting to respond to her unwelcome intrusion.

Her feet rolling softly into each step, Fiadh progressed following the trail of blood with her hand still wrapped firmly around Caerdrich's leather.

The room beyond the doorway was wreathed in darkness, no windows reaching up to cast light on the bare stonework ground. She squinted as she slid sideways through the opening, careful not to disturb the door or brush against its frame. Within Fiadh could make out a line of cots framing the room, simple wooden frames holding hay mattresses above the floor.

There was, lying sprawled on that floor at the foot of one of these cots, a child. Lifeless, drained, limp. The blood ran from them across the centre of the room and through the doorway in which she stood. Just one left to hint at the fate of the others who had disappeared from this village over the past months.

It was evidence of the fate a part of her knew had already fallen upon them. But, still, faced with confirmation of her fears, she knew this was not everything. Caerdrich did not stir to something as banal as death. Something lay deeper still within the horrors of this place she had yet to uncover. Even with their silence the blade remained a useful companion.

She saw the child clearer now as she crossed the threshold, saw the rugged gash running about the child's throat mirroring that of the priest slumped at the altar above. But, as Fiadh knelt at their side, she could see the wound was not of the same kind. It was sharp and deep, made by blade rather than bite.

Caerdrich had guided her well. There was more to this than the feeding ground of a twisted fey.

Her eyes could not help but run up to the child's face. Hazel eyes still wide, frozen in fear, fixed on a distance seeking aid that would never come. Or, at least, could not come soon enough. She couldn't shake her gaze from them. Her heart felt like it had fallen through a hole in her gut, and the cold cut close. Everything else seemed to fade away around those sightless, haunted eyes.

The scuff of her boot on stone startled her, breaking a silence she had not realised had fallen so completely. There was no sound of wind here, no creaking of the timbers of the temple above. She walked to the wall and ran a hand along the joint between the stonework and the wood above. Frowning, Fiadh gave it a knock. There was no response, no hollow *thunk* of knuckles on floorboards.

Continuing along its surface, more knocks returned more solid taps. This floor was more than just a floor. It was packed with soil.

This space was designed not to let a single sound journey into the temple above. It wasn't the work of any witch or spirit. Those who erected the temple above had sealed this space, and it was in the silence below the earth that the children had been hidden.

So, who had let them out?

Above each of the cots hung chains, each a single hook holding bands of iron. Cold iron. Like the doorway to this chamber, like the one at the rear of the temple above.

Fiadh's search took her back to the doorway, running her free hand across the surface. Her silver eyes pierced the darkness and saw the gleam of grey metal running across it, the bolt that enabled the room to be sealed from the outside alone.

The metal was darkened in places as if scorched. In isolated spots at first as if a flame had been put against it gingerly, careful to avoid touching the wood beneath. Then there was a wide expanse of the burn, a hand's width across, marked in raised bumps of ash. It was as if someone had rubbed a lit torch against the bar, creating a layer of ash across the iron that might shield its surface.

She moved back into the corridor and across to the other door. There were no such marks here. The locking bar had been returned with what might have been quite some difficulty, perhaps clumsy and panicked. The scuffs against the frame betrayed that it had been sealed by someone unused to handling the mechanism.

Fiadh loosened the belt about her waist and pulled it free, wrapping it about her other hand with several twists. There was no telling what had burned the surface of the iron, and her years on the road had taught her that such precautions were a wise step to avoiding inflicting the same pain on herself. With the belt tight around her hand, she grasped the locking mechanism and pulled.

The stench that rose to meet her was fouler still than she had expected, and her arm instinctively came to cover her face as the door cracked open just a sliver.

There was more here, though. The hairs on her skin stood on end, chills running from her fingertips to her skull. It lingered, something deeper than the smell, a rot that ran into the very stone at her feet. It flowed freely through the space, and it was all she could bear to stand still for a moment and not bolt back up the steps.

Fiadh's eyes shone, their silver peering into the gloom that ran free of the crack. It glowed with spite and radiated cruelty. Waves of revulsion flowed through her; no human should stand on such a threshold.

It was why they offered a Crow gold to stand here instead.

Her knuckles were white between the straps of the belt as she gripped the hilt of Caerdrich tightly, one foot reaching out and pushing the door open.

The room was smaller than the previous one but no less shrouded in shadow and oppressive silence. Fiadh spied a series of candle stands against the walls and a desk which had once held the papers now scattered across the room. They lay strewn across a dark stain on the ground just beyond her feet, a wide circle containing another and yet another within it. Within each circle were scrawled symbols in the same darkness, but where it came to her feet the circles were broken, scuffed, smeared across the paved floor.

But the patterns didn't hold her gaze, for there was something far darker beyond them. The gloom that only her silvered eyes could discern from the shadows was spilling from an object framed against the far end of the room. A bronze apparatus had been erected and secured against the floor and ceiling: a frame as large as a man. Hanging from it was a tattered shroud of translucent cloth, shifting in a breeze she could not feel.

From behind it, the gloom fell, spilling over every surface, caressing every sheet and object as it poured through the door and into the corridor behind her.

Fiadh's mind raced. What nature of place was this? What lay beyond the shroud that would drench this place in such darkness? What did the symbols mean? She needed to know what this was and close it before it could poison not just this temple but the village beyond.

She moved as fast and efficiently as she could, her heart racing and cold sweat breaking out across her brow. She swept up papers from across the floor in turn, desperately running her eyes across them. They were a mix of different scrawls, from the polished and delicate to frantic scratches.

They were in different hands, some crumpled and faded as if stuffed away to be brought here. This was not the work of a single man but many.

All writing in a text she could not read.

Fiadh swore as she continued to flip over page after page, looking for anything written in a language she could understand. There was none. The letters were as she'd expected; some of the words seemed as if they should be Àrdish but twisted and ornate – some kind of archaic language shared by the priest and his colleagues. All of it.

Enough with the words, then, she flipped back through looking for pictures or diagrams that would give her some clue as to their purpose. There were some, mostly collections of symbols and geometric shapes that resembled the scrawling on the floor, though she could not tell if their purpose was for measurements or some ritualistic procedure.

But there was one thing that stood out. A collection of papers tattered and darkened by age which displayed an ornate orb, illustrated in detail and from different perspectives, arrows and script indicating where it had been altered and moved from position to position.

Why hold such instruction without an object to carry it out on?

Fiadh dropped the papers and began to move across the room methodically, eyes piecing the dark, scanning the floor for such an object.

There it was, back up against one of the corners of the room a small metal orb the size of a fist.

It glinted in what little light there was, highlighting the intricate carvings across its surface. No, not carvings, each curve of metal was a separate piece interlocked into the device. One piece shifted under her palm and Fiadh hissed as it caught on skin and a droplet of blood ran into its cracks.

She cast her eyes about, at the indecipherable pages on the desk, at the blood of children gone staining the engraved floor, and that veil hanging before the darkness that poured forth like smoke.

She was done with shouldering this mystery in silence. She swore, feeling the heat rising in her and the hot rage of the injustice that had occurred here.

"Caerdrich, what fey is there that could operate such a device?"

She knew the answer, but she had asked anyway. An extra moment of seeding doubt she no longer held. It was no fey who had used this space, who had stolen the children of the Three Willows, who had trapped them down here in the dark and cut them open one by one in a ritual designed by those who had never stepped foot on this ground.

Fiadh turned once more to the veil, that infernal contraption that held it aloft, whose design had cost this village too much to grant it nothing but loss.

The blade's chill became a harsh cold, the very air around them seeming to frost and the bite turning her hand white. Caerdrich beckoned her beyond the veil, in pursuit of the darkness.

What lay beyond it? The souls of those lost? The children who had disappeared from these chambers, sent on as sacrifice to whatever fearsome god this dead priest had shut himself away to serve?

Her eyes fell to the orb again, cast down, and her mind drifted back to the burns across the iron brackets at the door, at the single body left in the adjoining room.

"He never opened it."

The realisation came to her suddenly. He had shut himself away, despite being sent here to serve the village, along with the creature who had previously been seen free at his side. A fey that would burn at the touch of cold iron.

"He never could, he couldn't work out the key to pass beyond the veil. All his efforts came to nothing. That's why he reached out, that's why he ..." Realisation kicked in.

... listened to the whispers that came in the night.

She turned to the doorway behind her once again. That's why he died. Killed to free the children that remained. Murdered on the cusp of his completion of whatever ritual he was guided to by the whisperer beyond the veil.

She thought back, to the doorway torn down at the front of the temple. No fey who chose to kill by bite achieved that. Something else was brought here after the death of the priest. Something capable of taking the children away. To a place beyond where neither the priest nor the villagers could find them. On the very eve of the Seanadh. Fiadh remembered the farmer's words; there was a place they knew from before. The woods with a place for the old gods deep within it.

It was time to leave this dark place. Caerdrich would know the path. The blade had survived generations passed hand to hand in these very woods and hills. They would lead her onwards.

But what of the fate of this place? What if the misguided and lost returned to hear the whispers, to follow their guidance to tear aside the veil and attempt a journey to what lies beyond once again? How many more dead eyes would gaze up from these halls, their futures snatched away by the greed of those chasing knowledge that would cost more than they had any right to offer?

Fiadh spat her response to the darkness from behind a snarl. There will be no one to return to this place, she would leave them no place for them to return to.

"I'll burn it to the ground and let the gods fight over the ashes.

***

Dìleas bore her through the trees as fast as he was able, the branches tearing at her hair and leathers, crashing between fir and birch, his hooves dancing across earth and roots. Fiadh's knuckles were white on her pommel, her heels held tight against Dìleas' haunches. She could feel the dawn rising behind her, the sun's light racing her to the heights. Even now its glow would be lighting the peaks, running down their sides, spilling towards their goal.

If the light reached them before she did, they would be gone, spirited away from her grasp, never again to rejoin their families.

They would not be the first to be lost, nor the last. But this time she could not, would not, let this chance get away.

They were not alone among these ancient woods. Howls and barks like a hundred hounds rung between the pines. They may have left the village to its fate, but the old guardian had not abandoned the trees and the altar that lay beyond them.

"Where? Guide me, blade."

She felt Caerdrich's presence, the pressure at the edges of her mind that pulled and pushed so that she might follow the long-lost path.

The trees were pressing close, and Fiadh's vision swam as the light was driven out by the grasping branches. Their trunks hemmed close, forcing Dìleas to swerve from side to side to evade them. Carved faces gazed back at her from them, emotionless eyes whipping past from beneath great antlers.

The face of Cernos lived in this shade; it was the spirit of Cernos that pursued her, baying and barking in the dawn's light.

But they were rising, every gallop of Dìleas bearing them higher away from the forest floor and towards their destination. The sound of the beast of the woods fell away behind them as the warm glow of dawn began to break through the canopy and light their path. Ahead roots made way to rock, and the dirt was replaced with stone steps placed upon the side of the ascent.

The steps were overgrown and broken but her steed was no beast of burden or wagon horse accustomed to the paved tracks of the lowlands. He picked his way higher swiftly and with the confidence of the shaggy breeds that were reared among the peaks and hills of the Seann Àite.

Finally, they were free, the branches giving way to clear skies and the steps to a wide-open space where the stone had long ago surrendered to the grasses and weeds that had reclaimed this hilltop.

Fiadh dismounted and gave Dìleas' sweat-drenched haunches a pat as she stepped towards the centre of this ancient stone circle. Old cairn stones had tumbled and cracked; furrows carved into the stone floor that were now overtaken by lichen. They shone with dull light as her eyes passed over them, far fainter than the runes that had graced the circles of home. It had been many years since the people of Three Willows had truly tended to this place with the respect it was due.

The altar, which once must have been the pride of the community that had called this region home, had been split into two crumbling chunks. On one half, on seemingly the only structure still standing upright where it was intended to be, sat clay bowls and plates long devoid of any contents. The remnants of a past Seanadh, perhaps.

Beyond it was what she was seeking. Rising ahead was the sìd, a great mound of earth punctured by a yawning mouth held open by slabs of flagstone. As the sun passed the horizon it could well be an opening to the realm of the Daoine Sìth. For now, it was exactly the kind of place you might use to shelter those unable to build shelter for themselves.

Fiadh stepped cautiously forward, Caerdrich's scabbard once more in one hand, her other on its hilt. The dawn's light had not yet reached the mouth, cloaking it in shadow that her eyes could not adjust to while out in the open.

But she could hear them, the scuffs of leather on the rock, the whispers of children who had been beckoned to stay quiet but couldn't quite grasp it, the hushes of their elders who had heard the arrival of hooves outside.

She gave Dìleas a rap on the rump, letting him wander on and off the flat and back into the trees in search for something to graze upon, and crouched low, waiting for any response from the shadows. Nothing, yet. More whispers as they heard the horse move away but then nothing else, not even the barks of the guardian she had left behind in the woods.

Then there was movement, a figure venturing out into the light, one hand held over their head to shade their eyes from the rising sun.

She froze, eyes fixed on Fiadh's crouched form with one hand on Caerdrich's scabbard and the other outstretched for balance.

Slowly, with her free hand raised and palm open, Fiadh fought against the chill that ran up her arm from the blade and placed the scabbard on the ground, the frost dancing across the stones and dew across the grass freezing upon their stems. The blade's anger bit at her fingers but now was not the time to placate them; she had the feelings of others to soothe first.

Her jaw clenched with the effort of holding a smile even as the cold gripped at her hand and stabbed up her arm. Still the girl stood frozen, eyes wide and darting between Fiadh and the darkness of the opening behind her.

"Still, child, I'm not here to hurt you," Fiadh said in the softest tone she could conjure. She took a step forward, hand still held up and open. "I've seen the temple. I promise you will never have to go back to that place again. I'm here to return you to your parents."

She took another step and the girl stiffened and ran back into the dark. Fiadh swore, wondering how she could have better worded her intent. Too late now. She straightened, and with a lingering glance at the blade lying flat among the dead vegetation about it, headed towards the opening.

Within was a chamber far smaller than the gaping entrance suggested might lie beyond. A single space with what may once have been a stone table in its centre, now little more than a mound protruding from the rough-hewn rock.

In the corner, cowering in a huddle with the girl who had ventured to the entrance attempting to shield them all with nothing but her outstretched arms, were a dozen children curled in sudden silence.

She crouched, sitting back on her heels, and tried desperately to bring a genuine smile to her face. This wasn't her speciality, but children seemed to like adults who were at their own level rather than looming over them. Right now, though, it didn't seem to be calming their fears.

There had to be something else she could do, surely? How had she felt those many years ago when her own home was taken from her, when she had heard the whispers and witnessed the intent of men long led astray?

Hungry, that was one feeling she could remember with complete clarity. Fiadh pulled her pack down from her shoulders and, after a moment of rummaging, came across some scraps of two-day-old bread, salted meat, and a pair of apples. It was meagre fair but with some luck she'd be dining out on the coin of their parents for some time after today. She pulled it free in the loose cloth that wrapped them and tossed the collection in the direction of the children.

The eldest of them barely moved, their eyes fixed on her, but the younger ones' attention was drawn immediately to the apple that rolled free and across the stones.

Not enough, yet, but their trust would be hard to earn. It had been shattered by someone far closer to them than a strange warrior from a far place, dressed all in black.

The apple came to rest in a groove and Fiadh saw it lit from beneath, more symbols carved into the floor than outside. Here, though, she knew them well. Without the weather to soften them and vegetation to crack them time had not broken this script. Her fingers traced the edges of it, reading the words.

> *"Whenever the night is darkest,*
> *However long the winter might draw on,*
> *Fear not, children of the woods,*
> *For the sun will always rise again."*

There was no need to read the words once more, to search for meaning in foreign script here. This was her tongue, the language of the folk who had once called the Three Willows home, the words of these rolling hills and deep forests. In years gone by, they marked this place as a home and shelter against the encroaching cold. They had lived here, and at dawn and dusk brought gifts in thanks to the lord of the woods who kept watch over them until they departed.

This place was once the hearth of a god long passed into mist. But another had returned to tend to the village of Three Willows, one who for generations kept watch over their children until they were snatched away. Fiadh's eyes followed the script as it ran around the stone mound and out towards the entrance.

Another who comes in the form of a fox, perhaps?

It stood at the mouth of the cave with golden eyes fixed upon her, its shadow cast far by the light of a brightening sky now spilling through its entrance. The fox of the Willows had come back for the children of the village, even when their own families had fled.

Its gaze lingered for a moment longer before turning and padding away in a wide circle clear of the black scabbard that still lay in the centre of the stone circle.

Fiadh turned back for a moment, hesitating as she found the eyes of the children still set upon her. They did not trust her. She would not, in their place. But they may trust the fox, who had delivered them to this place from the horrors that lay below the now smouldering ruins of the village temple.

Perhaps if she could win its trust, she could win theirs.

As Fiadh stood and walked back towards the entrance, she saw that the fox was not alone. It had walked to the far side, where the cairns had tumbled into the trees, and it walked into the shadow of a far greater and stranger creature.

The beast stood as tall as Dìleas, but it was no beast of burden. Slit eyes peered at her from the face of a snake, its serpentine neck fading into the mottled coat stretched thin over the lithe and muscle-bound body of a predator. The split hooves of a deer pawed at the stone, but the low chorus of warning that emerged from its throat as she entered the sunlight reminded her that those feet would rather trample her than bear it in flight.

Those hundred howls had come not from a pack, but from one creature alone. The guardian of the woods, this questing beast, the spirit of Cernos.

At its side, the fox turned and hesitated but a moment before it rose onto its hind legs and began to shed its animal form. From the shadow rose a woman, but not a woman that would mingle among humanity without disguise. Fur still clung to her hips, and it was the clawed pads of a fox that graced this hallowed ground. Pads that had graced not just this place, but the halls of a temple before it.

The eyes flickered the gold of the fox before fading to a ruddy brown. This, then, had been the companion of the priest who the villagers had so distrusted. The very same being who they had offered gifts to for the Seanadh, whose entrapment by that priest had surrendered their fields to rot.

With her hands turned towards Fiadh she could see the black and blistered skin of her palms. The burn of cold iron against fey flesh. The burns of having pulled free a single bar from a single door to free the children who had been locked within.

Fiadh was kneeling, now, though she couldn't remember when she had chosen to do so. It was to her bowed head the fey spoke.

"Welcome, Crow, we were not sure that you would come."

The sound of Cànan, her own tongue, was like a song after so long conversing in Àrdish.

"But for what purpose?" she continued. "You have already set fire to the evidence of wrongdoing in the Three Willows. The rot came for their crops, the woods came for their children, now a Crow comes for their temple. Yet still you come here and despoil this ground with your accursed blade. For what purpose?"

The beast chattered, the breaths of many creatures mingling in a staccato growl as Fiadh's eyes glanced across at the black scabbard.

"We have an arrangement, the blade and I," she said, not raising her gaze from it.

"No good will come of it," responded the fox.

"It is not good that we seek together, but I shall try and do some good along the road."

"We cannot simply let this transgression pass. Others displaced those who we watched over, but none have been so bold as to bring such a blade onto this ground. None have been, so none shall be. Do you challenge us, Crow?"

Fiadh kept her eyes cast down; her hands relaxed. She could not challenge the guardian alone, but the blade could, should she move fast enough to reach it. But the beast was faster than she, and who could tell what wrath Cernos might bring down on those who would spill the blood of his own at the foot of his hearth?

"It need not come to that," she said, as softly and steadily as she could manage. "I might die, but so might you, and leave this place to fall to those who would destroy it and raise it anew in their own image."

There was silence, for a moment. The fey tended not to respond as humans would, their thought impassive and opaque, and they had no reason to pander to human expectations on their own ground.

"We cannot simply let them return, you know that, Crow. We have seen what fellow men will do to them. We have seen the cruelty, the selfish designs of those who would use their suffering to serve their own ends. We cannot simply stand by and risk those we have taken into our care."

"See it in their eyes," the fox continued. "See the pain and consider what you ask of us."

Fiadh turned her head to see that the children had come to the mouth of the cave behind her and gathered in a huddle supporting one another, the eldest still standing at the front, shielding the youngest.

But that wasn't all her eyes saw. One of the foremost of them, a girl who stood to the front with all the confidence of age but the stature of one barely a dozen winters' old, looked back at her with eyes that did not fully reflect the dark rings of the others. There were flecks of silver in those eyes. Silver that would set a child to age far slower than those around her, silver that would one day overtake her irises and grant her the gift to look deep into the darkest of places.

Eyes Fiadh shared.

They are only children, she thought.

So was I, came the response from the back of her mind.

It wasn't the same, was it?

She stood and walked back to the group. They shrunk back from her, all apart from the two eldest and this one exceptional child whose chin was raised high in defiance.

Fiadh knelt before the girl, placing a hand on each of her shoulders, "what's your name, girl?"

"It's ..." the girl hesitated, her eyes searching Fiadh's own for her intent. "It's Orlaith."

"Who is your mother, Orlaith?"

She shook her head sharply. There was no mother waiting in the town for a lost daughter with silvered eyes. There never was. The Àrdish have few ways of treating a suspected changeling, of which abandonment was a fate gentler than the others. Whether living or dead it wouldn't be long before a girl like Orlaith was stolen away by another like the dead priest in a ruined temple.

She looked into Orlaith's eyes. There was fear there, of course there was, but there was grit there as well. She could thrive here, perhaps, as many others might not. It was that or be abandoned once more to the violence of frightened men.

It was settled, then. If the fey needed to have saved something from a village plagued by the rot of crops and whispers, then they could save this one. One who had already been abandoned by the people who had denied her a true place to call home.

She stood slowly and turned to face the pair. "Orlaith will stay among your kind. You may raise her as your own, as past children of the forest have been raised. But the others will return to their homes. With their own kind where they belong."

The silence followed once more as the fox fixed her with its deceptively brown eyes. The beast circled her once, pausing for but a moment before loping into the trees beyond.

"You have made a proposal we can accept, Crow. We shall protect her as we have done all before her. But the Three Willows will not thrive if they cannot make peace with the ruins they have wrought upon themselves."

Fiadh walked over to her black scabbard, aware of the eyes on her but moving with all the certainty she could muster.

"Their pact is not mine to give", she said, her hand folding over the icy leather and passing its belt over her shoulder. "I cannot grant it. But I can promise you that I will return those you release into my care safely."

She turned towards the fox, who now stood alone between the toppled cairns. "I have only one question for you before we depart."

The fey nodded her acceptance.

"What was behind the veil in the temple, in the room of the seal you broke to permit the guardian of these woods to tear open the way for you to depart?"

The eyes of the fey fixed her with a stare fiercer than before, the stillness of her face breaking only for a moment as the muscles tensed in her cheeks.

"Nothing," the fox said, her hand waving away the question. "A curtain on a wall, that was all. The focus of so much suffering was just the obsessions of a broken mind." They raised a hand dismissively, as if the happenings below the temple were only a mere nuisance.

"Depart, Crow, before the sun opens the way to Fearann Eeile and we change our minds. But know this, the blade you carry will never deliver what you seek; it will not give you peace nor solace. Only death follows it. We will meet again, you and I, but I fear you will have lost much to escape the shadow of death that falls over you."

Fiadh did not push further. With a whistle she heard the hooves of Dìleas bearing him up from the trees and she turned to her new charges. It would be a long morning's travel back to the tavern on the beaten path, but at least it would be the last walk of this wretched journey.

***

The once-lonely tavern was now bustling. News travelled fast, and families who had fled to Dun Caraich had flocked back to the roadside where the children of the Three Willows waited for them.

There were tearful reunions. Adults threw their arms around their children, searching their eyes for the harm they knew had befallen them. More there, besides. They had been returned from the fey and no true Àrdish would accept such a gift without checking that they had not been duped by a child with the form of their offspring but the eyes of another.

But there were also adults searching over and over again through the children who remained in increasing panic. They would not find who they were looking for.

Too many of them wouldn't.

Fiadh stood leaning against Dìleas some distance away. She knew how this worked. No one wanted to be faced with the reminder that they'd needed to bring in an outsider to save their own when they could not. In time, though, the foreman she had spoken to only yesterday would drag himself from the others and slump in her direction.

He would not meet her eyes, nor entirely face her as he rummaged deep into a satchel and pulled free a purse ringing with the metal held within. His gaze continued to glance up at the horizon, where smoke still rose in a trail up from the village beyond.

"So, there wis a demon in that temple, then?" He muttered, looking deep into the purse as if he hadn't counted out its contents more than once already.

"That there was."

"A fat lot ae use the faith did him if it cuidnae even keep a monster oot." He drew the purse strings tight and paused with it in his hand for a moment. He looked out again at the lingering smoke before holding it out in her direction, his gaze turning to the milling families down the road.

"That it didn't," she said.

Fiadh waited a moment before taking the purse. She considered making some joke, anything to break the tension. But she couldn't feel any of the warmth she'd drawn by teasing the man just yesterday. She had her coin. That would be enough. Now she could ride free of this place and hopefully put the eyes of the child below the temple far from her mind forevermore.

There was a break in the reunions on the road. Someone stamping back and forth, red robes of a layman of the Order sweeping around, dragging in the mud. He stopped for a moment in the crowd before turning his head in towards them, eyes alight with rage. Storming in their direction, he began jabbing a finger towards her.

"Whaur is she?" he snapped. "Whaur's Orlaith?"

Fiadh did not move from her relaxed lean against her saddle, but she noted the split wooden stave he gripped in one hand, its miniature hung about his neck, a mirror of Oeric's own. She noted the haphazard stomp of his furious steps, and the manner in which his neck protruded forward from slumped shoulders.

"Whaur is she, ye witch?" he said, waving a hand to quiet Oeric. "Whit huv ye done wi her, whit accursed ritual did ye carry oot in yer bargains wi the deevil?"

"Simon, she ..." Oeric began, before the man's flailing hand again silenced him.

"Ye burned the Laird's hoose! Ye took her frae me! Ye hud no richt! Witch! She wis mine by richt ... by, by richt ..." he stammered as Fiadh stepped away from Dìleas towards him.

His eyes darted back and forth between hers and a moment of realisation shot across his features, eyebrows rising. "Ye werenae here fur the bairns at aw!" he said, finger jabbing towards her chest. "Ye were here fur the Laird's work, fur Faither Wærmund's work, beneath the ..." His words were cut off into a gurgle as Fiadh's fist struck his throat. He staggered back for barely a moment before the gurgle became a strangled yelp, as he collapsed to the ground when his knee gave way beneath Fiadh's foot.

"Whit huv ye done?" Oeric shouted, rushing to the side of the felled man. "Ye broke him, oor layman!" His stoic demeanour was gone, the stiff restraint he had displayed ever since they met falling away all at once.

Simon gurgled his complaint, stave lying abandoned, hands wrapped around an unnaturally twisted limb.

"Ah'll huv tae gie yin ae ma ain men in his place, Ah brocht ye here! Ye burned it aw an noo ye strike him doon. It'll cost me a year's harvest, ye owe us ..."

"I owe you nothing." Fiadh cut him off, packing the purse into her saddle bag and hauling herself onto Dìleas' back. She could feel the blade's satisfaction, the chill touch of their strength running down the arm that had laid the priest low. They hungered for more, to be drawn and to do far worse to these men than even she had let herself inflict.

But not now. There was far farther they must travel, far from this place, far from the machinations of the High Chalice. She could not afford to draw more attention from them than she already had.

"You had a worm in your midst, Àrderman," she continued from above him. "A worm who spread rot through your people. If you wish to reclaim the Three Willows, you'd best leave him behind."

She looked down at the prostrate form of the layman with a snarl. "Let the wolves and ravens have him. They'll gain more from his bones than you ever did from his whispers."

Fiadh squeezed Dìleas' flank and with a whistle he pulled away and down the track, leaving the barked complaints of Oeric behind her.

In the distance, she knew, a fox looked down on the tavern and waited for those who might return to the Willows and the smouldering remains of a dark past they would do well to put behind them.

That was a future she would have no part in, nor would she waste thoughts for a village that lost itself long ago.

Fiadh ran her hand down and into her saddlebag, running her fingers along the rough fibres of the grey veil sequestered there. The mystery of what lay beneath it called to her, a journey for another place, and another time. One small step on the long path she and the blade must tread.

❈

NAMES OF THE DEAD

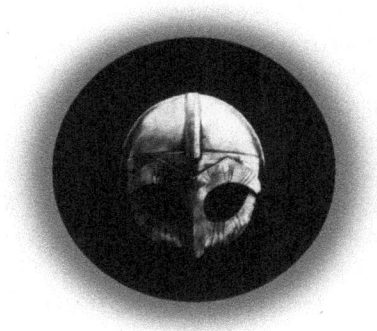

The sea was still as glass beneath the ship as it drifted into harbour. The port of Ghav Rhien loomed over them, the stone walls and towers of its fortified heart protruding from the cliffs above. It was both a statement and a memorial to the one hundred sieges over the centuries. No one had come to the isle with drawn swords and left it with both their blade and pride intact.

The soft swell of the water lapped against the pebbled shore and the scent of salt and seaweed filled the air. This was a place of rest for many a traveller – a home to many more whose travels had ended.

Fiadh's eyes cast over the bay with a warmth she felt deep in her chest. There was something about home, with the meeting of the granite and the sea, and it had been many a season she had sailed past Ghav Rhien and looked to it with yearning. Today, finally, she had been given a good reason to make landing here.

There was someone waiting on that harbour for her. Old men in white robes and the symbols of faith didn't tend to watch over docks in the middle of the afternoon on a whim. He stood as he always had, hands clasped before him, below the embossed bronze ornaments that hung about his neck and glittered in the sun.

As they drifted in against the jetty, Fiadh stepped onto the woodwork before the boat came to a halt, dropping ashore with her sack and scabbard over one shoulder, a skip and a smile to the grim features of her one-man welcoming party.

"Brianan! It has been too long!" she said, arms wide in welcome.

Brianan did not appear to share her enthusiasm.

"Fare you well, Crow?" Though his words were warm, his tone was cold; his arms remained wrapped in his robes. This was a frostiness she'd encountered before – the chill of someone whose mind was occupied with the misfortune of others. "When I put out the call, I did not imagine it would be you who returned, after all this time."

It was more than just his grim features that set her on edge. There was something else here, a sound that rang just at the edge of her hearing, beyond what she could grasp or accurately describe. An eerie keening that drifted and hung over the water.

"I ..." she hesitated, trying to shake the sound from her head. "I fare well enough, old man. My bones aren't quite aged enough to bother me when the storms roll in." His eyebrow rose at her words, though the scepticism was at least a marked improvement on no expression at all.

His look was made no friendlier by the cruel upturn in his lip – the result of a scar that ran from his chin to a milky-white eye and his temple. A legacy of an age where the fili had wielded more than books and tales of old gods.

"Your face may not bear the lines of age, Fiadh, but you have changed. There is pallor in your skin, like the light of life has drained from you. I fear there are some things we were never meant to see. You, like Eònan, may have seen too much in too many journeys around the wheel."

She scoffed at his melodramatic tone. He'd learnt to intone his words with the weight and cadence of a millennia, even if he were only discussing what food graced his plate. Such habits learned from the filidhean didn't slip easily. But her outward mirth hid her true feelings, as his words struck a little too close to the truth. It had been too many years. Brianan had been a young man tutored by a more learned storyteller when she had last left this isle, and she had felt the strength of Caerdrich slipping from her as the years turned by. She may look far younger than the bard, but she could feel the years as well as his retreating hairline had clearly done.

"I travel all the way here," Fiadh said, skipping ahead and turning to continue while walking backwards up towards the town beyond. "Risking my very life to these treacherous seas at your beckoning, and you greet me with jibes at my age. Dear Brianan, you spoil me so!"

Brianan's mood remained cold as the deepest winter. "I assure you, Fiadh, I would not have made such a request lightly. The clouds hang low over Ghav Rhien, and I fear my ability to lead it to the right path is swiftly waning. It is my hope that you may breach those clouds and bring some light back to this place."

He had continued to speak even as Fiadh turned away and flipped a coin into the waiting hands of a merchant in exchange for an apple, continuing to walk in expectant silence as she fell in step with him.

"So," she said as she began to carve slices from her purchase. "Doom and darkness, driving out ancient evils and restoring us to the natural order of things. What kind of curse has fallen under your watch, old man?"

The route around them began to wind as they left the harbour market and made their way past the scattered homes thrown up against the hillside that dominated the isle.

"I would not have called upon a Crow for a simple matter, you know this." The druid was a smaller figure than she remembered. The years had drained away much of his stature and the slump of his shoulders belied the familiar determination of his eyes. "I am not so old that I cannot handle such matters myself."

"I apologise for wounding your pride so," Fiadh said, turning to spin an apple slice towards a child curled beneath one of the straw awnings, smiling a little at his instant delight. But the smile was short-lived. The keening of the docks was drawing closer now, and though those around her could not hear it as she could, she saw that it had drawn a shadow over the people of the hill. As the wail drifted over them, eyes were cast fearfully to the fortress above and shutters were closed even against the sunlight and still winds.

This was not the way people responded to sudden frights coming in the night, but rather that of a community held under the foreboding air of a threat held over them for seasons.

"He cannot sleep, the Rìgh. He is plagued by shadows that come to him in the night and speak to him alone. He wakes with fits of anguish, preoccupied by the past at the expense of the present." Brianan said. His eyes cast upwards and past her to the walls as he spoke.

"Eònan has long since ceased listening to my counsel, after my failures to guide him from his dark thoughts with what little help I could offer. There is another here, now, who has his ear. I fear others are guiding him down a misjudged path and into the arms of those who wish him no good fortune."

Fiadh followed his gaze to see helms glinting on the battlements, mismatched spear tips and shields gathered in watch over the path.

"Those are not Daoine," she said.

"They are not," Brianan replied. "The Rìgh in the depths of his darkness has cast suspicion on all those who once stood at his side. I am one of the few who remain. The Àrdish and Sjøfolk, the very people he sacrificed so much to defend this rock from, now man his keep and drain his coffers."

"Yet you have remained?" Fiadh asked.

"I fear not for many more days. This is my final cast of the dice. Your Order are who I have turned to in my last moments on this isle and my last under the eye of Eònan, in what I believed to be the vain hope that some of you might remain. I will not leave here regretting that I did not do all I could to save my liege from his torments."

He was a grim and sour individual, but Fiadh had always respected the fierce loyalty and honour that Brianan held close to his heart. There were few she knew would fight harder for their duty, even to those who had long ceased to deserve it.

"Some people are doomed to linger on their past mistakes. I will not be one of them, Fiadh. We cannot change what we have done. We may only come to terms with it and let it change us," said Brianan.

"And what if we cannot save him, what then?" she asked.

"What's done is done," he said, the words intoned with all the authority of a man who had spoken them many times to audiences of the faithful.

The doors to the fortress loomed over them as they reached the crest of the hill, great slabs of wood shipped from oaks far away piled upon one another in the form of a gate. Two men bedecked in mail and capped helms stood on either side of the opening and nodded to the druid in recognition, letting the pair past and into the courtyard beyond.

Quite unlike the bustle Fiadh remembered, the clearing within the walls was practically empty. Further guards were scattered here and there, glancing suspiciously in their direction but just as frequently over their shoulders as if their shadows crept up upon them.

The hall of the Rìgh sat cupped in the shadow of a cliff that hung over the fortress: a squat complex, built generations ago by the first lords who seized control of the waters around the isle, its many timbers cracked by the waters of a hundred storms and decorated with trails of moss and vines. Above its door a carved mural displayed the battles of Eònan's ancestors against men, serpents, and great monsters of the deeps.

Now their successor had shut himself away in fear of shadows and cries in the night.

Like the gate before, the guards at the hall's door nodded to Brianan and drew back the bar that held the door shut. It may be his final cast of the dice, but the druid still clearly claimed the respect of those who remained at the Rìgh's side. With a nod in return, Fiadh followed Brianan into the torch-lit interior.

The hall within dwarfed the other structures of the isle, the staunch pillars legacies of the centuries it had stood here. Over time the complex had spread from this meeting place, connected to it by a half-dozen corridors radiating outwards from it. In the silence within, Rìgh Eònan sat slumped in a throne of ornate woodwork, with yet more carvings of the monsters and heroes of Ghav Rhien's past looming over him, locked in eternal combat. He had aged in the years since Fiadh had seen him last, the proud brows and chin now wreathed in scraggly white hairs. Beneath his iron circlet his hair fell long across his shoulders in thin wisps.

The men standing about his seat were not the old champions who had stood at his side for a hundred minor skirmishes over the isles. Gone were the trusted advisors of his forefathers and the famed warriors who carried their names. Instead, there was a scattering of young men and women of every possible people and garb, a gathering so disparate they could have been collected by hands grasping at random from across the known world. They stood in silence, their eyes darting nervously between their lord and their new guests.

All the better to ensure they could have no possible loyalties nor affections here that came before the Rìgh. Only one man stood closer to the throne – a red-haired giant of a man with a single hand upon the back of Eònan's throne. The similarity in the crags of their brows and set of their jaws was unmistakable: his son, surely.

There was another among those around them, however, who set Fiadh's hairs on end. At the left arm of Eònan stood a gangly figure so overwhelmed in their red robes that they might as well have been hung from a rack. Beneath their cowl was a mask in white marble, and a string of bells draped from their shoulders to their waist.

From their neck hung the symbol of Alwealda, spun to appear in the form of a two-headed key. The priest's mask faced them, his eyes hidden behind the expressionless visage.

Here, standing before the silent gathering, Fiadh could hear the keening she had heard below more clearly: a high wail carried through these halls, an otherworldly cry beyond the hearing of the scattering of men and women gathered, but nevertheless she could see its presence set them on edge.

The wail wasn't voiceless, then. There were names in the air, drifting in and out, wrapping themselves like spectral hands around the shoulders of those gathered here. She could see the men around the Rìgh standing uneasily, shuffling their feet, glancing towards one another and into the corners at nothing, rubbing at sleep-deprived eyes.

Over them all the wail continued, carrying names along with it. *Caoimhe, Domhnall, Rhona, Fionn.* They repeated in that order, always the same, always drifting just at the edge of the wail that she alone in this hall could pick from the air.

"Come," came Eònan's croaked acknowledgement, his hand raised itself in an exhausted wave in their direction. In concert Fiadh and Brianan bowed their heads and walked forward, their footsteps echoing in a silence only broken by the uncomfortable shifting of the guard.

When they were halfway to the throne, Fiadh took the druid's lead to kneel before the withered remnants of the warrior sat upon it. It had been too long since she had last seen him, too long for him to recognise the face of the raven-haired woman he had seen last when they had crossed paths in the town below, one who would have changed far less over time than he could understand.

"It has been some time since you last came to my hall, Brianan, old friend. You once stood at my side, yet now instead you spread rumours and messages far afield to tell the tales of my woes."

Eònan's rasp grew harsher the longer he spoke, though if Brianan was stung by those words he showed no sign of it.

"Yes, I know what you have been doing. I have heard of your missives and calls for aid to complete the work of protecting me from the darkness that has seized my domain. The work you failed to do you now ask others to complete in your place."

Fiadh desperately wanted to see how the servant of Alwealda was responding to this tirade but stayed bowed alongside Brianan in silence. Now was likely not the ideal time to let curiosities breach whatever stillness they had found in the midst of Eònan's paranoia.

Brianan remained strong as he replied, "I return with Fiadh, of Tur Eumor. She might yet be able to find the source of your dark dreams, I thought..."

"A Crow? You bring me a Crow, old man, as your final bid to redeem yourself in my eyes?" Eònan cut off the druid with further weak waves of his hand before he continued his thoughts. "After you failed to drive out the keening of the dead from my halls?"

"A Crow!" Eònan laughed, but there was no mirth in his rasped cackling, the sound was grim and cruel. "After all this time, it is you who would bring a servant of the Ríagan to the doors of my very chambers."

Fiadh knew that tone, the tone of someone who felt powerless finally seizing on something they could wield control over, something they could hold over someone else and feel strong again. There were few more dangerous things on this earth.

"You've led me to my death, druid," Fiadh hissed under her breath.

"I have faith," he whispered in reply. "You didn't become the last of your Order without some skill in avoiding the hangman and the stake, Crow."

Fiadh cursed and she cast her gaze back to the baleful eyes of Eònan glaring down at her. "I'm the last Crow because the rest of them had friends like you."

"I made a deal, Brianan," the Rìgh continued. "A deal to make sure the Crows never again set foot on my isle and meddled in affairs they had no right to be sticking their long beaks into."

He pulled himself to his feet, shaking hands clinging to the arms of the chair and teeth gritting against the effort, but his eyes never left the pair kneeling before him.

"I didn't watch the Tur burn just to have my advisors welcome them into my halls and plague my very shadow."

Fiadh flinched at that. He had been there? Rìgh Eònan had been there when Tur Eumor fell, at the destruction of her home and sanctuary? Her teeth ground together as she bit back the fury and hurt, the pain bringing tears to her eyes. All this time, all these years searching for the bastards who had come across the sea and brought ruin on the Tur, leaving her a wanderer. Brianan had been serving one of them this entire time.

Head still bowed, she could see the priest of Alwealda lean in and begin to whisper to the Rìgh. She could see it clearly now, the darkness that hung over the lord, the dark rings beneath his eyes, the weakness that left his back arched even when stood, the eyes filled with suspicion and anger. This wasn't the strong ruler who had secured the isle from innumerable foes by the point of a spear in years past. This was a man gripped and ruled by his own fear.

As the priest whispered their reply from behind that etched marble mask, Eònan's withered gaze fell upon her and their eyes met, albeit briefly. Beneath the veil of hate she could see the desperation of a man surrounded by strangers who could not aid him against whatever spirit haunted this hall. A man who in his darkest hour had driven away those who had failed him, only to turn to those who would weave whatever remained of his hope for their own ends.

Perhaps, all those years ago, those very same whispers had brought him to the Tur and upended her own life into the dark and chaotic seas.

Eònan snarled and tore his gaze away, feebly waving off his devout advisor. "Take them away, give them lodging elsewhere. I no longer wish to see either of them in my hall. I wish to think; all this clamour clouds my thoughts. I must think."

The Rìgh's face twisted and twitched as his eyes searched the hall, over the heads of those gathered before him.

"Enough! None will question my judgement, I will have silence!" he snapped, those about him starting at the sudden command. No one present had spoken. But Fiadh could hear them, just as the Rìgh now could. Those names continued to drift across the hall, the keening falling in and out, jumbled in the midst of indecipherable mutterings and whispers.

Eònan gripped his throne hard in one hand and the other cast about in the air like he sought to free it of thoughts not his own. "Away, away, I must think, I must have silence. All of you, away!"

Brianan nudged her arm and stood. She joined him and they backed away from the throne even as other servants began to filter out of the hall through the corridors leading them deeper into the complex. This was clearly far from the first time they had been instructed to depart with such abrupt and unprompted vagaries. Few remained where they stood, the priest of Alwealda and a handful of his mercenary champions among them.

Fiadh grabbed Brianan's arm roughly the moment they had moved down a passage and out of sight of the throne. His eyes widened at the harshness of her grip.

"Who are they, Brianan?" she snapped in as low a tone as she could muster.

"Please, Fiadh, I didn't know, none of us did!" Brianan stammered, before realising he was answering a question that had not been asked. "Wait, who are *who*?" the bard finally replied, eyes glancing back from where they had come, half expecting more ears to be leaning into his words.

"The names drifting on the wind. They portend the dead. The cry of a caoineag grips this place. Something has trapped it here."

The druid nodded understanding to that. "Who is portended to die?" he asked. "Is it Eònan? Townspeople?"

"The names, Caoimhe, Domhnall, Rhona ..."

"Ist!" Brianan cut her off suddenly, finger raised. "Never speak those names again here, Crow, lest you be left to hang from the ramparts before the night's end."

Fiadh roughly brushed his finger away. "You and I both know that unless I can lift this curse that fate is what is intended for me. Who are they?"

"It makes no sense. Those can't be the names you heard."

"Why not?" she snapped.

"They're dead." His eyes locked with hers, reinforcing the earnestness of his words. "Have been for years. Since before you even washed up on these shores and into my life. They're the Rìgh's family, killed when Jarl Vestamr seized the islands. That first name you spoke, that was his sister."

"Why can't their names be spoken?" Her grip drew him further from the hall as their heads leant in towards one another, keeping their whispers safe from the servants still making their way from the throne.

"He never truly recovered from their loss," Brianan said. "He was a bright young man in his youth, always first to look to the horizon and ask how far his ship could take him. Their deaths changed him, casting a great melancholy over him. He may bend the knee to Vestamr, but he never truly forgave him; those deaths have hung between them ever since and will follow them until one or both are sent to their graves. His son, Ruadh, he called the priests to try to rid his father of whatever curse had been set upon him by his sister's kin."

Footsteps began to sound from the hall behind them, cutting short Fiadh's questions.

"Are you sure they were killed? They cannot have survived?" she asked.

"As sure as I am that I stand before you, Fiadh. I saw them laid to rest, I assisted the master who carried out the burials, learned from the song of the filidh who sang their tale. They are as dead as the rock we stand upon."

It wasn't possible.

A caoineag haunted the nights of places where the ends of those dear to inhabitants were due. Their cry could bring the chill of death upon a household, preparing them for the loss that was to come. But never would their wails come beneath the risen sun, nor continue for months on end, nor would the names on their tongues be those of the already dead. If Eònan did not have her killed by the morn it was possible this caoineag would, if disturbed in the midst of its powerful grip over this hall. For the first time in years Fiadh felt the faint stirring of panic rising in her chest.

It was broken by the arrival of one of Eònan's party of mercenaries and two servants. Brianan nodded his acknowledgement to them and departed down the hallway, abandoning her to this new heavily armed company. This warrior was one of the slighter one of their number, but his armament was that of an experienced fighter, and the crisscross of scars across his arms betrayed a storied career before his arrival in this forsaken place.

"Please, the Rìgh has insisted you be treated as our guest and stay till the morn. You may leave with the tide. We will show you to your chambers," one of the servants spoke, gesturing further down the hallway. So it began, she thought.

As they joined her, Fiadh's ears pricked as the mercenary muttered to himself. It wasn't quite loud enough for her to catch the words, but the tongue was unmistakable. He wasn't speaking in Cànan, the language she shared with the people of this isle, but in Àrdish, clearly believing that he could do so without being understood by his company. Brianan may have left her in a death-trap, but this could be a lifeline at last.

"Very well." She did her best to smile at the servant and fell into step alongside them.

Fiadh slipped into Àrdish, certain that the mercenary would know the others alongside them weren't particularly learned in the southern tongue.

"Southerner, are you?" she said, finding genuine cause to smile as the mercenary desperately attempted to hide his jump of surprise.

"Aye, whit's it tae ye?" He spoke low, eyes flickering at the two servants with more suspicion they would understand than she had.

"What's your name?"

"Annis." His eyes narrowed. "Whit's *yours*?"

"Fiadh."

The servants were paying them no mind as they continued down the hallway. No doubt they had experienced more than their share of mercenaries swapping chat in their variety of tongues and had long since learned to tune it out.

"You don't speak Cànan?" she said.

"Yer tongue? Yin wurd here an there. Ah git by in Àrdish an whit Sjøtunge Ah picked up oan Vestamr's ships. Ah dinnae need tae ken whit yer laird says tae ken whit he wants. He's no a complicatit man: 'Bide here; awa' there'."

They walked in silence for a moment as Fiadh considered how to phrase her request.

"How much do they pay you for your service?" she asked.

He hid his reaction well this time, eyes flitting to the servants leading them down the hall: a good sign. "Whit's it maitter tae ye?"

"I'll triple it, for one night of work."

If the mercenary had not prepared himself for the shock, he might well have shown it at that, but the most Fiadh got in return was a couple of more regular blinks and the slight crinkling of one eye in thought.

"Yin nicht? Whit fur?" His acting wasn't convincing, the suspicion and temptation were both clear in his hesitant tone.

"Because if you don't say yes, I'm going to die, and I would very much like to stay on this forsaken spiral for at least a few more turns. I've got good reason to give you what I've got." Fiadh did her best to meet his eyes as they continued to walk side by side. "So, what will it be? Triple your wages for just one night and maybe learn a thing or two about the workings of a Crow?"

"If ye huv tae die, whit wid Ah be daein followin ye there?"

He wasn't wrong. There wasn't much use in a bag full of coin if the closest you ever got to it was dangling from the belt of the man holding you under in the drowning pools.

She had to word this carefully. "There's a spirit hanging over this place, you must have felt it." He nodded, a good start. "It's not going to leave unless I rid this hall of it tonight."

"An if ye dinnae?" he replied, turning the words over in his mouth.

"You all die. It has the name of every soul on this isle on its lips."

His eyebrows practically hit the ceiling in the most dramatic expression he had pulled so far. The servants took a sharp turn ahead of them and they turned into a dead-end with a single door. It was time for a decision.

"The Laird haes nichtmares. He tosses an turns in his sleep. Ye think this spirit is behind thaim?" They came to the door but Annis raised a hand to quiet the servants as they turned towards them.

"I do," Fiadh replied, looking the mercenary dead in the eyes

"Ye ken how tae stop the mares?"

"Sometimes," she said. "If there's a spirit behind them."

He frowned thoughtfully. "Guid tae ken."

Annis turned to the two servants, who were looking somewhat put out from being held waiting at his hand while the pair spoke in a language they didn't understand. He rattled off a couple of sentences in Sjøtunge and they deliberated a moment. Finally, the servants nodded reluctantly and moved past them and back where they had come.

Annis watched them depart before turning the latch on the door, letting it swing open, and gesturing for her to enter.

"Ah'm tae stay wi ye, mak sure ye dinnae git up tae ony funny business while yer in the Laird's hame. While Ah'm here Ah micht as weel mak sure yer no disturbed," he said. His expressions were unreadable, a wall of stern features and implacable deep blue eyes.

Fiadh nodded. She didn't need to know his exact reasons behind having her back right now, only that she had bought herself some brief reprieve, one that Brianan had not offered. She turned and entered the room. Annis followed and closed the door behind them.

Fiadh slumped roughly onto the cot that made up much of the sparse adornment of the chamber, dumping her sack, adjusting the scabbard slung over her back, and pinching her nose hard in thought. She had won some time, at least, but it would be useless unless she could lift the shadow hanging over Eònan before he sent his champions to finish the job that began at Tur Eumor.

"Are ye a Völva?" Annis broke her thoughts, and she looked up to see him standing awkwardly in the middle of the room, arms folded and looking down on her.

"The Sjøfolk might call me that, yes," she said. "But no, I do not practice the Seidr as they do. It is a talent I have not come to master."

"Ye ken Jarl Sigurd treats his Völva weel, treats thaim like his ain wives, jist aboot."

"Hah, I bet he does. After this I might even consider his attention." There was absolutely no chance that Fiadh would ever give Sigurd the opportunity to give her such attention. She'd heard other tales about how his court treated foreign magics.

She sighed heavily. Her time was growing shorter by the moment and dusk was approaching, bringing with it the thin sliver of an opportunity to fend off her fate.

Rising from the cot she began to unload her pack, arranging its contents in careful rows, ignoring Annis' curious eyes inspecting her work. Here went her brace of knives, there her rolls of parchment, a sack of dried foodstuffs from the voyage and her water flask.

In the centre came what would be vital for the hours ahead. Chalk, a small spherical metal device, and a roll of ancient woven cloth.

"Whit's that?"

"Nothing you need to know about," Fiadh replied, leafing through the parchments and lifting one, unfurling it, and setting it out on the floor next to her. It was covered from top to base in scrawlings and diagrams – her scrawlings, dozens of notes she'd made over the years.

She had dedicated so much to this, searching far and wide across the Seann Àite for the keys to this puzzle, for what knowledge existed about the door it unlocked. Now, for the first time, she had reached a point where there might be no other option than to discover what lay behind it.

She looked to her new companion.

"I need you to do me one more favour, even if your companions don't come for me tonight," she said.

Annis twitched an eyebrow in her direction in what appeared to be his form of an acknowledgement.

"If I do not return by the morning, the way back will be closed. I will not be coming back. Should that happen, burn the veil and destroy the orb. Should they be left intact, other things may return with the rising of the sun, things that neither you nor anyone else in these halls is capable of facing."

"Haud aff till dawn, burn the cloth, break yon orb. Ah've hud harder jobs. How are ye gan tae git oot ae here?" he ventured.

Fiadh lifted the rolled cloth and unfurled it into the tattered veil she had found so long ago. Turning, she walked across the room and carefully laid it down in the centre of the floor.

"Through that," she declared, pointing down at it.

Annis looked at her as if she had brazenly told him that her mother was, in fact, a fish.

Fiadh shrugged and continued with her tasks, first removing her leathers and boots, leaving herself in just her sleeveless tunic, leggings, and the scabbard of Caerdrich across her shoulders. She stretched her arms out wide and enjoyed the feel of the stone flooring underneath her bare toes.

"Yer leavin yersel affa bare fur a rammy, Craw," he said.

"Where I'm going, I'm not going to need them. For now, I just need some air."

She set about across the room, returning to her parchments from time to time and using the chalk to mark out points and then draw the circles that ran between them. Along each line she began to chalk out the text she had detailed along the sides of the parchment, Cànan script from long before her time.

She had written these lines often enough – they were etched into her memory, but she still returned to check them over and over again, ensuring that every line was correct, every mark exactly where it should be. As she finished, she stepped back and took a spot facing across the chalk and through the window beyond at the slowly dimming sky.

Annis had stood silent through it all, his back to the door, watching the entire procedure with careful bemusement. But he had stayed, that was something, and should at least lend some hope that he would stay till the morning.

"Whit noo?" he asked as she pulled Caerdrich from across her back and laid the scabbard in her lap, the brief chill dancing across her fingertips a reminder that this was as far as the blade would tolerate being moved away from her.

"We wait until the sun touches the horizon. Then the way will be open to me, for a time, and every minute will count before I can find my way back. Till I am done that door must not be opened and these markings must not be disturbed. If I do not return, it must be destroyed."

"So be it," he replied.

"Aye," she said with a sigh. "So be it."

***

The time passed slowly. Annis stood with greater calm and patience than Fiadh felt as she sat facing the window and watching the sky shift from blue to violet. Caerdrich grew cold as the time approached where she would be able to reach across to the world of the caoineag to put the spirit to rest.

Or destroy it.

With time her scratches in chalk began to shift and glow with the dull orange of the setting sun. It was working, for now at least. She looked up to see Annis' eyes fixed upon her, staring as the silver of her eyes began to shine with the coming of the dusk. He was not the first to stare, nor, she hoped, would he be the last.

When the time came the chill of the blade became a sharp stab of frost, gripping her thighs and fingertips. Fiadh stood, grasping the metal orb from the bed where she had set it aside, and approached Annis.

"Your hand, please," she said as he looked at the delicately carved sphere. He held out a palm and she placed the orb upon it. With a sharp twist the intricate mechanisms shifted, and Annis jerked his hand back with a hiss of pain, his blood running from a nick from the thin notched blade that extruded from its surface.

"Sorry, my own blood wouldn't do," she said, as if those words sufficed as an apology.

Without checking to see if Annis had need for any further comment, Fiadh returned to the chalk etchings, reaching across so as not to disturb them and twisting the orb yet again at the midpoint between them, directly above the veil laid down in the floor's centre.

It clicked and a small needle emerged from its opposite side. A drop of blood fell from its tip, dangling briefly before detaching from the instrument and hanging in the air, suspended by nothing.

As Fiadh stepped back across the chalk's threshold the droplet began to distort and expand, flattening into a thin translucent sheet and stretching to stand as tall as she, the remnants of the sky's light casting through it to bathe her in a crimson glow.

Caerdrich froze, the air around the blade shimmering with ice shards as the water of the air was dragged from it. Fiadh's fingers went blue around the scabbard as she gripped it tighter, the pain of the cold stabbing up her forearm.

Annis was transfixed, eyes wide, hand on the hilt of his own blade, his back against the room's door as far from the chalk as his feet could take him.

Fiadh gave him one last look through the bright gleam of her eyes. "Hold the door, Annis," she said. "Hold it fast like your very life depends upon it."

She turned back, fixed her stance, and leapt into the blood-forged portal.

The darkness was immediate and shocking. One moment she was bathed in the twilight's glow, the next she was surrounded by a vast expanse of nothing. Even her feet seemed to be set on nothing in the pitch darkness, though she felt as though she was standing on the same stone tiles of the room she had left. Fiadh looked down to discover that it was not only the room that had disappeared. She was bare as the day she was born and formless – an approximation of a human figure made of her eyes' shimmering silver.

Caerdrich still lay in her palm, the blade shining bright and unsheathed like the sun's glare off fresh snow. Gone was the cold, replaced by the strange feeling that she was suspended in nothing at all, as if the very air had been pulled away.

As the seconds passed, slowly but surely, her silvered eyes began to decipher shapes about her. There was the cot where she had left her sack, the window looking out onto yet more darkness, and Annis holding himself upright against the door, fright filling his eyes as he looked directly past where Fiadh stood.

Caerdrich did not light her path, their glow seeming only to fall upon own shifting figure.

There was no time to waste. Now that she had her bearings it was time to bring an end to this curse that had fallen upon Ghav Rhien.

She did not need to move Annis aside or pull open the door beyond; instead, she moved through it without resistance. It danced as she passed, as if it were cast in the form of a waterfall of light that her passing disturbed, and it splashed its shining substance across the hallway beyond.

She moved through the corridors like dust carried in a draught, sweeping past those inhabitants still gracing the halls. She could see the servants sharing hushed whispers at the passageway beyond, the priest of Alwealda gathered at the entrance to the hall with a handful of mercenaries bearing a broad collection of sharp and cruel weapons, each held at hand, but not yet drawn. They would be soon enough.

In the hall itself she heard the keening return, no longer the wavering whispers and mutters of a cry from the beyond, but words as clear as if they were being spoken into her very ear.

"Dearest Caoimhe, Domhnall, Rhona, Fionn,
the dead who lie but walk anew,
the fallen who rested now let me in,
to watch over the guilty few."

Fiadh had had enough ghostly riddles for a lifetime and wasn't about to start deciphering one now with her time drawing so perilously short. The keening continued even as she drifted through the hall and towards the Rìgh's chambers beyond, the words repeating again and again in her ear, clawing at her for attention.

The way to the Rìgh was barred by two of his champions, both looking uneasy, turning their eyes to one another and to the doorway at the sounds coming from within. She could hear Eònan's voice, his hoarse murmurs and shouts.

She moved between the guards and took her final step to her destination.

The chamber beyond was decorated with the spoils of a lifetime of victories. Gold-tipped spears flanked one wall, embellished shields the other. Hanging above the rich fabrics of the bed that dominated the room was a grimacing wooden head bearing an iron helm.

But Eònan was not alone. Four shadows stood with their heads turned towards his form lying upon the bed. His eyes gazed up towards the ceiling, filled with fear and anguish.

Upon his chest a final figure crouched, seemingly formed of the very darkness of the beyond itself, its spindly limbs clutched close, claws of pitch gripping the Rìgh's temples, its head tilted forward to stare directly into his eyes.

Fiadh now knew what she faced. A mare, a Sjøfolk legend, a spirit come to prey upon the lost, drive them to madness and steal away their souls to fly the skies of winter. It had no place here in the Seann Àite, beneath the eye of the Rìagan. It had not earned its right to stand among the spirits of this land and claim souls as its own.

"Eònan," she found herself calling to him. But he could not hear her, his mutters and shouts of fear and desperation being leached from the very air itself into the mare, whose back heaved with vicious laughter.

The four shadows paid her no mind, swaying as they stood, two tall and two short, like children. Caoimhe, Domhnall, Rhona, and Fionn. The lost family of the Rìgh, returned from the tombs in which they lay to haunt their kin and drive him to his own demise.

She took a step forward, letting the blade light the space between her and the spirits. What was not meant to be could be banished, driven out, and the peace it had disturbed restored. She had heard the tales, been raised on the stories of the heroes who cast back the spirits of foreign lands. Now, she could do the same.

The mare's silent laughter ended, its claws gripping tight and toes curling back from Eònan's chest. Its head began to twist upon its shoulders, revealing a fixed grin turning to her slowly, etched into its dark features like a knife had carved it out.

"You're not meant to be here," she snarled, fingers tightening about Caerdrich's hilt. The mare's head turned around, and its gaze seemed to swallow the light around her, dragging at the frost-touched glow of the blade.

She raised Caerdrich, gripping their hilt in both hands, and ran in between the shadows to swing the blade forward and down upon the dark spirit. Its grin looked up a final time, its eyes boring into her, and for a moment she froze, hanging in the air, suspended with Caerdrich's blade raised overhead.

"Neither are you."

All at once the room seemed to expand away from her, a dark pit opening up beneath her, and, with a final scream, Fiadh was pulled down into the dark.

***

She was in a long, stone corridor. But it wasn't the rough mismatched stonework of Ghav Rhien. Instead, it was smooth, perfectly carved granite, granite carved from the very mountain through which it led. Torches flickered in the dark and the smell of sea spray had been lost to the rough taste of charcoal in the air, the thickness of years of dust kicked up by her footsteps.

There was no mistaking the cold stones of Tur Eumor, or the long halls of its inner sanctum. The corridors leading to ...

Fiadh halted as she realised her hands were empty. She pointlessly patted at her own form, as if she would find Caerdrich hidden in the folds of her shadow. This is where she had found the blade, all those years ago. Why here? What business did the mare have in these halls?

She snarled at the darkness beyond the torches. Whatever it was, it could not have the blade. No good would come of uniting a haunting spirit with that ancient steel.

She turned away from where she had walked in her own distant past, away from the choice she had made to draw the blade from its stone confinement.

But within a few steps Fiadh realised this wasn't quite the hall from her memories. There was no turn in the stone ahead of her, just an endless series of the same nooks and sconces disappearing further into the dark. With each she passed another appeared out from the shadows. She came to a stop, turned, and found the hall behind her remained just as close as it had been before she began.

It was some kind of trap, a labyrinth forged in the mind of the mare, designed to lead her back to the blade. Maybe it wanted Caerdrich for itself. Maybe this was some kind of trick to cause her to give up the blade for some cruel designs it could wage with that strength.

It was playing games with her. Wasting her time even as the Rìgh's men advanced on her chambers, as it continued to drain Eònan's will and lead him to desperately seek the aid of the worst parasites of the land.

She was done playing games.

Fiadh strode towards the hall. She knew what awaited her; the memory was burned into her mind. She had walked this path a thousand times herself, without the need of a mare seeking to torment her with it. She had tormented herself with the memory, and she'd be damned if any being was going to take that curse and make it their own.

The hall was exactly as she had left it, the same dust-coated stone, the same black drapes of the Sciathán Dubh hanging from the walls, the same white cloth draped over the plinth where the blade lay, the same three-faced statue of the Ríaghan looking down upon it all. It did not whisper to her, not this time.

She advanced upon the dais, hand tearing away the cloth and revealing Caerdrich. No longer in their bright unsheathed form, but instead within the engraved black scabbard she carried upon her shoulders to this day. It all came back to this, to this moment where she had heard the blade whisper to her in the dark, guiding a desperate girl to its chamber, promising her deliverance even as invaders tore through the great fortress' grounds and hunted for the acolytes within. Her elders might well have turned the course of battle wielding this most powerful weapon held deep within their halls. Instead, she had taken it, turned from her flight by their whispers, and they had promised her vengeance.

Caerdrich had raised her from where she had fallen, and it would aid her again to free her from the mare's grasp. She reached forward, wrapped her hand around its scabbard, and tore it free of the plinth.

The world seemed to tilt on its axis. Suddenly the plinth was above her, the corridors formerly behind her now beneath her. Fiadh hurtled down the drop, her stomach thrown into her throat with such force she didn't even have a chance to scream. With Caerdrich in one hand, she scrambled to find some, any, kind of purchase as the torch lights flew past, their flames now blazing up in the direction of the Ríaghan's hall.

But now the corridor opened below to moonlight, the sounds of battle raging beyond as the mountain's stone gave way to the wide grounds beyond the walls of Tur Eumor.

Fiadh tumbled and slid across the dirt and grit, her feet desperately kicking out to gain some purchase. Her free hand dragged clear of every crack and rock as if she were falling straight down instead of along the ground.

The torches flashed in the night, lighting the silhouettes of figures engaged in a desperate fight to survive, blades held aloft, spears flying through the night. The screams of people left defenceless as blades crashed down upon them and the crack of lightning rending the stones of the walls that protected them.

Still, she spun across the ground, past the courtyard, directly towards the cliff overlooking the tumultuous waves. Her scream echoed out into the nothing and for a moment she hung in the air over the vicious crags of rock far below.

Her hand found something to grasp hold of. The loose dirt holding a root in place against the side of the cliff gave way and left her hanging by one arm, her torn and bloodied fingers wrapped tightly around that lone root.

Hanging above the raging waters, just as she had been all those years ago, tossed aside by the sorceries of those who had carved open the walls with the fury of the skies. Just as she had done a hundred thousand times in her mind, running through that moment and all the ways she could have done things differently. All the ways she could have been stronger, been able to haul herself back onto the edge and carry Caerdrich back into the fray. All the ways she could have held on for just a few more moments and been lifted free by her sisters who would surely have seen the bright blade shining in the dark.

But she was stronger now; she wasn't swallowed by the blind panic of a child facing this fall for the first time. She had been here before, and she knew how to beat it.

She flung the blade up and over the top, swinging her other hand up to the root to steady herself. Her feet found purchase on the rock, and she took a deep breath to steady her heart before the heave over the edge.

There was another crack, a flash of blinding light as another bolt struck from the heavens and cleaved through soil and rock. Caerdrich tumbled into the hollow and her breath was pounded from her lungs as the ground lurched and swung her away only to crash back into the sheer cliff face.

Fiadh could feel the panic growing again, her heart thundering against her ribs, her eyes spinning back and forth trying to spot any sign of escape through the bright spots left by the strike. Her arms grew cold, and her fingers numbed as blood fled her limbs and face.

There had to be a way up, this time, there had to! She had done this before, in her thoughts, beneath every sky on the long road, in her dreams beneath every star. Her hands started to claw at the rock, but every handhold fell away at her touch, every surface turning slick as if coated with rain.

And then, the rain came, torrents of it, slamming down and drowning the din of battle with the roar of thunder above.

This is not what happened. This is not what should have happened. None of it was right.

What's done is done.

Brianan's words came back to her unbidden. They rang around her head even through her desperate, gasping breaths, past the pain of her hands slipping every moment down that lone root.

What's done is done.

She hadn't clambered back up. She hadn't thought to throw the blade, even if Caerdrich had let her. She hadn't found a foothold. She hadn't been there as the last defenders of Tur Eumor fell, leaving only a ruin in their wake. Leaving no one to watch the sea when the mare came to the isle of Ghav Rhien.

She had fallen, blade in hand, robbing the citadel that had shielded and taught her of its most potent defence. She had been swallowed by the freezing waters and never again returned to the charred shell nor seen the remnants of its keepers and those ancient halls.

Fiadh had dreamt every possible way she might have saved the Tur, every far-fetched strategy a child could have drawn on to charge into battle against an army that wielded the sky itself as a weapon.

Then, like now, Brianan's wisdom had aided her to lift herself from the dark delusions and denials of loss.

Caerdrich was in her hand once more, sliding across the rock into her waiting palm. She closed her eyes, took a final breath, and released her grip. The wind thundered around her as she fell, the surface of the water striking her back like a hammer, before swallowing her and dragging her beneath the waves. She opened her eyes and saw only the roiling waters lit by the blade's ghostly glow.

Caerdrich began to freeze, spindles of ice snaking out, tearing loose only to reform anew in an expanding web of frost. Fiadh kicked desperately towards the surface, hand clawing skyward even as the cold began to seize her.

She broke the surface, sucked in a gulp of air, and the waters parted around her, rushing away into the darkness, and leaving her standing alone in the dark, the light of Caerdrich lighting nothing but emptiness.

Gradually the world began to reform around her as ghostly shadows found their substance. The bark of great trees began to solidify around her, the darkness making way for the green of their foliage and the grass at her feet.

Where was she now? What other mazes did the mare intend to lead her down?

Fiadh wrapped her free arm around herself, shivering against the chill that still gripped her from that frozen sea. The memory of the ice was etched into her mind closer than it had been for years, the cold feeling as real as if Caerdrich's frost was still wrapped about her.

There was no respite here. Flakes of snow were beginning to spiral down from between the leaves above, the grass shimmering with frozen dew.

The vegetation was verdant, too alive for such cold. It was if the cold had been pulled with her from those icy depths, or that this was no forest of her world at all. No moon or stars shone here to illuminate the forest beyond, no night's light to brighten her silvered eyes. She held the blade aloft and, lit by its cool glow, began to walk forward through the brush.

There was a crunch of feet on twigs ahead and Fiadh ducked behind an oak, hiding the blade's light between herself and the bark. She craned her head around the corner. This was no memory. Never before had she hidden among the boughs of some other worldly forest gripped by an unnatural winter.

Ahead, down a slope and moving with youthful abandon, was a girl. Hair as black as pitch and pale arms poking out from beneath roughly hewn hides. She moved with confidence as if her eyes, like Fiadh's own, could pierce the dark.

Behind her, stalking on the far side of the trees, was a figure with skin as white as starlight. In their hands they held a wicked two-handed blade as long again as their bare torso. From their head fell hair in a brilliant silver, and their ears protruded from beneath it in long points.

Fiadh moved in parallel to them, mirroring its movements as they followed either side of the girl in the glen.

She tracked them for a while, hand bearing the blade held low to hide its shine from the clearing, trying to see what she could do from where she was. She was too far off to ambush the pale figure across from her, and to shout from here would be to distract the child while warning the one stalking across the way.

Why here? What could the mare want from her, showing her this distant scene from another time and place?

Distracted by her thoughts, Fiadh wasn't paying close enough attention to where she put her feet. She froze as she heard the crunch beneath her step, eyes immediately going across to the valley floor and to the girl whose eyes were now cast up into the trees from where she stood.

She hesitated only a moment before ducking behind a tree and struggling to calm her breathing. She had recognised that face, those flecks of silver in those wide dark eyes.

Orlaith, here, in this mysterious wood in a dream spun by a mare.

She leant around and looked across the gap around the other side of the tree, but the pale man was no longer there, vanished into the foliage beyond.

She could stay here, walk to Orlaith, protect her, ensure she did not come to harm.

No, she realised, she couldn't. She could have done that a long time ago. She could have remained at the Three Willows and kept watch over the child and ensured the fey kept up their side of the bargain. But she didn't. She rode away, continued with her life, for years never returning to that place.

Now the mare was tormenting her with that. Like lifting Caerdrich from their plinth in Tur Eumor, like her fall into the ocean below, she had made those choices. She could not take them back in a dream. Her heart strained, screamed at her to walk around the tree and down to take the child into her arms and apologise for having left. But it was not Orlaith. It was a dream and no matter what she did, the mare would drag her back to do it again.

There wasn't time for her heart.

So, she took a breath and, without looking back, walked away into the trees. They faded away before her, disappearing back into the shadows even as she continued to walk through the dark.

"Where are you?" her shout surprised even her, seeming to echo back from walls she could not see.

"Reveal yourself! Face me, you coward! I am done with these games. I am done with you!" She slashed the air with Caerdrich, their glow leaving behind a trail of sparks.

She screamed into the dark, a wordless, formless howl of rage and grief. Tears came to her eyes as her hoarse throat gave way to sobs, broken by more screams at the nothing around her. The emotion spilled out from her, the heat of her anger ebbing away.

In the distance a light sparked into life, the orange glow of flame gradually growing as she raised her eyes to it.

Feeling drained, but lighter for it, Fiadh approached.

A lone fallen trunk barred the way towards the light and upon it sat a figure, sitting away from her, the fire's light extending out beyond him as though cast from his eyes. A great fur cape sat upon his shoulders and Fiadh could see the blade in his lap, already dripping blood onto the grass at his feet. Red hair fell upon his back and over it sat an iron helm.

The same helm that hung in the chambers of Eònan in the halls of Ghav Rhien.

The scene shifted. Shadows of the Rìgh stood from where he sat and moved into the home beyond, with hands raised. She saw one shadow stabbing the blade into the ground and walking away, another shouting into the home's empty doorway, one drawing blood from his own hand and displaying it into the night. The last fell upon his own blade.

Through it all, Eònan sat on that fallen bough, watching in silence.

The flames beyond crackled and popped. From time to time, she saw shadows grappling on the edges of the light, blades rising and falling, the echoes of screams from voices long forgotten.

Whispers hung in the air, crowding the space between her and the Rìgh, beckoning and tempting him to lift his blade and advance into the house to claim what he was owed, protect his people, be the leader that they deserved. In this memory, in this far away time of Eònan's past, he too had heard those whispers coming to him from the darkness.

Fiadh advanced cautiously, but as she raised her blade to light her path, she found that Caerdrich was once again in their scabbard, that she was clothed in hardened leathers and her tough boots crumpled the ground at her feet. The symbol of the stag riding a wave adorned her chest. In this place she had become one of Ghav Rhien's own guards, another figment of Eònan's own dream.

With care she advanced, sliding into the edge of Eònan's vision, and as he remained still, she came to sit beside him and gaze at the flames lapping against the walls before him.

They sat in silence for a moment, Eònan's eyes fixed on the bloodstained hands wrapped around his blade, Fiadh's own on the fires leaping up the walls and thatch, neither giving warmth nor burning away the wood.

"You were not here, were you?" the Rìgh finally said. "I recognise your face, but not from this place. Not from this night."

He looked up and she saw shock register beneath the anguish, his eyes widening as they saw the silver gazing back.

"The Crow? Here? Even in my dreams." His hands twisted tighter around his blade, blood pooling between his fingers, but he did not raise it. "It is true I sent my men to bring an end to you, finally, but foul magics have brought your spirit to me even from beyond the grave, to bring vengeance for your death at my hand."

The shock twisted and faded, giving way to sorrow.

"What poetry it is that vengeance would come to me here, before the display of my reign's cruellest act, to wash away the blood that has stained me so with my own."

"I'm not here to kill you, Eònan, though perhaps it is what you deserve. Nor have I come to offer you some kind of deliverance," Fiadh broke her silence, the firelight dancing in her eyes. "I think it is past time that you left this place behind, don't you?"

"I can't," he replied.

Fiadh turned to see he had raised his head and was now staring directly ahead, into that dark doorway, past the dancing fires and battling shadows.

"I've tried everything," he said. "I've walked away, I've taken my own life, I've run into the fires myself and burned as I attempted to free them. Nothing I have done is enough, nothing can remove the stain of what I have done."

The whispers continued to swirl about them, coming close, feeding temptations and coercions into their ears. They promised fame and riches, they threatened death and being lost, forgotten, to the sea.

"They were my kin. Vestamr came and with his coming came their deaths. I saved Ghav Rhien from destruction. They paid with their lives for our isle's future."

"You killed them," Fiadh said.

He turned to look at her and met her eyes with those words. Beneath his helm it was not the eyes of the Rìgh of Ghav Rhien that looked back, but the black pits of the mare.

"I had no choice," he said, his voice contorted and strained, as if being pulled from a place far away.

Fiadh cast her arm out at the scene that his memories had cast before them. "Yet you have spent all this time showing what other decisions you could have made. Each time you are returned here to start anew and make a new choice, and each time you do not make the choice you made then. You *had* a choice."

Those foreign eyes turned back to the flames, and it dawned on Fiadh what had occurred here, why it was that the caoineag wailed day after day in the halls of Ghav Rhien, slowly driving the Rìgh and his house to madness. Caoimhe, Domhnall, Rhona, and Fionn. They weren't dead, not to him. They continued to haunt his mind even as the years passed. The mare had found that guilt and denial and made it real in this place, where the dead could live again and plague the mind of Eònan. They had been dragged from the grave to live again and haunt this man, and as long as he held them here, unable to accept the path he had chosen, they remained trapped at the border between life and death.

The caoineag cried for them, not for Eònan. It cried for their release from this dark place.

"What's done is done." She spoke Brianan's words as if they were her own. "You cannot deny the past, nor can you change it. You used this blade, and you wrought death with it. That cannot be changed."

"Then why am I here?" he asked. "If not to change what I have done, why return me to this place?"

Fiadh shrugged.

"Why are either of us here? You tried to have me killed, and when I tried to drive the mare from your chambers, I was dragged through the moments which my mind has clung to most. Perhaps the twisted intent of the mare is to trap us here using our drive to change what cannot be changed."

She turned to him and met that empty, haunted gaze with her own. "Why did you seek to have me killed? Why now, and why then? Why did you burn Tur Eumor?"

Eònan hesitated, his body stiffening at the question.

"It may not have been long after the return of Vestamr," he said. "But it was not my past I wished to change at Tur Eumor, it was my future. I spoke with the Norns in the hope of freedom from what I had done, and they gave me no answers. They did, however, foretell that one day a Crow would come to me and bring with them the finality of death. When the Raven came to me with her designs to destroy the halls of the Ríaghan, I could finally be assured no Crow would ever bring about my end."

"The Raven indeed came to my hall, and with the Norns' prophecy fresh in my mind, I promised her my ships with which to besiege the Tur. I watched the sky fall upon it across the sea and have never felt such dread, but with it I felt a release from that curse. It fell, and with it I felt like I had saved myself. Yet here you are."

"So, I am here to deliver the finality of death," Fiadh replied, standing from where she had sat at his side.

"Perhaps, yes, my time has come. Fitting that it might be my own hand that delivered it. I was not owed my freedom from it. I could not free myself of the curse of blood shed by drowning it in more blood, after all. I should have known that." Eònan did not meet her eyes once more, instead staring into the sky beyond, as if preparing to see nothing at all. Opening his hands, he allowed his sword to tumble to the ground.

"That would be too easy," she said at last, releasing her hands from the hilt of Caerdrich.

He started at that and brought his gaze back to her, his eyebrows displaying a surprise that those black pits could not.

"You are not here so you might be struck down in some kind of twisted penance for your actions," she said. "I am not here to deliver that to you as a reward for the lives you cut short, for the life I may never have due to your choices. You are here to face what you have done and accept it, finally, after so many years making excuses and denials." Once she had begun, she felt unable to stop. "You butchered your own kin because of the threat they posed to your continued prosperity on this isle. You helped the Raven burn the house of a god because another threat had dared to be raised to your rule. You do not deserve salvation."

Fiadh kicked his sword back to his feet from where it had fallen.

"Lift your blade, accept the choice you made and make it anew. Maybe then you will be freed of this spirit and have a chance to earn your forgiveness. The mare may be gone when you waken, but your guilt will not be gone, and you will have to live with that till the end of your days. You may never atone for the death you have wrought."

Eònan's mouth opened and closed as if words should have emerged but he simply had not thought to create them. He looked down at the blade, his hands clenching and releasing in his lap. With a final pause, he gripped its handle to pull it from the grass, pulled his shoulders back, and stood.

"If this works," he said, eyes fixed on the burning thatch. "If I am freed of this spirit, what can I offer you in return?"

"Ideally, I should like to live on this earth a little longer," she replied. "One day, I may speak your name and ask something else of you, and you must answer my call then. I place this geas upon you, Eònan, and may you never know the consequences of breaking it."

Eònan nodded, and, with a final look in her direction, walked into the flames.

Where he had waited a small creature sat, black as pitch, spindly limbs curled up underneath it. A fixed, jagged grin turned to meet her. It looked at her for a time, those twisted features revealing nothing of its intent. Then, finally, it lifted one arm in a wave. The mare faded and with it the flames, shadows, and Eònan himself vanished from view.

In the darkness, for a moment, Fiadh felt a sense of peace. The pressure on her chest was lifted, the burn in her throat from her screams had eased. For that blissful moment, her thoughts were empty of the whispers that had trailed her for so long.

Then she felt the scabbard of Caerdrich become chill once more and, with a curse, she began to fall.

***

When she blinked open her eyes the whole world was crimson. She was back in her chambers in Ghav Rhien, dawn's glow shining light onto the ceiling.

She was ... *wet*. Slick from head to toe. With her free hand she wiped her eyes free and looked down to see she was coated in slick, bright, blood. Horrified, Fiadh turned back to the window and found that the gateway she had opened before had collapsed with her return, splashing across the floor.

There was a clatter from the doorway, and she turned to find Annis standing absolutely still, eyes fixed upon her, from the other side of the frame.

Only the frame. The door itself was split into pieces, some lying across the floor and some hanging from the remaining hinges. One body lay inside the room, moving very slowly and groaning from time to time, barely inches from the chalk that surrounded her. Another lay underneath Annis' feet in the doorway itself, the blood trail showing they had been thrown face-first into the door's frame.

Annis stood with the same look of frozen shock that he had had when she first opened the portal. One torn-off leg of the cot that had previously held her belongings had fallen from his fingers, the cot itself now shredded and impaled by one end of a spear shaft.

He was not alone. Beyond the door stood two more of his colleagues, between them the priest of Alwealda, hand clutching his face, blood running between his fingers where half of his mask had once been. The group had halted mid-motion, blades raised, one bearing a shield still holding Annis' axe and barring his path.

Fiadh twisted her face into a snarl, gnashing her teeth, and raised Caerdrich, held again within their scabbard, towards them.

"Begone, priest," she said, dropping her voice into a growl. "Run from this place as swiftly as they can carry you, before I seize your soul and drag it down into the pit with me!"

The silence was broken only by the sound of blood dripping from her clenched fist. But that was enough. Still holding his shattered mask close the priest fled, almost tripping over his vestments as he vanished up the corridor, followed swiftly by the remnants of his companions.

Annis watched them go, a look of bemusement replacing his shock as he turned back to her, hands raised in question.

"Thanks," Fiadh said, trying to wipe her hand free of the blood she had pointlessly smeared across her face.

"Yer welcome," came Annis' reply, as he lifted one half of a white marble mask in his other hand and gave her the first smile she had seen from him.

In spite of herself, Fiadh laughed.

***

The waves lapped at the shore, washing back and forth over the pebbles beneath the docks. Fiadh stood looking over the sea, enjoying the breath of fresh air running over her skin.

The ship was ready, her pack loaded and the crew gradually shifting the last of their cargo of fish and wood carvings from the jetty. She had a keen ear for whispers, a trait which had kept her safe over the long years, and she had heard that Eònan had passed peacefully in his sleep in the night. The geas she had placed upon him, perhaps, would never be answered. Ruadh, his heir, would be too busy ensuring loyalty from the mercenaries in the fort to be concerned about the fate of a Crow no one in the halls had wanted to stay for longer.

Brianan stood with her, as he had done for some time, looking in silence over the water. It does the mind good, he had always said, to take some time to drink in the world around you without feeling the need to break it.

That might be true, Fiadh thought, but she did have a question.

"Brianan?" she asked.

"Yes?"

"There's one thing beyond the veil, something Eònan said that I can't shake from my mind," she said.

"The dreams of another are a dangerous place, Fiadh. Be careful what you bring back with you." His voice was as stern as ever. The shadow may have been lifted from Ghav Rhien, the caoineag laid to rest alongside the spirits it had cried for, but the druid forever spoke as though he carried the world upon his shoulders.

"Eònan he ... he said a Raven came to him many years ago. This Raven, they burned the Tur, or at least he said that they did. Who are they?" she asked.

She could see Brianan looking at her out of the corner of his eye, weighing his answer. He knew, possibly more than he would ever reveal to her, but even a little could guide her to where she needed to go.

"Ach, no matter. Dead men hold no secrets," he said, finally. "The Red Raven. She goes by many names, has ruled one of these hundred isles for longer than I have lived, plying her trade as a useful ally for whomever might be in need of one on these tumultuous seas."

He sighed and joined her to watch over the water. "Given how long she has ruled, it may be that the Red Raven is more of a title than a name. I did not know she was at the Tur, but then, the stories would have it be that she has been at many places even when she could not have been."

He paused for a moment before adding, "Do not chase her, Fiadh. The Raven is not spoken of in hushed tones for her tendency towards generosity and good will. If she were indeed behind the burning of the Tur, it would be a gift to bring her the one acolyte of the Ríaghan who got away."

Fiadh offered a thoughtful frown. "Maybe then I must bring her an even greater gift, some trinket she might have seen that is more within the reach of a Crow than a Raven. Aren't we infamous for picking up the shiny scraps left by those long departed?"

Brianan laughed at that, and it was a warm, chesty chuckle that brought a genuine smile to her lips.

"There isn't anything that might change your course when you have one, is there? I see my work here is done. You have my thanks." He turned to her and offered a hand. "You may not know it, but what you did here matters more than you could believe. So many will rest easier tonight."

She took his hand and they shook, pausing a moment to exchange smiles they had not shared for many years. With a final nod, Brianan gave her shoulder a squeeze and walked away back towards the fortress above.

Fiadh returned to her place, letting out a sigh of breath she had been holding for far too long, looking out at the sails dancing on the distant waves. She heard the footsteps coming from behind her but did not turn, raising her gaze only to fix on the mountains of the Seann Àite beyond.

"Ye huvnae left?"

Annis stood alongside her, taking the place the druid had vacated. He crossed his arms as he cocked his head, staring off into the distance trying to spot whatever she could be looking at.

"Not yet. It's a lovely day, figured I might as well enjoy it for a while," she said.

"Aye, 'tis that. It'll be a guid day fur a journey."

She paused for a moment, considering how to phrase her question to him for the second time in as many days.

"Do you want to come with me?" she said, keeping her tone light. "I could use someone like you watching my back. How many did you turn back at that door? Four? Five? I may need that distraction again one day, maybe a few more times."

There came that matter-of-fact shrug again. "Are ye guid at whit ye dae?" he said, with an eyebrow raised sceptically.

"If I weren't, I wouldn't be offering to share half of what I get. If I'm not, you can feel free to find someone else who can offer you more coin," Fiadh said, turning to look at him.

Annis' eyes drifted to the pair of sacks lying in the bow of the ship alongside her and then to her eyes. "Ye kent Ah'd say aye."

Fiadh's smile broke wider at that. He had taken long enough. "I knew that troupe of misfits wasn't giving you the escape you needed. You're too curious to turn away from a chance to know what happened in that room. I know you don't want to go back to standing beside the throne of a sad old man again."

She tossed the bag Eònan's men had delivered in his stead in one hand, peering thoughtfully at it before tossing it over to her companion. Annis caught it without breaking her gaze.

"I know you're wondering if there's more gold where that came from," Fiadh said. "There will be. So yes, I knew you'd say yes."

A thoughtful frown and nod came with that. Then, without a further word, he turned and jumped into the waiting ship.

"So," he said, eyes on her again. "Whaur's next?"

※

A GIFT OF THE SEA

The trail down into Tur Pailt was slick with rain, every flash of lightning lighting up the water cascading off the rocks. Fiadh and Annis had long since dismounted and guided their steeds down the path with care, mindful of the yawning gap beside them and the roar of waves crashing against the base of the cliffs.

"Whit brings us tae this forsaken steid, Fiadh?"

"A job, Annis. It's always a job. A man who's lost a brother sent me a letter in the hopes a Crow might find him, even though an Rìgh, as usual, could not."

"An Rìgh?" Annis replied, his southern accent mangling the words in her tongue. "That's the Laird Pailt?"

"The very same. I'll put down five pieces that the Laird didn't shift from his tower an inch for the effort," the slick rocks shifted beneath Fiadh's feet, and she swore as she regained her footing.

"Ye ken the man?"

"I know him. He was a feared man once, Rìgh Tuath, Laird of lairds over these waters, with the rulers of every isle as far as you could see paying homage to him. Now every petty merchant in this crumbling backwater sees themselves as the true power of these seas." Fiadh had to shout over the din, and a crack of lightning and an immediate rumble answering it helped emphasise her words.

Tur Pailt was a shambling place, sheltered within a cup carved into the cliffs, buildings scattered about the cove as if they had been thrown up against it by the waves. A lone tower struck out from the shore, the fire burning at its peak shining a solitary light beneath the tumultuous sky, bright enough that Fiadh could see it even as the howling winds burned her eyes.

They ventured down the twisting path, hugging close to its granite sides and past shutters sealed tight against the weather. The Rìgh's stronghold overshadowed them, its broad stone bulk standing out against the wood and slate of the buildings around it.

The home the letter had directed them to closely matched the description they had been given. It sat beneath the empty arms of a birch, its green painted door illuminated by the flashes of lightning.

Fiadh gave a nod and Annis approached it, giving the door several firm knocks. The roar of the sea and storm didn't hide the squeal of furniture being moved within, as if the door had been blocked, before the door whipped open in the face of the wind. Beyond the door a blurry silhouette of a figure within waved them in.

Their host struggled to push the door back and Annis was forced to lend an arm to hold it in place as he pushed drawers against it to hold it shut. The lock bar that might have held the door had been torn free, the bent remnants propped up nearby.

"The Crow?" he said between heavy breaths.

"One of them, yes," Fiadh replied, perching on the rough-hewn table set across the far side of the fire pit. Despite the wind they had let in the pit still smouldered, the remains filling the chamber with much needed warmth and an unfortunate stench of well-cooked fish that must have preceded their arrival. She peered through the wafting smoke between them and examined the man before her. He was small, almost gaunt, eyes sunken into dark sockets.

There was an awkward silence as the man turned on crutches seemingly cobbled-together with leftovers from a boat's oar and tiller but etched with delicate swirling carvings and patterns. He leaned upon them, standing on the one leg not missing from the knee down, and glanced back and forth between the visitor who had just made herself at home at his table and her companion who stood cross-armed at his own door.

"Ceud mìle fàilte, please, my home as if it were yours. I am Eadan, you must have received my notice? My brother, Rònan, has been lost. An Rìgh has not sought to find him, and I am no seafarer myself." The man's hands clasped one another as he shifted his weight uncomfortably over his crutch.

Annis, as was his role, did a stellar job of looking stern and imposing even as the man continued to mutter in Cànan, a tongue her companion could barely grasp a single word of. In this company, however, the act was maybe a little bit too much.

"Lost?" Fiadh asked, finally relaxing her legs by hoisting herself up to perch on the edge of a chest leaning against the far wall.

"My brother was lost to the sea, I fear."

This was new. People didn't reach out to a Crow to fish for corpses, let alone for a reward promising not just coin, but silver. This must have been a brotherly bond like no other. His name would mean little, she thought. A dead man's name would not identify him.

The man noted her quizzical look and hurried to clarify what he meant. "He was in search of an item of great power, meant to tie the very soul of the sea to the bearer's will. I believe he was convinced that it lay not far from these very shores."

"So, are we looking for the item, or your brother?" Fiadh said, running his description through her mind. There were tales aplenty of trinkets and relics that were meant to seize control of the untameable seas, but none for generations more substantial than a song or a con. This was likely no different.

Their host looked genuinely astonished by the question, and he appeared pained, as if any motive other than finding his brother had not even crossed his mind.

"My ... my brother, of course," he stammered. "I don't have any need for whatever power he went searching for. I told him he was a fool to go searching for it, that nothing could truly win him what he seeks. But he went anyway, without me or my aid, and now he is lost."

Guilt, then. There were few stronger forces more able to separate a man from his silver.

"And what did he truly seek, your brother?" she asked, nodding to Annis that he could relax. There was no threat here.

"A woman, of course. Whatever else would that disaster of a man be chasing out into the raging seas?" Eadan sighed, shuffling over to the chair Fiadh had left nearby and dropping heavily into it, his crutch left leaning against the table.

"A woman ... and not just any woman ... *the* woman," Eadan continued with some bitterness, the words coming slowly, as if he had to drag them out from where he'd have preferred to leave them, discarded. "The one he raved on about any chance he had, the one already in the arms of the most powerful man of Tur Pailt, whose beautiful ethereal eyes he had met between market stalls, whose fleeting glances and moments he valued before all else. Before even his own life, he claimed."

"For those eyes he went out to seas off the Àirde Sgreamhail, declaring he'd return with the sea itself as his servant to whisk her away, to carry her to his new kingdom of the waves."

Fiadh's eyebrows went up at that, frowning in thought. Those were mighty grand words even for a young man newly besotted, and at no minor risk either. The screaming cliffs were not known for their hospitality, nor were the tales of men snatched below the waves at their feet a myth. When Annis raised his own eyebrows in response, she translated into Àrdish briefly: "Lad with eyes on a lass went to sea for something shiny to win her with."

Annis nodded matter-of-factly to that. It wasn't the most original of stories.

"So, you're offering us enough to buy yourself a fèinne just to find your fool of a brother and return him?" she asked, pandering to his desire to see his brother alive once more. Truly, this long lost at sea, long enough to seek aid, be denied it, and seek out a Crow instead, his remains were either washed upon some rock or he had long since sailed for another shore. She cast her eyes around the room as the man gathered his own thoughts. It was a simple place of no more than a handful of chambers. A place of some comfort, true, built sturdy against the seasons and with space aplenty, but not burnished with a wealth that suggested there was much to be thrown into the grave of a man possibly lying fifty feet beneath the waves.

"How come you by these riches?" she asked, peering into the shadows of the room.

"What does it matter? I've invited you, armed, into my home, shown you where I store my coin. Is not a little trust to be reciprocated?"

"Sure, and since we didn't barge in here, kill you, and steal your coin," Fiadh's voice lowered, "maybe you could sate my curiosity before I set out into these fearful seas to look for your brother in a nest of monsters."

He gulped at that. "I'm a carpenter, I make designs and figurines for wealthy patrons. No one else does, this side of the mountains, so they fetch a fair price."

She cocked an eyebrow. "No one else carves people from wood?"

"No one like me," he replied, with some confidence coming back into his voice.

There was a silence for a moment as Fiadh looked across the chamber again, weighing up the potential that there was something more to this. This would not have been the first time an offer of coin beyond their usual taking turned out to be some kind of trap, or a con spun to make a display of a changeling drawn into the wheelings and dealings of spiteful men.

He broke the silence. They often did, eventually, unnerved by silver-eyed fey guests and the implacable silence of Annis.

"You're not the first to come by, on seeing my notice," he said, his eyes no longer meeting hers.

Here we are, she thought, and more quickly than she had anticipated.

A nervous glance from him in her direction caught her curious gaze, prompting him on. "Hooded men, Crow, red robes from the south, asking if one all in black with silvered eyes had passed by since my notice went out. They didn't speak Cànan so well and muttered to one another in the tongue of your companion, furtive like, as if they were expecting you to leap upon them from the shadows at any moment."

Now this was a tale worth the journey. Fiadh immensely enjoyed hearing how the story of Ghav Rhien had been spun in the months since she had left that haunted isle.

"They were searching for you, or any word of your passing," Eadan continued. "That blade you carry at your shoulder; I recognise it from their description. Caerdrich, they called it. They call you the blood weaver." He shuddered; his eyes cast to the floor. "They say you have a spindle to draw out the life of innocent men, and that you bathe in it to stay young."

Fiadh barked out a laugh at that, both Annis and Eadan jumping at the sudden sound as she clapped her hands together.

"A bath!" she shouted with open glee. "Oh, I absolutely *would* murder someone for a bath!"

There was no laugh from the pale faced Eadan, and Annis looked, not for the first time, as if she had finally lost her mind.

"You have won me over, Eadan," she continued. "It takes nerve to invite a 'blood weaver' into your home and offer them gold, all to win back a brother lost at sea. I appreciate nerve, and I'll take your coin for the pleasure."

"You ... you want to help me more knowing that the High Chalice is searching for you here?" Eadan looked more nervous than he had done since they'd entered. His free hand gripped fast around a pendant hanging from his neck.

"I want to help you more now that I know you're not hiding anything from me. Who knows, maybe your brother still lives out there on the seas and your faith in his survival might yet be repaid." Fiadh turned to Annis and broke the news that they'd be setting out on the water soon, and to find their horses and packs and somewhere safe to shelter. His expression matched the weather they were due to head out in, but with a nod and a final puzzled look at the woodcarver he let himself out.

"So, any more detail on where he might be? And what I might return should he be lost, to prove his passing to you?" she said, standing and wandering around the small abode, looking for evidence of the man's artistic talent.

"He ... he said he had to search the seas off the cliffs. There's a wreck out there, impaled on rocks a few hundred yards from the shore." He paused for a moment, as if asking for her permission to continue. "It's been there since before I was born. They say the Daoine Sìth sailed to an ancient home beyond the waves upon it, and their magics still bind it from decay to this day. He will have had his ring upon him."

He brought forward his hand and she turned to look upon it. A roughly hewn iron ring sat around his middle finger, two fish carved into its surface. "We have worn them ever since we were children, as a mark of our love for one another. He'll be wearing it out there, somewhere."

Having memorised the ring's design, she continued the search for his work and finally found one, a small carving of a horse no larger than her hand, with the hindquarters replaced with the tail of a fish. It stood out from its surroundings; the wood was delicately carved and smooth enough to reflect the glow of the embers even as it rested on a table-top hewn so roughly as to risk splinters. It was exquisite! The detail of every hair of its mane picked out, every scale of its tail. She had never seen anything quite like it.

A man of such talent, bound to one who would throw it all away on a folktale. The heart was so often loyal beyond the wisdom that might guide us, she thought.

"The cliffs? I know where they are. I have just one thing to ask of you before I depart," she said, gently returning the figure to its place upon the window ledge.

"What's that?" he replied, a slight tremor to his voice.

"Is there a chance you have any wax?"

***

"Found a place for the horses?" she shouted, pulling the hood of her cloak down hard against the wind.

"Did Ah say Ah hudnae?" came the reply, Annis not bothering to turn as he picked his way through the shore's rocks and pebbles.

"Well, no, but ..."

"Weel then, there's yer answer."

Annis didn't speak much at the best of times, but he'd been particularly quiet today, ever since they'd left the carpenter's home.

"You need to smile when death comes knocking, Annis," she yelled over to him, sliding away down towards the water. "It'll come often enough. If you don't smile when you can, you'll end up never smiling at all. If the Ríaghan wills it, we'll pass."

"Is this bloody rain the Ríaghan's wull as weel, then?" he said, turning towards her as she slipped away further towards the shoreline, the water running through the close shorn stubble of his scalp and over eyes squinted against it.

"The Ríaghan hasn't spoken to me since I was a child. I haven't heard her voice since the fall of the Tur," she shouted up towards him, the grind of wet pebbles shifting under her feet cloaking her words. "I have heard many other voices in the dark, but never hers," she continued, as much to herself as to her companion. "I hope, once those responsible for the death of her heralds have been reacquainted with Caerdrich, I might hear her voice again."

There, ahead of them, was what they had been searching for, winding their way from cove to cove between the cliffs. The rowboat had been dragged up past the seaweed that marked the high-tide line, lobster pots and nets crowded into one end of it.

"I told you we'd find one!" Fiadh said.

"Aye, ye did." he replied, joining her, and looking over the small craft, barely large enough for a single seat between the oars.

"But whit if ye faw in?" he asked, sceptical eyes taking in the waves lapping at the shore.

Fiadh stood up from where she had been checking its underside for any leaks or cracks. "Feel my hand," she said, holding her bare fingers out towards him.

He looked a little taken aback at the request.

"Go on, hold it."

His lip twisted slightly as he held out a hand and gently wrapped his fingers around hers. He hid it well, but she felt the muscles of his arm tense at the sensation, the warmth of his skin vanishing into the cold depths of her own.

"Does that flesh feel like your own, Annis, flash that should fear the creeping cold of the sea?"

"No, it feels like a bluidy corpse."

She wasn't expecting that, and his words stung more than she was prepared for. She pulled her fingers free of his loose grip and hid them within her cloak once more.

"A corpse is what I might well have been when I fell from the Tur, Annis. I gave away something of myself to walk on land again. The sea didn't claim me then, and I have faith it will not do so now."

Annis' brows were knotted with concern as he looked sceptically towards the rowboat and the sea beyond, then up to the cliffs that loomed above in the moonlight and that lone rock framed upon the horizon.

Fiadh stood with him in silence a moment. The sounds washed over them, the rhythmic crash and roll of the waves, the faint ringing of water striking the pebbles and running between them, and the far-off voices of those who watched from the cliffs that her ears could hear but his could not. The voices reminded her of a rhyme from long ago, when she had listened to these same sounds from far above these dark waters.

"Don't worry for me, Annis, I have been into these waters plenty of times before. Besides, I have you completing a vital task, here to guide me back to the shore," she said as she unshouldered her sack and knelt to move through its contents, pulling free a lantern encased on three sides with metal and on the fourth in coloured glass. "Because the cliffs ahead earned their name in our tongue from horrors far more deadly than cold water and sharpened rocks."

"Now," she continued, standing and holding the lantern towards him. "I need you to ensure this is lit and remains lit until I return. The rain will cloak the rocks so I cannot see the route back, and I will not be able to hear your voice."

Annis took the lantern from her hand, letting it hang as she took up flint and steel and began to light sparks within its chamber. As it caught the oil-soaked wick and she closed the glass window at its front, she reached back down and pulled out the wax Eadan had spared her.

"Any questions before I head out?"

Annis screwed up his nose and looked back out at the water through the rain dripping from his eyelashes. "Nah, Ah'm guid. Ah'll staun an git drookit, an point the licht at the sea. Ah'll wait fur ye tae row back wi a deid yin, then wander back an git oor reward."

Fiadh nodded as she massaged the wax between her fingers, struggling to soften it against the cold. She kept kneading it in one hand as she set about unloading the nets and pots from the boat, tossing the last of it aside just as Annis put one foot against the hull and gave it a shove towards the waterline.

The sodden pebbles underfoot crunched and squealed as she put a shoulder against the wood and gave it another shove out onto the water, her own boots holding back the water but not the chill that pricked at her calves as she strode into the lapping waves.

Hopping aboard she made herself at home. Two oars were fixed in rowlocks on either side and a handy bench sat between them for the work ahead. She settled in, thumbs pushing the wax deep into her ears. Another shove from Annis sent the boat on its way out, and she gave his grim furrowed brows a final wave as she took up the oars, glancing back from the light into the darkness stretching out behind her.

Immediately, with her ears clogged against the din of the storm, she could hear her heart throbbing, the sudden bellowing rush of her own breath as she wrenched the oars into place and began to row herself out to sea. The sounds came with every pull she took a breath, and with every pounding second, she glanced over her shoulders at the stretch of waves that tossed her craft like a plaything rolling in her palm.

She could see the cliffs begin to rise from the pebbled beach, their pitch-black crags framed against the dull grey of the clouds beyond, shimmering under the rain's tumult.

In time they made themselves known, moving across the rocks at the base of the cliffs, their scales flashing back the grey of the skies and the light that bounded upon the waves. Fiadh could see their mouths open, calling to her as her vessel touched each crest before spilling down the other side once more.

The Merrow of the Àirde Sgreamhail were coming for her, their song sounding across the waters, beckoning her to join them in the depths. She knew what songs they sang; she had heard them before as an older Crow held her shoulder tight, looking out and listening from a distance. She knew their song's pull, the way it had pricked and tugged at her mind, drawing her to join them, to plunge into the depths and swim with their melody.

To die there, like so many others tempted to their end.

They knew their song went unheard, their scales flashing as they ducked in and out of view between the waves, spiralling ever nearer to her craft. She fixed her eyes ahead, back towards that lonely golden light on the shore, where Annis awaited her return. She had heard about their beautiful faces, more beautiful than any she could ever know, their perfect features appearing between beckoning fingers to coax you into their reach so you might never escape their song again.

The mighty pinnacle of rock that jutted from the centre of the bay was beginning to loom ever larger now, its black expanse beginning to block the way onward. The effort to steer the boat began to gnaw at her back and shoulders, her neck aching as she struggled to drag the boat back on course as waves knocked it this way and that, her forearms burning even as she flexed and rolled her fingers against the wood to rest her grip with each pull.

She caught them in the corners of her vision, their scales breaching the water one by one, fins briefly flashing and letting gentle sprays fly free to challenge the rain. They were circling, drawing in like a net enclosing her pitiful craft knocked about by the shifting waves.

The great rock was not alone above the waves, its passenger growing clearer with every stroke of the oar and every glance over her shoulder. A ship rose from the sea, impaled on that pyramid of stone, its bow embracing it with shattered timbers. Its hull seemed to glimmer as the beams of moonlight struck it, the green that wrapped the woodwork shining like emeralds.

It was enormous, like no ship she had ever laid eyes on before. Greater than the trade ships the Àrdish sailed from southern shores weighed down with cargo; greater than the largest longships filled with horses and powered by a score of oars the Sjøfolk sailed from their far-off home.

The rowboat shuddered as it ran aground on barnacled rocks, jerking Fiadh forward and onto her feet as she scrambled to keep hold of the oars. She pulled them in, running them under the seats at its rear and hopping onto the rocks herself, giving it a final haul up and out of the water. Looking back over the water she saw nothing but waves, no sign of the Merrow, as if the rock itself had dismissed them back to the black cliffs circling the bay.

It was not only the wreck of the ship itself that had shone that green hue. Seaweed clung to it, hanging in sheets from the wood and pouring out onto the rock as if the two had long become one, looming together over the sea. Fiadh ran her fingers over the wood, its surface slick with water and algae. Sharp barnacles and limpets wreathed the lowest reaches, blurring the line between wood and rock.

She planted a foot into the crevice the ship's bow was embedded into and reached up to the woodwork, working her fingers into the carvings and giving them a tug to secure her hold. She pulled herself from the rock and up to the side of the hull, her free foot gaining purchase against the rough shells on the rock.

The climb was slow and difficult, the handholds slippery and her grip tired from the rowing. But the rain was easing, and her silvered eyes found cracks and shadows in the green glow of the woodwork, openings for her fingers to grip and boots to push from.

A final shove took her over a gunwale and onto the deck, the entire surface wreathed in thick seaweed, twisting in green, red, and brown patterns. Below her the sea's surface writhed, the waves writhed into whirlpools and eddies as it ran around the broken remnants of the mast.

There, held above the water's surface by a stand that extended into the cruel grasp of eagle's talons, was a horn bound in bronze and leather as long as her forearm.

Fiadh stepped towards the mast, gradually sliding her boots through the weeds with her hands spread out for balance. Her eyes lit upon the engravings on the horn's surface, of bare-skinned men with circular shields and long spears challenging one another, of horses formed from the froth of waves, of a script that flowed in both sharp edges and curves in an ancient tongue.

As she neared it, she felt the strength that dwelled within, the air that shimmered before its mouth, parting the rain before it. The scripts on its surface glowed with the faintest of lights, as if dulled by the passage of aeons.

She reached towards it and her fingers felt the prick of the magics that filled the space around it. Fiadh was not alone feeling its power; Caerdrich felt it too. The rain about her sharpened as the tips of every drop froze with the blade's awakening, biting at her cheeks. The blade yearned for the magic, they called to it, bidding her to draw nearer. She shook away their demands. Not yet. Not so hastily.

So, this was the subject of the brother's journey. An object of great power left behind by the Daoine Sìth before they vanished below the earth and into the world beyond our own, a legend that had proved truer than most. One whose command could not only win the love of the one he sought, but also compel others to clear his path to her. Had he made it this far? Braved the waters he'd have known far better than she, withstood the call of the Merrow and looked upon this great relic as she did now?

He could not have been the first to be drawn to this place, to this emerald ship so close to the shore. But still the horn sat, undisturbed upon its stand. Where had he gone?

As if to answer her thoughts, the wood beneath her feet shifted and quaked, the entire bulk of the ship shuddering as if someone had grabbed its bow and tugged it towards the sea's surface.

Fiadh turned and steadied herself, twisting her heels into the deck to steady herself in a wide fighter's stance. She could see it through the gloom and tilt of rain, the sheen of light scattering over shifting scales, a great body slick with the downpour and sea spray, its bulk running over the woodwork of the figurehead, gripping it tight.

From the scales emerged flesh and from that flesh the torso of a woman towering above the ship, arms held wide, hair dark as night, spilling over her form from a frost-white brow.

The Ceasg smiled, her teeth gleaming the rainbow of pearls and glinting with the sharpness of blades.

"We meet again, Caerdrich!" Her voice sprang across the air and into the back of Fiadh's head, scraping beneath the drumbeat of her heart and the thunder of her breath. The wax in her ears did nothing to diminish the sound. "How long has it been since I raised you up from these depths? One thousand moons? Two?" The blade did not answer, but their readiness remained, their call to her to turn back and seize the horn even beneath the gaze of a new, monstrous, companion.

The skin of the Ceasg shone with the oil of a creature from the depths, her eyes bright in the darkness like stars grasped from the sky and placed into the sockets of a skull that could be seen beneath translucent skin.

"Now you bring me a new plaything, blade, how generous." The muscles of her tail bunched beneath those shining scales, flashing their greys and whites beneath the light of the moon that had begun to peek from behind the rain clouds above. They coiled around the figurehead tightly, threatening to snap it from its perch and carry it into the currents below.

"It was ... it was not the blade that brought me," Fiadh said, her voice catching in her throat as she gazed up at the towering creature framed by the emerging moon. "I brought myself."

The blade did not share its desires so directly, not in the years since it had spoken to her upon the Tur. Their bargain did not stretch so far as such guidance, it seemed. Nor now did it deign to speak, its frozen touch no longer gripping the spray nor its thoughts revealing their connections to this master of the depths.

The Ceasg leant forward from her perch, her hair spilling downwards but drifting in the air like fronds of weeds suspended in the water.

"I am sure you believe you did," the Ceasg's words trailed, as if every statement were a suggestion tugging at her like the song of the Merrow beneath the waves. "I know what you are, little bird, I know you fluttered down from your nest upon the Tur. I know your wings were clipped and singed by the Raven's fiery breath. I know you are not strong enough to have come this far alone."

The words sliced through Fiadh and left her weak at the knees, the blood running from her face.

"I have come here in search of another, great one," Fiadh said, her voice weaker than she had intended, barely above a whisper. "A man's brother came here in search of the horn ..."

"Your words bore me, little bird." The voice sprang back and cut off her words. "I have become accustomed to the verse of the fili who have come to me in search of wisdom and tales, whose tongues dance on the wind and woo me with their weaving speech. Why do you not sing for me, small one?"

Fiadh was frozen, for the first time feeling the cold of her rain-soaked leathers seeping through to her skin, the icy bite of Caerdrich at her back scraping at her bones. The first words of songs began to flash in her mind.

But it was not a song that finally emerged from her lips to this ancient survivor of a time long vanished, but the rhyme she had learned from the shores, her shoulder held by her teacher, that proud warrior of the Sciathán Dubh.

> *"The wings that rise from Tur Eumor,*
> *That sweep aloft and over shore,*
> *To keep their watch out to the sea,*
> *Here, hear how the Crow came to be."*

The Ceasg withdrew up towards her figurehead, a smile dancing upon her lips. "The little bird speaks but will not sing. No tunes to carry your spirit away on the winds, to prevent me from casting your body to my children with the tide."

"You lifted the blade from the sea," Fiadh replied, placing a hand on Caerdrich's hilt. "You know their power. You know that should I come here to take from you what I had not earned, I would come with their blade in my hand, not sheathed upon my back." Her voice broke free of its whisper so that she was now shouting above the crashing waves, her hand releasing the sword's hilt and returning to her side. "I come only seeking what was lost by another, so that I may return it to their hand."

"You come seeking the man who claimed what was lost by the sea so that he might call it his own," the voice answered, swirling in her mind. "Do you come to make that claim as well? Do you come seeking to deceive the sea, to steal what is not yours?"

Fiadh's mind raced. She knew this creature could snuff her before she could draw Caerdrich from their sheath. Their presence at her back had bought her time, for now, but only for as long as the Ceasg continued to find her more interesting than tiresome.

The horn was here. So, what had Eadan claimed? What had he sought to take which the sea had already lost? That he had sought, what the horn was only a tool to win ... the girl at the market! Perhaps it was not something the sea had lost, but *someone*.

"That which you have lost, she still lives in Tur Pailt," she said, trying as hard as she could not to let the uncertainty she felt seep into her voice.

"I know where she is, little bird, I feel her when she comes to the shore and looks out upon the waves that should be hers by right. She was taken from the waves, stolen." The pearly teeth shone as that final word twisted and sank in her mind, bleeding darkness. "Your questing boy sought the horn to claim her as his own. He promised her return, but the sea knew his lie, so the sea claimed his life as payment. He may try to claim her once more from the beyond, if he is so convinced of their destiny to be together."

The Ceasg's expression was that of gleeful contempt, a smile more menacing even than those shining eyes peering from dark depths.

The 'boy' had come here looking for something to take the woman, Fiadh realised, not to win her. She was of the sea and somehow trapped on the land, held there in a way not even the Ceasg could release her from.

She had heard of this before. Some tales spoke of people managing to identify and capture those of the sea, taking something from them that prevented them from returning to the waters. Something they could not take back, something that had to be returned to them willingly by those who held it.

"His ship is not here, is it?" she asked, hoping to buy herself time to identify a way out, and a bargain that could be struck.

"Here? Hah!" The Ceasg's laughter was cruel and spiteful. "Half a man and barely half a sailor. His pitiful craft is long shattered and scattered on the waves."

"Now this, this craft you stand upon, this is a ship!" For all the Ceasg claimed to love the tales of the fili, it was clear she was keener still to have an audience to whom she could tell her own.

"I have ruled over this ship for generations before he so much as danced along the sand for the first time," she continued, casting her arms wide as if she still saw it afloat rather than ground against the rock. "The navigator of this vessel was a scholar, an adventurer, a name that will ring through the ages as a titan of his day." She was seized by her own thoughts now, paying Fiadh little mind. "Oh, for a man like him again, sailing on the waves with gods at his shoulder, bringing me tales of seas which do not move with the tides, of oceans swum by creatures I may never witness with mine own eyes."

"Instead, I face nothing but greed and lies." The Ceasg flung an arm out as if to act out her throwing the sailor into the waves. "If he had truly loved her, he would have gifted her the sea. He would have returned her skin to her, freed her to return to the home that was taken from her. But no, he held only lust and the need to possess her. His greed was to take what had not been given. He drowned in that greed, but even as it filled his lungs, he screamed for what he wanted for himself and had not a moment of doubt that he she was owed to him."

Her skin? Fiadh thought. A selkie, perhaps, beings who take the shape of seals in the water and humans upon the land – who might be trapped upon the land should their fur be stolen from them after they had shed it upon the shore.

"I would ask for one thing alone," Fiadh said, fixing her eyes on the Ceasg's own even as her heart raced at the very idea of asking for more. "I would ask for something to take home to the man's brother, to remember him by. As despicable as his brother was, he is alone, now, and even should he be joined by another to share his life with, it may calm his heart to hold a reminder of what he had, and which is now lost."

It was frighteningly still as she looked deep into those pin drops of stars shining from within the Ceasg's eyes. There was no expression in them, no emotion to give away her intent.

"What, pray, would you ask for by which this pitiful excuse for a man might yet be remembered upon the land?"

"I come only for the ring he bore upon his finger so that I may prove his passing to those on the shore," Fiadh replied, flexing her fingers to restore blood to their tips. "A ring bearing the mark of his brother, of two fish intertwined, so that he may be laid to rest in the memories of his loved ones."

"The ring, that is all," she continued. "The one I describe to you. It was the mark of his brother, who, despite himself, held his brother dearly. If I could return it, I could set his mind at rest, if little else."

"Very well," the Ceasg conceded, "you will have your band, it is of no consequence to the sea. But he will remain taken, to feed the denizens of the waters he sought to steal from."

"He saw nothing to exchange, only what he could take to keep and to own," the Ceasg continued, barely caring for the attention of her audience. "Let his fool's tongue rot, for only I rule this sea!"

Fiadh saw an opening, a chance for more information that she had not imagined she might find out here upon the water, of a name that Eònan and Brianan had spoken to her, that of the true architect of the fall of Tur Eumor. "What of the Red Raven?" she shouted up. "I have heard it is she who truly rules these waves."

The wind seemed to quiet to a whisper as the Ceasg's eyes dimmed, cast directly towards Fiadh's own as her sinuous body leaned down towards her, those pearled teeth fixing into a snarl, her muscles bunching about her neck and down to the violent veins bulging from taloned hands. Fiadh steadied herself, fixing her expression in one of desperate determination, digging her nails into her palms to steady the shakes which threatened to seize her as she felt the Ceasg's pungent breath all along her body.

Then the Ceasg recoiled, her sudden movement shifting the entire ship beneath Fiadh's feet, and her laughter keened into the moonlit sky.

"Oh, you are clever little bird," her voice sprang back as she loomed, her shadow once more framed by the moon above, "to taunt me so. But you are not clever enough. I have a deal with the Raven, and you will not beckon rage from my lips by dangling her name before me." She paused, as if weighing the life held before her against something Fiadh could not yet see. "Still, I have owed the Ríaghan a favour for a long while, and perhaps it is this day I might settle my debt. Ask me your questions, child of the Sciathán Dubh," she said. "And let me pay my final debt to your departed gods with words, to match her own favour to me."

"Where is she?" The words escaped Fiadh's lips as though they had been waiting for this moment all along. Her heart sank as the words were answered by a bark of laughter.

"This merry circle of gifts and favours between us spins like a whirlpool, child, that may one day drag us all down into the depths," she said, a cruel grin etched into her features. "I cannot answer this question, for that is the one gift I granted the Raven, that no one could possibly discover the path to her keep without magic greater than I can wield. You may find it, one day, from a being capable of granting you that very wish. But it will not be by my hand."

"Whose will it be from?" Fiadh said, the words coming in a rush now, her mind whirling and stabbing at the vast nothing she knew of the Raven, nothing but the ravings of a man haunted by ghosts and the dark prophesies of a druid who refused to grant her more information. It grew greater now, understanding all the knowledge held by this creature of the seas.

"A creature of gold and wishes, that dances upon the graves of the dead and the light of the sun. A creature trapped as I am on this side of the glimmering arc."

"What is the arc?" Fiadh asked, her hand subconsciously reaching for the sack at her hip where the fabric she had taken from the red cloaks resided. She remembered the passages she had opened with it, and the way shadows had poured from behind it beneath the temple in the Three Willows.

"The arc is what guards your world from Fearann Eeile, the lands the gods of old reside in. You have passed through doors to the arc to the place between, where dreams and mischief are wrought." The Ceasg leaned closer, those bright eyes lighting Fiadh's face from within her leering skull. "I smell it upon you, I can taste its dark residues seeping from you like a stain. I can hear his voice, the one beyond who whispers, seeking always to tear a hole in the arc and bring his people back from beyond, from where they were rightly sealed after the great battle. The Raven knows this and knows that to permit the way to be open again would be to see her power on this earth challenged by the very gods spilling forth anew."

Fiadh shook her head. The machinations of gods and monsters were beyond her. They would not get her closer to her goal, or that of Caerdrich, to avenge the fall of the Tur. There had to be something here that would bring her closer, that could be pulled from the Ceasg's tales.

"You saw me fall from Tur Eumor, great one," she said, restraining a wince as she met the bright eyes that loomed over her. "Who else was there alongside the ships of the Raven and those of Ghav Rhien? There were three, I know, but one remains lost to me."

"Remember the banners that flew over the Tur when you fell from the rocks, little bird," came her answer. "They struck a bargain by summoning the Raven once and they could do so once again."

Fiadh thought back, trying to remember the glimpses of battle at the Tur, the ships that had arrived on the shore and warriors who had poured forth to begin their ascent to the ancient fortress of the Sciathán Dubh. She remembered the sails bearing the sigil of the Red Raven. She saw the shields bearing the crest of Eònan of Ghav Rhien. She saw the banners sewn with a ship and a lightning bolt.

A banner she had not seen since the fall. How had she not remembered it before? How had she not searched for it long ago?

What spells did the Ceasg weave that brought it to her now, and could they be trusted? Were they truly her own memories, or creations this being planted to shape its own designs on the realms of the Dullahan Sea? Were they planted to lead Fiadh to her own goals, or to take her away from the horn and out again to her death willingly, without the protection it might grant her?

The Ceasg smiled. "Your thoughts reveal too much, small one. I may not hear the words, but I can feel the storm, the yearning, the pull of power to seek something more. It is not simply the ring for which you have come into my domain."

"Nothing more, I am not here for her, nor am I here for the sea." Fiadh steadied her eyes as best she could, willing her thoughts to still, to turn away from the bargain struck with the blade and its call to the horn.

The moon shone free now, its light scattering across the waves and bathing the ship in its pale glow.

"You lie to me, little bird, you know the price paid for such deception, and yet still, you lie." The Ceasg's words lapped at her thoughts, gently pulling at her to step back towards the waters. The words swimming in her mind were not sounds alone. They could feel her thoughts as well, they stroked the truths she had not given, coaxing them forth.

"I ... seek the horn, as well, yes." The words leapt free of their own accord.

The Ceasg smiled, the smile of a predator that has ensnared their prey. "Now, prove to me your worth, little one," she said. "The man you sought could not look me in the eye and tell me the truth, for he could not accept the truth within him, that his desire was selfish, not noble. That he was little better than a slaver, bent on possessing a woman regardless of her will."

"Show me you deserve the waves more than he, servant of the Ríagan, warrior of the vainglorious Sciathán Dubh! They call you Crow, upon the land, do they not? How far you have fallen from the songs of your masters. Tell me your truth. You seek the horn, no? But for what purpose, selfish or noble?"

"I seek it for revenge," she said, lifting her face to look straight into the Ceasg's eyes, as dark as the water's depths, each carrying a spark of the moon's light.

"Your own, or for another?" the Ceasg asked. "You are not alone in this journey and, though I need not ask, my curiosity compels me. The sea will know, and may it take you should you fail. Even Caerdrich could not free you should the sea find you wanting, for it was not the blade that lifted you up from the frozen waters below Tur Eumor."

"The blade and I have a deal, yes," Fiadh replied. "Their revenge and my own is intertwined. The justice we seek will be found together."

"But of course," the Ceasg hissed. "It is truth you speak, but there is more truth to it than even you know. You walk so far, young one, yet you see so little."

Its words were meaningless, no more than kindling to the flame of its fascination with tales and song. Fiadh had what she had come for, and more besides. She would be leaving with her life, proof of the brother's death, and information that could lead her to the Raven at last. Now only the return remained. "Will the Merrow grant me passage?" she asked, daring to turn her head to see if she could spy the lantern upon the shore.

"Oh, no, little bird." The Ceasg's words swam in her mind once more with undisguised satisfaction. "Who am I to deny them their prey? No, you must find your way home through their waters without my interference. Should you fall into the deep, then it will be clear you have not earned your return to shore, and the sea will keep you both."

Fiadh shivered, almost able to feel the damp touch of the sea creatures grasping and dragging her towards the sea floor. The Ceasg spoke of fate and portents, but she knew the sea was a fickle thing that cared little for such trifling concerns as the visions of the Ríaghan and the weave of the Norns.

"A deal!" she shouted. "I can bring you what was once yours, return her to the sea, and in exchange I shall take the horn so that I might call on the waves in my own time of need."

The Ceasg chuckled, its heaving form sending tremors through the wood at Fiadh's feet.

"Clever bird!" came its voice. "All this time threading through your true purpose and finally you seize what might bring you what you truly want." The Ceasg stretched and Fiadh felt it, the fading of Caerdrich's icy grip, a blade satisfied.

"A pact it shall be, Crow, you may depart my ship with what you seek. But should you walk the land again, and reconsider whether to keep your side of our bargain ..." The Ceasg smiled, those shimmering teeth shining like precious stones in the moonlight.

"You may have the horn, wield its call to the waves, but the waves are but a part of the sea. I can wait a hundred years for you to face your fate if you do not return what is owed to me. Can you spend the rest of your days living in fear of every loch, every storm, every tide? You know better, I think, Crow. Do not dawdle, I will await her return with eagerness."

The Ceasg drew back, the moon's light sparkling across wet scales and teeth alike.

"Fly, little bird, and should you part with the horn without bringing the sea its due, I will come for you, one day. The sea always claims what it is owed."

Those final words slithered from the creature's lips as she slipped behind the bow, scales sliding over the wooden flesh of that proud figurehead pointing to the sky, and silently into the lapping water beyond.

Fiadh stood alone once more, her feet set wide upon that slanted and shattered deck, alone with that great engraved horn held in eagles' talons. It must have rested there for years, decades, centuries even without being swept out to sea. Through the darkest storms and the greatest tides, it had sat waiting on this deck, whether waiting alone or dragged from the grip of those who had sought to make it their own.

This is what the brother had come for, and now she would hold it, a tool for seizing the waters that had borne those dark ships across the waters to the feet of Tur Eumor. A power not even the Raven could wield, an advantage, after waiting so long in the shadows and scrounging through the dirt left in her wake.

The Ceasg had warned her the sea would judge her, but she knew the sea well. She knew it was vengeful and vindictive, capable of snatching away lives in a moment to claim what it wished or to repay a slight against its name. It could swallow up towns and peoples along its edge just as easily as it had provided for them, it would bear people on great voyages of adventure and discovery only to dash them against the rocks before they could return to share their tales.

She knew the sea, and the sea knew her. It understood vengeance, and it would understand her call to be true, driven by that singular cause alone. She would not call it without cause, and she would return what it was due when her time had come. Just as she had pledged to repay its due should she return to place her feet upon the land. It would not find her wanting, and if it deemed that insufficient, she now held the means to bear her beyond its reach.

Fiadh reached forward and pushed her hand through the shimmering air around the horn. The magics dimmed as her hand neared it and faded to nothing as her fingers touched the engraved metal that wrapped its form. It would not return till the call to the sea echoed from it.

Caerdrich lay silent, the cold gone from the air around her. The blade recognised power and respected it, even if they sometimes did not respect Fiadh's own. Perhaps, however, they had crossed paths with this horn in an era before her time, out upon this wide sea where emerald ships had once carved the waves. One day she might hear those tales, when the sword's thirst was finally sated.

She sequestered the horn away in the sack she hung beneath her cloak and spared only a parting glance at that shattered figurehead still reaching out towards the moon before jumping over the edge of the ship and making her way back down the wreck she had clambered up to reach here.

The rowboat still sat half-beached upon the rock. When she neared it, Fiadh saw what she had sought here in the first place. A small iron ring sat upon its lone seat, still dripping with seawater as if swept to its rest by a chance wave dashing against the rock. She took it, ran it through her hands, and stashed it away beside the horn.

Time, finally, to depart this frightful and ancient place. With a shove, she, the horn, and the blade were back out over the sea, her oars returning to the water to begin distancing them from that green-wreathed ship.

A glance over her shoulder away from the moon's light revealed her destination, the faint golden light shimmering in the distance, far from the shadow of the cliffs.

Annis still held the lantern high, at least.

The stillness of the water brought by the storm's passing brought her some respite, a chance to catch her breath and collect her thoughts. Her strokes with the oars helped steady her breathing, the pounding of her heart easing to a gentle rhythm.

Yet it was in that quiet within that she could hear the keening from the cliffs, working its way through the wax, caressing her skull, setting hairs on end. The Merrow knew she had returned to the water.

She spared another glance towards the shore, seeing the mists that carried their wails clouding the surface, obscuring the way, leaving only the faintest golden glow of the lantern on the beach.

They were circling her once more, the mists pressing closer, the water slapping against the sides of her craft even though the water beyond sat still. Fins and scales began to break the surface, dipping in and out of view as the keening grew to a tumult, demanding she listen, to tear out the wax and give in to the cries.

She could feel the claws pawing at her leathers, one drawing up and brushing at her hair, drifting along her cheek. She shuddered at its touch but gritted her teeth against the fear, refusing to give them her gaze or let them distract her. To let them have her attention for even a moment would be enough for them to drag her down into the cold with them.

Fiadh closed her eyes, steadied her breathing, and focused on the rhythm of the oars. She set her mind on the feeling of lifting them from the water, reaching forward, touching them down, and pulling back, on the tension running through her forearms as she drummed her fingers on the wood to ease the tension of her grip. She flexed out the renewed burning sensation, running from her shoulders to the hollow of her back, rolling free of it as she brought the oars back, tensing against the pressure as she pulled back.

One stroke at a time, pushing through the mist, her ears dead to the sound beyond her wooden vessel. Towards the light still shrouded in mist.

Then she jolted forward, the rowboat coming to an abrupt halt as it slammed up against the pebbles, the crunch of wood on stone sending vibrations shuddering up her bones.

Snatching up her sack, patting it to check the ring and horn were still safely within, Fiadh leapt over the side and scampered up the beach, putting as much distance as she could between herself and the water. She tore the wax free, immediately hearing the roar of water and wind, and of her feet sliding about on the rocks. Finally, the pebbles were lit by the golden glow of the lantern, which stood alone, propped up on the top of a long branch of driftwood.

Annis himself sat halfway up the beach, perched on the pebbles, one hand holding a lump of wood and the other a dirk, surrounded by chipped splinters and slivers he'd loosened.

"Whit?" came his complaint as she stomped up the pebbles towards him. "Ah wisnae gonnae jist staun there till ma airm gave oot." He gave a shrug. "Besides, Ah wanted tae ken if Ah cuid mak a fish oot ae this wood." He waved it in her direction and pushed himself to his feet. "Turns oot ah cannae. Ah'm no sure how onybody wid mak yin. It looks a richt mess."

"I could have died!" Her own voice caught her by surprise, sounding more as a dry croak than the authoritative tone she had intended. "If there'd been no light to cast the way, I could have been led anywhere, you'd have been waiting here till my corpse washed ashore!"

As she strode up to him Annis stood, and Fiadh was more disgruntled than ever to be confronted by his chest, having to crane her neck to look him in the eyes.

Another shrug, and Annis waved in the direction of the torch. "Ah can see it, Ah held it fast. Ah kept an eye oan it, dinnae fret, Ah'd huv kept it staunin till the sun came up an drooned oot the licht."

Annis looked at her, his nose slightly crinkled.

"What?" she coughed, feeling the sting of salt scalding her throat.

"When the moon's oot at nicht yer eyes licht up, even when yer facin awa fae it. Ah ken the eyes ae cats or deer micht shine wi the licht ae a torch. But yer eyes shine their ain licht. It's no richt, it gives me the wullies. Ah dinnae like it."

She knew how he felt, for once, looking back over the waters towards the rock framed in the moon's light. Fiadh had no doubt that if she and the Ceasg ever crossed paths again, it would be when the sea had called for her to be returned to it, permanently. Those star-bright eyes would follow her, a memory to haunt sleepless nights as a reminder that far greater powers rested in the corners of this earth than her and the blade she bore.

But not on land, for now, at least.

"Aye, Annis, it's not right, but you're going to have to deal with it for a while longer at least. For now, we have a merchant to visit," she said, beginning her crunching steps up the pebbled beach.

"A merchant?"

"Yeah, one who took something from the sea that wasn't his to take. It's about time he returned it."

***

Fiadh sat on her heels behind the dock's wall, peering around a barrel left at its base towards the merchant's sprawling home. The road before it was cobbled rather than mud, still slick with the rain and sea spray from earlier in the night.

A low wall sat around its base, two floors of fine log-hewn structure rising beyond them in a trio of buildings boarded by shutters embellished with the merchant's personal sigil, a clear challenge to the power of the Rìgh.

Annis stood languidly behind her, leaning back against the dock.

"How mony?" he grumbled, rubbing the tiredness from his eyes.

"Just one," she whispered in reply. "But one's plenty if all they need do is raise a shout and anyone with coin in his master's ventures comes running with axe and pitchfork."

The guard was practically asleep at his station, his hardened leather helm from beneath his hood reflecting the blues and hints of gold from the encroaching dawn. His head was slumped, but he'd clearly found a nook in the loose stonework that prevented him toppling in his half-slumber.

"So, how do we do this?" she said back to her companion, who looked moments away from drifting off himself.

"One guard at the door," she continued. "Might be a chance to get in around the back? These kinds of places always have another entrance ..."

"Nah, dinnae worry, it'll be quiet," Annis said, brushing past her shoulder and barely pausing in his stride as he walked directly across the paving and up to the entrance.

The guard jumped for a moment, hand gripped fast around his spear, and looked ready to challenge the intruder when Annis' palm fixed over his face and slammed his head into the wall behind him.

He crumpled to the ground, silent.

Fiadh jogged up beside him. "Is ... is he dead?" she said as he nudged the prone body with a foot.

Annis shrugged. "Mebbe, Ah'm no sure. Ah'll pit money oan his bein back oan his feet shortly, wi a poundin heid an a sense ae impendin unemployment."

"We don't kill here, Annis, that's not what we're here for. We don't need to drive these people into the hands of the High Chalice," she said, her voice still subconsciously a whisper.

Annis turned his head with eyebrows knotted in scepticism. "Then mebbe ye ought tae huv mentioned it so Ah'd ken it afore noo, Craw."

Fiadh shook her head and gave the path on either side of them a final look for any incoming trouble before moving through the open gateway and up to the door of the merchant's property.

The door itself was a simple affair, not locked by key as many of the properties of the wealthy to the south had come to be of late. Fiadh ran her hands over her knives, stopping at one with a long blade and handle, long blunted by its use as a tool and more suitable for this kind of task than as a weapon.

She slid it gently along the gap between the door and its mounting, feeling it drift and then bump over the bar that held it in place. Crouching, she took another blade and pinned it lengthwise along the door and into the frame.

Then, at Fiadh's signal, Annis stepped forward and rammed both hands down on the first blade's handle hard. Barely a moment of resistance followed as it pivoted, and they heard a clatter from within.

Fiadh pulled her blade free and beckoned Annis forward, following behind as he swung the door loose and they entered the room beyond.

Their welcome came swiftly.

"Who are you?"

The merchant stood framed in the candlelight of the stairs, dressed in only a tunic that barely covered his particulars. The veins of his neck protruded beneath beetroot jowls and eyes bulging with rage. Salted whiskers completed the comic display.

The room was far more spacious than the carpenter's. A fire pit sat embedded in a stone-framed wall, a table with seating for a dozen men filled its centre, and smooth-hewn wooden beams held up a ceiling which could well support more rooms above. The hearth holding the smouldering coals was embellished with trophies and gifts that must have come from far across the seas, bearing runes and scripts that were alien and ornate.

Above them all, framed high above the fire, was a folded fur as long as a man, pinned in place by wooden pegs hammered deep into the stonework.

"We're here for your captive, you are free to stand aside," Fiadh responded, gesturing Annis towards the hanging sealskin.

"I will not!" came his growled reply as he stomped down the steps. He must have been a larger man in his day, maybe once inches taller than Annis and broader still, though his bulk had long since slid from his muscles into signs of a far more comfortable existence.

"Annis, if you would," Fiadh said.

He looked, bemused, between her and the merchant, having barely moved from the door.

"The skin over the hearth please, it's what we're here for and you're taller than me."

He frowned, nodded, and moved in its direction. The merchant stammered for a moment and then moved as if to block his path.

Annis jabbed a finger in his direction. "You'll haud yersel there, wee man," he growled, "or else Ah'll be pittin yer heid through these here coals."

The merchant came to an abrupt halt. Fiadh could not have told whether he spoke Àrdish, there was every chance he didn't, but the message seemed clear enough regardless.

"Wee man?" she whispered to Annis as she accompanied him towards the hearth, keeping her eyes on the man who seemed trapped between simmering rage and fear as Annis' hands approached the hearth.

Annis shoved a stool over towards the hearth and clambered upon it. "Aye," he said. "Wee is a state ae mind, no a stature, an this yin here is full tae the brim wi it."

Fiadh stopped moving as she saw motion behind the merchant. He was not alone at the stairs. Crouched behind him, one hand around the wooden pillar and at arm's reach from the man, was a figure clad only in a light shift. Her long limbs spread in a stance somewhere between a coiled predator and prey preparing to flee.

It seemed they had the attention of the one they had come for.

Annis grunted as he hauled himself up closer to the hide and began to tug at the wooden stakes that held it in place. "Careful," Fiadh hissed. "Bring it down in one piece. It's worth more than we can pay to return it undamaged."

The merchant stammered again and began to stomp across the room. Fiadh spotted what he was moving towards: a hatchet set upon the wall. She moved swiftly, a hand running to the blades strapped along her torso, pulling one free and pointing it towards the man.

"Hold yourself there," she spat in Cànan. He barely spared her a glance, not so much as slowing his steps as he clasped both hands around the axe's long haft and pulled it free, snarling.

He turned towards her, and they stood there in silence for a moment, his furious glare meeting her steady one, her blade held out towards him and his across his chest. He was slower now than he may have been when he had last wielded a weapon, but he held it with the certainty of a man who had once carved his own way through the world.

Fiadh had used her blades when needed over the years, but she was no fighter. Annis was paid for that particular role, and more often than not his size was imposing enough to discourage it. If it came to blows, she was not sure she could avoid that curved blade, and from the size of it she couldn't be certain a single blow would be enough.

"Ah huv it!" Annis words split the air between them, and she shot a glance at him as he proudly held the hide over his head, unfolding it into long brown sealskin as he stretched it out almost as wide as his arms could hold it.

"Great, now put it down, Annis," she said, keeping her blade hand steady towards the merchant.

"Whit? Ah thocht we needed it."

"We don't." Fiadh jerked her head towards the stairs. "She does."

The figure on the stairs had made her way to them in almost complete silence as she moved gently on the bare balls of her feet. Her eyes were fixed on Annis, flitting between his face and the skin he held overhead.

"Ah dinnae think she needs a ..."

"Don't think," Fiadh snapped. "Put it down."

He looked uncertain as he gently lowered his arms down, all three of them flitting their eyes back and forth between the others in the room. But as he began to set the sealskin down at his feet, the merchant broke the silence with a bellowing "NO!" and made to barge past Fiadh towards Annis.

Another among them was faster still, however. As soon as the skin touched the floor, the silent figure lunged across between them and, before Fiadh could so much as turn towards her, had seized hold of Fiadh's hand and twisted the knife free from her grasp.

The sudden twisted grip had Fiadh stumbling to the side, free from the swing of the merchant's axe which came down between them. It was the only swing he would get.

The knife spun from one hand to the other and slashed across the man's bare arms, crisscrossing them, streaks of crimson flying across the walls and floor. The merchant released the hatchet and stumbled back as the slices continued to cut ribbons from his arms, raised to shield his face.

The knife fell, and, taken up by the selkie's other hand, it plunged into the man's thigh and twisted, pulling a cry of pain free from him as he fell to one knee and then dropped prone to the floor. The selkie continued to press towards him, her foot planted on his chest, shoving him to the ground. The blade screeched as it met stone in the ground beneath him, the sound weaving with his screams.

Fiadh's heels kicked at the ground as she tried to shift herself clear of the grappling pair. She felt Annis' hands grip her under her arms and haul her back and clear as the sickening sound of the blade scratching the flagstones set her teeth on edge. She cringed, torn between fixation on the animalistic display of rage and turning her head away from it as the selkie's hands rose up and plunged down, beating the merchant's head against the ground.

Then the girl straddled him, pinning his arms to his sides between her thighs as he attempted to writhe free, screaming as every movement tore the blade in his leg further through his flesh.

The selkie snarled, her hands fixed over his face. Her muscles bunched as her thumbs pressed down on his eyelids, palms clamped firmly against his cheeks to hold his head in place. She kept pushing even as his screams rose into a shriek, blood seeping out of his sockets before, with a sickening pop, her thumbs plunged into his skull and his entire body spasmed and fell still.

"Fuck," Annis whispered in shock. The pair of them had stayed frozen between the doorway and the hearth, Fiadh still sprawled against the wall at his feet, neither able to tear their eyes free even as the selkie rose from the merchant's still body, crimson droplets falling from her hands.

"He will never covet another with that twisted gaze again," she spat as she stood over the merchant's unmoving form, the words dancing in the musical Cànan the Ceasg had spoken directly into Fiadh's mind. "He'll travel to Tech Duinn blind and wander there forevermore, never able to find the way on to rest."

"Fuck," muttered Annis again, still frozen at the hearth and none the wiser for the words spoken in a language he did not share.

The selkie moved towards him and he broke his stillness to back away from the hearth, the skin still laid at its mouth. She knelt before it and lifted it gently, one hand trailing across the fur with care and longing, her fingertips smoothing the hairs even as they seemed to follow her touch.

Where once the hide had been inanimate, the skin a faded leather as if tanned to be stitched, it now sprang to life, warm and soft, the skin moving along with the selkie's fingertips as if it were to rise up and wreath them with its warmth.

She stood, the living skin held across her blood-stained hands, and turned towards Fiadh still breathing heavily upon the floor.

"You did not come to lay claim to what is mine, girl?" she asked, paying no heed to Annis though he stood close by and with a hand upon the hilt of his blade.

"No." Fiadh shook her head, rolling back to her feet and dusting off her clothes. "I have come on behalf of the sea so that you may return to it."

"For what?" The selkie's tone was harsh, suspicious, even as the words danced from her lips.

"The deal has been struck already and I have what I sought from the waves," Fiadh said, meeting her gaze, searching the eyes that swam with blues and greens. "I have nothing more to claim, only that I may ease your path back to the water."

The selkie's gaze was still, unreadable, and with no further words, she turned and made her way to the door and out into the soft golden light of the rising dawn.

Fiadh leant and pulled her knife free from the still leg of the merchant, trying not to meet his eyeless visage but unable to escape its slack, empty gaze. There was something less scarring to it than the faded eyes of the dead she had seen before, but the violence of his end would stick with her, she knew, as a reminder of what the sea could bring to the shore.

As she turned and moved through the door, she heard Annis behind her, turned to see him cradling the merchant's axe with some mix of guilt and joy in his smile.

"Stealing from the dead, now, are you?" she said, more amused than anything else.

"Aye, weel, it's no lik he'll be needin it, an given how it did him nae guid Ah've nae doubt his spirit wid want it taken far awa. Nae reason fur me nae tae dae him the favour."

Fiadh shrugged. If the gods wanted to punish him for it, she was sure they'd find a way. Maybe at least this way he'd have a weapon to fend off whatever curse they put upon them. She had plenty lined up for them both already.

The selkie stood still where the pebbles of the shore met the land, the shore grasses and her shift waving with the breeze, her head held high as she looked out over the waters, skin in hand.

Fiadh walked up beside her, hearing Annis come to a stop on the path where he no doubt intended to keep watch while staying far from the reach of those blood-stained hands.

"You have the horn, then?" the selkie asked, not taking her eyes off the warming horizon.

Fiadh nodded, enjoying the sound of the lapping waters for a time. "I do," she said, eventually.

"What will you do with it?" she asked, turning to look at her.

"I have a promise to keep that I hope, with its help, I might finally bring to rest. It's been too long, and I've travelled too far, to let it wait any longer," Fiadh replied.

The sun was beginning to break over the horizon, causing Fiadh to wince against the glare shining off the waters.

"What of the man who went searching for the horn before I came here?" she asked the selkie in return. "His brother said he came here for you, waited for you at the dockside."

The selkie responded with confusion for a moment and then with a snarl filled with contempt.

"I remember him." Her tone dripped with derision. "We never exchanged so much as a word, but I felt his eyes on me. I know that look, that impotent greed so much more intense than desire alone. He did not search for love, he sought only to possess something that was not his own. That is how he saw me, as a thing, no different to how the merchant did."

She removed a hand from beneath the seal pelt, raising it so Fiadh could see the dark mark that ran across her forearm, beyond where the blood halted. She could see the shape of a hand, fingers wrapped around it, like it had been burned into her skin.

"It was not the merchant who marked me so, but the sailor," she spat. "He grew the courage to grab me, once, tried to drag me away. I was wailing my pain, feeling my skin being pulled away from me still pinned to the merchant's wall, but he kept pulling at me even as I warned him I could go no further. He only let me go when he saw the mark begin to spread and knew what he desired would be too marred by the loss of my skin for him to enjoy, should he have dragged me further."

The look in the selkie's eyes was merciless, cold, what they had seen for a flash as she'd lunged across the merchant's hall and taken Fiadh's blade from her.

"Is he dead?" the selkie asked, her gaze fixed on Fiadh now. She nodded her reply.

"They were no different, he and the merchant," she continued. "No amount of wealth could divide the cruelty each held within them. Both would have claimed my skin, never to return it had the sea not intervened."

"So no, I do not feel regret for his passing," she said, answering the question Fiadh had not thought to ask. "He wished to claim power over the sea to sate his greed, and in turn, the sea took him as its own. A fitting fate."

Fiadh reached into her sack and rummaged for the small piece of metal she was searching for. She pulled it out and turned the ring over in her palm, letting the iron glint in the dawn's light and touch upon the two fish intertwined on its surface. So simple a gift, given with so much heart, and given away with so little.

A crunch of shifting pebbles alerted her that the selkie wasn't looking along with her. She had begun her descent towards the water, the furs in her arms beginning to shift and run from her hands over her arms, gradually enveloping her skin as the shift fell away.

Fiadh watched as the fur encased her like a shell, pulling her arms and legs close, her feet forming flippers and whiskers springing from her brown cheeks. As smoothly as she had walked from the hall, the seal slid into the waters and vanished from view, barely leaving so much as a ripple on the surface behind it.

Fiadh turned the ring over in her hand once more and turned back towards the merchant's hall, seeing Annis had watched the selkie's departure as well. They exchanged a nod as she approached, and Fiadh looked back over the water once more, seeking that lonely rock in the distance, framed by the rising sun.

Annis coughed, and when he next spoke it was in baritone verse.

> *"Ah yince kent a lass,*
> *who came fae the sea,*
> *borne by the waves,*
> *carried hame tae me.*
>
> *But ye dinnae haud a lass,*
> *by leash or by gold,*
> *else they'll sprout wings an' fly,*
> *and lea yer hearth cauld."*

They stood in silence a while longer, looking out over the waters as the glimmer of sunlight lit the crests of the waves as they swept over the pebbled bay.

"Ma faithir taucht me that yin, a lang time ago," he said to the silence. "Ma mither left afore Ah kent her, but Ah aye thocht she likely bolted frae him. Ye cuid see it in his eyes, ye ken, that yearnin fur something he kent he lost through nae fault but his ain."

Fiadh wasn't quite sure how to respond to that. She'd had no parents of her own, nor had she allowed herself to come to know any of the families who had given her refuge in the years following her fall from Tur Eumor. The concept of staying alongside anyone for years, decades even? She'd seen too many gone before their time to have any faith that they could ever stay. There had been many before Annis. No doubt there would be many more after him.

"Would you have gone to sea for a lass like that, Annis?" she asked, tilting her head towards the shore.

He shrugged, shaking his head. "Nah, she wisnae ma kind. Ah prefer those wi a wee bit mair ... heft, if ye ken whit Ah mean."

Fiadh shrugged in turn. She didn't, truly. These people's urges for one another, enough to turn to such cruelty or even throw away their lives for, was as alien to her as the life of a selkie beneath the waves.

"But ye ken, that lass cuid mair than hauf handle herself, mebbe she'll fin herself someyin afore lang."

"... afore lang?" Fiadh pinched her nose as she tried to understand Annis' unique phrasing. "She'll be older than the oldest house in this entire town, Annis."

"Aye weel, ye cannae jist write an older lass aff lik that, onybody has it in thaim tae change."

Fiadh snorted and turned away from the water, giving the ring a final look before handing it to Annis.

"See that the brother gets this, Annis, and that we get our due," she said, tipping the iron band into his hand. "Tell him that he perished, dragged beneath the waves by the Merrow, and that I fell to the same fate. That you were the only one of us to get to shore."

She raised her hood, aware that, with the growing light of the dawn, it was only so long before people began to emerge from their homes around Tur Pailt.

"Yer deid noo?" he mumbled, looking over the ring himself.

She snorted at the question.

"As far as this town is concerned, yes. I died at sea. I'm sure it's not an expected way for a Crow to go, dragged down by the very monsters they hire us to rid them of. You heard him, yesterday, the High Chalice has been looking for us already, and maybe they could use a disincentive to continue their search."

"So, Ah'll catch up wi ye at the horses. Whaur next, Craw?"

"Next, we look for a ship's banner with a lightning bolt over the waves. There's another who believes us Crows long dead who I believe needs to discover that he left one behind."

※

THE WOVEN THREAD

The freezing mist cut through their soaked and heavy leathers as they wound their way around the boughs of trees stripped of life by the coming of winter. The path they trod was barely distinguishable from the rocks and grass stretching out either side of it – more of a trench worn into the soil than a road.

Fiadh paused her steps, her nose crinkling at a smell rising to meet them, so thick it stung her eyes. Crouching below the mist's haze she gestured to Annis to pause as she searched for its source, finding little but a lone lump wrapped in leather blocking their path.

Annis walked forward carefully and nudged the lump over. As it rolled, the cloth gave way to charcoal-green flesh, rotted through to the bone, a putrid stench rising with the flies from the remains of the limb and foot. The decaying leg rolled a little further as Annis took a step back, raising an arm over his nose.

"Those arenae animal bites," he said, pointing down at the rotten edges, his voice muffled by his sleeve. "A blade did that, a bluidy sharp one, too ..."

"How can you tell?" Fiadh asked, walking over to peer at the find.

"Ah've seen plenty like it afore. You huvnae? Look," he pointed towards the flesh where the thigh had been parted. "Clean through. Ah've no seen onything like it. Like it was burned by the blade ..."

They both had the same thought, scanning the foliage on either side of the path for further remnants of the deceased. But it was clear. The limb must not have been more than a few weeks old, bloated and still providing ample food for maggots writhing over its surface.

It was then that Fiadh looked up, through the canopy to the rays of sunlight filtering through the bare branches. There she saw it, the limp figure impaled upon one of the jutting timbers, jaw slack and an eyeless gaze fixed down towards them, not a single intact limb still attached to the torso arched against its fixture.

"Annis ..." she whispered. His gaze turned to her and followed her line of sight.

It was not alone.

Some were months old, skeletons barely held together by torn cloth and leathered remnants of connective tissue, others barely days old, bloated and swollen, still clinging to the branches on which they had clearly been thrust upon, still alive. Some reached forward, meeting their death amidst a desperate last act to drag themselves towards a swifter end falling from the trees, leaving black stains trailing behind them.

"Aye, Ah'll be huvin none ae this," Annis said, his voice a whisper. "Ah've been tae mony a barrow an grave, but no like this. It reeks ae all kinds ae death."

Fiadh and Annis moved in silence, turning away from one another and towards the trees, hands on the hilts of their weapons, feet trailing low to the ground to muffle the sounds of their footsteps.

A great forked trunk split the path before them, the evening sunlight striking through the clearing around it and illuminating the display of a man suspended between the rising boughs.

His arms were spread high, strung wide by twisted branches, beneath them wings lit golden by the sunlight were stretched, streaks of red running across their surface like lightning.

No, not wings.

The skin of their backs had been flayed from them, pinned wide, leaving the bones of their ribs jutting out towards them, cut free of their spine. Viscera stained what remained of their breeches, the flesh of their arms disintegrating under the corrosion of weather and carrion feeders.

The pair of them had halted in their tracks, transfixed by the macabre display.

"Annis," Fiadh whispered. "We need to move."

There was no response from her companion, his bulk frozen in place as she felt him tremble.

"We don't know if whoever did this has moved on, given some of the dead have been here barely days. They've been returning to place new ones in the trees," she continued, turning her head slowly to search for the lurking threat among the dark limbs branching around them.

Annis nodded his understanding and began to make his way around the split trunk, continuing to follow the trail beyond it. From here they could see where it reached the cliffs beyond, the horizon darkening with the fall of the sun.

Far below lay their destination, ships passing in and out of the port town of Kempe Fell. Had they done this? Was this some roving warband put to the blade and left as a brutal warning to any other that might infringe on the territory of one of Vestamr's prime Jarls? It was like no display she'd ever seen, so far above the settlement and so complete in its vicious demonstration.

Caerdrich grew chill at her back, the black-scabbarded blade seeping their icy fingers of warning into her bones. No, this was no show of barbarity by the people of the town. It was a display intended for them.

Fiadh spun too late to run, seeing only the great wings of feather and steel rising above the trees, mere moments before the being they heralded plunged from the sky. Annis dove to one side as Fiadh threw herself flat, barely avoiding being tossed from the crags and down towards the rocks below.

She was on her feet in a moment, turning again towards the cliff's edge. Annis was even faster, his axe clutched in both hands.

The monstrous wings rose over the cliff, between them hanging a figure clad in scale and chain from head to toe. Their feet hung poised beneath them as they drifted towards the rocky outcrop.

The gust of their beating wings forced Fiadh back, taking her knees and holding her forearms over her head to break the wind. The ground leapt as they landed, a ringing like the chime of bells as the blades that adorned every feather of their wings folded over one another.

Gazing down at them, towering twice as tall as Fiadh, her death mask was expressionless. The cracked white stone was shaped into a surface portraying the lips, eyes, and nose of a woman. Great curled horns sprouted from its sides in bone, between them a helm of a thousand meticulously interconnected plates, each etched in runes and shaped into a beautiful landscape of spirals and arches that could have blessed the halls of the most ornate temple.

But there was nothing behind the mask. The eyes that surveyed her were voids, nothing more than openings into the darkness beneath that helm.

In her clenched, plated fist rose a spear even more decorated and detailed than the magnificent helm. At its head a bright blade stood proud, flanked by two others that jutted outwards from the flames of a sun that graced the top of the spear's hilt. Fiadh's eyes widened as she recognised the weapon, and thereby its wielder. Only one wielded the deadly and prophetic Lance of the Dawn: Tyra of the Sgiath Athar did not need to announce her name with the features of a mortal woman.

"Speak, false one." The voice that boomed from the helm was metallic, as if ringing from deep within. "What cause have you to trespass on the business of the Othair? No gods remain to instruct you, no people calling their names in this place. What is your purpose?"

Fiadh grimaced. There were questions of curiosity and then there were questions to justify decisions already made. These were the latter; there were no correct answers open to her now.

"My purpose here is not with you, oh great deliverer of warriors lost, I come here in search of another." Fiadh kept her eyes fixed on that helm, her mind racing as she spoke. What had she been taught all those years ago on the Tur? Did the Sgiath Athar respect strength or subservience, respect or submission? Even as glimpses of the texts she had pored over flashed through her mind, those black pits gazing down upon her stole them away.

"You come here in search, as do I," Tyra said, not even caring to turn her head to Annis. Fiadh followed her lead in the vain hope it might keep her companion from being used as another display in the trees. "I have heard of your coming here, searching for the very same one I seek."

Fiadh was taken aback, for the Sgiath Athar did not concern themselves with the trials of the living. Those of them that remained chased the bloody glories of warriors who fought in their names, but only upon their death. It was said their souls would be collected for the armies of their god for a great war.

A war that had already occurred, and a god who had died long ago.

Tyra's helm creaked as she cocked it slightly, though with the stillness of her stone mask it could well have been either in amusement or consideration. "The whispering god speaks in many voices, for those who care to listen. The kobold-kin spoke with me, high above the giant's fall. They asked for freedom, and I granted it. In exchange they gave me you, false one. You will bring me what we both seek, and in turn I will not cast you from this place and leave the last of the black wings of the Ríaghan smashed upon the rocks."

The blood drained from Fiadh's face, fear seeping deep into the empty pit of her stomach. She held her palm outwards and flat, willing with all she had that Annis would see it and neither flee nor seek to strike. Either would leave them as bloody smears against the cliffs.

At her back Caerdrich grew colder still, the chill running up her back and pricking at her cheeks and the back of her skull.

Tyra's head cocked back the other way, as if looking straight over Fiadh's shoulder.

"I remember you, blade," her voice intoned. "I remember your final words to me. You told me you would scour the earth, that you would tear down every mountain, uproot every tree, burn every civilisation in your path until you had your vengeance. Yet I stand upon such a tree, its roots boring deep into the mountain you have left untouched, as you have been reduced to a trinket borne by another. How disappointing you have been."

Her death mask turned to regard Fiadh again, "What do they call you here, she of the black wing? Changeling? False child?" the last word dripped from her mask with derision. "Doppelganger?"

Fiadh struggled to keep the disgust from her face. Yes, such words had been thrown at her more often than she could count, often accompanied by spittle or the point of a blade. More frequently in these times, however, came 'witch' or 'devil'.

"They call me Crow," she said, keeping her face clear of emotion.

Tyra drew herself up from her crouch to loom ever taller over the two of them. Still, she bore Annis no mind, as if the warrior was not even worth her consideration, with or without his axe.

"Crow? Fitting. Left to wander the lands picking at the remains of the dead for coin and secrets. It is time to press your skills to my use tonight, Crow." Her tone was matter of fact, as if Fiadh had already agreed to be at her service. The murderous prowess of the

Sgiath Athar had made that consideration a forgone conclusion. They had little choice, and Tyra knew that full well.

"I was sworn to come to this place and retrieve a great warrior whose passing was foretold to have occurred two moons past, with blade in hand defending their right to rule," she continued. "One fit to join the Einherjar. A ruler with fair hair who once rode alongside Vestamr in his conquests as one of the five champions with whom he conquered these isles."

"But instead, I find one of raven hair sat upon the throne, successor to no one, warrior of no lord, wielder of no blade. Though the verse of the Norn foretelling their passing speaks of five at the side of Vestamr, only four are still spoken of in the tales now told of his victories."

"My mind is being toyed with, some dark magics of this place being woven to trick me, to trap me in confusion and doubt. I will not have it!" The calm tone was gone now, twisting into frustration, fury even. "No amount of blood can be spilled to fill the void of a soul in the ranks of the Othair, yet it shall be blood that will stain these paths until my duty is done."

"I will leave here with the soul I am charged with, black wing, or I will leave with a host forged from mine own blade. Maybe I will take yours, too, as an offering to the Othair in penance for my failure."

Fiadh stilled her trembling hand even as the frozen grasp of Caerdrich set her hairs on end. There was a chance, perhaps, that the blade could well strike down Tyra. There was also the chance they would both be cast into the sea in the battle that would follow. Better, now, to seek what they had both set out to find than invite death to take them both upon these cliffs.

"I can find the one you seek," she said, careful not to lose eye contact with those empty hollows within Tyra's helm. "It can be done. You will be delivered the spirit you are destined to find."

Tyra's wings rose and unfurled again. The chimes of the blades jutting between white feathers sounded out across the outcrop.

"The kobold-kin told me you would. You will deliver me to where they lie, and you will do so before the dawn's light strikes the hall of Kempe Fell. Move swiftly, doppelganger, for if you do not then I will take from this place every soul that rests here this night."

With a single beat of her wings, the Sgiath Athar flung herself overhead and past the trees beyond, vanishing behind the boughs from where she had come.

Fiadh stumbled as she heard the wingbeats fade, falling to one knee as her breaths came in gasps and her ears rang. Her mind was racing but the thoughts wouldn't form any coherent message, only flashing by in pieces and snippets of words that might have formed a plan.

Annis's hand wrapped gently around her shoulder and the thoughts began to still, slowing along with her breaths and the beating of her heart. They had been here before, she knew. This was not the first time she had brushed against the monstrous powers left behind by long lost gods. One day such an encounter might well finish them, but it was not today.

Taking a final deep breath, she stood and removed his hand. She walked over towards the root-infested crag Tyra had perched upon and looked downwards at the sharp descent to the sea, beyond which lay the town of Kempe Fell.

It was spread around the bay, one of the largest towns of its kind along the coast and isles of this sea. One structure dominated its shoreline – a great hall that jutted out over the water held up upon the docks themselves, the rocks that had split the bay now forming its foundations. From those docks were raised a banner, over and over again. A lightning bolt over the waves. This was the place, the seat of the final Jarl who had led the fleet against Fiadh's home high on the cliffs of Tur Eumor. She and the Sgiath Athar were searching for the same soul.

At one end the long wooden piers continued out onto the water, sheltered from the crashing waves of the open sea by a natural seawall that cupped the bay. The piers themselves were encased in a dramatic display of Kempe Fell's conquest of the waves; a gigantic skeleton of some great sea beast erected over them. Its ribs formed the buttresses of their shelter, its spine arcing overhead to meet the roof of the hall, the formidable, tapered jaw piercing the water at the dock's end. All about it ships were moored, people small as insects from up high travelling back and forth between them and the market stalls that accompanied them.

"There's a song aboot this place," Annis said, standing beside her.

"Is that so?" she replied, scanning the bay for any sign Tyra had left of her own search.

"Aye, a guid song, the Sjøfolk sang it, aboot the battle oan the rocks in the midst ae a storm, whaur they dragged the sea monster fae the waves, an ... an ..."

"Well, what?"

"Ah cannae remember. The Laird fell, an his throne sat empty, but Ah cannae remember the words tae it. It wis a guid song as weel, pity."

Fiadh responded with a shrug as she continued her search, and finally her eyes lit upon something new, the flashes of red, a collection of men cloaked head to toe in crimson. It seemed nowhere, no matter how far north they travelled, was free of their reach.

She cursed; Annis responded with a raised eyebrow.

"They're here," she said. "The High Chalice, the bastards. I can't tell if they're following me or I'm following them."

Annis crouched and peered down towards the bone-sheltered dock, though from here his eyes would not be able to pick them out as her silvered ones had done.

"It's them, I'm certain of it. That's why Tyra cannot find her ward. Stealing souls from their rightful place is everything their faith is about. They feel entitled to them, declare them their own with nothing but their claims of sin and absolution to justify their contempt of us."

"Steal ... souls? How wid ye even steal a soul?"

"I've spent many a year digging through the arcane contraptions and tomes they have developed over the centuries. So many under the guise of seeking knowledge but all with the same purpose: power and control." She shook her head, fighting away the memories of her time chasing impossible dreams in the south. "It doesn't matter. Hopefully, they think me dead off the coast of Tur Pailt, and it's best we keep it that way. I need some way of getting down there and moving around without them recognising me. At least until we can uncover what they're up to and put an end to it," she muttered, dropping into a squat beside him.

"I'll have to have a story to tell other than who I am, if they have their claws into the Jarl of Kempe Fell. I will not let this be like Ghav Rhien. I'll go as a seer perhaps, someone who throws bones to tell the merchants and mercenaries portents of their future. I've seen those con artists at work, I'm sure I can fake it well enough."

When she turned her head, she saw he was peering intently at her.

"What?" she asked.

"Yer eyes," he said, brow knitted into what she assumed must be his thinking face. "They stick oot lik a sair thumb. Cannae be huvin that. That siller licht wid tell everyone within a league whae ye are yince the nicht comes."

"Then what are you suggesting we do? I can't just cover ..." she paused as his eyebrows raised in reply.

"I'm going to have to cover them, aren't I?"

He nodded and began rummaging into his pack, pulling out a long section of cloth. "Here," he said, standing and offering it to her. "It's meant fur cuts an scrapes, but it'll cover ye weel enough. Naebody's goin tae bother a blind lass followin a mercenary aboot. Naebody wull pay ye ony mind."

Fiadh took the cloth in her hands and cursed, casting another glance down towards the docks, considering her options. Go, and be faced with an attempt to find a lost soul without being able to see, where her silvered eyes were her best tool to search for the magics that might be left by any being able to steal a soul away from a Sgiath Athar. Leave, and Tyra would hold that grudge and come searching for her. She could not escape her for long. After years of searching, to have it all end gasping her last breaths impaled high up over the cliffs. No. She owed them more than that.

"Do it," she said, holding the cloth out to Annis. He set to work, binding it under her hair and over her ears where it was unlikely to slip as they moved. The darkness felt like it was closing in as soon as the cloth pulled tight across her nose and cheeks, her eyelashes brushing it as she blinked, casting her eyes about to see if light would filter through the strands.

"Ready?" she heard Annis' gruff tone behind her.

She felt out around her, her fingers brushing his arm, her ears hearing her feet crunch over stones and grass as she stepped forward, the salty scent of the sea crashing below overpowering all else but the stench of the wet leathers they wore. She could sense so much but still had no idea if she stepped out once more whether it would be onto the firm ground or straight out into open air.

"Ready," she said, turning towards that arm she had felt behind her. "But you will have to guide me. I'm relying on you here, Annis, until I have an opening to seek out this lost spirit Tyra has set her claim upon."

She heard the sudden exhalation as he barely managed to conceal a chuckle.

"You're going to guide me straight into a wall, aren't you?"

She could almost feel his customary shrug through the air, "Mebbe aye, mebbe no."

She cursed again, knowing even if he weren't so childish as to go through with it, he would enjoy keeping her on edge throughout, regardless.

"Well then," she could sense the barely concealed smirk beneath his words. "The man guides the Craw. Won't this be a tale for the bairns someday."

***

They approached the hall through the winding, roughly cobbled streets of Kempe Fell with Fiadh's hand loosely holding Annis's elbow, letting him lead the way forward and trying to follow his steps so as not to bump into anything or anyone along the way. She had clenched her eyes shut beneath the folds of cloth, partly to avoid the irritation of its fibres, partly to better focus on her other senses, to seek clues as she passed.

There was a bustle around them, the screech of wooden boxes and barrels being shifted back and forth, the heavy steps of people laden down with their cargo. It was joined by the chatter and roars of laughter of people far more relaxed than she had expected of those living in the shadow of a monstrous butcher in the crags above.

The talk came in many tongues. There was Cànan, Àrdish, and Sjøtunge mingling around them without a single one of them caring to temper themselves for the other. She could make out some of it, stories from the waves, of family disputes in the harbour, gossip from across the lands, and news of a new landing by raiders bearing riches from distant shores.

Whispers ran beneath it all like a current, mutterings of souls lost to the rocks and seas, those who had lost their lives clambering the battlements of temples and towns far afield.

But none spoke of the winged nightmare that had already claimed so many of them. Those who did not know had nothing to tell; those who knew clearly did not dare to say.

She could tell when the voices and bustle became more muffled that Annis had led them into the sprawling hall itself, tapping his foot against the steps to let her know they were coming. There was more boisterous clamour ahead, as the smells of salt and fish were swamped by those of a crackling fire pit and the meat sizzling upon it.

One voice sounded above the others, a southern accent flipping between the tongues of the land with unearned confidence, mangling each as willingly as the last with gleeful abandon. His deep tone boomed across the hall, declaring himself to everyone who seemed to so much as drift near him, regaling them with tales of how he came across the great treasure he kept alongside him, punctuating his tale with meaty slaps of the box that jingled the coins stashed within.

He clearly spotted the two of them as they entered, delighted at new company to show off his conquests to.

"Ho! Man wi the cuffs aboot yer wrists, yes, you!" His accent made the Àrdish he yelled dance in a way she was not used to compared to the dour tone Annis tended to lend to his tongue. The timbre was foreign to her, from far to the south perhaps, far further than her own travels for knowledge and coin had taken her.

"You look lik a big lad, well-kent aboot the coasts aroond here nae doubt, sword fur hire, perhaps? Whit say ye? An adventure awaits!" Fiadh lurked as best she could in Annis' shadow, but even without sight she could discern the grin that came from behind the man's words, and she jumped as his hand slapped Annis about the shoulder.

"See this? One season's raids brought all ae this! Enough wealth tae find ye a steading onywhere ye could wish fur across this blessed isle. One season oan ma ships an ye'll be thankin whichever gods ye pray tae that I found ye in this here hall …" There was a pause then as the man's heavy footsteps found their way round to where Fiadh was attempting to appear as small as possible.

"Heh, clever man. Ye found yersel a blind lass, the only way ye could find yin whae'd look past that ass-kicked face!" Fiadh almost jumped again as that booming laugh rang out again over her head, gritting her teeth as best she could not to stand straight and stare down this oaf with her true eyes unveiled to him.

Annis, as was his wont, had yet to say a single word in the whole exchange and part of her wished she could see the acerbic expression he had likely fixed their companion with throughout.

Their companion was not given an opportunity to continue as a round of hushed tones swept across the hall, the hubbub dying down amid the sound of a few scraping chairs. In the quiet Fiadh could pick out footsteps from a collection of figures at the head of the hall, from where the great skeleton that hung over the docks must be suspended.

Fiadh groped about her shins until she found the leg of a stool and drew it over to perch on; all the better to hide behind the shadow of Annis and listen for who had entered the hall and shushed those attending. Surely this must be the successor of the soul Tyra sought, and so an opportunity to trace the fate of the deceased.

The thumping of a staff hammering against the floor was followed by the scraping of seats at the head of the hall and the few remaining voices were silenced. A voice rang out, heavy with authority but wearied by the weight of years and office.

"Ahar! I've done nothing but hear about your exploits every step of my journey from my chambers to my throne. Come before me. I would hear of them from the jackal's mouth rather than the cackles of your pack." The woman spoke in a thick Cànan, with a Sjøfolk accent. Perhaps a leader of one of the Gall-Ghàidheil warbands Vestamr had brought across the sea with him in his conquest of the isles, now seated as a ruler of Kempe Fell and its surrounding waters.

The loud man who had accosted them shifted, the sound of his bulk moving past causing Fiadh to draw her feet under her, unsure where his heavy, swaying footsteps would land.

"My lady, great Sæunn" he replied, the boisterous boasts replaced instantly by a tone of excessive reverence as he slipped from one tongue to the other. "Whatever tale you might wish for, I shall deliver to you, just as I deliver to your halls the riches of distant shores, collected so that it might shine all the brighter in reflection of your beauty."

The audible scoff from the head of the hall echoed across the silence. Fiadh was desperate to find a chance to remove the cloth shielding her eyes and cast them about to spy where the red-cloaked Order might be lurking. Not being able to search for them made her nervous. A couple could well be standing over her shoulders as Annis desperately tried to warn her with futile glances and hand gestures.

"Ahar, if I was being disturbed only to listen to another round of your fawning I would have remained in my chambers and simply listened to you lay more on your own person for your new audience ... Tell me, which stragglers have you dredged up from the depths this time? Who are these new visitors you have charmed with your wit and sparkling treasures? I do not recognise their steps, not yet in my years upon this dais. Have them attend me."

Fiadh nearly jumped from her stool as she was nudged by an elbow that must have been Annis's for all its lack of subtlety. She grasped it and followed as meekly as she could manage as he led her forward to the front of the hall. Years? It made no sense. How could she have been sitting on the throne for years if the Jarl Tyra sought was only two months dead?

Ahar shuffled ahead of them, awkwardly shifting out of Annis' path. "These two? They're ... erm, they're ..." He clearly threw some kind of gesture in the direction of Annis, whose loose understanding of Cànan was far from sufficient to follow the conversation.

Annis coughed. His words sounded strained, stumbling through what he could from having followed Fiadh over the seasons. "We are walkers ... erm, travellers ... from the south, lady, come to give looking and prophet to all those who hear so that they live a good future."

"You hear, Ahar, they've come for your job!" The chuckle that followed gave Fiadh a chill. She had heard that tone before. The grim relish of someone who had long since stopped finding enjoyment in much but the humiliation of others. "What use do I have for you when all I need is this strong southern lad and his ... what exactly?"

"My ... she is a prophet, lady. Where her eyes cannot see as we, um, I can, she sees further than we, I mean ..."

Annis was not a gifted spinner of tales or of her tongue, but this struggle was a new kind of uncertainty to her.

"She has a different kind of sight?" came the question breaking the silence.

"Aye, m'lady."

"I see," she said, with a wry tone of voice Fiadh couldn't quite decipher. Another silence followed, Annis's hand tensing upon her shoulder.

There was a cough from further back in the hall, the scrape of a stool, and she felt Annis lean in to speak. "We're dismissed."

Her face felt hot with frustration and intense self-awareness, unable to read the faces of those around her but fully aware of how many gazes might be fixed on her, reading her every expression and movement.

Annis guided her back to where they'd been as she distantly heard Ahar resume his boasts and lavish compliments upon the lord of the hall. Her head was swimming, spinning between attempting to track her surroundings and desperately scrambling for a plan of how to survive both a hall infiltrated by the agents of the High Chalice and deliver on the demands of a butcher who would gladly see them and every other person here dead.

One she could not do without keeping her true nature concealed, the other she could not manage without having her sight restored to her.

The sound of idle chatter returned to the hall as Annis nudged a stool beneath her. She felt his bulk landing alongside her through the floorboards as she kneaded her temple with thought. The Sjøfolk would not recognise the silver cast of her eyes, but the Àrdish might, and her own people certainly would, though they might not report her to a foreign priesthood just yet. All the while seeking a dead Jarl who as far as could be told from the denizens of the hall might well have never sat upon the throne, perhaps no more than a simple fallen warrior from raids present or past. One among a throng of the dead, whose soul may long since have passed to another realm to join whichever gods they had worshipped.

Annis coughed and gripped her arm, drawing her to turn towards the table they had sat themselves beside.

"So, travellers," she recognised the thick accent of Sæunn across from her and felt the heavy steps of her guards taking their places alongside her. "We have unfinished business, you and I. For a seer and her ... companion ... you are surprisingly quiet in the selling of your trade to a willing audience among this hall. The High Chalice will not touch you here, you are my guests as well as they are, and I will not endure the imposition of their sacrament upon those unwilling."

"My lord," Fiadh said. "Should you wish to hear your fate from a fáidh bhean such as I, I am afraid ..."

"Enough!" The hiss from the ruler of Kempe Fell silenced her. "You are a worse liar than even your friend here, and I will not be further insulted by your attempts."

Annis stiffened by her side but did not move except to put a hand gently upon her forearm beneath the table. Whatever was happening around them, however little the others within the hall had noticed the turn in their discussion, there was clearly no swift way to escape.

"Do think I don't know why you are here?" she continued. "Do you not have faith that my men have enough loyalty to warn me of the strangest of companions entering my realm? You, who come from the forsaken path of the cliffs in the wake of that fell creature that has followed my kin from across the sea, to demand on its behalf what I cannot give? None have passed through alive since the turning of the leaves, and I am to believe that a blind seer and her lap dog passed through unharmed? You think me a fool."

Sæunn continued, the frustration in her voice tinged with rage. "It demands one of fair hair, a warrior who has led us, but there is no such ruler in these halls. None ruled before me, and none have ever taken my throne in my time. I rule alone, as I always will with no children to succeed me, but now I shall reign under the protection of the one Lord."

"I will abide by the ways of my kin and will not break the hospitality you have been offered. But know this," Fiadh heard the rasp of Sæunn's breath as she leant close across the table, "should either of you draw a blade in my hall, raise a hand to my people, blaspheme against the god who watches over us, or outstay your welcome beyond the dawn, what remains of you will be cast out to feed the sea."

There was a screech as the bench across from them was shoved back before Fiadh could even think of how to respond, Sæunn and her guards departing as swiftly as they had arrived.

Fiadh buried her head in her hands, eyes now wide open, futilely staring into the cloth towards the floor, feeling little comfort from Annis's hand upon her back. Why were they here? Stepping so close to the path she had found, to the secrets she had yet to uncover, all to have it snatched away waiting for the inevitability of death with the dawn.

There had to be something, anything, that she was missing. A piece of the puzzle of this hall she had not glimpsed. What was the fog that clouded the minds of its inhabitants? What manner of being could hide a soul from not only the Sgiath Athar but also those who knew it in life?

She could hear Annis obscuring their presence among the crowds, exchanging hails and cheap jibes with the collection of mercenaries and traders filtering in and out of the hall, trading coin for drink, and challenges for snark. The sound of warband leaders and representatives of other lords filing before the throne to make their pitch to its occupant echoed around her, the clamour of commerce from the markets sprawled beyond the hall's doors pouring in from the other side.

She could smell the tang of salt all around, the earthy tones of smoked meats and wet leather. The floor creaked with the footsteps of those passing, bouncing as a tankard was slammed upon a table nearby or when someone particularly heavy dropped into a waiting stool.

But still, she could see nothing.

Except that wasn't exactly true. Not anymore.

Beyond the blinding cloth covering her eyes something new was forming; a textured half-light bright enough to be seen even through the binding, sweeping beneath her.

She turned her head from side to side, watching it trail and shift across the ground. But it was not her movement that drew it, it was not some casting of the dusk's light across the stone floor. It drifted between the tables like mist carried on a breeze, curving about them like the edge of a spiral. It was so bright that it pierced through the cloth; though she knew those around her would not see it.

She raised her head to focus on those around her. Annis' shadow blocked out the light beyond him, but it was not blocked by the others. The light pulled at them as it passed as if dragging the essence from each person it touched. For some it drew wisps from their hands and faces, and then for others ...

She looked up to where the throne at the head of the hall surely sat, where its occupant had retaken her seat. There the light fell from her like a waterfall, cascading forth from her to join the tide that whirled and spun at her feet and swept through the hall.

The light spun clockwise about the hall, seeming to spill forward from the halls on its left and out through the right and back through the entrance through which they had come. It had purpose, pulling itself together into woven strands, seeking out where it frayed then binding together to proceed in its path.

The weave of light. Someone, something, was pulling on the very fabric of time and fate in this place. Tyra was right, there was more to this place than a simple den of raiders and merchants. What was the High Chalice up to deep within these halls? What contraption had they built that could not only use the weave to access places they should not enter but also bend the very weave itself to their will?

"Annis," she whispered, placing a hand on his thigh.

He tensed his hand on her back in acknowledgement.

"I need you to keep our companions occupied for a while. There is something here I need to find which you cannot see. I need you to buy me until the dawn before they think to come looking for me. I am sure you have your ways."

This time his response was a chuckle. Yes, he had his ways.

"Now?" He asked.

"As soon as possible, please," she replied.

"Hear me!" His shout made her jump and it was immediately followed by a clatter as his stool spun back over the floor.

"Tae all folks here an afar, tae oor gracious host an tae the hearth she keeps warm this nicht. Tae the gods whae walk among us an gift us wi their favours ..."

Fiadh's eyebrows shot up. This was somewhat more of a distraction than she had anticipated. She could hear the shuffling robes of the red cloaks as they began to move against this flagrant challenge to their authority.

"Tae their continued health an plunder, skål!"

"Skål!" came the roar of approval from the hall, with the clatter and grind of benches forced back and horns lifted to their air.

Annis gave her a thump on the arm; time to move.

Fiadh slipped from her chair as smoothly as she was able, using the way people and objects blocked out the light's weave to guide herself between them, crouched down to remain hidden as she saw the dark forms of figures from the sides of the room moving in.

"Tae the feast, skål!" Came Annis' bellow from behind her, and another roar and clatter in response from all around her.

"Tae the drink, skål!"

One heavily robed figure ahead of her was bowled over by another leaping over to seize a pitcher nearby. Fiadh hissed as a splash landed on her shoulders. But she kept moving ever on towards a far entrance around which the light coalesced.

"Tae companions, new an auld, skål!"

The roared response was now accompanied by laughs and a fair few bodies thumping back into their seats heavily.

She was almost there now, carefully staying crouched down out of sight between the burly shoulders of the warriors jostling one another and shouting out their suggestions for the next toast. They were crowding closer, making it all the more difficult for the heavily robed figures to get any closer to this new disruption even as moving against the tide remained easy.

The doorway ahead was unhindered, the pungent smell of salted meats cooking upon fires beyond wafting out into the hall. A servant's passage of some kind opposite the chambers of the Jarl.

She slid through, trailing one hand along the stonework to keep a sense of space as she moved, her eyes following the bright weaves that flowed along the floor, spiralling about her feet and around corners ahead.

"You, fáidh bhean, stop!" A voice came from behind her, and she turned, seeing nothing but a black silhouette against the streaming light. "This is no place for you, you're to remain in the hall until morning, it has been decreed."

Fiadh reached up to his face, pressing her fingers against his cheek and jaw even as he recoiled. "Yes, yes!" she intoned. "I see it now, your path. You will love, but you will be consumed by it. It will gnaw at your very soul and leave you alone in the face of god's judgement, yes, this is your path."

He jerked away, stumbling a little even as she continued to reach towards him, play-acting a compulsion to reach for his face. With a couple more steps backwards and a mumbled attempt to restart his challenge he was gone, disappearing back into the crowd of the hall, returning her to her search.

The light wound tight around the walls here, following steps down deeper below the hall and into the cellars and passages below it. The stone here was rough-hewn, uneven beneath her touch, piled upon one another and standing against the trials of time through inertia alone. It was ancient, remnants of a civilisation that had reigned here long before her time – perhaps seaside homes, perhaps a barrow mound laid bare by the elements built as a human imitation of the sìd portals to the place beyond.

The wind blew hard against her face as Fiadh pursued the light further, the way ahead clearly open to the elements. She figured the path ahead was opposite the harbour path they had descended to arrive here, deep into the shadow of the hall that rose above, balanced upon these ancient stones. But this old place was not her destination, not yet. The light continued to flow past her, dancing over the crashing waves and towards the cliffs at the far side of the bay.

The stone was slick underfoot, here and there grasped by weeds and lichen that caused her boots to slip and threatened to cast her out into the waves. One slip too many made her tear her blindfold off in frustration. If any more guards lay in her path, she would have to deal with them as who she was, not through her fool's act of a fáidh bhean.

The sight before her was one worth seeing true. The cliffs reared over the raging seas, dashed with streaks of gold and violet where lonely sunbeams flashed across the water. The frozen rain fell in icy, sweeping arcs from the sky, shaped by the buffeting winds.

Out before her a stairway stretched, carved into the cliff face itself, wrapping around its lower reaches, climbing up and out of sight beyond the bay. That was where the light led her, where the weaves of so many in this town were being pulled to. There, she hoped, she could finally find an escape from the eyes of the Sgiath Athar and find whoever it was who had been hidden from her sight.

The steps that wound up against the side of the cliff face were all but completely exposed to the wind and waves whipping frozen water against the rocks. She clung close to the rocks within, taking each step with care knowing that a single mistake could return her to the grasp of the Ceasg waiting still somewhere out there, ruling over the oceans. Still the weave flowed past her, guiding her forward, breaking into the open air before hugging again to the stone.

The final flickers of sunlight provided no respite, its lonely rays breaking below the clouds upon the horizon only to be dashed against the crashing waves and frozen rain. If this were some spirit from beyond, she did not have much time to find it. When night fell, when the dusk was replaced by darkness, the path to other realms would be closed and she would not have time to wait until dawn to try once again.

Around the side of the cliffs, she found what this long stairway had been built for. A cove was formed, a secret hollow in the cliffs as if a giant had reached out and gouged a furrow right into the rock. At its base the waves ran over and between columns that filled its floor, angular slabs that slotted together like segments of a disturbed game board, breaking the waves and spilling out into the open sea for a way before disappearing into the depths. Far above them, nested in isolated alcoves dotted about, were rooms with exteriors left completely bare to the elements.

From here she could see the iron bars that wreathed the doors beyond. They were cells – lonely, exposed prisons for those who had fallen foul of the rulers of Kempe Fell. The exposed hollows were not a path for escape, but rather an invitation for those entombed here to cast themselves against the rocks should they be unable to endure the misery of their confinement any longer.

The stairs plunged into the rock here, leading down into the dark even as the weave of light spiralled out into the open air, directly drawn to one of the cells furthest along the hollow. It lay at some distance from its companions, as if separated deliberately so that no other could hear from its occupant over the crashing waves and howling winds.

Fiadh, unable to follow the weave into the open air like her corvid namesakes, followed the stairs. It was some respite to finally be free of the elements here, and though the water trickled down the steps the air was drier here, the rocks grey with salt clinging to their surface.

Her silvered eyes lit up the darkness, seeing deeper into the hewn passage in shades of charcoal and ash. At points rings had been embedded into the walls, although whether as fastenings for guide ropes or manacles, it was hard to tell. Torch fastenings sat rusted and abandoned, some still holding the withered remnants of the wood that would once have lit the way.

The route followed the curve of the hollowed cliff face. On occasion it opened into chambers long abandoned, littered by a few rotting chairs, tables, and pallets. Guards' quarters perhaps, refuges from the docks for its rulers, or interrogation chambers.

Further still the entrance ways to those exposed cells began to pass by. Heavy wooden doors remained sealed, swollen by rot tight against their frames, iron bars letting the wind whip through and further chill the dark passage. They were not the one she sought, not yet.

Even as the passage diverged into several others plunging deeper or higher into the rock, her route was clear. Far ahead she could see the golden glow of the weave illuminating her path, where surely this maelstrom of light found its destination.

The path ahead was barred by another swollen wooden door, unlike those she had passed before where nothing lay between the cell and passage other than the sole portal locking their occupants within. Its bar was loose, as though never locked, but it was stuck fast against the stone it may otherwise have swung loosely within. It had been some time since Fiadh had last hacked her way through old wood to find her way forward, but it was hardly a complex skill easily forgotten.

In minutes, enabled by the remnants of an old guardrail, the door hung in shattered pieces about the path. The sweat had frozen to her skin. Forgotten droplets forming painful beads of ice against her chilled flesh instead of evaporating as it would have from Annis' skin were he here. That inner warmth was long lost to her, and over the years the experience had grown no less uncomfortable. Her work completed, she tore back the last plank still blocking her progress, gathered her belongings, and continued forward.

This cell was unlike the others, the corridor up to it holding several braziers barely hanging from rusted chains from the hewn stone above. A small table or desk of some kind was set just before the door as if to be used as study for the subject beyond. The chamber door itself lay wide open, its upper woodwork long gnawed away by rot, water, and wind.

Beyond lay what she had sought. In the room's centre, bare to the thrashing gales, the light pooled as it poured in from the cliffs beyond. It spiralled in close to a point, where it was swept up and spun tightly about a single thread, as if wound around a spindle whose centre was not a wooden stave but instead a black pit that swallowed the light greedily as it turned.

The golden light illuminated the cell with an unearthly radiance, every surface strewn in bright dust as if filaments of the weave had been scattered by the strength of its spin. Someone other than the fates spun destinies here, but for what purpose? What manner of being would draw upon the petty squabbles and ambitions of merchants and raiders with such earnest intent?

The entrance she had crouched behind was free of the torrent of light, so bright she wondered if people without her eyes might still see it bleeding into their own world. Lit by the weave, she could see the details of the room before her. Close to her the bare rock was barren but for barely legible scrawls carved along its surface. To the right there were tallies, some fool counting down the sunsets until either their body or their will gave up the fight; to the left, rags held in place with what looked like the wooden handle of some tool that had been used to carve a small hole in the stone. Where the wrecked door may once have stood firm, she could pick out the marks left by the desperate clawing of fingers, the blood long washed away.

She moved carefully into the chamber, staying well clear of the spinning weave, unsure whether stepping into the current might have her spun away from this reality too, a forgotten victim of this place just like all its occupants before her.

She was not alone here, not quite. Propped up in the corner furthest from the sharp drop to the waves far beyond sat the sad remnants of someone who must have called this place home for a while before their demise. A desiccated jaw hung slack gazing at her, the flesh clinging to it and holding it back in some cruel imitation of a laugh, mummified by the cold air and salt.

Its remaining hand still held the other end of the wooden spoon that pinned the cloth fast in the cell floor. If there were a sorrier weapon to die with in hand, Fiadh could not imagine it.

She sat alongside the corpse to examine the room from their perspective, imagining what it may have looked like for them before the end. It was strange, at least, that they sat this far from the hollows carved along the far side which suggested a cot, perhaps, or some shelter from the wind before it had been swept away. Perhaps they had not been alone in this cell, or maybe they had crawled out here to die with the sun on their face in their final moments. Not for the first time Fiadh wondered what it must be like to feel true warmth from the sun's rays – not simply a respite to the chill that reached out from within her, a momentary break from the dreaded reminder that she should never have risen from the icy depths below Tur Eumor.

The glimmers of sunlight cast across the underside of the roiling clouds could still be seen despite the coalescence of the weave before her. If she were to do this, she had very little time indeed.

There was sufficient space to set up her requirements. Chalk emerged quickly and she began to etch the circular pattern burned into her mind from that day beneath the temple at the Three Willows, at each point entering the sigil that the tomes collected over the years had led her towards, the angles and relationships careful and specific. Then came the centrepiece, the veil that had hung from that accursed contraption, claiming to be a scrap of the very weave from which this golden light was now sourced. The gold dust scattered upon the stone was drawn to it, pulled into its fabric, vanishing within the strands as if to give some credence to the tales in the full presence of her doubt.

But there was one thing this veil could do she had no doubt of. From her waist hung a small vial, its crimson contents glinting in the light. From her sack came the arcane contraption that had come with her all this way, a simple twist and spin of its mechanisms extending a needle, greedy to be used once more.

The vial held Annis' blood, an unfortunate necessity after the discovery her own was unfit for this purpose. She tipped it gently until a single drop fell to the needle's tip, drawn deep inside its structure. Another twist produced a second needle from its far side, the drop forming and falling to the centre of the etchings where the veil lay.

There, like so many times before, the drop hung in space before stretching and reaching outwards, forming a portal through which she could see the light beyond. At her back Caerdrich awoke once more, their icy will spreading across her shoulders and out into the air where the drops of rain spun into the chamber froze where they fell, hanging about her like fireflies reflecting the orange glow.

With a deep breath and a final glance to the cell's former occupant gazing up from behind her, Fiadh stepped through the portal.

***

The light nearly blinded her, spilling out in all directions like a star spinning its radiance out into the void, the weave unravelling, shattering against all it touched in great fountains of golden lustre, spilling flickers and embers all about her.

As a thread crashed against her, images began to flash through her mind. A small hand reaching out to hold that of a man on a ship rocking upon the waves. An older hand, spear haft aloft, burying its point through the chest of another, laughter ringing in her ears. The view of the hall of Kempe Fell from its throne, gazing down at that same hand that held the spear, now trembling, clenching fast against the shakes.

Fiadh cast her eyes about for an escape, willing herself to move away from the torrent of the unwound thread breaking out into this darker place. Her form, stripped of her belongings but for the bare blade of Caerdrich shining its own cool white light upon her back, shifted without need for steps, floating up to the far corner of the room in which she had stood to look down upon the display.

From here she could see she was not alone in this space. Another had come here before and had set itself to work ordering the weave as it broke through the passage from her world into this one, tying it back into place, pinning its strands back into the spindle of light that spun and crackled like a fork of lightning held fast to this one spot.

Its head shimmered, spinning this way and that upon its shoulders, flickering between the tasks it continued repeatedly.

Numberless arms sprang from its shoulders, threading, weaving, picking at strands of the light to pull and twine them around one another, yet more searching the stone paving of the floor, holding palms over its face as it sobbed, casting them into the air with grief and despair.

That head, she saw now, had noticed her entrance. Time and again its eyes, brighter still than the strands it spun, stared balefully towards her as it muttered and shouted.

Fiadh knew this thing, this creature of another time and place. She had read of it, long ago, from the old writings in the hallowed halls of Tur Eumor. An Taibhse Ùine did its work in this place, a keeper of souls lost in time. A thief of the strands of fate, all but hounded into oblivion by the servants of the three keepers of destiny. Some called those keepers the Norn, others Moirai, but for all they were jealous wardens of the weave of time they spun.

Yet one worked here still, stealing away this light of the weave in this cell at the edge of the world. Tyra had been right. A thief had stolen from her and the Norn, hiding itself in this place between worlds.

The light that poured in was not of a kind that her eyes could see on the other side of the portal. Intertwined, shaping the light as it flowed, were people. Though she could not recognise any of them through her blindfold back in the hall, Fiadh felt as though she was finally able to put some faces to the voices of Kempe Fell.

Dominant among them, light pouring from them and flooding back in all at once, was a single figure who was themself locked in a loop. Walking up to where the shattered door lay was a woman, tall and proud, with shoulders thrust back and a swagger in her step, her hair dark as pitch. Another followed in her wake, one hand tracing along the wall beside them, fingertips trailing on the stonework.

In the doorway the first figure's face turned to a snarl as she peered through where the opening into this chamber must have been. She turned and placed a hand gently on her companion's cheek as she spoke a few words. Her companion's eyes never quite seemed to meet her own, but they were wide, and her mouth opened just a touch. Fiadh knew that look, though she had never experienced it herself: Adoration.

With those silent words the companion departed, switching hands, and letting the other trail along the stone at her side.

The proud woman pulled open the door, her face twisted into a cruel grimace, but she paused there for a moment, an expression of confusion on her face as she looked to where the skeleton lay, and across to the remnants of a cot that lay across the floor.

Through it all the spirit in the chamber continued to work, though its head spun and muttered, its loop had calmed and begun to coalesce into some kind of focus. Its eyes rested on her, stoic, its mouth sealed as if sewn shut. Its yells echoed around the chamber, several voices at once as if layered over one another with each spin of the weave. Through it all one voice began to form a coherent stream, slicing through the others.

"The time has long passed since I was of any concern to the Sciathán Dubh. Your kind hunted mine across time and worlds before you, too, fell to the ambitions of another. You have not come for me; no one shall again come for me."

Fiadh steeled herself against the wave of curiosity that flooded her mind. This being knew more of the world than any earthly thing could possibly learn, had seen time flow from its very beginnings to its end. It could well know where she would be and where she would end, what of her journey would succeed and what would end in failure. But she knew the Taibhse Ùine did not part with their secrets by request, and those who pried came to regret it.

"Gabh mo leisgeul, I have not come for you," she said, careful not to offend such a being in a space it controlled. "I come seeking another, a no one, who seems neither to have walked this earth nor passed into the next. Another claims them, and lives rest on their place being found."

"This will not be the first nor the last time you have lied to hide the true nature of your cause. I wonder if you even know what pulls you here, for surely a lie to another with such ease might rest upon a far greater lie unto yourself."

Fiadh gritted her teeth. Each time she came across these beings of another age they spoke down to her as if to a child, as if she had not fought her way here by every step. All as they frittered away the aeons barely thinking to concern themselves with such trifling things as the passage of years and lives in a world they deigned to visit.

"You draw from the people of Kempe Fell, you weave their time and fates free of the great will. You know it cannot alter their path, yet you steal from their path regardless. Why?" she asked, keeping her tone as measured as she could endure.

"Steal? To have stolen from you only what you sought to take from another seems a fitting fate for those who believe they can take whatever they wish. Fitting for those who believe their power is such that to take it is their birthright. Is such a fate theft? What entitles you to cast judgement? What authority guides you to decide my fate before yours has even been read?"

Before she could think to decipher the ramblings of the spirit, Fiadh felt herself stilled, her limbs forced back against the shimmering walls of the cell. Gently, as if teasing a thorn free of hair, hands of the Taibhse Ùine began to pull at her, thin strands of gold drawn from her being so that its shining eyes could cast their gaze over them.

"Ah yes, the lonely remnant of the Sciathán Dubh, the child abandoned by her gods and her elders, left to die beneath the blades of the Sjøfolk and the thunderous laughter of their god of storms. A final witness of the machinations of the Red Raven." The head twitched and jerked back, the mouth leaping open and shut as a disjointed laugh barked all around her.

"I was there, you know, what fateful coincidence that is! Locked within an iron cage upon her ship, I watched the flames rise, I watched you fall, small one, hands clasped around this storied blade and vanishing into the waves beneath the flames. I did not speak of what I saw, for I knew your weave. I know you would be lost to the seas or lost to the will of the blade. I knew you would not be seen upon these shores for many years."

The eyes fixed upon her once more.

"What wonders might I find, what answers lie beneath those waters? Which claimed you, I wonder? The will of the sea or the blade? Whom now binds your weave to its intent?"

Its eyes flickered, both gazing at her and at the blade floating free of her now.

"They cannot hear me here. I know their name, and with their name I have bound them to the plane you call home to wonder what became of you here, free for a time from their call and claim. What would you do, I wonder, with this freedom, should you take what is mine for yours? But such is not your fate, nor mine."

"Both of you are trapped, spinning in a whirlpool of chaos between those attempting to seal the arc forever and those who wish to break it and unleash the gods of old upon the world anew. Yet here you stand, chasing your petty vengeance unknowing that with every step you are dragged deeper into the depths of this war. This great scheme that you catch only flickers off as it washes you away."

Fiadh snarled at that, at these beings with their perspectives of generations, of entire centuries passing them by, knowing nothing of the pain and torment of those who danced and were dashed against the fates they so easily dismissed as matters of too little import. Why should they care for such trifling concepts as loss and revenge when to them the life of a Crow passed in an instant, when the rise and fall of Tur Eumor was little more than a flash of memory no more defining of their time upon this world than a fine meal too early interrupted.

What right did this creature have to judge her?

"You sailed to Tur Eumor aboard a ship. What lord sealed you within it to witness the flames that he lit upon my home? I ask not for my fate, nor yours, only the petty details of time already passed so that I may sate my vengeance." Fiadh did her utmost to bite back the spite lingering beneath her words. For too long she had endured the Daoine Sìth meeting every step of her journey with their condescension and cruel dismissals.

The Taibhse Ùine did not notice her tone. If it understood such things at all there was no sign of it. But one set of its arms had begun to weave a new thread from the spindle that beamed from the cell's centre. The golden strands divided before coalescing into the form of a woman, standing proudly at the chamber's entrance, sword upon her hip. Her raven hair flowed near waist-length and her face was etched with a look of abject contempt. Fiadh recognised that face, that of the woman who had walked to the chamber with her companion before.

She shimmered out of focus before forming anew, closer, kneeling near where the skeleton lay in the earthly plane. She wrenched something away, standing to turn and shout to the other side of the room. The shout dissolved into a smile; her eyes ringed not with mirth but with cruel intensity.

"Signe Grímsdóttir, the ruler of Kempe Fell, champion of Vestamr, burner of Tur Eumor, captive of mine own." The face of the Taibhse Ùine broke from its focus to leap back and forth between the silent howl of laughter and the many tasks it continued to pursue.

That smile shifted, becoming wide-eyed shock just for a moment before her form was washed away in the light. Then again, she was there behind Fiadh once more, walking up towards the door with her companion in tow.

"A fitting fate, you must agree, for such a spirit that claimed to have triumphed over fate, to have trapped me free of mine sìd so that she might rule over the very Norns themselves. She claimed power over knowledge and time so that she might feed their reputation and esteem. Claiming such power, yet so limited in imagination to wonder only how it might benefit her fireside tales. A fitting fate for a fool to claim so much to be remembered, only to be forgotten even by those who loved her most."

Fiadh watched that face cycle through her movements again, from their place in the doorway, to the body, to that cruel smile. In a final shimmer she watched the threads dragged forward before they snapped into the first image once more of the woman's walk to the doorway, and she understood.

These were the last moments of Signe Grímsdóttir, torn from time and the weave of fate by the Taibhse Ùine they had trapped in that mortal plane. Something in those last moments had freed this fey's powers over the weave, and they had used that strength to summon a spindle capable of trapping the Jarl as they themselves had been trapped before.

They had erased not only Signe Grímsdóttir from the world in that moment, but from every moment before or since. They became a nobody, a blank in time and memory. There was no soul to be collected, for they had never existed. There was no predecessor on the throne of Kempe Fell, for they had never sat upon it.

The Taibhse Ùine remained here, still trapped in this cell even through the veil, repeating its spell over and over, forever drawing every hint and suggestion of Signe's rule from every denizen of Kempe Fell. A fitting fate, perhaps. However, it was one that doomed Fiadh and everyone else in that port to the wrath of the Sgiath Athar whose quest would remain forever unsated, their own fate never fulfilled.

Part of Fiadh's will fell away. All this time, all this way searching for the Jarl who had sailed under the lightning bolt banner, and they were already dead. Not only dead but stripped away from this world as if they had never set foot upon it. Her vengeance against one of those who had razed her home had already been taken by another.

Emotions crashed over her: exhaustion, relief, anger, determination. There was another, she was not done yet. There was one more who had led those ships – The Red Raven. A being of such power that she made deals with the gods of the sea and rallied the servants of another to sail against the nest of the Crows. To complete her journey, she would have to find a way to break that power, and to escape the wrath of Tyra's spear.

"A fitting fate," Fiadh said. "But how did she come to seal you in this place and visit such a fate upon herself? The Sjøfolk are not famed for their grasp of our ways, nor the secrets by which your kind pass from this world into the next. Perhaps with time I could unlock the way, and prepare your path to return?"

The gaze was fixed back upon her now, the ghostly reflection of Signe's final moments fading away. "What cause would the last of the Sciathán Dubh have to aid a challenger of the fates to return? After generations extinguishing every challenge to the will of the Ríaghan?"

Fiadh weighed how much to offer in return. It had been here many years, trapped, shorn from its place of power and willing this spindle to continue its work drawing from the weave. There was so much it might not know, and that knowledge was a precious advantage over a being whose purpose was to know more than could possibly be known.

"We are not alone in this place, spirit," she said. "Another has come to claim what you have taken from the weave, one that cannot cross into this place to claim it. Should I not return with word as to where it has passed, my life is forfeit, as are the lives of every soul from which you pull. They will not be satisfied; they claim that their fate is to take the soul of Signe Grímsdóttir."

The face of the Taibhse Ùine shimmered once more, screaming, laughing and twisted by rage, all at once. When it spoke again its voice held more grit than before, the growl coming as if fed between rolling stones.

"Fated! I know the fate of Signe Grímsdóttir. I have woven it. I have spun its threads to the only destination they could ever have been fated to travel. None decide the weave but the weavers; none speak the path but those who roam it. I will roam again, my visitor, and I will see what fate shall befall this presumptuous intruder upon mine work."

Fiadh stayed silent. There was no need to interrupt an old spirit who had found reason to speak.

"A hundred moons past the followers of Alwealda first came to this place. Their schemes and portents cast a spell over the new Jarl Signe and her companions. One by one they fell, their fates decided long before by their foolish inclinations to follow the word of a ruler distracted by promises of immortality. Tormented by loss, Signe searched for a way to cheat the fate she had delivered to herself and to her forsaken followers, and Alwealda gifted her his blessing. So, she waited until the moon met the sun and unleashed the waters upon mine sìd, sealing the way beneath the white rock, sealing me upon this plain and within the iron cage her new faith had forged for me. Free me, fallen one, from this place, so that I might see the fate of this world once more with mine own eyes. One final time before I take what is mine and depart beyond the arc to join the already departed."

"What if I do not?" Fiadh said, seeing little in this demand that might help her escape the vengeful intent of Tyra upon the cliffs. "What if I flee this place and leave Kempe Fell to its fate; free myself from your demands as you remain in this place weaving nothing but ghosts from the ruins along the sea?"

"I see your fate. You will do it, for you see no other path."

With that a single hand waved to dismiss her and Fiadh felt that same feeling that came before the fall, her heart leaping to her throat, her stomach lurching as the black pit opened beneath her.

"Careful, silver eye, one does not simply cross into this realm without consequence. The sacrifices you made to reach here begin to make many things seem worth the price you paid."

As she fell, the final words followed her down.

***

Fiadh stood once more in that cell open to the frozen wind and rain, accompanied only by the skeleton still fixed in a permanent bark of laughter.

She was slick with the blood of the portal even as it collapsed back into that single drop and fell to the floor behind her. No matter how many times she made the journey, the return would never feel comfortable, the sudden sense of weight and the sticky remnants of her passage coating her skin and clothing.

She tried to paw away the blood that smeared her face, dripping down before her eyes, but managed little more than to smear it further. Not for the first time she was taken aback by how Annis seemingly stank more inside than out, if such a thing was even possible.

She sat for a moment, pondering her situation, the red stain slowly spreading across the stone beneath her. The Taibhse Ùine may not know people well but it seemed to know her calculation before she had made it, even as it busied itself drawing from the past of another. To run, now, would be to leave empty handed and run the risk of being hunted by a Sgiath Athar, the hunters of the Othair, longer than she could ever hope to escape.

To free the spirit could be to unleash a new enemy upon the world, one still vengeful for the part the Sciathán Dubh had played hounding their kind from the earth. She could not be certain the spirit's contempt for Tyra would trump that or leave her safe to continue her journey.

Pondering, she stood and sought out a sign of where she needed to go. Crouching at the edge of the drop to the crashing waves below, she enjoyed the whipping water beginning to wash the crimson from her face and arms. It was almost immediately below her, right at the centre of the hollow carved into the cliffs – the white rock, a lonely finger of chalk jutting out between a maze of hexagonal slabs of granite slabs around it. A destination, at least, and that was better than too long spent worrying about finding solutions for where there so often were none to find.

Fiadh stood once more and rummaged through her pack, pulling a long rope from her belongings and testing the metal bars of the chamber doors beyond the cell. One, still sturdier than the rest for its relative shelter from the elements, became her choice of purchase. With the knot tied tight and the rope tested with a boot against the wall, Fiadh walked the remaining loops back to the cell and tossed them over the side, watching them fall just short of that lone white line.

With a sigh, and hands wiped against the rock to rid them of the slick gore coating them, she began the descent, placing one foot after the other against the cliff face as her hands worked one over another to rapidly descend the rope's full extent.

All along the shrill wind screamed about her head, rain stinging as it lashed her bare arms and neck, the buffeting gusts threatening to send her swinging back and forth as they shredded around the cove. Caerdrich, still bound firm against her shoulders, barely shifted, held fast by the multiple straps that bound her torso to their scabbard.

At the rope's full extent, she sat barely an arm's reach from the point of the white rock, still a dozen yards from the crashing waves below. Again, Fiadh imagined what it would be like to hang above the waters knowing that the Ceasg may still hold her indebted, that the Merrow might circle the depths just beyond sight ready to drag her down. The shudder she felt did not come from the cold.

There was no pathway above the water line. The hexagonal columns stretched out in either direction, hugging the granite of the cliff, jutting out of the water this way and that to break the passage of the waves. Where they met the white chalk they fell together, opening a deep cavern below the cliffs, the faint light the moon cast through the clouds vanishing into darkness. Knowing where her destination must lie, Fiadh took a deep breath, pushed twice upon the rock, and dove into the depths.

The water knocked her this way and that as it rolled and punched forward towards the cliff, the salt stinging her eyes as Fiadh desperately searched for where the entrance must lie. The cavern's opening lay deeper still, lit only by her silvered eyes as a dark space where the granite and chalk met just out of reach. She kicked and pulled through the water, fighting so as not to be dragged away with each swell of the waves, before being thrown forward and closer with their trough. Five strokes were enough to bring her fingertips to the cavern's edge, enough to pull herself with the rock and through its opening to the tunnel beyond.

The submerged entrance was short and within moments Fiadh broke the surface to find air in the darkness, a pebbled shore lying before her even as the water level rose and fell as if breathing into this secret space.

As she dragged herself from the water, scrambling over the shifting pebbles, there was some relief that the drips ran down smooth skin, no longer matted with the cloying blood of her companion.

The chamber ahead was small, barely opening into air before descending back into water. Fiadh realised the pebbles she stood upon were not washed up against a floor of rock but instead stones that had been piled up upon one another, building a wall that held the water back to where it was now, higher within the cave than outside of it. The tide must be falling, now, as the water lapped upon the pebbles.

Climbing further, she dipped her hand into the water beyond. It was still, without currents. The water was held here as a pool, filled by the high tide, and remaining high even as the sea receded.

Beyond, as she lowered herself into the ice-cold pool, she found what she had been sent for. Just below the waterline, to what may have once been left open to the air with each low tide, another smaller opening led into the cavern. Inscriptions on clean-carved stones surrounded the portal, the entrance glowing with a silver light, just as those outside the Three Willows had done long ago.

A sìd, portal from this world into the next, home of the Taibhse Ùine now trapped in the cells above. Blocked, not by earth or stone, but by the salt water of the sea itself. Grímsdóttir had been taught a trick even the Crows had not imparted in Fiadh's years sequestered in Tur Eumor. A secret that held far more power than she could have known.

Bracing her feet against the lowest level of the piled stones, Fiadh wrapped her hands around one of the highest and pulled, dragging the stone from its place, and letting it tumble past her into the dark pit below. Even as she reached to the next one the water began to rush past her, re-joining the falling tide. As each stone fell, the water she waded in dropped closer against the etched portal at her back, each moment revealing more of that ancient, shaped stonework that formed its entrance.

As the water fell below the carvings they began to shine again, the white light cast from them dancing upon the water as Fiadh continued to work down the wall block by block. The pebbles beyond were swiftly washed out into the open water as the trickle became a torrent.

Her work completed, Fiadh straddled the water rushing over the natural rock left at the base of the wall, turning to watch as the full circle of the sìd revealed itself, the dancing light around the entrance making the darkness at its centre all the clearer. Beyond there, she knew, lay the plane beyond the arc, to where all the Daoine Sìth had fled during the fall of the world, leaving only isolated stragglers behind them. Sometimes she wondered what it would be like to travel through herself and be among her kin, both those that had left and those who had fallen.

But not now, not yet. Not when there was still work to be done.

She turned away, feeling the gust of wind when the final engraving broke into the air, pulling her back. But this sìd was not for her. She could only hope that its owner would remember the deed done.

***

The return to the cell was exhausting, the climb far harder than the descent, and by the time Fiadh reached the lip of the chamber her limbs were screaming with agony, her lungs and throat aching with the gulps of frozen air that tore at them with every breath.

But here, still, the spindle of light continued to spin. The way was clear. The sìd of the Taibhse Ùine might be free, but the soul of Signe Grímsdóttir was not. She knew it was only a matter of time before the memory of that name was also dragged from her mind, as it had been from everyone else's.

If she had once known the name of the Taibhse Ùine to summon the spirit, she no longer knew it, and she was out of time. The sun was set and the path to cross with the aid of the veil was closed.

There was no other option now but to escape.

Fiadh gathered her things at pace, without the will or energy to untie and retrieve the rope that had given her access to the cavern below. With ritual equipment and clothing both bundled roughly into her sack, she slung it over her shoulder alongside Caerdrich and began an exhausted lope along the corridors and stairs.

If not for her eyes the path would have been perilous in the dark, though a murmur of thunder over the water warned her that it would not be long until the path was lit by the flash of more lightning.

As she strode back through the passage into the halls of Kempe Fell, Fiadh did not bother to look away as she passed servants, their eyes fixed upon her and expressions agape. The time for subtlety was over; they did not have the time to hide themselves from people whose lives would soon be brutally cut short.

The return to the hall was a short one. There was no need to retrace her steps – she could hear the clamour from deep within the hallways beneath it. The sound of drink-soaked songs and boasts echoed around the stone and she was struck by the stench of honeyed drinks liberally sloshed across the tables and floors.

By now Fiadh was certain the agents of the High Chalice had seized Annis and sealed him away to be subjected to whatever punishment Sæunn saw fit for his blasphemies. Given the merriment there was a chance he had been sequestered to a cell somewhere within the halls to await his fate while they sought her out and let the raiders and warriors have their fun. She had to move fast, albeit carefully, now. Find where they had stowed Annis, get out, stay clear of the slaughter to come. In and out, as fast as possible. A simple plan Fiadh knew full well would go far from smoothly.

She brushed past several more servers in her path, ignoring their stares as the warmth of the raging fire pit in the Great Hall began to dry her skin. The red cloaks would see her, she knew, and the Jarl of Kempe Fell too. There was no time to wait for them to be warned.

The sound of the hall hit Fiadh like a wave as she reached its entrance, the noise filling her senses for a moment as the scale of the gathering beyond became clear. There were dozens, no, hundreds packed into the space, thrown together in clumps almost shoulder to shoulder as drink and food was snatched up aplenty.

There among it all, stood upon a table in a long line of men belting out Sjøfolk songs, was Annis, horn held high.

Fiadh stood frozen in disbelief. How had he ... what had he ... It didn't matter. She shook her head, continuing into the room and beginning to elbow her way forward through the crowd. She had a clear path to him now and being hidden below the shoulder-height of men crammed together kept her well out of view of the Jarl's seat and the red cloaks likely still stood around it. This was simpler, at least, and she could ask questions later.

Shoved back and forth by the weight of the crowd around her, the stench of the armpits and ale-drenched shirts of others was overpowering, and the desperation of forcing her way through it and the scream of muscles already exhausted from the climb brought tears to her eyes.

Fiadh's eyes shone silver like the moon, and those around her were beginning to notice, even as she was buried among them.

The crowd opened as she made it to the tables, staggering slightly as the slick floor beneath made her boots slip forward further than she had intended. Annis was there, oblivious, shouting out odd words from half-heard lyrics of the tune the Sjøfolk led.

"Annis," Fiadh shouted, though her voice was lost in the din. "Annis! For fuck's sake, Annis!"

That last yell was finally enough. He saw her, and with a smile grabbed the back of the head of the man besides him and planted a kiss on his lips before releasing the bemused mercenary and dropping down to the floor beside her.

"So, lass, ye made it. As ye can see, Ah earned ma gold. The red cloaks ken better than tae git between hired swords an their ale. Job's done, time fur ye tae enjoy yersel fur yince!"

"Annis," she hissed, desperately trying to be heard over the songs without being spotted by the crowd around her, increasingly noticing the pallid skin and silver eyes. "There's no time, we have to go."

He looked at her with confusion knotted into his brows before the implications of what she said began to dawn on him.

"Ye didnae find thaim, the spirit? The Valkyrie is still coming?" He cast his head towards the crowd around him, who were taking steps back from the intensity of their conversation. "We cannae jist leave thaim aw tae die, Fiadh!"

"What do you expect me to do?" Fiadh rapped her knuckles against his chest, trying to force sense into him with every word. "What she's looking for can't be found. They're not here; they're gone. Tyra cannot be reasoned with. We're finished."

"Whit happened tae 'we dinnae kill', Fiadh?"

Fiadh's expression snapped between shock and anger in an instant. "It's not the same, you know it's not, don't you dare throw my own words back at me."

"Then we fight, an if we dinnae everyone here wull die. Whit bluidy use is that blasted icy sword across yer back if ye dinnae use it?"

Fiadh locked his eyes with her gaze, her hand clenching his arm tight, "Listen close, Annis, and understand me. If I am forced to draw Caerdrich to fight for my own life, everyone here will die. Not a single soul will leave this hall, no man, woman or child. If we leave, some may live, but do not make me draw this blade. They cannot be sated."

The space around them had grown now, the songs fading and being replaced with panicked and confused mutters.

"Annis, stop looking at them, look at me," Fiadh reached up and gripped his chin, turning his head towards her. "We leave and some may live; we stay, and we die among them. I will not allow Caerdrich to take their lives by my hand. Let's go."

They were interrupted by a loud cough in what was now a quiet hall. Fiadh and Annis both turned to its source, the Jarl of Kempe Fell sitting slouched upon her throne, her face cradled in one hand. A great cloak of wolf fur hung across her shoulders, two heads still filled with sharp fangs hanging down over her chest and the red dyed cloth beneath. Above her cradle-hand, gazing down towards them but not at them, her eyes were glazed over with opaque grey.

Fiadh's blood froze as she watched those eyes stare off beyond them, and the Jarl's free hand gestured one of the red cloaks forward.

"She's blind?" she whispered. "You let me play-act as a blind prophet in front of a blind lord?"

"Ye dinnae pay me fur quick thinkin, Craw," Annis replied under his breath. "Ye pay me tae smash in heids an mak a racket."

Sæunn's grey eyes stared out at them, a calm fury brewing beneath their surface. They had breached her trust, her demands, and there was no time to play for or space to escape the will of the cloaked priests alongside her or the grip of her housecarls, lined up by her throne, spears in hand.

One of the red cloaks stepped to the edge of the platform the throne rested upon, looking down at her. She saw the transformation creep across his features as he met her gaze with his own, his eyes registering the bright silver and widening, the blood draining from his face. Behind him another, marble mask across his face, registered his own shock by stumbling back, bells strapped across his chest chiming as he struck the wall behind him.

"W ... witch!" the front man declared, hand raised towards her, a single finger jutting out accusingly. "Crow! Messenger of the devil!"

Fiadh snarled, for all the good it would do her. They thought her a monster; they would never be tempted from that path. If they wanted a monster, she could provide them with one. Whatever it would take to break her free of this forsaken place.

Rising from her seat, Jarl Sæunn took the arm of one of her guards and began to take steps from the dais towards them even as the red cloak continued his rant, growing in confidence.

"Behold," he declared, now casting his arms wider to the hall around them. "The Crow in our midst, carrion feeder, blood weaver, she would have us cast aside the Lord and follow her silvered eyes unto hell."

"Be not afraid, those of faith, for you stand under the protection of The Lord Most High. She cannot harm you here where her spells will fail, and her whispers fall upon unhearing ears. Fear not! We will take her to face the judgement of Alwealda."

"Annis?" Fiadh said, setting herself into her best impression of an intimidating fighter's stance as he stood stoically, arms crossed. Sæunn was off the dais now, being led towards them by five heavily armed mercenaries.

"Aye?"

"You can smash heads and make a racket right now, right?"

"Aye but we'll still end up in a cell at the end ae it," he replied. Beyond the guards the red cloaks continued to rant from the dais, spinning all kinds of new and spectacular horrors she was meant to have accomplished with various incredible powers she'd never had, and if she had done would surely have used them to escape this predicament.

Fiadh's hand trembled, though she fought to still it. A part of her, deep at the back of her mind, wanted that hand to reach to her back, pull the scabbard down to her hip, and feel the ice of Caerdrich spring into her grasp.

The memory of the last time the blade was drawn was faint, now. So many years had passed, so many leagues travelled over land and sea searching for a way to repay her debt to them.

How easy it would be to leave this place, blade in hand, and forget it had ever existed along with the ghosts she would leave behind.

She looked at their faces, the gaze of the Jarl passing through her, her guards' stern looks as their hands went to the hilts of their weapons. Beyond them, around the hall, people who so recently had been singing and dancing now stood in silence watching a witch being brought to heel. She looked to Annis. Caerdrich did not care for who travelled alongside her. His life would surely be forfeited along with the rest.

Sæunn's hand fell upon the arm of her guard, steadying their hand before they reached out to Fiadh. The Jarl would not have her guests dragged away before facing the wrath of her judgement face-to-face.

She did not deserve to die. None of them did. Not for this, not for her.

A voice pricked at the back of her mind in reply. *Are you sure?*

Her hand shook again, and she willed it to still as the guards moved in, Annis still stationary at her side, waiting for her word.

Then chaos broke out.

The wall behind the dais erupted forward, beams and stone flying through the air. The red cloaks who had remained at its base disintegrated, red mist dashed across the rubble as it tumbled through the air, splashing in sprays of crimson among the crowd.

Where the wall had stood, lightning flashed and thunder rumbled as one, the wind driving rain across the fallen stones and broken limbs that protruded from between them. Revealed by the opening, the great arcs of bone that loomed over the docks beyond reared upwards. Above it all, framed by the dark clouds and bearing the shining Lance of the Dawn, floated Tyra of the Sgiath Athar. Her death mask gazed down upon them; the veined marble fixed in cold contempt.

Her voice boomed in unison with the thunder, her spear a blinding point that lit up the room as if it were the day.

"Your time has come, denizens of Kempe Fell, as was decreed, as your ruler has kept from you, as your messengers were sent to be made a display of in your name."

"Now," the spear point lowered, directed at the scattered remnants of the crowd of the hall. "I will take what I am fated to retrieve, the soul of the one who ruled here as the shores fell to Vestamr. If they are not delivered unto me then I will take those who are of their blood. I will take from you until I have found what destiny has laid in my hand."

Fiadh had landed beneath one of the benches at the side of the hall, shielded from a stone block only by the beam that had landed first and was propped up by one half of a table that hadn't collapsed under its weight.

Her mind raced. They could still get out. Tyra wasn't interested in her or Annis, they were not of the Jarl's blood. She looked around trying to spy where her companion had ended up. There he was, sprawled further back flat out against the floor, motionless.

She cursed. If they had moved together, escape was possible. Carrying his bulk out with her wasn't.

She looked around desperately for Sæunn, in the hope Tyra might notice the Jarl of Kempe Fell before she did them, but she paused. An image had come back to her. Of two women, wreathed in light, of a gentle touch and a look of adoration in the eyes of the Jarl of Kempe Fell. The glimpse of lovers parted for the last time.

Not only was Fiadh not of the Jarl's blood, but none of them were. Sæunn was without children, rising to the throne in the place of the Jarl not through blood, but by having sat beside her on the dais before. She was the only person left after Signe's disappearance that the people of Kempe Fell remembered sitting at their head. There was no bloodline left to hunt.

The Sgiath Athar would kill every one of them in this hall and find none whom she could take as recompense. Then she would come for Fiadh, as well. She knew too well the single-minded butchery of those not gifted what they felt they were due.

Tyra had landed among the rubble, gazing about the wanton destruction she had delivered, the broken bodies and moans of pain emerging from beneath stone and timber. The rest of the hall was silent, shock and horror freezing the denizens of Kempe Fell where they had fallen, a scant few seeking to crawl to those exits not blocked by the shattered remnants of the wall and roof. The wolf cloak of Sæunn was within the rubble Tyra had passed, a single hand wreathed in red dyed cloth, twitching and grasping faintly at the air.

There was no way out, no escape that would not leave her hunted across land and sea by one who travelled faster and saw farther than she ever could. No possible respite from this proudly barbaric and dedicated weapon of foreign gods.

Fiadh winced as she dragged herself from under the fallen beam and brought herself into a crouch, her vision swimming with the pain of bruised bones and the stench of blood mixed with the thick dust in the air.

"Doppelganger!"

Fiadh winced as the word sliced through the ringing still sounding in her ears, Tyra's words booming like the thunder she left in her wake. "So, you join us, empty handed, unable to deliver what I am owed. What now, Keeper of the old Order? Do you fight, or do you kneel and accept the end has come for you?"

Fiadh's hand shook again, that voice at the back of her head returning anew as the air around her grew cold.

"I will not fight, nor will I kneel, butcher of forgotten gods," she said, trying to keep the waver of doubt from her voice "What you seek is not here, it was not taken from you. You have simply lost it."

Tyra paused in her descent for a moment at her words, as if astonished that someone could even think to offer a depiction of events that did not match her own.

"False thing!" she said, her voice dripping with scorn. "Liar! Born of deception and pretence. Draw your blade, let the fading light of Caerdrich face the dawn and be struck down like all the others. Show this doomed hall where the true power of this middle realm lies."

The cold turned to frost, and Fiadh's shoulders slumped with the weight of that challenge and the decision she faced. Stand by and be struck down by Tyra in the hope it might sate her bloodthirst. Draw the blade and bear the lives of all in this hall on her own hands. She shook her head, imagining what it may have been to claim her vengeance with the truths she had learned of this place. Despite everything it would be better, still, to die of her own will than let herself be consumed by the will of another.

"Caerdrich!" The Sgiath Athar demanded, her voice betraying the rage her stone visage would not. "Show yourself, meet my challenge or be returned to the waves from whence you came."

"They won't answer you," Fiadh replied, walking to stand between Tyra and Annis. "No one will. You're alone, a remnant of a vanished age, seeking something that isn't here on behalf of a god who is no longer waiting."

The Sgiath Athar moved faster than Fiadh could react, sweeping across the space with a single beat of her wings, one wing striking forth, casting Fiadh from her feet and stabbing her downwards before she even had time to fall.

Fiadh struck the ground hard and slammed down into the slabs of stone with a crunch of breaking ribs. Her vision swam red, and pain shot through her, beating out the last air from her lungs as a scream.

Above her, flashing crimson as she blinked away blood, that stone mask stared down relentlessly, a bladed tip of one wing thrust through Fiadh's arm, another pinning her hand deep into the stone beneath, not even caring to lower her spear.

"Anyone else?" Tyra said, looking up and around the hall to those struck silent by horrified shock and awe. "Is there no one who would step forward and deliver what I was due, no one who might stem the blood of your fellows before you join the pyres of your brethren?"

Fiadh tried to move but Tyra twisted her wings, tearing forth another scream of pain.

"Is there no one else?"

"There is one."

Fiadh started at the familiar voice echoing through the silence of the hall, turning her head to look up towards the door as a single figure stood, wreathed in grey robes.

She could see the shimmer, the way the figure within the robes shook and jerked back and forth between the hall and the place beyond the veil. The spirit from the beyond had returned to them.

But here, to those around her, it appeared as a simple man wrapped in grey robes stood alone.

Tyra twisted her wing once more as she turned to the new visitor, drawing a gasp from Fiadh as her vision swam with tears of pain mixed with the blood she could not wipe away.

"You come to give me what I am fated?" Tyra asked. It was more of a statement than a question.

"I do. I can take you to what you seek and deliver you to the place their destiny has found them. Fate finds strange ways to reunite people." Its voice was still now, no longer the cacophony of sound Fiadh had encountered beyond. One voice spoke alone.

The figure held out their hand. "You are destined to be together, are you not? I can take you there. You need only take my hand."

Tyra tore her wing free of the floor, causing the pain to wash over Fiadh with such intensity she could not even find the breath to scream again.

Tyra hesitated, the time stretching out between them even as the crowd looked on, the silence broken only momentarily by the whimper of one still pinned below the rubble.

"We are fated to be together," she said.

"That is your destiny," came the spirit's reply.

Tyra reached out, paused for a moment more, and took their hand.

Time froze as they connected, light rushing by and into the folded grey robes as a new black pit opened up, swallowing the light even as it wove into tight strands around them.

The grey hood turned to Fiadh, the voice echoing out a final time.

"I've met someone like you before, child of the Sciathán Dubh. The silver eyes, the look of someone who hasn't found their own fate yet. Yes, beyond the arc, wandering, a younger one perhaps. They are not destined to be alone. Not yet. I shall not deny you the words that might lead you to them. Let the weave guide your path."

There was a flicker, a flash, and they were gone.

***

Annis staggered forward a few steps, the high-pitched whine in his head disorientating. He held a hand to his temple and another to the bench beside him to steady his steps. The hall was abuzz with activity, the wounded tended to by those more able, mercenaries clearing the rubble and seeking survivors below the ruined remnants of the south wall.

The lightning strike was like nothing he had ever experienced before. A roar that had tossed him off his feet, a flash that had disintegrated everything before it. It was as if the gods themselves had split open the heavens and delivered their judgement on this place.

The red cloaks had been found wanting, it seemed. Not one of them was spared from devastation.

Sæunn had been carried out as she had clawed her own way free of the debris, gasping for air. They were forgotten, for now, whatever judgement she had intended to lay upon them now buried with those who had stood beside her on the dais. He had heard her protestations at being removed before those trapped alongside her had been recovered and those scattered across the hall could be attended to. Her housecarls did their duties well, removing her from the danger of the still crumbling walls and rafters and leaving the booming voice of Ahar to rally the effort in the hall. He would have done the same, once.

Fiadh was propped up on fallen beams, cradling her side with one arm as a servant from among those who had rushed to the hall after the strike gingerly stitched her wounds.

Annis suppressed a grunt of pain as he continued his path towards her, the world swimming a little and an ache gripping his joints with every attempt to move any faster. Pausing to catch his breath, he gently pressed his fingers to his ribs, twitching at the burst of pain that erupted at his touch.

Whatever it was that hit him had been big. The lad beside him that night had fared all the worse, no more than his boot still jutting out from below the chunk of rock that had fallen upon him.

Fiadh was still grimacing as he drew close, staring straight ahead as the servant carefully threaded a needle through pale skin, hands trembling as they tried to hold close the cold flesh of her arm and bind tight the wound where something sharp had clearly punched clean through.

"Fiadh," he said, momentarily weighing his words before giving up and forging on. "Wis this us? Hus yer Ceasg pal decided tae gie this place a visit?"

Fiadh glanced up and the look in her eyes was steely, before mellowing to a dismissive eye roll. "No, Annis, this wasn't us. I don't know what it was. But whatever it is, our plan to stay disguised is dead. People will talk, the High Chalice will hear of this, they'll send more, we need to go."

"Efter ye've been stitched up, ye'll need tae heal a bit, ken? Oot there in the cauld it wullnae heal," Annis dropped himself heavily onto a nearby beam, running a hand across the stubble on his scalp. "Word travels slower than we dae, we'll be well clear, Ah ken a lad wi a bonnie ship whae'll gie us passage."

"Ahar?" Fiadh looked at him with an eyebrow raised.

"Aye, that's the yin."

"I don't trust him, Annis. He talks too much, his crew drink too much. There's only so far the promise of gold can keep a mercenary's lips sealed." She snarled as the needle bit in again, the servant trying to control their jump at the noise.

"Ye dinnae need tae trust him, Craw." He probed at his ribcage again, trying to gauge the damage. "He'll git us whaur we need tae gan, an then we can be gone afore he maks port at anither harbour.

He isnae gonnae try an keep ye captive oan his ship, he hus a fear o yer magics. Fear is gonnae keep the man in mind surer than gold."

Fiadh shrugged with her free arm, her eyes darting back and forth as they tended to do while she thought. The moon's light lit up the glint of her eyes like jewels, and not for the first time Annis suppressed a shiver at how they seemed to stare out with brilliance but without life behind them.

Then they stilled, her eyes widening with an intensity he knew too well.

"I know how to beat her, Annis." He knew who she meant before the words left her throat. "The Red Raven, I know how to bring her to her knees and take everything from her just as she took everything from me. All I need is a way to get to her, and I know exactly who can show me."

He sat quietly, knowing better than to interrupt. Her eyes were wild now, staring past him, as if picturing exactly what she could do.

"A spirit spoke to me here, before the strike," she said. "I don't know how, but I know that the sea is the key. The sea can block their calling, trap them in this place and make them vulnerable." She grabbed his shirt with her free arm, pulling him to her eye level and fixing those bright, dead eyes on his own. "It all comes back to her, all of it. Every thread. I'm going to make her regret her failure. The end to all of this is coming at last. Then, only then can we rest."

Annis had learned to keep an impassive expression when Fiadh returned to the focus of her obsession, the inspiration for their departure from the trail of monsters plaguing lairds and villages across the isles. This wasn't his business, and the less he fed the fire behind her eyes the less likely they'd be diverted once more away from the promise of coin and a warm hearth.

Fiadh was distracted from him already, her grip on him looser and her eyes staring off beyond him deep in her own thoughts. Annis gently unfurled her hand from his shirt and stood again, looking around the ruined hall. There was something about their travels that had denied him the belief in coincidences. This didn't just happen to a place, not to those where they had passed through.

He turned and began to look for some corner or room nearby so he could finally rest his eyes. Fiadh might not be ready to rest, but any chance for a kip was a chance to be taken. Dawn would be here soon, no doubt, and with it a brand-new day.

Who could tell what disaster would befall where they walked tomorrow?

❉

EYES OF GOLD

It was dark here, this place between worlds, beyond the veil. Where once the brilliance of gods would have lit the sky from horizon to horizon, with only an empty void stretched above her. The light of Caerdrich at her side barely stretched beyond her to pierce the shadows wreathed around them like smoke.

But there was comfort in the dark. Her mind was quiet, as if held in the gentle hands of the stillness extending around her. Fiadh had rested here more often of late, taking her time to return from this forgotten realm. It was said her kind once passed through it often, travelling back and forth beyond the shimmering rainbow arc she could see faintly across the sky, beyond the horizon.

It called to her, gently, quietly. With every shimmer she felt as though a breeze caressed her form, coaxing her forward. She closed her eyes and let out a breath, submerging herself in that feeling for just another moment.

But the harsh light of Caerdrich still shone through her eyelids. Its chill still crept through the air and alighted upon her skin, the cold ache gripping her bones, keeping her from drifting away with that brief respite. She could not remain here, not yet. Nor could she pass through the one-way journey beyond the arc. There was too much still to be done. Too much the blade still demanded of her.

She opened her eyes and let herself rise from where she had knelt, willing her body upwards to float above the waters. Her body was woven light in an approximation of her true self, her own dull glow barely visible beneath the blaze of Caerdrich. She focused, searching the distance for what she had been seeking for months of journeying into this realm. Here, at last, there was something that might yet unlock the way forward.

High above her, looming as if suspended from the sky itself, a small clearing of trees shone with a faint aura of gold, the air around them clear of the darkness that spilled across the land around her. At their feet an object shone more brightly – a spark in the darkness.

Months at sea, stopping at every port, stepping beyond the veil at every chance in search of this. A golden spark that might finally light the way to her destination. A way to break the protection of a god of the sea itself. A single ray of hope in the darkness.

It was with a start that Fiadh realised she was not alone, gazing upon that spark. Whether it had been awaiting her arrival or had happened upon her in this moment of searching she could not tell, but another had come to this place and had stepped beyond the veil. Nested below the glade deep within the darkness, two vertical slits of light peered out from that silent shadow, fixed upon her without so much as a blink.

She was far enough to escape its powers, but not far enough away that it would fail to see her and the bright light of Caerdrich at her side. It was time to depart this place and find surer ground among the living.

Her feet met the dark surface, letting out a ripple as they did. Crossing her arms tightly around her, Fiadh closed her eyes and focused on the veil she had passed through to reach here, letting herself continue to fall through the ripples until they closed over her shining blade.

Reality claimed her with a jolt, her stomach falling and her heart leaping into her throat. Fiadh staggered forward, her boots skidding on the rock and the glare of the sun blinding her instantly.

She spat, the taste of iron still clinging to her lips as the blood of the passage through the veil dripped from her chin and fingertips. No matter how many journeys she took, the sensation of the return would never feel natural, nor would the twisting sensation in her innards as if they had been gripped by a fist thrust up from the earth.

Each time she felt weaker with the return, the ease of movement beyond the veil taken from her.

Each time, a reminder that the strength Caerdrich gave her was fading a little every day.

Stepping forward, Fiadh moved towards the lapping sea at the edge of the rocks, wincing through the red droplets until she could fall to her knees and splash the water over her face. With her sight restored it was a short descent into the waves, submerging herself and Caerdrich's scabbard just free of the seaweed-wreathed shore.

The feeling of the water sloughing off her viscous coating was sweet relief, as was the return to weightlessness with the gentle waves rocking her back and forth. She clenched her teeth against the sharp pain as the cold worked its way into the raw skin stretched across the deep cuts in her palm and across her face. The salt water was good for it, the sailors on Ahar's ship had claimed, but no matter how many times she bathed, the way the cold clawed deep under the skin never felt comfortable, nor did the scars heal over any faster.

She gasped as her head broke the water once more, feeling the wind as she ran her hands back through her hair, her fingers teasing out the remaining congealed blood. This experience always made her feel like the return wasn't worth it at all, that she would be better off just staying there, where the world faded away and she could drift as she pleased through a void meant for her kind alone.

Fiadh stayed in the water a while longer than she knew she should, letting the ache of the salt grip her more tightly until the feeling begin to drift away from her limbs, before finding steadier purchase on the rocks and hauling herself back onto the weed-wreathed stones.

Stretching in the early morning sun, she felt the prickles of feeling returning to her fingers and began to gather her clothes, drying herself on the woollen lining of her cloak. Caerdrich's dark leather lay as it always did, safely looped over her shoulders even when all else had been removed, the carefully waxed leather still impervious to the water she entered.

She pulled her head free of her tunic's neck just in time to hear the sound of a strange new stream forming nearby.

"Fuck, Annis!" she exclaimed, spotting her companion barely twenty feet away and relieving himself into the sea, breeks around his ankles.

"Whit?" he called back over his shoulder. "The fishes pish in it an aw! Whit's a man tae dae? Haud it in an pray fur deliverance?"

"Did you at least wait until I was out of the water?" she growled, tugging her own breeches up and reaching for her boots.

"Mebbe," he said, finishing and putting himself away.

"Bàs an fhithich ort!" she grumbled in response, throwing Caerdrich across her shoulders and turning towards him to wait before she collected her things.

Annis' brows creased as he wandered over, in what Fiadh had learned was the best indication there were actual thoughts processing behind them.

"Ah ken that yin!" he exclaimed as he drew up beside her. "Wishing death upon me, richt? Something tae dae wi the raven? Dinnae forget ye promised tae deliver me frae it as lang as Ah stood by yer side."

He glanced at her and barked a laugh at her clear astonishment at his newly discovered translations.

"Ahar taught me," he explained as they clambered across the rocks and back to the small flat outcropping she'd laid out for her passage.

"Ye keep sayin it so Ah figured Ah should ken whit ye're mutterin aboot."

Fiadh frowned. She hadn't realised she'd been swearing all that often, or even speaking her thoughts aloud. A habit she'd have to keep a firmer grip on if her travelling companion was picking up the tongue.

After Fiadh collected the various components that made up the ritual for her journey beyond the veil, the two of them clambered across the rocks and back in sight of the boat pulled up in the bay ahead. Ahar's ship, which had been their home for months now as it moved from port to port, trading goods he had collected from his past season of raids in the south.

Annis broke the silence as they made their way across the pebbled beach. "Did ye find onything, this time?"

"I may have done," she said, knowing her reply was cryptic. Annis may have been her companion for some time now, but it was not his place to know yet. Too often she had seen companions turn their backs when promised breakthroughs were revealed as dead ends. "I know where next we need to go, and it isn't far – is that enough for you?"

They walked in silence for a while longer while he pondered that, running his hand over his shaved scalp in the manner that seemed to accompany many of his emotions.

"Ye spend mair an mair time beyond the veil," he said. "Less an less wi the people wi us at every port we dock at. Ye dinnae look fur new contracts, ye've lost interest in the advance ae the High Calice. If ye were lookin fur something, mebbe it isnae there at aw."

"It's there. It's always there," she said as she felt a cold wash over her with the renewed realisation of the gulf between them – his draw to be among his kin upon the ship and shore, and how little she was interested in joining them. How little he understood of her path. She had never cared about the High Chalice, even as their machinations had complicated the journey, it was not the red-robed priests who had burned Tur Eumor. "I'm not meant to be here, among you all. My kind were meant to have departed long ago, far beyond the veil. It still calls to me. It always will do, until I have completed my work and earned my place in the beyond."

"Earned?" His response came fast, nearly cutting her off.

Perhaps he was nervous that she would depart without paying him his due for his company all this time. She had kept the pay regular. Years spent plying her trade inland had given her some time free of the need for new work, but he couldn't know whether that would last the full journey to her destination.

"I keep my promises, Annis. There is one I have yet to fulfil. When that is done, at last, perhaps, I may have earned my rest," she said. The words lacked the weight of conviction because the truth was that she did not know. The tentative words were as much hope as she could muster.

The silence drifted over them again as their feet crunched over the stones. The waves lapped gently around the hull of Ahar's ship and the faint sound of its crew beyond came to them on the wind.

"Ye said that ye leave somethin behind in that place?" Annis said. He remembered things, a strength that had come in useful more than once when her own mind wandered and was distracted by journeys to come.

"Yes, I do." She was watching her feet as she thought over her own words. "I leave uncertainty and doubt behind me. With every journey I learn more of what is to come and what I must do."

His grunt of reply didn't betray what he thought of that explanation.

The crew had disembarked and established their camp in a sprawl of makeshift tents and bedrolls along the shore. Most of them, a dozen or so, were gathered around a campfire they were using to dry out clothes and boots still damp from the last crossing. Few paid the pair much mind as they trudged back into the camp. This coming and going with each landing was an accepted part of the journey by now.

Annis began to exchange greetings with the crew as they passed. They had clearly bonded over time, as confused as most of their companions were by the role he'd found himself in; they respected the appeal of steady work that offered lower risk than the losses that came with each raiding season.

Their greetings were entirely for him, however. Most turned their backs rather than meet her eyes, and there was only one who acknowledged her return: Rian, a young pox-marked lad, who threw her a cheerful wave from where he was busy ferrying stew between the crew.

He was one of two Annis had become especially close to over the winter. The other was Hengist, a swarthy-skinned warrior who spoke with Annis' same Àrdish accent. The two older men seemed to have taken Rian under their wing and made it their mission to teach him before the next raiding season, lest he become yet another forgotten name who passed on and off Ahar's ship. So many had passed already that Fiadh had long since ceased to learn them, save the few that Annis kept beside him. He had told her the lad's entire village had been taken by the plague years ago, leaving him alone when Ahar's ship had landed, expecting to take the riches of the temple. Instead, Ahar had taken the child, insisting his survival might grant protection from disease to the whole ship. The boy seemed to have seized upon Ahar's faith and responded with a boldness and enthusiasm that belied his age and the fate of his kin. That alone, perhaps, might have inspired the pair's affection for him, though she sensed there was more to Annis' care than that.

When Annis spotted them and headed their way, Fiadh instead spun off towards Ahar himself. He had placed his omnipresent ornate wooden seat in the direct path of the rising sun and was basking in its warm rays. At his side was his long-term companion on the waters, Svana, an iron-forged mercenary from across the sea.

As she noticed Fiadh's approach crunching across the pebbles, she gave her captain a single disapproving look before marching up the beach, not even acknowledging the Crow in passing.

Ahar didn't open his eyes before greeting her approach.

"Fiadh?" Her Cànan name rolled off his tongue in his easy but accented way. He was, almost above all else, a studious learner of nearly every language she had heard of. "Is it the mornings that are growing longer or is Annis treating you better with your special time ashore these days?"

Fiadh's hands clenched as she came to a stop and ground her heels into the pebbles. She knew the large captain knew better than to believe her relationship with Annis was romantic, but she had yet to find a sturdier response to his jibes than to grind her teeth and wait for him to tire of it.

"We'll be headed out on the tide again," he continued, his eyes still closed, and arms stretched out either side of him. "Out and round towards Skysted. Grimr's patrols should be past us now. Be ready to leave afore noon."

"Annis and I won't be coming. We'll catch you on the return," she said, muscles coiled tight in anticipation of his scathing response.

His eyes opened at that, a sceptical glance escaping his squint against the glare bouncing off the still water.

"Aye, is that so? What for?" he said.

"We have business up the mountain. We'll be back at the shore by the time you return," Fiadh said, glancing back to where that mysterious grove had appeared to her.

Ahar's eyes turned up past her and to the crags that loomed over them from above the glen that fed into the bay. Beinn Mathan was an imposing peak that reigned over the entire Northern Isles with its bulk and two promontories that curled over the water like mighty paws ready to smash open the waves. It held a special place in the history of the Seann Àite, but even with Ahar's extensive reading he was unlikely to have delved into those depths.

"You'll pay for my diversion, and I'll be gifted my share of whatever treasure you find up yonder?" Ever the businessman, Ahar worked in coin and always collected his due. Few ships had sailed as long or survived as many raids as his, and that longevity did not come without a keen mind for what was profit and what was trouble.

"Always," she said.

He responded with an exaggerated shrug. Everything about the man was exaggerated, from his penchant for bare-chested sun lounging whenever light so much as flickered free of the clouds, to his broad gold-etched belt that identified him far more swiftly than his distinctively foreign features.

"If you take any of the others, keep them fed on your own coin and return them in one piece. We won't need all of them. No more than a handful, yes?" he said, squinting up at her through the sunlight.

Fiadh nodded and turned to trudge back up the beach without worrying either of them with a more formal farewell. Ahar was a charming man in his own way, a boisterous storyteller when he was in the mood. But he was also insightful in a way that made her nervous – his eyes more than capable of spotting things she did not know she was giving away. Even pleasantries ran the risk of piquing his curiosity, so she felt no need to offer him any.

"Annis," she called as she passed the bonfire. "We're going."

"Whaur tae?" came his reply, shouted up from behind a bowl of some stew or another he'd procured from the crew.

"Up the mountain, a couple of day's journey and then we'll return to the ship," she said.

Annis nodded his confirmation and then turned to give a further nod down to Ahar. Fiadh's gaze followed his to the raider, who had turned to watch them go. He returned Annis' nod, communicating a message she was not party to before casting a hand in the direction of Svana, who had crouched on a dune nearby. Her own response was a rude gesture she had seen commonly thrown between members of the crew. Annis did not follow her steps immediately as she set off from the beach, but instead barked a few things in Sjøtunge, a language of the seafaring raiders Fiadh had never seen much purpose in learning herself, at the others gathered around their fires. Before long Fiadh found herself not only trailed by the usual solo companion she was accustomed to but was now also followed into the dunes by a small retinue, the boy and Svana among them.

As Annis fell into step with her, Fiadh looked back at those following them; he noted her gaze with a gentle nudge to the shoulder.

"Ah figured a couple ae days ashore cuid dae some ae the crew guid," he said with a confidence and familiarity she felt was at odds with their guest status aboard the ship. "An mony ae thaim huvnae seen the view frae the peaks afore. Wid be a shame fur thaim tae miss it."

The two of them jumped up and into the reeds that crested the dunes as Fiadh looked sceptically around for the dark-haired man she'd seen with Annis earlier. "That lad from before, Hengist wasn't it? Is he not coming with us now?"

Annis barked a laugh. "Nae chance, he's guid fun wi a horn in his haun but wid be a liability oan the road. Ah found a few others whae ken whit they're daein, an the lad cuid learn frae thaim."

"Fine, whatever, I don't care." There were a half-dozen with them, it seemed. She couldn't afford to cover the rations for this many every time they came ashore but a single time was doable. "Just know they're your responsibility, not mine. I chose you to accompany my journey and you alone. I will not make sacrifices to protect them."

Annis grunted. He didn't always agree with her perspective, but he didn't need to. They'd lasted this long on that understanding.

***

The trail ahead snaked up through the glen and crossed the stream that wound its way between the boulders deposited along its route. It was said in eras past that the entire valley would have been coated in the ice that had come down from the mountain above, flowing the same path the stream did today. It was fortunate, Fiadh thought, that at least they would not have to make this climb in the cold that created such a monstrous edifice of that forever-winter.

On every crossing they made over the rough fords of the valley floor, Fiadh cast her eyes up the valley and towards the mountain that reared over it, trying to recall where that spark of light had shone towards her beyond the veil. With every step she wondered if those eyes still watched her.

She paused for a moment, hissing as pain shot through her hand. It did this from time to time, the changing temperatures seizing it as she warmed up with the climb or cooled from standing still for a time. As she kneaded it, Annis caught up to her once more.

"Still?" he asked, leaning against one of the many boulders that littered the sides of the stream. "The healer telt us it wid be jist weeks afore ye'd be healed."

Fiadh weighed up her response. Saying nothing at all when she was clearly in pain would be noted. "I'm not from this place, Annis. Time moves slower for me, and with a lighter touch. So, these wounds will take me longer to recover from, even as my hair doesn't grow white with the years."

"How auld are ye?" he said.

She was taken aback by the direct question. For so many years to have passed and for him not to have asked struck her as a curiosity sated, rather than biding his time for this opportunity. She glanced up to search his eyes for intent, only to find him gazing aimlessly up towards one of the great paws of rock that reared above them.

"Have you heard the tale of the Three Willows?" she asked.

"Aye," he said, his tone still distant as he mused. "Ma faither telt me aboot it when Ah wis a wee yin. It began the red cloak's reign in

Canmarr, an they burned it tae the groond thegither wi aw the people in it. They scattered the ashes across the land, declared it ju ... judi ... judico ..."

"*Iudicatus,*" she interrupted, remembering when she had heard the news herself in a lonely inn and the rage that had grown within her on that day. "Condemned. I was there, Annis. Before it all happened."

"Afore ..." That broke his reverie, his head turning and his eyes widening, a rare sign of surprise from the big man. "But, but that wid mak ye ..."

"Pretty damn old, I know, and tired. So very tired."

Fiadh pushed off the rocks and continued on the path as the others following them drew nearer, keeping distance, seeing no need to involve them in her tale.

"You measure seasons as the coming and passing of winter," she continued, hearing his heavy steps follow her back across the stream. "The old gods measure seasons too, but rather than the winter you know, instead it is the coming and passing of whole generations. The arrival and departure of great waves of ice, the appearance and disappearance of entire peoples under their eyes. Their births, lives, and deaths flash past as if they were your years to those beyond the veil."

The path split in front of them, divided by the stump of a great tree that had been felled years before.

"In your seasons I am very old," she said. "But in theirs? I have barely seen enough winters to be more than a child in their eyes. How old am I? I don't even know by whose measure I was meant to be counting."

The stump had not been left untouched since the felling of the great oak that may have stood there before. All across its surface, hammered in along their sides like rows of scales or teeth jutting from its surface, were a wide variety of coins of every design and metal Fiadh had seen on her travels. Here and there she could spy the head of some Rìgh who had ruled the Isles, a southern King, even the wreathed crowns favoured by the rulers of the old Empire. No longer simply a tree, the stump resembled a part of some great drake, part-buried and drawn into the earth with the years.

"Whit is this place?" Annis' voice came from a distance behind her, and she turned to find him looking up towards those great curled promontories of rock and the path that now led towards them.

It split from the glen's path they had been following and almost immediately was lost in a cascade of fallen rocks and boulders. Just beyond it the rocks fell into an even pattern of rises and plateaus, each nearly as tall as a man. Gigantic stairs that rose with the cliffs either side of them, winding their way up and into the mountain. But every time her eyes passed over them the boulders seemed to have more form to them, less a random cascade than a structure breaking free of the natural form of the mountain. She stepped back and nearly gasped as the patterns fell into place, a vision from a tale she knew so well but had never expected to see.

They were not boulders fallen from above, but limbs, heads, the twisted fallen bodies of enormous figures whose very flesh had been turned to the stone they had landed upon. They were scattered either side of the stairs, some breaking upon the steps themselves and crushing the even progression into landslides that smoothed its rigid boundaries into the cliffs around it.

Their features were faded, weathered by an age of wind, rain, and ice. Moss coated those on the lowest reaches. Most were cracked and fractured by roots that had pulled them apart to make room for trees that clung to the crevices between them.

Their faces lay fallen, some almost restful, others with eyes staring blankly into nothing, still more left arched into screams as the rocks broke through their flesh before becoming one with them. Their bodies were twisted and broken, many bearing great wounds that split their torsos apart, or caved in their skulls.

They were the final remains of a once proud people whose hubris had led them to annihilation, fated to gradually be worn away until no one could tell them apart from the mountain whose heights had claimed their lives.

"The Giants' Fall," she said, walking over to Annis and joining in his awe. "They climbed the stairs and sought to overwhelm the gods, but they were struck down one after another and fell upon the steps they had challenged. The final resting place, at the feet of the very peaks they had ruled from when this land first broke free of the ice of another age."

Their companions gathered around them, one by one joining in their stunned silence upon the spectacle. It was said that this was not the only remnant of that great battle, that far across the seas lay yet more edifices to that turning of the tide where the giants of the old order marched upon the gods of the new. A titanic battle that had claimed the futures of both and unlocked a future free of all of them.

"Is that whaur we're goin?" Annis said, finally breaking the silence.

"It is," Fiadh said, taking the first steps up the path. "I hope you're all prepared for a long climb."

***

The climb was arduous, the great steps being too large and smooth for a person to climb alone. Instead, they clambered to either side of them, up the scramble that had littered the way and slopes formed of fallen limbs and torsos. The party behind her frequently halted to lift one another up over the ridges. More than once, Fiadh found herself confronted by the empty stare of wide eyes nearly as large as she was tall and not once did the experience fail to raise a chill in her veins.

Their journey was interrupted just as the stair took a sharp turn away from the paw and across the mountainside, deeper into the valley. Here a mound of rocks stood, some precariously balanced upon one another, carefully placed from the largest to the smallest.

Beside it, licking its paw as if the arrival of their group was the most normal event in its day, was a cat.

As they arrived upon this latest plateau the cat interrupted its cleaning to sit upright and gaze down upon them, all black but for a great tuft of white upon its chest. There was something unnatural in the way its fur ran across its features, how one ear seemed longer than the other, how the eyes glinted larger and deeper than one would expect. It was as if someone had drawn an approximation of a cat, having only been told tales of them, and reality itself had brought that image to life as best it could.

A cat sìth. This was no miller's pet to keep rodents at bay nor a wild animal wary of humans trespassing upon its secluded domain. It was a creature of the barrow mounds, a granter of blessings and a taker of souls, enraptured by fire and gold.

Annis stiffened at her side as he spied it ahead, a quiet hiss escaping between his teeth. "Ah dinnae like cats, they look doon oan me as if Ah'm their lesser!"

Fiadh laid a hand gently on his forearm as a warning not to continue forward. "That's because," she replied, "sometimes you are, Annis. Perhaps to this one most of all."

"Why come upon us, cat sìth?" she called up, as the cat continued to gaze down upon them impassively.

"I have been searching for you for a long time, sword-bearer," came their reply, a voice as smooth as silk running down to them. Annis shifted sharply, his hand immediately upon the handle of his own blade.

"Do you tell every traveller that?" Fiadh said, hand tightening on Annis' arm. She recognised those eyes from beyond the veil, those golden slits peering down towards them. This fey had been waiting for her. They knew she came with Caerdrich, and they had not fled. No doubt Annis' axe would do them no favours here.

"Cats cannot lie," came their answer. As the myths said, no true fey could lie, bound to truth by the gods long departed. How faithfully that binding remained so long after their power had drained from the land was still in question, however. They would have to tread carefully; even truths could be told with nefarious intent.

"Do fey cats no tell riddles?" Fiadh nearly jumped as Rian's still unbroken voice shouted up his own query, stepping out of Annis' shadow as the others joined them and began to whisper about their new visitor.

The cat seemed to ponder a moment, eyes fixed on Fiadh and their paws gently clenching and relaxing against the stone. "Would you like a riddle?" they asked.

"Aye, Ah wid," the boy said.

"Very well."

The cat's tone turned sonorous, reverberating among them as if spoken from within a deep cavern.

> *"Soft beneath wary teeth,*
> *A brilliant prize you will not sheath,*
> *Found in rivers, mines, and sea,*
> *You will be rewarded to lose me.*
> *What am I?"*

"A dwarf!" The voice of Arne, one of Svana's men, came from behind them so swiftly he almost cut off the final line.

"Artrí's blade! Bound tae rise again!" said Rian, excited at a chance to reference the old folktale of the south that Ahar was particularly fond of telling.

Fiadh was astonished, her eyes flitting back and forth between them, unable to imagine how swiftly this crew had decided to play games with this ancient and devious fey within moments of coming across them for the first time. Svana, obviously of a similar mind, had grabbed Arne by the back of the neck hard enough for the man to cease any further contributions.

The cat sìth gave their answers no heed as the crew quickly turned to berating one another for how those responses and more could not possibly be an answer to the riddle and instead their feline eyes continued to bore into Fiadh's own.

"It took you longer than I expected to reach here, sword-bearer. I almost began my search for another." Their silken tone caressed her mind, gentle and comforting. An invitation to forget the many tales she had been told of their kind and the fates suffered by those who followed their promises to untimely ends.

"Why wait for me, what purpose could I serve for you?" Fiadh said.

"Walk with me," the cat replied. "Let me show you. I believe what we seek may well be one and the same."

They turned their back and jumped up to a rock leaning over the path before them, not caring to turn to see if they were being followed. Fiadh patted Annis' arm and clambered up the next step swiftly, accelerating her progress until she could come into step with their new animal guide.

"What do I seek, cat?" Fiadh called up.

"A path forward that you have been denied. You have been among mortal kind for too long, black wing, and you have developed their passions for whatever you are told you cannot have," the cat said, never turning their head to acknowledge her directly.

Fiadh's brows furrowed at that. They could not tell lies, perhaps, but what truths they were asked for might well be buried in the very riddles they were famous for.

The cat was leading them on a path that diverged from the stair itself, and it was becoming apparent why. Water had breached a section above them where a giant arm had crushed the rocks below it and with time it had carved away the steps below into a sweeping fall that passed by and out over the glen below. The cascade vanished into a mist that drifted down upon their path and her companions stopped momentarily to gaze at the shimmering drops and the colours that danced among them, swapping stories of old beings of light and mountains and all manner of things that might yet be the answer to the cat's riddle.

Fiadh's silence, at least, seemed to spark some change in the fey. They came to a halt at a corner in the path, where it overlooked the bay on which Ahar's ships could now be seen departing the beach and setting out to sea.

"You and I seek the same thing, black wing, we both seek a way to travel forward in a world not meant for our kind. Both of us are blocked by those who still wield power, long after this world was left by those who brought us to it. I have a solution for us both, should you wish for it," they said, their tail flicking gently as their gaze passed from her down to the ships below.

That word, *wish*. They were right, they did know what she was searching for, and so they dangled it before her with the smug satisfaction for which their kind was so well known.

Fiadh wrestled with how to follow the thread without revealing her full hand. This fey clearly had quite enough leverage on her already without being granted more so easily.

The others joined them at the crest overlooking the bay and as they caught their breath Fiadh looked up past the cat and to the peaks above. Up there, somewhere, was the glint of what she had been searching for months now. Something to break the pact between the Red Raven and the Ceasg; something with a power primordial enough that it could unweave the strands of fate between those two beings and uncover the lair of the last protagonist of the burning of her home, the razing of Tur Eumor. She needed a wish, and there were few beings left in the Seann Àite who could grant one.

Few enough that she had little choice but to follow this fey to the peak, something the cat clearly knew full well.

"How came you across this wish, cat?" she said, looking for where the path might follow from here.

Those bright, unblinking eyes turned to her again before it answered, "that is a tale for another time, black wing. But I have another tale to tell, one both of this great peak and the lessons others have learned before."

An answer, of course, would have been too simple.

The cat sìth turned and the rocks behind it ... shifted. They did not move, but they came apart as if where they had been before had been no more than a mirage, a waking dream blinking away as the sun fell more clearly upon them. There the path proceeded, as if it had always done, winding its way back towards the Giants' Fall.

Annis mustered barely a shrug as he followed the cat through the new passage. Fiadh could hardly blame him; she had put him through stranger fare in their time together. The others, however, whooped and gasped in wonder. Rian ran his hands along the rocks as if he expected they might pass right through them. Only Svana stayed silent, her face creasing with concern as she muttered some choice words in Sjøtunge the others may not have heard.

But Fiadh did, and for the first time she wished she could understand those words. There might be something the Sjøfolk magics of seiðr could tell her about their own experiences with these fey. This was not the first time she had witnessed Svana recognising the threat of magics her companions were too awestruck to grasp.

Fiadh moved through the gap herself after watching the others pass without incident, trying desperately to see the corners of the illusion with her silvered sight, but finding none. A neat trick, clearly left to be revealed just at the right moment to underline the fey's capabilities more clearly than words and hide the path to whatever secrets they had hidden high in the peaks above them.

"Did the cat say they'd tell us a tale, Annis?" came Rian's voice ahead, as Fiadh wove to overtake the others to rejoin the head of the group.

"They did. Talk, cat, it is traditional fur the heid ae a journey tae tell tales ae their previous passages," Annis said, ever one for framing a request as if it were a demand.

The cat sìth seemed to consider that for a moment, stretching the pause until it might break before it replied.

"To tell the tale of this place we must return to a time before your peoples began to tread upon the old place, to when fey and man mingled as one under the eyes of great beings who styled themselves as gods over the land. To when the mortal Daoine were as new to the hills and peaks as you are to them today. When the hall of these great gods sat upon this peak, its sides the walls of a great fortress, the mightiest of all the sìth'" It spoke as if each sentence held the weight of an age upon them, intoning the words with rhythm at the very border of verse. Fiadh's eyes darted to her companions, and she saw they were enraptured, barely glancing to the rough path to maintain their footing.

She remembered, then, that it was said that the first storytelling fili had learned their crafts from a cat sìth who lent them a strand of the magic that bound their words. It did not matter, now, that some words were spoken in the old tongue, and that the magic of those words wound their way around the minds of men with a compelling touch.

"Satisfied in their reign over creation, the gods divided the realms of the world among themselves. Some claimed the seasons, others the seas and forests, still others the very concepts that ruled the minds of people and fey alike. One did not and stood apart, though their power had proven vital to the victories of their kind over those who had come before. Cuthac. Cuthac the seer, Cuthac the watcher, Cuthac the mad."

The path had wound back to the fall and the group had to move in single file for a time as they squeezed between the crumbling steps and over the fallen palm that had crushed them, its fingers long having fallen away down the stair below. The wind was stronger here, the edges of the glen offering them no shelter from the sea wind as it whipped up the sides of the mountain. Caught by a gust, Fiadh faltered, her legs buckling at the sudden change in direction, her stumble halted by Annis' steady hand grasping her shoulder. Steadying herself, she gritted her teeth. These moments of weakness were coming to her more frequently, now, leaving her both thankful for and resentful of the need of her companion's consistent presence.

Across the other side the cat waited for them, patiently, its stare never drifting until each of the party were across and continuing their journey up the path.

"Cuthac had seen too much to be content with the present. He believed there was more than the weave of the triple goddess could reveal to him, more than the Rìaghan knew," the cat said, their nimble paws carrying them over the rough outcroppings above the path as their audience clambered breathlessly behind them.

This was a tale Fiadh knew well – the arrogance of the god that believed they were above fate and its keeper, the Rìaghan, the mother of the Sciathán Dubh. Who Fiadh had been raised to follow in her every word and teaching.

"He scoured the earth to find the means to see beyond what fate laid before them and came across a great smith in a distant land who might craft him that means: a mask that once worn showed him such horrors as to burn the very flesh of his features into its metal."

Several members of their party visibly flinched at the vivid image that sprang as if summoned into their minds. But none looked so shaken as Rian. Fiadh remembered, then, the grim tale of his past that Annis had spoken of. She imagined it may be some time before he'd leap at the chance to be told another tale such as this.

The cat, however, did not pause. "Cuthac saw a great vision," they continued. "A portent, that a great deity would rise from the desert far to the south and would sweep into the Seann Àite, conquering all before him and consuming all who would not obey him.

Desperate, Cuthac climbed this great peak and went to the Great Hall of the Gods to warn them. But he was not the first. Caitlin, the hand of the Rìaghan, the black wing cloaked in red, had come to them first, already tainted as she was by the whispers of Lot."

A chill ran down Fiadh's spine as nudges passed between the Sjøfolk among them. It was a name they recognised, of course. A name that had come across the sea with their ships, that had been painted across their bows for luck and guidance. A name that, unbeknownst to them, had arrived long before to spread its shadow across these shores. Svana, alone, did not share the nods and smiles of recognition. Maybe she, too, knew that shadow. But it was not the only name that Fiadh had recognised.

"Caitlin counselled the gods that the Rìaghan's vision was clear, the weavers had followed the threads of the weave of fate far into the future and there was no one who would best their champion, the great Eirian Cleddyf Llachar, in battle. He who had travelled across the lands of the fey seeking all who might challenge him and finding none who could stand against his blade. All who would stand before him would fall. It was written in the weave. So, when Cuthac came to them they only laughed. None could challenge their rule here, they proclaimed, they had seen off so many other pantheons who had sought to stand here in their place, never mind one lord claiming to rule alone. They witnessed Cuthac's scarred features as he removed his mask to plead they listen, but they turned their backs, disgusted by how he had fallen.

"The gods of summer and battle, stone and lovemaking, wind and rage, they all laughed as he departed, and none laughed harder than Eirian, the bright blade, who had cast the many who had dared challenge the hall into the waves.

"So Cuthac retreated, deep into his visions of how the new order would drown his people, would drive them off to new lands beyond the sea, would starve them and burn them. The words of the Rìaghan did not align with what he could see, and he could not marry the certainty of her conviction of the god's invincibility with his visions of their downfall. He knew no more than they that the Rìaghan had been betrayed, that the truth of the weave had been twisted by the words of another speaking through Caitlin's tongue. Cuthac saw the world as it truly was, and he could not reconcile it with the words of the weavers, nor the claims purported to be made on behalf of the goddess of fate. The visions broke him, and so he swore that he would show the gods just how precarious their hold was.

"He made a deal with a schemer across the sea. A schemer of many names: Lot the Golden; Lot the Radiant; above all Lot the Cunning. The same whispering tongue that had spoken to Caitlin and promised her a freedom she had never dared to dream of. Together they rose giants from the waves and Cuthac marched on the Great Hall at the head of an army of the Formori, armed with a plot that Lot had crafted and his sure-staff, a weapon which could never miss its target.

"Alone among all the gods, Làmfada and Cernos had not laughed at Cuthac's warning, and they did not laugh when the giants marched upon their gates. But they placed their trust in the weave, and when Eirian dismissed their aid, they led the other gods within the great sìd, their faith lying in the champion the fates had brought to them. Of the fates themselves, and the Rìaghan, there was no sign upon the mountain, for Lot had spun their own machinations upon the keepers of the weave."

Fiadh clambered over a large rock that had fallen onto the path, noting the lichen giving way to ice as they clambered higher into the mountain. The Rìaghan had departed, her reason and destination remaining a mystery even to her own order for generations to come, for she never returned. Other Crows had said she was tending to fate, ensuring that it would not be torn asunder by the events of that fell day upon the bear's back. But none remained to share that story, and Fiadh did not have the will to take their place.

The cat sìth had moved some distance ahead of them as the group made their way over the fallen stone. Fiadh sat and caught her breath as Annis and another of the larger sailors helped the other members to crest it. When Rian crossed he looked curiously after the cat, his brows furrowed with consideration of its tale, before speaking.

"Whae were the giants, the yins frae the sea, the yins the cat caws Formori?" he said, eyes still gazing after their storyteller.

Fiadh stared, not expecting the question after months aboard the ship in which the crew tended to do their best to avoid her whenever possible, let alone speak to her.

Rian seemed none the wiser to her momentary surprise as she gathered her thoughts.

"The giants were beings who came to this land long before us," she said, looking back to the cat making its way over the rocks ahead to distract herself from his rapt attention. "Cruel beasts whose battles tore open the earth and reshaped the mountains, split the world, and let the sea pour into the crevasses. With time the largest of them fell and became the very hills and peaks we walk upon, and their brutish children were driven back by those who would become the gods of this land and those beyond the sea. They were driven into the sea so that the land might belong to the fey, and it is with their passing that the many waves of peoples came here to build the Seann Àite on their remains."

She paused to breathe for a moment. There were times in the past where such a climb would have been easy for her, where the strength of Caerdrich could have carried her leagues without pause.

Those times were long behind her now.

"An so, wi this new god they came back frae the sea? Were they truly aw gone?" Rian said, taking a seat opposite her, upon a small ledge that strutted out over the long drop behind him, casually knocking a stone out into the air with a kick of his heel.

"They died, all of them, every last one was struck down upon the stair," Fiadh said, looking back towards the great steps and the broken remnants of the stone bodies that had fallen upon it. "Never to march again."

"A sad way fur an ancient people tae end, is it no?" the boy pondered, looking down the fall and into the glen below.

Fiadh stood and brushed imaginary dust away from her leathers. Her mind turned to the fires that rushed through Tur Eumor, to the hand that had held her shoulder for the last time looking out at sea hearing the sirens' call, those dark sails filling the sea as an enemy of a different kind came to end everything she had been raised to hold dear.

"No, not sad, a relief. They were monsters, bent only on the eradication of those who had taken their place and building a better world without them. Their deaths were a necessary end," she said, looking up to find not only Rian's eyes on her but others besides.

"It's not just that they would one day be a threat again to all on these shores," she continued. "They also deserved to die; they chose that fate. They had together considered what they wished for and what they wanted was the death of every soul upon the mountain so that they might butcher and burn all that the gods had protected. They who had been so easily goaded to kill would do so time and time again. It's said some fled; I am glad they never made it to the waves. They decided their fate when every one of them took the first steps towards the summit."

When she turned towards the group that had gathered behind them, she found Annis' gaze, the hesitant concern written in features that so rarely showed much emotion that she could discern. No, not concern, after all. His eyes wavered a little on hers before he turned away and set his oversized palm on Rian's shoulder, moving the boy back to the path onwards up the peak.

The others moved by silently, not meeting her eyes. Svana, last of all, passing as if she were not even there. What had been in Annis' look, she thought, watching them pass. Was there a sadness to it? A regret?

The next portion of the climb passed quietly, as the sun moved across the sky to fall behind the mountain and leave them in its cold shadow. Few plants clung to the rocks here, their place in the crevasses filled with snow packed densely from seasons of fall.

It was on a flatter section the fey came across them again, their fur swimming in the breeze as if it were ink drifting on a stream, their paws seeming to float across the stone as they moved across the palm of one of the great paws of the great bear itself. Giant fingers of rock stretched over them like claws reaching for the sky.

"Ye didnae finish yer tale, cat," Annis said, breaking the long silence.

"I did not. It is tradition, is it not, to leave a pause before the final act?" the cat sìth said, though its tone made clear that it did not expect an answer. But, regardless, it left a pause as the group gathered beneath the outcrop it was perched on.

"Eirian and his companions set about them with blades as bright as the sun, carving a path through the giants that dared face them at the height of the stair," the cat said, their eyes not wandering across their audience as many storytellers' might, fixing instead firmly on Fiadh's own. "After slaying many dozens of the giants and monsters, Eirian grew bored of his victories. When Cuthac finally came forward, the mighty warrior did not consider the mad god worthy of his great sword. He gave his lover, the fair Elisedd, the opportunity to defeat the traitor god and bring an end to the battle, so that the other gods might return and witness his great victory and perhaps raise his beloved to stand alongside him. He turned to Elisedd and placed in his hand the very sword he had been gifted from the stars.

"So, Cuthac and Elisedd came to blows, each wielding the weapons they were gifted: Cuthac with the sure-staff of Lot; Elisedd with the sun-sword of Eirian Cleddyf Llachar. Night and day passed upon this very rock as the two battled. But try as he might, Elisedd was no god, and he could not harm Cuthac, who struck the boy down and cast his body from the peak."

In the corner of her eye Fiadh saw Rian visibly shudder as he looked down and off the mountain, Annis' hand upon his shoulders guiding him back to the tale.

"Eirian, filled with grief and rage, set about him with such fury that the other gods fled behind the veil as he made great battle with Cuthac, the bodies of the Formori who fell to him in droves beneath their feet. He flung his companions down the mountain to pursue the giants, even as so many of his own fell in the fight without the light of his blade at their backs. They fought until every giant that marched upon the hall had been broken upon the stair, with not one left to return to the seas from which they had risen."

Once more the cat's tone deepened, its echoes bouncing back and forth from the rocks until it seemed to come from all around them.

> *"Bright burning blade aloft,*
> *The warrior struck fast and true,*
> *It landed with a mighty crack,*
> *Upon the skull of great Cuthac.*
>
> *His madness did torrent forth,*
> *His cries split earth and skies,*
> *A great rainbow of brilliant flame,*
> *Swept across the divine claim.*
>
> *The arc of light did breach the veil,*
> *Beneath the madness he unleashed,*
> *The shining path beyond was sealed,*
> *Buried by Cuthac's final wail."*

"At last!" The cat's exclamation broke over the still echoing words. "The sun-sword broke the skull of Cuthac, Eirian tore the mask from his ruined face, and so Cuthac's visions consumed him and broke what remained of his mind. The visions that spilled from his splintered skull coalesced into the arc that blocked the way, flooding the great sìd into which the gods had fled, sealing them behind it forever more. Cuthac clung to the visions, desperately trying to gather the truths of the future he had unleashed, but he became lost in them. The fallen god, unable to live with what he had seen, yet sealed on the wrong side of the death that might have freed him, fled the mountain. He was pursued by his visions of many-winged demons and wheels of eyes and fell into the Vale of Dreams which became twisted by his baleful touch. Some say he crafted the Vale as a prison, so that he might never inflict such harm on his own again. Some say it is a homage to the old world he had led to fall."

"What do you think, cat?" Svana almost growled the question.

The fey seemed to ponder that for a moment. "I believe it is foolish to attempt to comprehend the broken mind of a dying god." The cat finally took their eyes off Fiadh and looked south out over the sea beyond the mountain peaks.

"And so Cuthac," they said, "by means of his own visions, ensured there would be no gods to stand upon this mountain when a new foe marched north from the south. He ensured his own prophecy in his refusal to stand by alone and permit his visions to come true.

"Eirian Cleddyf Llachar stood upon the pinnacle of his victory. All who had stood before him had fallen, as was foretold. But he was alone. His companions had been dashed against the walls of the great fortress pursuing the giants down the stair. The other gods who had placed their faith in his prophesied victory were trapped beyond the veil. His lover lay dead in his arms, still impaled by the great spear from beyond the waves. It was there that Lot came before him and their silver tongue wormed tempting and comforting words into his mind, promising him all he could possibly want should they lay down their weapon and forsake the cowards who had fled beyond the veil, should he truly wish to be free of the torment of his heart-rending loss. He could not know that the very spear that pierced the breast of his beloved was Lot's own.

"The great warrior made a deal. A deal to make him as hard as a rock, as deadly as death itself, and cool his emotions to ice that he might have his revenge and never feel loss again." The fey looked to Fiadh once more, as if daring her to miss the intent behind the tale.

"Lot agreed. So, they brought the great warrior before the Aodann Òir, who transformed them into a weapon, crafted from sky-metal stronger than any earthly stone, unable to feel anything but the cold rage of revenge, and so deadly that to draw them is to condemn all present to death. And so, their tale of grief continued, marked by a long line of slaughter that followed in their wake."

Fiadh glowered back at the fey, knowing how close they were treading towards unveiling truths to her companions that she was not prepared for them to know. Knowing that the cat sìth could, with a simple rhetorical flourish, turn their audience into a dangerous pack torn between fight and flight. Did they know she would be powerless to stop them, her arms so weakened by the journey that the cold iron at her sides would fall long before they reached them?

"But the warrior felt the change even as his wish was granted," the story continued. "Felt the metal clawing over his skin and the ice begin to consume his heart. He saw that he had been deceived, and that he had one wish remaining, and with that wish the reborn weapon brought upon Lot everything they had lost. They made Lot ethereal, unable to touch the world of the living, unable to kill so much as a fly, and unable to prevent themselves from feeling every emotion with the intensity of aeons. So, Lot became the whispering god, reduced to a voice on the wind, the shadow within the veil. The two champions were both laid low, mirrors of one another's fate, and as Lot drifted away in the winds the great warrior lay still upon the ground of the hallowed ground, alone."

There was a pause then, a silence that was left behind the words whipped away with the cold wind whistling between the great fingers of stone rearing overhead. The cat's tail flicked sharply behind them; their gaze as unblinking as when they had first met. For a time, there were only the two fey, waiting to see what they might learn from one another's eyes.

"Some say that Lot truly wished to help the champion of the gods." The cat broke the silence. "Some say that they wished to turn him into a weapon for their own devices in the war to come against the god of the south. Some say they saw the only true challenge to their power who remained this side of the veil and knew full well that his wishes would demand too much and therefore lose everything."

"What do you believe?" Fiadh asked.

"You know, I never thought to ask them. Maybe I will, one day." Fiadh could have sworn she saw the ghost of a smile playing on the fey's feline features. "But it did not matter, for Lot was gone, for centuries to come known as no more than words dripped into the ears of the few who came seeking knowledge in the darkest shadows of our realm. Eirian the blade lay here for a time, beneath this rock, buried beneath the snows of seasons. It's said that one day when conducting a burial for their liege, one of the great Lords of the Sjøfolk lifted them from the ground on which they had fallen. They felt the power and knew this to be the cursed blade the people of the Seann Àite spoke of. They seized it up and crowed their victory over the gods of old, exalting in how they would now wield their own champion against them to conquer the whole world, until all knelt before the throne of Othair. They too, now, were a god walking the earth."

"Aye." Annis' voice snapped Fiadh away from the fey's eyes and back to their company, who had gathered around them. "And whit came tae be ae this new god?"

"Ah, well, you see," the cat drew out their words, letting each one linger in the air. "The other lords doubted his claim. They mocked him and goaded him in his own hall, until he drew forth that dark blade ... and as one they killed them all, men, women, and children, theirs and his own, leaving his own clan nothing but murmurs of a memory and the dead piled high in his hall. Devastated by his loss, the lord cast himself from the cliffs to be dashed against the rocks below."

"If everyone wis deid, how did ye ken the end ae that merry tale?" Annis asked.

"Men are not the only ones who walk the earth," they said, "and there are more than only the gods watching their fates rise and fall."

"Ah thought the gods were mighty an guid," Rian said. "Staunin ower us through guid an ill."

Svana scoffed, and she was joined in her amusement by several of her Sjøfolk sail hands. Few told tales of gods more pointlessly cruel and flawed then the peoples from across the waves.

"Gods are as you make them," Fiadh said, cutting through what false wisdom the fey was sure to impart. "They're exactly as good or cruel as you wish them to be, as it is your stories that shape their tales and ascribe events to their will. What they truly wish for matters little. You'll decide their intentions and consequences yourselves even if they've long passed beyond the means to make their wills known."

The fey tiptoed a little closer to the line it had trod so far. "Even if they find another to bear their wills for years to come, like the ghost of this very fortress, the final Caer of Eirian Cleddyf Llachar."

Fiadh felt as much as saw Annis tense and turn his head towards her. If there was one thing she had always relied upon him for, it was his sense for threats honed by years as a mercenary upon the waves. Suddenly, now, that was a skill she had never considered she might need to evade.

For he had read between the fey's lines and seen a familiar name being hinted at, a threat far closer than he had imagined when this tale began.

"Come", said the cat sìth, turning and dropping down from its seat. "The sun sets, and we have not much further to travel until we reach our destination."

The group chattered as they followed the fey out from the small plateau and to the next stretch of rock that sufficed for a path. Further tales were being swapped between them, sharing similar stories of other gods and heroes of old, of other wishes and sorry fates for those whose arrogance had led them to believe they were destined never to feel loss.

But Annis and Fiadh walked in silence.

The path drew them into a sheltered alcove below the highest peak of the ridge, a section flatter than the rest of the climb and strewn with rocks and rubble held in place by ice packed tightly beneath them. Here the wind blew softer and less shrill, bringing a sense of tranquillity over the wandering party. Most of them still drew their wools and furs tightly around them. Fiadh's imitation of the motion was now second nature, driven by her need to ensure she was not conspicuous in her lack of concern for the cold.

She recognised this place, though she must have come to it by a different path as this was the first time she had felt this familiarity on their journey. Up against the steep cliff at the back of the clearing was the same stone structure, a broch, the squat stone tower nestled close to the rock, a section having been torn away by tumbling stones sometime in the years past.

Where once this space would have been carefully maintained it was now strewn with the remnants of shattered stone and clumps of ice. The intricate carvings that filled the circle were so worn that they appeared no more than erosion drawn by stubborn streams, their once brilliant starlit light that only her silvered eyes could see was now faded to a faint mystical glow.

Her companions moved on none the wiser, seeing only the chance for shelter at the broch, even as the cat sat themselves perfectly centrally in the stone circle. Great standing stones ringed it, the meaning of their placement long since lost with the memories of those who had erected them.

Here, perhaps, in an age long past, had lain the entrance to the great fortress mound of the Daoine Sìth, the fey peoples, whose kind was now reduced to a wandering Crow and a tale-telling cat. It was here, perhaps, that the gods turned their backs and left the fate of the world in the hands of a butcher whose own fate was to seal them away forever more.

As the others hurried over to the welcome shelter, Fiadh turned towards the cat, watching for a moment as they licked at a paw and ran it over their ears. Was it a pretence, some new illusion spun to deceive their company into believing this was, after all, just some harmless animal? Or was it a habit developed from years out here in the wilderness where their only company might well have been other animals of a more mortal kind.

"So," the fey broke the silence. "You know full well that this all comes with a price."

For once, at least, the cat spoke plainly.

"All favours between our kind do," they said. "Were you carrying true gold I'd know of it, so what else can you offer me on these high peaks?"

"Gold?" Fiadh asked, surprised by how ordinary the request was, even from a creature famed for their obsession with the substance. "What use does one from the sìth have for gold when the gods who wove their will in it have long since passed?"

The cat seemed unconcerned, preening themselves as they considered their reply.

"As the red cloaks of Alwealda move north there are stirrings in the veil," they said. "The one who whispers will not stay contained forever, and one cannot rest easy beneath the machinations of divine powers. Why not gather what may be of use in the times to come? At the very least the tall folk of the south seem to have great fondness for its complexion."

Fiadh considered that prediction, and the fey's request.

"You trapped an Aodann Òir, didn't you, cat?" she said, watching closely for anything that might hint at the thoughts that ran beneath those intense eyes.

"*I* did not," they said, not looking up from their preening this time. "But I do *have* one, one contained waiting to be freed and to bestow three wishes upon their saviour."

Fiadh crouched herself in the circle and ran her fingers along those rough-worn grooves of patterns from before her time. It was the most obvious of solutions, one of the few paths to alter the weave of fates to come – a wish granted by one of the gold-faced fey.

"You did not trap it, and you cannot free it, but you know where it is. That's what you need us for, to free what you cannot reach," she said.

"How incisive," they replied, and even in their flat tone the intent was hard to miss.

"So perhaps we can grant you something in place of gold?" Fiadh said.

The fey took note of that, pausing their preening and looking up to Fiadh with those cold, expressionless eyes.

"We free the Aodann Òir, gaining the three wishes, but as the one who brought us here and hid this place from others, we grant you one of those wishes, enough to bury yourself in gold if you see fit," Fiadh explained. She felt an itch, a suspicion, that this was the deal the cat knew they would receive all along.

"So, you shall have two of the three wishes of the fey, and the one you do not seek will be brought to me as payment in exchange for the price you carelessly did not bring with you. Then I will be free of you, and you of me, as soon as our value to one another is fulfilled," the cat said, their feline features giving nothing away.

"How will I know you will permit me two wishes, and how do you know that I will not deny you the last?" Fiadh said, wary of still more tales of betrayal that often led up to the seizure of a wish.

The cat looked at her carefully now, those still eyes giving away nothing of their thoughts.

"Call it a measure of good faith," they said, drawing out each word a little longer than necessary. "I will give you your wishes because I do not know what such irrational creatures as men might do to prevent any of us getting what we want at the scent of betrayal. I do not have the patience to endure an extended negotiation with the kind you have chosen to spend your time with, and having to find a whole new band accompanied with a fey I would be willing to deal with would be ... dull. You will not deny me mine because, well, you know better than to try, and you are in quite a hurry, now, aren't you?"

Fiadh studied the cat, a discomforting itch crossing her shoulders warning her not to feel at ease. Their suggestions were sound, there was no hint that the fey had broken free of their bond to never lie, but their words were a little too practised, too familiar to them. How many others had they presented with this very same agreement, with the same balm of superiority over their companions.

"How do you know I will not betray your presence here, your secrets for how you have trapped an Aodann Òir?" she said, aware her questioning would have its limits if she did not flatter the fey's ego. "It must be quite the talent to have rested in your mind alone for so long."

The cat sìth sat with Fiadh's question for a moment, their feline features giving away nothing but the consideration it gave in the silence it allowed to hang between them.

"From one remnant of an ancient time to another," they said, the words drawn out a little longer than before, the tip of their tail flicking sharply behind them. "I trust that you will not."

Before Fiadh had a chance to consider the proposal or the fey's intent, they continued.

"How long do you think you'll last, child of the black wing, with that blade gnawing away at everything left of you? You must know it wants you dead, as much as it wishes to kill everyone else remaining from the old world." The cat's eyes weren't meeting hers now, looking instead to the hilt of the black blade held, as always, across her back.

"Everyone wants me dead, cat," Fiadh said. "At least this one has some use for me to keep me standing until I can meet my end on my own terms."

The cat's momentary hesitation before returning to preening was as close such an animal might appear to offer as a shrug of dismissal, and they did not look to Fiadh again. She could sense that there was little to glean from keeping watch over it as it performed the part of a simple mortal creature. She turned, and with a final glance back at their spot in the perfect centre of that etched stone ring, rejoined the others huddled within the broch.

The confined space had swiftly come to stink of the dank leathers, wool, and fur wrapped around the group, their huddle in the sheltered space swiftly warming their clothes enough that the smell could seep out among them. One of the older hands was snapping up old wooden boards that had clearly fallen from higher in the structure over the years and was looking to light a flame among them.

Fiadh returned to the opening at the tower's front and squatted where she could still spy the cat even as the light faded about them, free of the smell and the suspicious glances of the crew. The warm glow of flames began to shine out either side of her, joining the cooler light of the moon out over the sea and the stars dashed across the sky.

"First watch, aye?" came Annis' voice behind her as he squeezed through the opening to settle beside her. By now it was simply a matter of time before she'd expect his appearance; he seemed to enjoy sharing time and words with whoever remained as the sun fell below the horizon.

"Are we splitting our time with the others, now?" she asked, pulling out a whetstone and a sgian from her harness that hadn't been shown very much love of late.

"Aye, we are," he said matter-of-factly, leaning his head back against the stones. Fiadh looked up again to the stone circle, but of their feline guide there was no sign.

There were a few scuffed footsteps on the stone behind her and the two of them were joined by a third companion, easing his way in on Fiadh's other side.

"Whit cause dae ye huv tae sharpen those things aw the time? It's no like ye use them at aw, dae ye?" Rian asked, sitting himself down and watching her work the whetstone.

Fiadh raised a brow, but it was Annis who spoke first.

"Aye," he said. "Ah never even saw ye sae much as cut at a man."

Fiadh shrugged, turning the blade over in her hand and inspecting the new glint to its edge, "Apples, I guess?"

"But ye dinnae even eat thaim?" Rian pressed. Now it was Annis' turn to raise an eyebrow, daring Fiadh to answer that question directly.

Fiadh gave a faint smile. Apparently, she wasn't the only one who was paying attention to their fellow travellers, after all. Who would have guessed it would be the boy who took note of her unusual habits? Most others avoided her presence at all costs, even in the cramped quarters of the ship. It was more often than not that one of the crew would gladly take her leftovers from her when offered and would do so without complaint or question. Especially if it was a new member each day.

"Not everyone's a fan of apples, or ship's biscuits for that matter. I'm smaller than the crew and have less work to do on the ship. I don't need as much to sustain me." The truth was, and she knew

Annis knew as well as she, that she did not require any sustenance at all. She wondered at whether she could even remember what pangs of hunger might feel like, or to finally taste a meal after months on the waves denied it. That longing for a need gone too long unmet, at least, she was familiar with.

"So why cut food tae go uneaten, or carry sae mony knives ye dinnae use?" Rian pressed. The boy was persistent but was also no threat to her, really. He told enough tales, many of them told to him by Ahar no less, that the crew had long stopped taking any too seriously.

"I never learned from anyone how to use them," she said, twirling the blade lightly in her hand. "But if you bare a brace to the right people, it helps convince them you mean business, and that you might know what you're doing after all. If you can convince them you know how to commit violence, maybe you'll convince them you're not worth being threatened with it."

She spun the blade between her fingertips, letting the moonlight strike the metal just right so it'd catch Rian's eye. That seemed to distract him for a moment, watching the blade turn over, enough to see he had not noted her evasion of the question of food.

"So, ye huv thaim sae ye dinnae huv tae use thaim," Rian said, content in understanding this, at least. "Ken, like a hoverfly, it bears stripes but hus nae sting."

"Is that why ye prepare food fur yersel but dinnae eat it?" it was Annis' turn to press, taking up the inquisition where Rian had left it.

Fiadh met his gaze, hands halting their work for a moment. Why press? It was unlike him to push on questions she had clearly left deliberately unanswered, still more so to do it on behalf of someone else. Perhaps she wasn't the only one here trained in faking, either.

Annis broke away from her gaze first, with a momentary shiver not quite disguised by a shrug. More willing to churn the waters than expected, perhaps, but still wary of her silvered eyes after all this time.

"You have picked something up from the months on Ahar's ship, after all," she said, half to herself.

It was not Rian who replied but Annis, moving his eyes sharply to meet hers. "Months?" He said, almost accusingly.

Fiadh responded with a bemused shrug before her brows furrowed, her eyes searching his for some kind of clue behind his obscure question.

His eyes flickered across the scar on her face and towards her injured hand. She instinctively drew her blade-wielding hand across it, shielding it from his sight. She could fake some things perhaps, but she felt the burn of too much self-consciousness, a feeling she thought she had left far behind with the villagers who had glowered and spat at her silver eyes and called her 'witch'.

"You know," she said, moving him along before his silence could stir another round of questioning from Rian. "Dark stains on the hands are the tell-tale sign of another kind of fey as well."

Rian, fortunately, took the bait, "Oh Ah've heard ae thaim! Fey in the guise ae village women, but secretly blood-drinkers, their hauns stained wi the taint ae their evil deeds!"

She chuckled despite herself, as much in relief at the attention drawn away from herself. So many things may have changed over the years but some of the tales stayed the same.

"Not quite, though you're half right," she said. "The glaistig often do take the form of common village women to spend their time among the people they protect, though their hands are more often stained by the earth they tend to or the animals they treat."

"The Baobhan Sìth, however, truly does gradually gain the stain of the horrors they inflict upon the people they prey on. But they do not disguise themselves too carefully. They are too proud, too contemptuous of those they see as lesser than them. Instead, they weave magics that trap the wills of those who stray too close and too trustingly," she continued, thinking back to the rare times she had seen the aftermath of places and people who had suffered the attention of those dark fey.

"It begins at their fingertips and spreads until their entire hands are blackened by it. Then, finally, when they are finished or found out, they destroy everything they couldn't feed from. They take pleasure in suffering, perhaps none more so than in the poor glaistigs whose folktales are interwoven with them, who might fall to the pitchforks and flames of people scared by cloven hooves and furred limbs without knowing what they see," she said.

"Fortunately, for the glaistig, most can take animal form to escape their would-be-killers ..."

"Whit manner ae beast can ye turn intae?" Rian said, cutting off her tale and earning a bark of a laugh from Annis, the tension of past motions finally dispelled.

"A Crow, boy, what do you think?" Fiadh replied.

"How dae ye ken sae much, onyhow?" Annis asked. The boy stared at her in wonder, clearly imagining feathers springing from her brow.

"What do you mean?" Fiadh said.

"Ah mean ye dinnae jist pick up every threat aroond here unless ye've seen a lot ae people lost tae thaim ower the years," he said, giving the boy a light shove to startle him out of his imagination. "How mony died sae ye cuid ken sae much?"

"A little morbid, perhaps, Annis," she said, though her mind couldn't help but think back at just how many deaths she'd seen on her journeys. "I read books, and I was taught, once upon a time, long ago, over the cliffs at Tur Eumor – where my order was meant to bring some stability between the forces of the old and the new – and so we had to learn how to keep both at bay."

"Some auld fellas wi lang beards an glasses an aw?" Rian asked, clearly remembering Ahar's tales of wizened old guides for mythical kings of the south.

Fiadh couldn't help but smile at the thought. "We were of all ages, though, like me, you might have struggled to see how old. Likewise, our goddess who founded our Order so long ago, whose image was so often either young or old, and sometimes both."

"An they kent sae much frae books?" Annis asked, his skill with reading still very much limited to his own name despite his time picking up Ahar's many tongues.

"Most of us, nearly all by the end," Fiadh said, looking out to the moon hanging still over the valley beyond the stone clearing. "But there were some who knew the old ways because they were there. Ancient beings, blessed with the favour of the Rìaghan, their skin pale as snow and fingers marked by the ink of a thousand pages of script and a thousand lines of runes traced onto the stone. All gone now, all departed beyond the veil and to rest alongside the Rìaghan herself. Perhaps one, or more than one, was lost for being mistaken for Baobhan Sìth themselves."

"Has onyone ever mistaken ye fur yin?" Rian asked.

"A story fur another nicht, mebbe, boy," Annis interrupted. "Ye've mair than enough tae spoil the captain wi noo. Ye huv anither watch tae look forward tae. Aff ye go."

He shooed the boy away with one hand and Rian obediently scurried back over the opening behind them. Fiadh wished, not for the first time, that she shared Annis' capacity for commanding the attention of others as he saw fit.

But, she thought, as she was finally left in some silence beside her companion, it was often far better to capture no one's attention at all.

***

Fiadh barely slept, moving a distance away from the broch as the watches changed, rather than lying among the crew within. By the time the orange glow of the dawn began to cross the stones she was wreathed in the dew that now coated the whole clearing, the standing stones barely visible through the fog clinging to the side of the mountain.

The group from Ahar's ships were gradually moving out from the broch and gathering their things. She winced as they trampled, without consideration, upon the already cracking remnants of the stone circle.

But her attention was drawn to the sight of glowing lights floating in the fog beyond them, blinking in and out just at the edge of sight as they beckoned her to come investigate their origin.

The group was already moving past her towards where the shadowy outline of the cat had returned to take their place perched high on a stone on the other side of the clearing, their eyes also looking out into the depths of the haze.

"Dinnae be tempted by bright things in the distance, lad." she overheard Annis saying as he passed, his hand on Rian's shoulder as he glanced over his own. "A sword shines jist as brightly as silver in the moonlight. There are only two ways tae deal wi fey: befriend them or flee."

Not all her lessons had fallen on unhearing ears, she thought, as she dropped down from the stone that had served as her seat and rejoined the group, weaving her way between them. The lights were not her concern for now. By the time they returned, the sun would have banished the fog and whatever lay within it.

The cat sìth stalked the stones above them and there were fewer gasps of awe this time as the stones before them began to meld into their surroundings. All kinds of magic could lose its wonder when people had witnessed it before.

The ascent ahead of them was quieter this time as the sun rose, though whether through anticipation or just the struggles to wake from an uncomfortable night, Fiadh couldn't tell. Their guide was certainly less talkative and was not drawn into telling further tales of mighty champions and old gods.

That did not prevent a few of them clustering behind the cat leading the way through the rocky gullies, clearly waiting on the next tale of hubris and dark portents. As they broke free of the channel and into open air, some chatter returned as they admired the view, a clear day revealing the whole bay beneath them and out to the isles beyond.

"Ah think Ah like you, cat," Rian said, clearly returning to a good mood as the sun warmed their ascent and clambering up to join the fey on the rocks above them.

"How strange," responded the cat, after a short pause and without breaking its step. "I don't feel anything about you at all."

Rian clearly took on Annis' advice then, deciding on the other option by retreating back down the rock and into the crowd. A couple of the men he joined below overheard as well, responding with sneers and mutters. One of them suggested just choking the cat and casting it from the cliffs, his loud whisper barely hidden to the others on the trail.

Svana shoved past Fiadh to move up to him. "Have you ever heard a tale of a man who has killed a fey cat, Arne? Maybe marched its pelt around for all to see?" she hissed, leaning in close to him.

He shook his head, shying away from her.

"Think about why that might be, wouldn't you?" she said, swatting the back of his skull for good measure. The cat themselves showed no sign of noticing the interaction, whether they had heard or not.

The group were quieter again after that, following the fey at some distance and allowing Fiadh to squeeze ahead. Once more their fey guide paused before a wall of rock and the way ahead was revealed as a mirage of stones. A narrow opening was revealed, the bright light of the morning shining through it. Squeezing through one by one they found before them a wide clearing, cupped by cliffs and stretching out over the valley below.

This, Fiadh knew almost immediately, was where she had seen that bright light shine from behind the veil. Finally, this was the place she had been seeking.

All around the clearing and through to the cliff edge stood a dozen young oak trees, sprouting straight from the rock as if they had driven their way through it in search of the sky. It was strange to see them situated so high in the mountain, though, she thought, no stranger than a talking cat who had crafted more convincing illusions.

In the clearing's centre sat their guide. Not looking back at them, but at the rocks hanging over the opening they had passed through. Fiadh turned carefully, turning her eyes up towards the heights, and froze.

Looming above, embedded in the rock and ten times the size of a man, was a golden mask, its edges burned into the very rock itself with streaks of black still flashing against the stone. It was fixed in a horrifying expression of a face screaming, dark streaks pouring from its eyes like tears.

"Fiadh?" Annis' voice came from behind her.

But she did not answer. She knew he could not see it, seeing only a strangely formed protrusion of the rock. But she could, her silvered eyes casting the light that illuminated its form. The cat could, too. She turned her face away from it, tearing her thoughts from that which could have twisted a god so completely as to leave their anguish carved into the mountain upon which they fell.

She felt them then, Caerdrich, felt their icy grasp creeping up the back of her neck and burying their fingertips into the back of her skull. They turned her face back to stare at that screaming visage, peeling her eyelids back to gaze upon the darkness that spilled forth from its eyes, shimmering with colour like oil upon water. Darkness only her eyes could see, madness only she could understand. The chaos of a mind that they had seen long before. With Caerdrich at her back and Cuthac before her, she felt the intensity of the rage still bound within the blade's scabbard.

"The mask of Cuthac, the mad one," the fey said, their voice carrying across the space. "Many have come to snatch it away from this place; none have left bearing it. But it seemed to draw the Aodann Òir to it like a moth to a lantern. So here it was snared."

"Are you also offering me such a deal, cat," she gasped, feeling the grip of Caerdrich finally beginning to release. "As Lot offered to Eirian? Are you seeking to trap me like another trapped the Aodann Òir?"

The cat looked down upon her, lip curled, and tooth bared in a sneer.

"For you?" they said. "For a spent sack of meat and bones, still slave to another? What possible use would I have for you? I would be rid of you as soon as I am able."

The companions reacted to that, stepping back with mutters and snarls, seeing once more before them not a friendly guide and teller of tales but the vicious, strange animal from another realm that had so dismissed their youngest member earlier. Its form shimmered, the black of its fur flickering and shifting as they backed away towards the rocks.

Not for the first time, Fiadh felt there was something missing from their tale. The mask had rested here for hundreds of years. Why would this be the first time an Aodann Òir had been drawn to this place, or the first this cat sìth had heard of it? She shivered even as Annis drew close and rested an arm over her shoulder, as the cat sìth padded over to the far corner of the space.

"Something's not right here, Annis," she said, trying desperately to suck in full lungfuls of breath.

"We're followin a talkin cat whae clearly hates ye," he said. "Whit mair dae ye want?"

"More than that," she said, pointing across the clearing. "These trees don't grow in rock. Let alone so near to one another, let alone so high into the mountains. This isn't some chance discovery. Magic has stirred here recently, far more recently than the cat's tales."

"Whit does that mean?" he asked, looking out to the others who were spreading out and peering at the trunks and acorns scattered nearby.

"It means we should wonder why no one who has been brought here for wishes has been heard of since," she said, straightening and taking a final deep breath. "Why have we heard no boasts of great wishes received, or warnings of those whose wishes cursed them? I need to think about our next steps carefully, and I need you to watch for anything those trees might be hiding from us."

As she moved forward, Annis didn't remove his hand from her shoulder. He walked in step while barking something in Sjøtunge to the cowering others. As they approached where the cat was walking in circles around a space flatter than the rest, Fiadh realised what she was looking at. A metal grate, cold iron bars flat against the surface. She could see where the grate had been held up against the rocks, and the trail of the snare that had dragged something across the rock to fall beneath it before it fell shut.

Cold iron. Toxic to the fey, but not to her kind, created to be sent among mortal folk.

She knelt down before it as the cat came to a halt and sat upon its haunches, just further away from the pit than the length of the grate above it. Gazing down into the space Fiadh's silvered eyes pierced the dark, and she could see the wink of gold shining below.

"Dae ye need a haun?" Annis asked, taking a knee beside her to investigate the bars.

"No," she said. "I need to be the one to open it, and, given its purpose I imagine," she ran a finger along its edge before gripping a bar and lifting it easily, as it squealed free of the rust at its edges, "there was no need to hold it down."

Below her, movement, as the golden being sensed its freedom and began to claw at the walls of its confines.

"Who trapped it here?" she asked, turning her head towards their guide. "Who created this cage, knowing that these fey would be drawn here? Who has both the knowledge and the ability to work cold iron?"

"Does it matter?" replied the cat.

It didn't, not now. The fey was right, time was running short. There was an investigation here that she may have undertaken long ago, but not now, not when she was so close.

"The usual rules apply?" she asked, keeping an eye on the small figure below.

"They do," replied the cat.

Annis cocked an eyebrow as she looked at him.

"Nothing comes free, Annis," Fiadh explained as she lowered herself, gauging the depth of the cage. "Any wish will take from you as well as give. So many, human and fey alike, have fallen foul of that bargain. But, if there's anything these creatures truly know, it's a sense of irony, and if presented with an opportunity they cannot refuse it. If you're clever about it, you can shape their answer to ensure you only lose what you are prepared to."

She padded the walls, getting a sense for how much weight they could hold before she could put pressure on them to reach down into the space.

"The greater the ask, the greater the cruelty of the loss you will suffer in turn," she continued, as much as a reminder to herself as a lesson for Annis. "It is best to accept what you will lose and make your wish in such a way as to give what you can predict rather than be cursed to live your life with an unexpectedly ironic fate. Now, please stand between me and the cliff," she said, settling herself into place as firmly as possible.

Annis shrugged and made his way over, leaning for a glance over the crag and the sharp drop into the glen below.

"If anything dramatic happens to me, throw the cat off it."

Annis turned ever so slightly towards the cat sìth, which had sat itself on a rock to look down upon Fiadh. The fey, forever unperturbed, rested its eyes unfeelingly upon her, not even acknowledging the presence of her companion.

She had spent so much time imagining this moment, running the decisions that must be made over and over again, carefully building the words she would say so she could gain what she wanted while giving away only what she could afford.

But now, on the precipice of writing that decision in stone, she hesitated. For a moment a chill ran down to her heart as the weight of her choice sat before her. She had not three wishes, only two.

The rules of this exchange were clear. They had been collated by her Order in centuries past when such encounters were as common as the gold that shone from the still face looking up at her from its confines, a plain expanse of metal where eyes should be, only reflecting her own.

The number was fixed; it could not be changed. You could not undo the weave that had come before you, only determine which strands would join it in the future. Whatever souls had travelled beyond the veil could not return. She could not wish back her departed Order, or the gods who created it. She could not wind back time to that fateful night and still the fires before they spread.

The Red Raven awaited her if she could only play this right. She could guide herself through the weave and pierce the cloak that had been placed over her hiding place by the Ceasg in a deal done so many moons ago.

She could finally divorce herself from the blade at her back. Be free for the first time since she had fallen from Tur Eumor. But what would she have to sacrifice? Would its power that bound her cold flesh to her bones be lost as well? Would she be able to face the Raven alone without Caerdrich's strength to carry her that far? What plans did the cat have for them all if she was rendered helpless by the cost of wishes used too greedily and carelessly? To take what she had travelled so far to claim she would have to let go of everything which would not clear her path. Anything that was not a part of that one final goal.

She had no choice.

Fiadh reached down into the space and gripped the creature within, below the golden plate that coated its face, favouring her uninjured hand. It writhed and squirmed under her hands, the bark of its thin limbs digging into her skin. With a heave she brought it to the surface, and she heard a gasp from one of the sail hands behind her as the bright reflection of its golden visage caught the morning sun, scattering the light across the clearing.

A true Aodann Òir, born from the fabric of the weave itself, shaken free to tumble across the world until they could find the corner of that great tapestry they were meant for.

This one had fallen very far from its destination. Its once smooth features were scratched and cracked at its edges. Its hands which clung to her forearms and scrambled for purchase were chipped, one wooden finger broken away entirely.

No more consideration. It was time.

Fiadh placed the creature in front of her, turning it so the sun no longer cast directly off its face, and she looked deeply into that expanse of gold, seeing her own features staring back. Those silver eyes glowing with unnatural light, the flesh as pale as snow, hair flecked with grey. Features of someone who had spent too long fighting against a world that had long been free of her kind. Features of someone who was so very, very tired.

"With your freedom before you," she intoned in Cànan. "I ask only what I am owed to release you back to the weave from whence you came."

The gold seemed to stretch to fill her vision, drawing her in until she was swimming in it, her mind set loose into the metallic void. Her stomach lurched with nausea as her mind seemed to fall through the space even as her body sat still, kneeling before the no longer struggling fey creature.

Then, finally, she came to a stop, on a platform in the swimming, aurous liquid. She felt the scrutiny of the Aodann Òir upon her. Patient, still, waiting for her first request. Fiadh tried to slow her thundering heart, taking deep breaths as she ran the words over her mind over and over again, as if she had not done so to herself one hundred times before.

I wish only this, she thought, careful not to speak the words aloud for her audience upon the crag to overhear. *I wish only the ability to see the way to the being in the sea before me who is called the Red Raven.*

The swimming gold flashed a brilliant light before fading once more. It flowed like liquid across the creature's face, gaps opening in the smooth surface as it seemed to eddy around wooden knots that now emerged from beneath it, the gold retreating within. One wish made, two more remained, one which was not hers to make.

That changed the game. No longer could she simply make her second wish what she had intended, let alone the third she no longer had. There was another playing, and with the power held by a wish there was little that could protect her from the power the cat sìth would wield when the Aodann Òir was theirs.

Except another wish.

Fiadh relaxed, the pressure of her choice easing as she realised what she must do.

I wish that you would do unto the maker of your next wish what they would wish upon others, she thought, focusing hard on that singular thought. Again, the gold flashed, and then withdrew, showing more of the wood beneath, retreating into the crevasses between the grain.

Then she felt the pull, dragging her from the depths, pulling her back to the surface. Her eyes opened and she found herself dragged back from the creature as the ground beneath her shifted, as the fey itself was secured tightly to the ground by stones jutting from the rocks to encase its limbs.

The cat sìth jumped down from the rock it had sat upon and nonchalantly circled the entrapped fey creature, not even caring to look back to Fiadh or forward to Annis, who had dropped into a broad fighter's stance beyond the wish maker. Their tail flicked the air above them gently as they drew closer to the Aodann Òir, their eyes never straying from that golden face even now so much of it had retreated into the deeply grooved wood beneath. Those eyes were wide, pupils nearly round, ears peaked and focused on what lay before them.

Fiadh watched as the gleeful cat placed a paw upon the rim of that polished gold and traced one razor talon across the woodwork on which it sat. She watched as the cat's eyes grew wider with intensity and greed, as it cast its wish down into the shimmering depths of that gleaming mirror.

With a glint in its eye that might have yielded a smile if cats could contort their features into such an expression, the cat withdrew, drawing its claw back across the edge of the Aodann Òir as the creature began to twitch and contort, the gold of its face finally sinking entirely within the wooden orb of its head.

Its limbs began to extend and grow, the wood stretching and sprouting new extensions that plunged into the rock below it, splitting the stones that the cat had used to contain it. Tendrils spread across the surface and its torso stretched up towards the sky. Finally, its skull split, golden flakes scattering to the wind as branches erupted and reached out in every direction, green buds already sprouting from its furthest extensions.

But it was fading from view. Fiadh's vision darkened, the edges falling into blackness as all else lost its colour, dropping the vivid greens and browns into shades of grey.

But one colour was still very clear. As the cat turned their smug eyes towards her, she saw them narrow and then shoot open, darting from her to the tree and then back to their own paws, each moving slower as they looked over them, the black fur giving way to gold that flowed across them, coating their paws, then their legs, then running up their chest and finally their face, locked in a vicious hiss directed towards her.

That was the last she saw of her surroundings, which were replaced instead with a glowing thread stretching from her and beyond where the edge of the crag must have been, before falling away to the bay below.

The path, only the path. The only sight left to her.

***

Annis caught Fiadh as she staggered to her feet, seeming to have lost any sense of where she stood and where the ground lay. Beyond her, Rian had thrown himself down in front of the tree that had suddenly sprung from the rock, yelling something even as Svana and a sail hand had run forward to haul him back.

She grasped at him, seeking purchase as her feet began to find solid ground again. As he led her to a nearby uplifted stone, tossed sideways by the sudden emergence of the new oak, he glanced back at where the fey still stood. Their cat-slitted eyes had disconcerted him nearly as much as Fiadh's silvered stare, but now their colour was gone, fixed blankly ahead as vacant golden spheres.

He sat Fiadh down at the rock, the Crow lowering herself gently, as if she had aged a hundred years in just the last few moments. They sat together in silence as the rest of the crew gasped and chattered about what they had just witnessed, a few even coming within a few steps of the golden statue that had once been their fey guide.

"So, Ahar will have what he wanted, at least," she finally said, grimly staring out over the edge of the crags. "He wanted gold so badly, well, now he has it."

He watched her staring out, at nothing specifically but also with a fixed determination, the same that had seized her ever since the night at Kempe Fell, ever since she had started disappearing more and more often beyond her blood-soaked device. Throughout, her fingers compulsively traced that winged symbol into her hand. As long as they had been together, she had drawn that mark, her fingers running them over again and again as she thought, a ritual he was not sure she was even aware of anymore. Ahar had told him it was the symbol of the Rìaghan, that old god of these parts whose followers had long been lost to war and age.

All except for this one.

The skin of that hand traced upon once had an almost human tone. He hadn't really thought about the warmth of anyone's skin all that much until he had watched that tone fade from her. How light passed through it to shine yellows and pinks lighter than you'd expect at the fingertips, showing the veins running across someone's palm. That colour was gone from that broken right hand, smashed by the storm years ago. It had turned almost the black of charred wood over time, gradually spreading from the wound that had never healed, the one that gripped her blade's hilt so tightly when she felt threatened by so much as a sail hand drifting too near her. In places it had crumbled slightly, showing nothing but grey beneath.

"How long is left until we find whit ye're looking fur?" he asked, tempted to sit by her but wary of setting off her frayed nerves.

"Not long, weeks, not months. This winter aboard Ahar's ship will be worth it before long," she said, voice dry, emotionless.

He didn't have the heart to have this conversation again, the one where he tells her it hasn't been months that they've been on Ahar's ship, but years. Years where her gold had slowly dwindled away, and their stay had been extended only by Ahar's conviction that having a Crow aboard brought him good fortune.

Years of ploughing the waves as Ahar rebuilt his crew and sold his bounties from place to place. It used to be that she'd pass through the portal every handful of stops for a few moments, then it was for an hour, then it was at every stop as he stood by and waited for her, someday, simply not to return.

She had been running out of gold, and as far as he could see she was also running out of time.

"Aren't ye feart, kennin whit that blade is, kennin whit it hus done tae its bearers in the past?" he asked, eyes running over that black leather hilt bound, as always, tightly to her shoulders beneath her wool cloak.

"I know that if I draw this blade no one can stand against me," Fiadh said, her voice darkening, the edge clear. "Only with the knowledge of that strength have I been able to travel so far, to push so hard, to get so close. Did you not imagine that I knew there were consequences to that power, Annis?"

Fiadh's hand patted the rock beside her until it found a small stone. With a flick she tossed it out over the cliff edge, but her head did not follow its descent, instead staring out still towards the sea.

"I knew the story, Annis," she said, softer now, almost as if she was dreaming of another time. "I've heard it before, a long time ago. The warrior got what they wanted. The Aodann Òir gave them exactly what they asked for. They became exactly what they wished to be, only to be locked away for centuries by an Order dedicated to finding an accord between the old worlds and the new. You knew that name. The ghost of the fortress, a name twisted from the words of peoples they left behind. The name of that warrior bound in metal was Caerdrich, and every warning of their fate was true."

She turned to him, and despite himself Annis took a step back, a chill running down his limbs as the hairs on his arms stood on end. Her bright eyes, for so long that disconcerting colour of moonlight, familiar even in their alien glow, were gone. Her dark pupils, once rimmed with silver, were now clouded over with a brilliant cataract of gold, fading towards her irises. Those eyes looked for him, but they did not see, glancing over him as if he were not even there.

"It gave me what I wished for," she said. "I can see nothing but the way forward. It gave me all I need."

"Ye ... ye gave it the opportunity," he said, tightening his fists to steady his voice and slow his pounding heart. He'd made a promise. He'd stuck by her, been the one at her back time and time again. She'd shown him places he could never have dreamed of, revealed secrets hidden just out of view. She had never asked him to sacrifice or to give anything to the fey magics she spun but for the single drop of blood kept in that vial across her neck. His life had been filled with longing to see the world, and for ends he could not understand she had simply given those sights away.

"I did," she said, turning away from him to look out towards the bay once again. "I wished only for this ... only for the sight I needed. No other. I knew it would be too tempting to resist taking everything else."

Her hands paused their motion and turned up, relaxing across her knees. She looked blankly down at them, slowly curling and uncurling her fingers, even as two of them refused her instructions and lay, near limp, across her thigh.

"This was never my story," she murmured, and Annis felt that now, again, she was no longer talking to him. "For many years I thought it was, but I was naive. Now I know my destination, the end of my chapter, and I will make sure hers closes with mine."

✹

THE RED RAVEN

The boat thrummed underneath her fingertips, the woodwork passing the pressure of the wind onto its sails and the waves onto its bow. The spray of the ship's break pattered across her face and clothes.

Those clothes, furs layered upon wool, concealed Fiadh's other arm deep within. It covered her increasing frailty and protected it from what she might not see was harming it, having lost all feeling in that hand months ago.

Now the single hand on the wooden railing guided her, for her eyes could not. Before her she saw no waves or ships, though she knew the fleet of Ahar now numbered a dozen or more. Instead, only the horizon lay ahead, a long line of darkness delineating the sea from the clouds, a bright golden string flowing from her towards it to indicate where she must go. Her one eye, given the gift of the Aodann Òir, saw nothing but the light guiding their way.

Another hand gripped her shoulder gently – the great palm of Annis, her constant companion over the years. Ahar had refused to follow her vision until he had gathered a force capable of storming the Raven's hidden stronghold. It had not mattered how often she had said she did not know what awaited them there; all that had mattered to him was the scent of gold and forbidden treasures. Treasures valuable enough to be sealed behind a spell that could hide an entire isle from those who charted these waters. They spoke less, these days. Annis was less curious about the world Fiadh lived in and she was less able to answer questions as she felt her energy fade with every sunset. Every time she felt she might not waken alongside the crew with the morning, she felt the spirit of Caerdrich, their blade still bound to her back, seizing her limbs and drawing them up to bring her to the ship's bow. Every day she would stand there, watching that light, the guide for Ahar's crossing and the host for the will of that great and ancient blade.

The Raven could not stand against the blade. None could. There would finally be vengeance for the fall of Tur Eumor, the destruction of her Order, and her own fall from the towering cliffs into a life at the very border of death. But, where once that thought had filled her with fury and determination, she now felt only the weight of the years upon her shoulders, the ache of wounds that could not heal and the memories of those she had not saved.

Her days were spent at the prow, but it was not *her* will that drew her there. She wished now more than anything else to find her will once more, or to be permitted, finally, to sleep.

Annis' hand tensed as they heard shouting in Sjøtunge, which he responded to with a single-word grunt. His hand tensed again, this time in a reassuring squeeze, but she winced as it grasped little more than the bones of her shoulder through her furs.

How long had she been fading away? It had crept up on her, appearing at first as no more than the exhaustion of travel coming more swiftly, then difficulty moving about Ahar's ship, losing the sure-footedness her travels had otherwise left her well-equipped with. She was now barely able to pull her wools over her shoulders without Annis' aid.

She knew he worried, in his own quiet way. But he didn't ask questions. Not since their time in the mountains when she had felt him piece together the past of Caerdrich. Not since he had known the danger they posed beneath the black scabbard, held at her back in his presence throughout this whole journey. But he remained by her, his steady hand upon her shoulder bringing the only mote of comfort she still held.

There was a burst of chatter, every language of Ahar's crew of peoples drawn from all along the coast breaking out at once. Through the fog of her exhaustion Fiadh was able to pick out the key focus of their excitement: land.

A familiar cadence of footsteps came from behind her as the captain moved his way up the ship to join her, never being one to hide the heft of his stride.

"At last!" Ahar crowed, his bellow making Fiadh wince. "You have delivered what you had always promised, Crow. What was it? Treasures and lands beyond my wildest imaginings? Well, I've been imagining this one for quite some time, and you have brought me here! Beyond the fogs, free of the rocks, a fey compass like no other."

He turned away from her to bark orders at the crew, advancing back down the ship. She heard the grind of the oars sliding into their locks and felt the shove as they dipped into the water and began to drive the ship onwards. The waters must be shallower here, the need for control greater.

The scent of kelp upon the shore began to drift across the water. Rocks must be just barely out of view, still shrouded by the mist before they could be avoided. How many had charted this course not knowing what lay ahead, their ships broken on the isle within the fog, never to emerge again to tell the tale of where the Raven's home had been hidden by the lord of the seas?

The vision came to her in a flash, of ships cracking open upon the rocks, their oarsmen tossed into the waves, their screams buried in the tumult. Then it was her, falling from the cliffs of Tur Eumor once more, Caerdrich's frozen scabbard clutched in her hand, the water closing in over her head. The feeling of the last breaths torn from her lungs as she sank, weighed down by her black robes and her hands bound to the leather hilt by the ice stretching out around them.

She shook her head free of it, feeling another squeeze from Annis' hand in response. He could not know what she had been through, but he had walked his own path long before they had met and would survive many years beyond her passing. The weave was nearly finished with her, but not with him.

She felt Ahar's heavy footsteps before she heard his deep chuckle.

"You can't see this, Crow, but I can. We've made it, the path is clear, the shore lies before us. You've paid your way, at last!" The laugh that rumbled in his chest was tinged with cold cunning. She knew that beyond his bright smile the mirth had not carried to his dark eyes.

"This may not be what you were seeking, Captain," she replied, turning herself back towards the golden line that spun out before the ship and curved up and over what must be the shore ahead.

"Aye, lass, is that so? What, pray, must I be seeking?" said the southerner, her mother tongue given a prancing tilt by his far-flung accent.

"A future, Ahar, to return to tell the tale," she said, barely able to lift her voice over the sound of the waves breaking against the ship's hull.

"You spin a dire fortune for us, Crow," he growled, though she could still hear the excitement behind the words. "What do you know that we do not? Are you ready to finally tell me what awaits us upon this isle?"

Fiadh had hidden nothing from them about their destination. She had no reason to, as even she knew no more than where it lay.

"If you leave this ship you take your lives into your own hands," she said, not quite answering the question. "I will not protect you. I will not promise you safe passage or long lives filled with riches. If you value your lives, you will remain here and sail away, never to return to this isle again."

"Aye," he said. "So, what's in it for us to stay? Surely you must give me reason not to turn my ship about and simply depart, leaving you at the mercy of whatever spirit you chase upon the hidden isle?"

"Perhaps you will watch a monster be slain," Fiadh said, playing upon Ahar's love of tall tales. "A monster neither you nor anyone of your bloodlines will ever have seen struck down. You will see it fall, or you will take your ship far from here as soon as we are ashore, lest the storm that is coming smash your ship upon the rocks."

That struck home. Ahar barked a laugh and began to step back towards his position upon the stern.

"I have out-sailed the Cirein-cròin, Crow," he shouted back, his steps beating out a rhythm through the wood. "There is no storm that can take me, not today, not for a hundred years. Take us ashore and let us witness your glorious battle with the spirits that herald thunder."

Fiadh paid his brazen confidence no mind. Ever the storyteller, Ahar would do what suited his own interests when it came to it. It would not be his boots striking the beach, nor carrying whatever treasures the Raven may have sequestered back to his ships.

If there were any ships left for him to sail back beyond the mist.

"Annis," she said, her free hand placed lightly on his arm, knowing the steady expression that likely looked down at her beyond the golden glow. "All I need is to get to the place where the Raven lies. That is where my journey ends, and what belongings I leave behind are yours to do with as you see fit."

She felt his tension beneath her fingers, but she pressed on.

"It will be beyond the beach, at the centre of this isle. From there on you are free to go, to be with your own. Any contract you feel you owe to me is finished." Her words were drowned out by the clamour of a horn echoing across the water, the final sign that their approach beyond the mists had been noticed from the Raven's refuge.

"Aye, lass," came his reply, more softly than she was accustomed to. "I'll git ye whaur ye need tae go. There'll be violence, noo. Stay here until it is done an Ah'll return fur ye. Ah've *got* ye."

His fingers curled around hers and gently removed them from his arm, placing them instead on the gunwale.

"Haud fast, we're here," he said.

The ship lurched beneath her feet and the harsh scrape of wood grinding over a pebbled shore filled her ears. Her hand brushed the air, looking to steady herself on Annis, but he was gone. All she could hear was the thunder of footsteps of the crew moving from their seats and over the sides, accompanied by the soft hum of blades being drawn from scabbards.

All the while, the gold thread beckoned her ashore.

So close, at last.

***

Annis' boots crunched into the pebbles beneath the water as waves crashed over his shoulders, soaking him through in moments as he heard others drop into the water from the ship. He wiped his eyes and clenched his hand tightly around the hilt of his axe, waiting for a break in the water's rush to begin the stride forward towards the shore where the bow of the ship rested.

The horn sounded again, its wavering cry echoing across the bay, and this time its meaning was clear.

The first arrow cracked into the hull of the ship, and Annis ducked behind it as several more followed from the head of the beach, striking the water where he'd been about to advance onto the shore. Then came the footsteps of their welcome party, crashing across the stones, almost ungainly in their haste.

He timed his swing with the momentary hesitation of the first of them reaching the ship's bow, stepping out and swinging his axe in both hands in a single movement. There was no chance for his counterpart to shout out as the blade buried itself in his chest, ploughing through cloth and ribs.

The man pitched onto his back and Annis planted a foot against his side to wrench the axe free, eyes up and seeking the next assailant. They were streaming down from the crest above the beach, barrelling full tilt straight into the waiting blades of Ahar's landing party.

One came at Annis, his mouth open in a wordless scream, hands clutching a spear levelled at Annis' face. It was a mistake. Annis stepped smoothly to one side, batted the haft of the spear away with his free hand and landed his own blade on the man's shoulder with a crunch. Ripping his axe free, he recoiled as blood sprayed from the wound over his head and chest.

The man fell limply at his feet. These were no trained fighters; they were villagers being thrown to their deaths. Where were the Raven's guards? Where were her defences?

Svana, Hengist, and half a dozen others had joined him from the ship by now, hacking their own ways clear and beginning the advance up the beach. They were cutting their way through fishing spears, filleting knives and wood axes, barely pausing in their march across the pebbles to swat away weak thrusts and deliver their efficient replies.

Could it be this Raven had placed too much faith in the mist to keep raiders at bay? Could the demon whose name so terrified Fiadh have been reduced to a village elder, her people cut down like sheep in the maws of wolves?

Annis dashed up the beach to join the others just as they crossed the reeds onto the dune beyond, the wave of defenders washed away and reduced to a trickle by Ahar's experienced raiders. They had crushed the keepers of fortress monasteries in their time, served

Vestamr as he carved his kingdom from the isles and burned the few who resisted his claim. This was no challenge for such warriors; there was no joy in it.

Then the first trap snapped shut.

One among them had walked forward onto the grass beyond the dune, peering deeper into the fog that still wreathed the land before them. The wooden spikes that sprang from the ground fixed his leg in place, jutting through his calf as he screamed at the blood spitting out across the ground.

The trapped man was nearly cloven in two when the creature from the mist struck. Its arm was a long band of exposed sinew, the bone jutting from where a hand might have been, forming a scythe that tore through cloth and flesh. The screams came more swiftly now as it turned, its torso grafted to the very back of its steed, its lipless grin fixing upon each of them in turn.

The scythe struck out again and the man's head vanished in a spray of crimson. The monstrosity turned and charged towards them.

They scattered in every direction, Annis diving behind the crest of the dune as the skinless limbs of the horse burst through its banks, its gnashing teeth baying as Ahar's raider's stunned silence turned to screams of horror. He heard the snaps and crunches of more traps crashing shut on those who had leapt into the grasses, and the strangled shock of those who had just witnessed this beast crash through to the beach where they had gathered.

Annis grabbed fistfuls of the dune reeds and hauled himself over the top, out of sight of where the monstrous apparition had landed. All about him was chaos. The raiders stranded beyond the beach were now battling for their lives against people clad in cloaks of grass that had hidden them until the trap was sprung. Cruel curved blades slashed out from beneath those cloaks as yet more of them rose from beyond, overwhelming the warriors trapped between the crest and the brush that they may otherwise have fled into.

The Raven had awaited them. She had been prepared.

Peering back over the crest from where he lay, Annis could see the crimson stain that spread below the hoofprints of the beast and across the sands, its grinning face jerking unnaturally back and forth, a half-dozen bodies scattered around it in various states of dismemberment. Where one arm's scythe dripped with the blood of those that had fallen in its path, the other twitched, bony fingers trailing nearly to the floor along the flanks of the steed beneath it.

The raiding party had retreated nearly to the waves, spread in a semi-circle across the beach. Only the boats offered them safety while they were unable to rescue those few stranded further ashore.

The creature screamed and the sound of a score of voices echoed out, cascading over one another from the horse's head that protruded forth from the front of the beast, mimicking human sounds like a choir of the damned calling them in desperation and fear.

He felt his breaths begin to come in gasps, a chill gripping his spine and stomach, his eyes flicking from that nightmarish mount to the red stain it left in its wake through the sands. For the first time since he had stepped upon a boat with Fiadh as his guide, Annis felt fear. How many had died at the hands of this terrible grafting of man and steed? How many had been torn apart by its bone scythe? How many now screamed from within it for the gods that had never come to reclaim their souls?

A hand gripped his shoulder and gave him a sharp shake. Behind him he heard Svana's voice, the authority of Ahar's second.

"Get on the beach, get them all ashore," she snarled, her mouth close behind his ear.

"Aye, an dae whit?" He turned his eyes back to the beach, taking in the pale faces of Ahar's gathered mass, frozen in fear of that monstrosity as it stamped back and forth.

"Everything can die, Annis," she said, her voice laden with the certainty of one who had seen more than their fair due. "Everything dies when you stab them where it hurts. Find out where it hurts and keep stabbing until it cuts out that hell-forsaken sound."

Her next instruction came in the form of a hard shove to his shoulder, and as he turned to watch her go, he saw her barking out orders, rallying what little remained of the crew who had made it inland to protect one another and hold the ridge.

Until reinforcements could come – the ones he had been tasked to deliver.

To think that not so long ago he had only been expected to sit and watch as a weird moon-touched lass drew circles and maybe knocked a couple of heads together.

He gripped the reeds he'd used to haul himself over the ridge once more, and lowered himself back down the way he came, careful not to draw the attention of the monster that was now turning back and forth before the crowd of raiders, looking among them.

Or, at least, one of its heads was. The horse turned this way and that, wild eyes darting across the faces of those who had not turned away in horror. The skull adorning the human torso jutting from its back instead lolled back and forth, eyeless sockets bouncing above that horrible grin.

Why hadn't it swept forward among the raiders and cut them down? Why was it waiting?

Everything can die.

Annis searched the crowd to find one of his companions, eventually seeing Hengist, backed almost up against their ship's hull. He waved sharply to catch his attention and Annis gestured pointedly to his eyes and then gathered up sand in his fist.

Hengist's response came with a nod, and the Sjøfolk man began to mutter to those around him. Faces of fear and confusion turned to fixed determination. Orders and a plan could sharpen the mind against all kinds of unknowns.

One broke the ranks before the others had a chance to spread the word, charging with a berserker shriek at the monster. It barely moved before the scythe struck out and tore him open from groin to shoulder, his axe toppling from limp hands into his own steaming entrails unleashed across the sand.

Annis took a breath, tensing and relaxing his hand around the handle of his axe, forcing his gaze upon the shrieking creature and the viscera strewn around it and to Ahar's forces beyond. There were enough of them; this could be done.

He found the eyes of one of the other captains on him, Ruadh, one of the Gall-Ghàidheil leaders who had been collected under Vestamr's banners. Annis crossed his arms in response.

Move in, move out, do not engage.

It was a raiding standard. Pull the attention of the defenders away and then move in towards the spot that was no longer being watched. Ruadh's response was a sharp nod.

Annis tucked his axe into its harness and collected sands into his fists, reaching for where it was coarsest and driest. As he did so, the raiders sprang into action. Those brave enough after witnessing the previous slaughter were darting back and forth, spears in hand, stealing the attention of that dreaded horsehead and its spine-chilling screams, only for another to dart in opposite and snatch its attention back.

He began to stalk around to where the outcroppings of the dune covered his approach as close to the beast as possible, waiting patiently as the raiders gradually regained their confidence, falling back into the calming repetition, like a ritual cast with their feet and spear tips. Gradually they drew nearer, spears darting out, ensuring that at no point was the beast being torn in its attention too swiftly to allow it to focus on any one of its potential victims.

The scythe-arm flashed out, cutting three spear points short, the hooves stamping at the ground and rearing up, head snapping back and forth.

His moment.

Annis darted forward, launching his way out from the dune and turning sharply to angle his approach opposite to the latest raider to step forward, in order to catch the beast's attention.

His feet hit the crimson stain in the sand and immediately dropped through the surface, the red sands reaching up in bloody tendrils to seize hold of his calves, his progress brought sharply to a halt.

His heart leapt, his vision narrowing to those mad, rolling eyes that spun towards him. His hand lashed out, the sand flying straight into those horrible spiralling white orbs, and it reared as the screams tore free through the ribs jutting out between its thrashing hooves.

The creature's hand swung about and struck Annis in the chest, pitching him back and slamming him into the ground, feet still held fast in the writhing blood-soaked sands. The air was punched from his lungs, and as he gasped for breath, he felt the sand begin to wrap around his arms and torso, holding him tight, his vision swimming as he desperately tried to grasp what was happening.

There were shouts as more of the raiding party rushed forward, filling the space created by the beast's blindness. He saw spears flash overhead, then splinters falling about him as the scythe whipped past, warm flecks of blood splashing across his face.

But the sands were loosening now, relaxing with every thump of the creature's hooves stamping down nearby, with every spear that passed by overhead, with every yelled reply to that choir of screams now echoing over a gasping gurgle.

Just as Annis managed to wrest one arm free, a body crashed down nearby, or at least a pair of legs did – the torso nowhere to be seen. He squirmed until the handle of his axe fell into his free hand, pulling it clear and bringing the blade down on the tendrils that held his other arm in place.

He was some distance from the creature now, the chaos barely discernible as the raiding party piled in past him. Further hacks at the sand freed his feet and Annis staggered upright as the blood congealed in the sand around him, his hand wrapped around his aching ribs while he sucked shallow lungfuls of air. He stumbled forward, his hand held tight against his chest, as every now and then blood flew high into the air from the scrimmage, and the crowd stumbled before surging back in.

His vision clearing, he watched as Hengist and three others seized hold of the scythe-arm as it swung back for another sweep, Ruadh towering above them all as his axe crashed into the seized arm, the bone splintering beneath the blade. He swung again, his red hair slicked back and darkened by the remains of those who had already fallen.

Again, Ruadh's axe fell, and again the bones splintered as the beast screamed. Again, it fell, and the limb was severed, breaking free, with everyone who had held it falling back as the beast reared and brought its hooves crashing down upon them.

Annis staggered forward, picking up speed and shoving his way through the ranks until he was close at hand, watching as a dozen spears plunged into the beast's flanks. One impaled the still-grinning skull high above them as the spear tip broke free through one socket while the remaining empty eye gazed sightlessly down towards them. He raised his own axe and brought it down as hard as he could onto the beast's back.

They hacked and they hacked, the blood spraying across their arms and faces, the bucking beast held down with spear and oar, its screams drowned in the sound of flesh being torn apart with every descending blade.

Then it was over, at last. What remained was little more than a pile of broken bone and torn flesh, the marks of its long and miserable death caked across the fronts of every last raider who had participated in bringing it about.

Wordlessly, they adjusted their grip on their weapons and turned up the beach towards the dune where the sounds of battle still echoed over the bay, stumbling around the eviscerated bodies of the fallen as they went.

Their work was not yet done.

They crested the dunes silently, clambering through the reeds and descending into the grass-caped defenders beyond like a blood-soaked wave. Svana's formation had held their place with a ring of shields and spears, and those that had gathered around them fell swiftly when trapped between the shields and the oncoming tide of axes and swords that swept down from the dune.

Beyond the bodies, the captains organised the crossing of the bog ahead, spear butts advancing to trigger the traps within and those who had already fallen were dragged out to the beach to join the dead on the sands.

Annis found Svana and she offered him a silent clasped hand and nod, eyes drawn to the blood splattered across his face and the hand held close across his chest. For a moment he wondered if this is how Fiadh felt every time she returned through her portals from the place beyond.

From here, past those making their way step-by-step through the peat, he could see the village beyond. A scattering of hardened-mud huts with thatched roofs, collected below the great dome of grass and rock that dominated the centre of the island. Stone slabs framed a gaping hole facing the homes from the flank of the hill, disappearing below a rocky outcrop mid-way up its side.

He knew little of the way of Fiadh's kind, but he'd be damned if that didn't look every bit like the lair of a great and powerful spirit of the land. No one builds themselves a giant hill fort unless they intend to make sure no one doubts just how important they are.

After some time, a shallow rocky path was visible through the bog and the raiding party weaved their way through it, plunging spears along the way to mark where the path ran. Between the scent of kelp and the peat held tight by the fog bank, the air felt heavy, each breath more laboured than it should have been without a strong sea breeze to carry it away.

Through it all the only sound was the trudge of boots and mutters of those pointing the way to others. Their eyes darted across the horizon, searching the silhouettes of the buildings, the mist-shrouded hills arrayed around them. Nothing replied.

The village was abandoned. Fire pits filled with steaming peat showed no embers. No doors were shut against them, and no windows were shuttered. The raiders moved from home to home, each one coming up empty. More gathered at the central hall, built seemingly with whatever few trees had clung to this isle against the storms, and forming the only timbered walls and tall beams of the settlement. Again, the great double doors lay open.

Annis stayed back as Svana and Ruadh organised the entry, hands readjusting their weapons, eyes flitting back and forth at imagined noises. But, as he sat and took in the clearing before the doors, the first sounds that echoed from the hall were cheers. Shortly afterwards, a crowd exited carrying aloft a chest practically overflowing with bronze, brass, and gold. Ahar's treasure was won: a journey justified; losses paid for.

Years earlier, the coins falling from the chest as it lurched on their shoulders would have commanded Annis' rapt attention. But now all he felt was exhaustion, the energy of the fight fading from his limbs and leaving an ache in his ribs. The coin would be divided later, and Svana would ensure he had his due before taking Ahar's share for keeping Fiadh aboard despite her own gold running short, long ago. There was no need for him to rush.

Crouching, Annis sat back on his heels, looking only at the deep boot-prints in the mud between his feet. In those grooves, just for a moment, he saw the shape of the empty sockets of a grinning skull, the long unnatural ribs jutting freely into the air, a disembodied limb falling to the ground. He screwed his eyes shut and shook his head, but there was no escape. The layered screams echoed in the back of his skull, the scythe-arm sweeping down again, and again.

He took a long, shuddering breath, opened his eyes, and began to look around for anything else that might distract him. No one would be rushing to disturb him. His bizarre errands for Fiadh over the years had become a common sight for Ahar's crew and no doubt word had spread among the others since the ships were merged into his raiding fleet.

He found what he needed to distract him nearby, half-buried in the mud, maybe dropped or thrown before the area was churned up by the raiders: two lonely prongs of wood jutting out into the air.

Tucking his axe into his belt, Annis bent and lifted the object free, finding it barely larger than his hand. He ran a hand over its surface, smoothing away the mud that coated it to reveal the intricate carvings beneath. A horse, carved out of a light-coloured wood, swirls and knots streaming from its mane into its coat. For a brief moment, in this quiet corner of the clearing, he was taken back to another time where he had seen another carved just like it.

"Annis!" The boy's shout lifted him from his reverie.

Rian was scampering across the space towards him, slipping and sliding in the mud, waving one arm over his head as if his shout had not already grasped his attention.

"Rian! Whit ..." he managed before being interrupted.

"Ah ken ye said dinnae come," he gasped after coming to a stop, hands on his knees. "But she insisted, she did! Efter the beast oan the beach, she said she hud tae come here."

"Whae ..." Annis began, but he already knew. With a hand on the boy's shoulder, he looked across to where she stood, wrapped tightly in layers of cloaks, crouched low with one arm bound across her chest and the other holding the wall of one of the empty homes.

Beneath that hood shone a golden eye, fixed on the great hill towering behind the hall.

"... Craw." He finished, simply, giving Rian's shoulder a squeeze as he considered what to do. So far, at every step of their journey, it was Fiadh's moon-struck eyes which had guided the way through the strangest of paths. Now, denied that vision of the beyond, she was more a liability than an asset, even in seeking her own ends. She knew where it was, but not what lay in wait for them.

"Lad," he dropped his voice, careful that it would not carry across the space. "Ah ken ye hide a great many things, but skill wi blade or ghosts isnae among thaim. Git yersel back tae the ship!"

"Ah can help!" Rian protested.

"Help? How?" he grumbled, eyes on Fiadh, wary of her trying to move across the clearing past the raiders showing off their claims.

"Ah've, Ah've been watchin her, Annis," Rian stuttered, gaining confidence when he regained Annis' attention. "When ye've been ashore, when ye needed things fetched frae the ship. Ah learned her ways, the signs she marked, Ah copied thaim doon an Ah'm good at learnin!"

Annis grunted, remembering the few times he'd noticed Rian hanging about after his errands for them were done, marking it down as simple boyish curiosity.

"She cannae see the way but mebbe Ah can be her hauns if she needs," Rian continued, his tone as earnest as it had ever been.

Annis frowned as he considered Rian's words and moved past him towards Fiadh's place at the entrance of the clearing. She knew where she was going. Anything else could be decided when they arrived.

"Fiadh?" Annis asked tentatively as he approached her hunched figure.

"We're nearly there, Annis," she gasped, her breathing laboured. "I can see where the path ends, I can hear the clamour of her refuge calling to me."

Annis looked around at the tumult of the clearing and swore to himself. As if he didn't have enough problems without the one who had been his guide so far now being unable to even distinguish between the sounds that were her only clue to what was happening around her.

"Almost there, lass." He returned his hand to its familiar place on her shoulder, opposite the fell blade that lay across the other. "A short walk an we've made it, whaurever *it* may be."

Fiadh nodded and he shifted his grip to guide her around the side of the celebrating raiders. As they neared the opposite side and the steps that led into the hill, a few peeled away to join them, mostly members of Ahar's own crew who had been with them through the years.

Hengist was the first to catch up. "This it?" he asked, matter-of-factly.

Annis grunted; his pace was slowed by Fiadh's need to feel the way down each stone step with her feet.

"Reckon there'll be mair gold fur us inside?" he continued, and when Annis turned to him, he saw eyes lit up with greed. The kind of greed that could lead a man to overstretch and get himself killed, whether over dice or a raid.

"Whitever is within is no fur us tae take," Annis said.

"Why no? We've conquered the isle, so whitever remains is oors by right," Hengist huffed.

"Are you prepared to bet your soul on it?" came a voice from behind them, as Svana made her way to the steps to join them.

Hengist stammered and muttered to himself. It was a lesson hard learned by the crew that contradicting the captain's right hand was the preserve of a fool.

The stairs descending erratically from the clearing in the abandoned settlement were formed of barely shaped lumps of stone. On their way they passed upright stones carved with scenes depicting some form of saga, various figures battling, meeting, praying, offering. Their sides were notched with markings Annis did not recognise, lines crossing the corners of the stone in regular patterns like a tally or script.

It was a while into the descent before Annis noticed a change in Fiadh's steps. It was not the exhaustion he had come to expect in her movement. Instead, she seemed to cease searching for the next step of the climb and stood more upright, and it was not long before she, too, noticed the line-marked stones. She paused at one, running her free hand's fingers along the etchings.

"Ye can see!" exclaimed Rian, practically racing to her side to capture any wisdom she might be about to impart about their surroundings.

"A little," she replied, still sounding as if she were speaking from a far-off place. "It seems we have come to the place where my wish has guided me, and whatever balance was struck with my sight departs with the way forward. We're here."

Rian skirted around her, trying to absorb what little could be gleaned from her words and gestures. Annis shooed the boy away with a wave and used the hand on Fiadh's shoulder to guide her back down the stairs. As much as the raiders may believe the battle was over, he did not trust this place yet.

The final steps revealed a cavern buried beneath the side of the slope, lit only by the gaping wound in the rock that opened the clearing's domed roof to the sky. It was a wide circular space of smooth stone wreathed with moss and vines. Standing stones stood around its edge, part buried into the rock, and in its centre a circle had been etched into its floor, with various symbols arrayed around it. Beyond what may have been the entrance to a cavern stood, but the space was blocked by stone of a different hue – a giant circular door graced by patterns familiar to Annis from Fiadh's rituals, and from the fabrics of the Daoine he had mingled with in the towns and villages along the way.

Fiadh walked ahead as those who had followed them gathered at the base of the steps. She began moving from pillar to pillar examining them, moving alone now but still seemingly unable to see clearly enough through the shadows without standing at arm's length from what she was attempting to decipher.

Rian scampered over to join her, taking in the maze of carved symbols for himself as the others made themselves comfortable. As time passed, Annis trudged back up the steps and clambered onto the grassy mound to seat himself beside the opening, looking back out on the scattering of homes around them. The light was beginning to fade quickly now, dimming beyond the clouds. It had been at Fiadh's insistence that they land so late, no doubt for some arcane purpose he had not thought to question.

Hengist dropped himself down beside him, announcing his arrival with a slap on Annis' thigh as they took in the view. They sat in silence for a moment.

"What wull ye dae when she's found it?" Hengist said, after a pause. "When she finally goes back tae whaur she's meant tae be."

Annis shrugged, "Ah dinnae ken whaur she's meant tae be."

Hengist grunted in reply and didn't continue, though Annis could tell he was tempted. Annis, however, preferred the silence. If only all his companions were so willing to indulge the silence Fiadh and Hengist had learned to respect, instead of feeling the need to explain their every wish and intent.

The silence did not last, however. The darkness had begun to sweep between the hills, the raiders in the village claiming what gold they thought they could get away with before the hoards would be returned to the ships. As shadows fell on the hall the chest began its move out from the clearing, only for those same shadows to begin to move.

Drums sounded from the valleys, echoing down from the sharp needles of rock that crested the hills, and the denizens of this hidden isle revealed themselves.

Hengist stood up quickly before Annis had time to make sense of what had alerted him, clashing the haft of his spear against the stone steps as a warning to those below. Even as he did so, the shadowed figures swept down towards the village, their form breaking into charging ranks of warriors in black cloaks, their short blades glinting in the fading light.

Why? Why now, with the day done, the gold taken, with Fiadh already within the hill? Annis ran his hand over the handle of his axe, filling his chest with air even as his ribs creaked against the strain. It did not matter. All that mattered was that they did not end what Fiadh had yet to finish herself.

Svana was first out up the steps and Hengist wasted no time shouting over to her. "Sjef, we're getting cut off."

He was right, the dark-cloaked mass was sweeping into the settlement between them and the rest of the raiding party. The retreating force had also noticed the threat, a rearguard swiftly coming together in a shield wall and marching step-by-step behind those bearing the chest that were still making their way through the marsh.

Annis stepped down to the ground and turned towards the steps as most of the rest of those who had followed them into the dark emerged. He moved between them, making his way towards the descent before Svana's hand struck his shoulder, nearly punching it back with the heel of her hand.

"Where are you going?" she hissed. "We're done here, we all have what we came for, it's time to go."

Annis glanced down to where the faint light of torches that had been lit below illuminated the small space. Fiadh was before the door at the far side, slamming the knife-edge into the stone again and again, carving a track with every strike, Rian crouched alongside her.

"It looks lik Ah'm gaun intae a hill," Annis said, unable to resist his usual shrug even as he saw the anger it inspired from Ahar's second.

"This is madness, Annis," Svana snarled "We don't go into the barrows of the dead, we do not meddle with the affairs of gods and álfar, we know the stories, we know their tales end in nothing but loss." She crossed in front of him, scar-etched features glaring up at his own.

"Ah made a promise an Ah intend tae keep it," Annis said.

Svana spat. "A promise to what? A monster!" She flung her arm down towards Fiadh and the boy. "Those who play games with promises lead all who play by their rules to miserable fates. You've been with her long enough; you've carried her to where she wanted to end it all."

She noticed his brows crumple at that and her hand snatched hold of his jaw, practically forcing it to follow her gesture.

"Look at her, damn you! She's crumbling away, there's nothing left of her, she's marching to her death and there's nothing that'll await you at her grave," she said.

Annis raised his arm and brushed her hand away, taking a step back from her glowering expression.

"Then it'll be a grave fur the baith ae us, an we'll huv tae dig oor way oot," he replied. He stepped away from those at the entrance and out to where the battle had rejoined the settlement below. The fighting had reached the clearing now, those raiders who had been too slow to finish their search for loot among the homes being overwhelmed.

"Go, Svana," he said, more quietly now. "Save yer ain an Ah'll save mine, an Ah'll see ye oan the ither side. Dinnae hesitate, an remember Fiadh warned a storm wis comin, so launch the ships as soon as ye can return tae them."

He paid no heed to her snort of derision and did not count the footsteps that followed her as she gathered her closest warriors and headed back out to where combat had been met in the settlement. When he turned, only a handful remained their fear of Svana's judgement outweighed by their curiosity as to what wonders might lie beyond the portal before them. Most surprisingly, perhaps, the giant Ruadh stood grinning among them, his freckled arms knitted loosely across his chest.

If what awaited them was the last thing they saw, Annis hoped it would at least be a sight that was worthy of that honour.

***

When the light sparked beneath her knife, Fiadh knew she had finally completed the circle, carving the final rune that had been scoured away by water, vines, and time. She knew her companions could not see it, but her heart leaped as the light spread from the stone beneath her fingers and swept around the hall, filling it with the ghostly glow of magics long faded from the world.

Within moments it ran along the carvings and to the great round door, lighting the whole surface in an intricate dance of knots and pictures of gods and tales of times long left behind.

How long had this way remained closed? Had the Raven remained shut behind the stone? How had she spread her influence out into the world, twisting the minds of warriors and lords across the waves to set sail and light the fires that burned Tur Eumor.

As the light of the engraved door filled the space, she noticed the darkness remained to her left. She turned, and it turned with her. Gingerly, Fiadh raised the fingers of her good hand to the left side of her face and felt the scar that had been carved into her features in the storm at Kempe Fell.

It continued across her cheek, breaking open into a wide, cracked gash. One that continued as far as her eye, an eye that no longer saw her hand crossing before it. Her stomach jumped as her fingers ran over the cracks, feeling no more than the pressure of her hand on skin that was stiff and unyielding beneath her touch.

Pulling her hand away, she frantically began to unfold the furs that were wrapped around her, peeling away the layers of wool and leather beneath to reveal the arm that had also been damaged in the wreckage of the storm. As she pulled the bindings away two objects dropped into them, tumbling to the floor among the cloths.

She felt her knees strike the stone before she realised she had fallen, the scabbard of Caerdrich scraping the floor at her back, her partial sight fixed on the broken remnants of the hand that she had not seen for so long, hiding it away from view while she had been incapable of admitting what she had lost.

Staring back at her was a broken ruin of a hand, the wound at its centre spreading up in a black crevasse that split it almost from her wrist to the two fingers that remained. She willed them to move, but they did not respond, instead answering her only with pain that stabbed up from her wrist, from flesh that only now realised what had been taken.

Her insides knotted and Fiadh retched, hunching over as her whole body rebelled, seeking to expel the poison of death's grip but finding nothing within her that could be exhumed. Her good hand slipped on the stones, her mind reeling, dazed, spinning so the ground was the sky, and she had no purchase to steady herself.

Then, a hand clasped her shoulder. Smaller and lighter than she was accustomed to, but the spinning stilled, and the world began to return to focus.

"Let me wrap it." She heard the boy's voice, though it still sounded so distant from her. She could not tear her eyes from those limp fingers even as he began to return the binding, only finally closing her remaining eye to the image as the cloth wrapped around them and he returned the wool half-cape to her shoulder.

Fiadh used her good hand to push herself to her feet, only then seeing that they were not alone. Annis stood with his back to them, blocking the entrance with his axe in hand, flanked by a group of others from the ships. Some she recognised, some she did not.

Closest to her, a giant of a man crowned with a mane of red hair had his own gaze fixed on the door behind her, his eyes following the runes. It took a moment for her to register the familiarity she felt of that gaze, of the steely determination and confidence of a man born into power. She recognised the eyes of Eònan beneath those heavy brows, the stature of a new Rìgh of Ghav Rhien.

Maybe she was not the only one here whose mind was filled with the promise of revenge.

Movement at the opening of the hall grabbed her attention and she saw Annis and the remaining companions backing away from it, the light dimming as more figures filled the space. Black-garbed warriors filed in, even as Annis and the other raiders fell back, outnumbering the party three-, then four-to-one.

Then they halted and stood in silence, watching.

"Whit are they waiting fur?" Rian whispered, as Annis stepped towards them, never turning his back on the hosts that had gathered.

He didn't answer the boy, instead asking a question of his own to Fiadh. "When wull the way be open?"

"When the sun sets," she replied, pulling a leather cord from her free shoulder. Hanging from it, glinting against her eyes in the silvery light of the runes etched into their surroundings, was the horn retrieved the first time he had accompanied her to uncover the mysteries of her past.

"Take this," she said, handing Annis the delicately engraved bronze instrument. "Whatever we find within, when she is distracted, sound it. It is our only hope once we are beyond this door. Do you understand?"

"Aye," he said, as he always did, no matter what her requests. "An why won't *you* be able tae soond it?"

"She will have eyes only for me ..." Her words were cut off as there was a shift in the space, the raiders clustering closer to the door and the black cloaks parting before a new arrival. Between them walked a horrifying chimera of bare flesh and sinew, blood running from gashes across its flanks and limbs even as they knitted themselves back together, a sightless skull lolling upon the torso grafted to the beast's back.

The sole eye the beast retained stared at her from the horse's head protruding before it. Fixed on her, waiting.

"Fuck," whispered Annis, and she understood completely.

The silence stretched between them. One group, exhausted and terrified, crowded near the circular door. The other, collected, faces covered in the company of that horrific beast, blocking the only other way out. Its hooves pawed the ground, a red stain beginning to seep into the carvings in the stone, smothering their light.

"Why are we no deid?" came Rian's whisper at last.

"Because they want us alive, for whatever awaits us beyond, for those of us whose arrival they awaited." It was the large heir of Ghav Rhien who answered him.

Fiadh did not have to see him to know his eyes were on both her and the blade across her back.

The light silhouetting the cloaked figures dimmed, their torches beginning to flicker and fade, but no one moved or dared disturb the silence further. Until, finally, Fiadh felt a breath of cold air upon her neck and turned to see the circular door beginning to give way, splitting into sections along the myriad designs in its surface before tumbling into the shadows beyond.

She met Annis' eyes for a moment, gave him a small nod, and stepped into the dark.

***

She was in a long, stone corridor. But it wasn't the rough natural rock of the Raven's isle. Instead, it was smooth, perfectly carved granite hewn from the very mountain through which it led. Torches flickered in the dark and the smell of sea spray was replaced by the rough tang of charcoal in the air, the thickened years of dust kicked up by her footsteps.

No, *no*! She'd been shown this before, she knew how this vision, this memory, ended – with her first time lifting Caerdrich's scabbard, her flight through the halls of Tur Eumor, her fall from the cliffs as her home burned, denied the strongest weapon that might have turned back the playthings of the Raven.

The corridor flashed, and Eònan's face gazed into the fire he had lit to consume his kin. The flames rushed out and coalesced to the sightless visage of Sæunn, the grief of a loss she could not understand etched into her face as she was lifted from the rubble of her home. It was all washed away, and a young man drowned, dragged beneath the waves screaming for the woman he'd laid claim to upon the shore.

The sights twisted, faded, and suddenly there was light, shining from the entrance of the cave to her back. She turned and saw the huddle of children, a dozen perhaps, gathered in a sudden silence. Then they were gone, and the light drifted instead through the fog clinging limply to burned timbers and corpses scorched black, twisted and frozen in the moment of their deaths. The ruins of The Three Willows, the land purged of every trace of her passage.

The beams rose, shaking off their ashes and forming around her, lifting her from the ground, sweeping away the fog and filling the space with the memory she had almost forgotten, from so long ago.

She was in a room just off a bustling street, the voices outside clamouring among rolling wagons and the laughter of drunks. There she stood gripping the parchment written to a newly appointed priest in a far-off village, standing over the body of the author she had struck down upon learning how close he had come to opening a way beyond the veil. In her hand she held the drawings of a golden contraption she now knew the path to.

The death that began her journey to this distant isle beyond the mist. Just one moment, knife in hand, coaxed to drawing blood by the feeling of icy fingers crawling up her neck from the blade at her back.

"ENOUGH."

The word erupted from behind her, smashing down the walls, sending the contents of the room flying across the empty space beyond. The deep echoes bounced back from the emptiness. Caerdrich had spoken, and the visions were shattered.

She was left, shivering, hand clutched over her head, kneeling in dark water that reflected her fractured features back to her. Two feet came to a halt in the pool before her and she took Annis' proffered hand to help her from her knees, revealing the expanse of this realm that lay within the sìd of the Raven.

The hall's floor was no more than a vast expanse of water, as if a shallow pool had been left to fill the void that stretched into the forever beyond them. Great pillars of perfectly smooth stone reached up either side of them, arching out far above and into the night's sky itself, where the full moon glowed unnaturally close, its light shimmering as it reflected off the water and lit the space before them. Beyond the horizon, however distantly it lay, a spear of stars jutted outwards, scattered as if spun out by a giant disk too far away for them to touch.

"What did you see?" Fiadh asked, her hand still in Annis'.

"Ah saw little of interest," he replied, his voice stony. "Ma faither wisnae kind tae me, but this place doesnae ken me."

The others were here as well, arrayed as they had been before, stepping through the doorway that they had entered, somehow only to be now standing here in the centre of this empty place. Rian hugged himself, arms wrapped tight with his eyes darting this way and that. The Rìgh of Ghav Rhien ran a hand down his face, eyebrows furrowed in a fury that unnerved her.

The others were similarly distressed. Two had already drawn their weapons and another simply stared up to the sky, his hands limp by his sides. Games, she knew. The Raven wished their minds weakened so they were more susceptible to her manipulations. Such was the ways of the Baobhan Sìth, the dark blood-drinking mirrors to her Order of the Sciathán Dubh.

The red-headed giant of Ghav Rhien was the first to take a step, and the noise of the water he displaced sounded like thunder, echoing out into the dark. From the shadows they responded: two dozen warriors in the same black cloaks of those who had blocked their way on the isle, manifesting as if woven from the darkness itself.

Fiadh snarled. Those black cloaks sat over the leather wraps worn by her Order so long ago. But from behind those dark hoods, it was not the gleaming eyes of her kind that stared back, but empty sockets ringed with white bone.

What monstrous fate had the Raven subjected the servants of the Rìaghan to, after their defeat? To trap them here, a sealed realm beyond the world they had sworn to protect, as mere shadows of their former selves. As a perverse trophy of her victory? As a reanimated guard of her own? Or simply as apparitions to mock the last Crow she had left behind?

"Where is she?" the Rìgh of Ghav Rhien bellowed. "Where is the Red Queen of the Eilean Fitheach?"

The black-clad figures, ringed around them in the same silence they had experienced from their living companions on the isle they had left behind, did not move. The leather handle of Annis' axe creaked under his grip, broken by the sound of water sloshing as another of the companions adjusted his footing and levelled a spear towards their welcoming party.

"Welcome." The word drifted softly across the space, comforting, gentle, and its source stepped out into the starlight.

She drifted across the water almost as if carried by it, her bare feet leaving ripples in their wake, her pale skin barely visible beneath the red cloak drawn around her shoulders and the hood pulled down over her eyes. Dark gloves hid her hands from view and as she drew closer Fiadh noticed she was not even as tall as her or Rian, her diminutive stature not quite hidden by the heavy cloth that trailed behind her, held aloft on a breeze Fiadh could not feel.

Two dozen footsteps away she halted, and as she raised her hands outstretched, a stone table rose from the pool between them, the water sloughing off its surface to reveal eight platters, one for each of them, with eight stone stools rising behind them.

"M'eudail, sit, please," the Raven said, her mother tongue dancing from her lips like a song. "My home is as if it were yours."

None of them moved. A couple of the raiders exchanged glances, but Fiadh and Annis kept their eyes fixed on their red-garbed host. Again, Fiadh heard the creak of Annis' hand tightening around the leather of his axe's hilt.

The Raven shrugged, raised her hands, and flicked her fingers towards them.

Fiadh's stomach lurched as her feet were swept up from underneath her and she was dragged through the air forward and deposited roughly down onto one of the stone stools. She found her hands placed upon the table either side of her platter, now suddenly filled with bread and meats. Beside her the other companions sat, similarly dragged to their new seats.

The Raven drifted forward to her own seat opposite them, and gently sat. One at a time she peeled the gloves back from her hands and began to pick at one of the wings magicked before her.

Her hands were stained black from the fingertips all the way up her forearms, and Fiadh felt her lip twitch back into a snarl. How many innocents had lost their lives to preserve her place in the world? How many had their blood drawn to maintain her youth and power? How many futures snuffed out, just like hers, to feed whatever machinations she had unleashed into the world?

She paused after a few bites, her head turning to each of them beneath the hood.

"Aren't you hungry?" she asked, her voice a smooth caress. "I assure you, there is no trickery here, my people worked long and hard to sustain themselves on this isle and this is the bounty of their faithful labours."

"You took this land ..." The Rìgh of Ghav Rhien began to growl.

"Ist," the Raven snapped, and his mouth clapped shut at her command. "It is not your turn to speak."

She turned back to Fiadh. "These mortals have such limited imaginations," she said. "They truly believe that just because they cannot remember a time before themselves, that it never existed, that the people whose graves they trample over never lived and toiled just as they did, that they stand on the legacies of the waves of those who came before. Different men, different beings, different gods. All claiming to have discovered the place that was truly shaped by those who came before."

She did not seem to mind the silence of her audience, nor did she grace any but Fiadh with her attention as she continued.

"To take this land, the soil, the seas, to describe it as if it was owned, and that I own it now. It's land. No one has dug it up and piled it into cellars to keep and sell for cloth or gold."

"This place, however? I built this; I own this. I poured my blood and sweat into the first cave that I dug into this very hill with these very hands, before his folk had even learned to speak. Those who have been born in its shadow are not mine by right. They swear to me of their own free will. I give those who swear loyalty to me protection, shelter and purpose."

She placed the leg she had been holding back down on her plate, considering the platter carefully. Her next words had a new edge, as her hand curled into a fist.

"I have not taken anything."

Her other hand drummed on the stone, but as she turned her head down the table she was met with silence. The red-haired giant, meanwhile, seemed ready to tear the table in half to reach her, his knuckles white against its surface. Her hooded face came to rest on him again, and, seemingly tired by the lack of engagement, she raised her hand once more.

"You may speak now," she said, exasperated, and with a flick of her wrist released a gasp from the now freed Rìgh.

"What is your name?" he shouted, filling the quiet with the voice he had been denied. "So I might commit it to my soul and haunt you long after my body is gone!"

The Raven shrugged, raised her hands as the Rìgh's mouth was forced closed once more, and drew her hood back from her head.

Fiadh's heart hammered in her chest, and she gasped in horror as the Raven revealed herself.

Her skin was pale as frost, her hair fading to a dark auburn beneath the red flame that spilt into a loose braid pulled across one shoulder. She was youthful, or at least seemed it, her smooth features suggesting a girl barely ready to leave home to find one of her own.

Above pink lips and a subtle touch of warmth upon her cheeks blazed eyes that shone with the silver of moonlight, brighter than any Fiadh had ever seen. Mirrors of her own, flashing with the very same gift of the Rìaghan. She was a Crow, a member of the devout Sciathán Dubh, keepers of the weave, warriors of its purpose.

She smiled, a small pull of her mouth towards those glinting eyes. Those eyes called to Fiadh in a way that unnerved her. Her mouth felt dry, her feet torn between standing to move closer and being pulled deep into the pool below to escape.

"She knows my name," she said, her eyes boring into Fiadh's own. "Don't you, Fiadh?" Those lips spoke, and Fiadh understood.

She knew the Raven's name. She understood, now, that it had all been connected. Everything from the fall of the gods to her arrival in this hall. All the scheming of this one fallen wing of the Rìaghan.

Her name was Caitlin, and she had been there from the very beginning.

But that smile was not friendly; it did not touch the faint creases at the edges of her eyes; it did not soften the arch of her brows that curved with such easy malevolence. The Raven was mocking her, toying with her prey, revelling in letting her audience dance for her amusement.

She'd been locked away in this realm of her own creation for dozens, maybe hundreds of years. She was bored. Boredom was a weakness. It led to distraction, so it might mean opening the only opportunity Fiadh had to break her spell and grasp the blade that begged to be the Raven's ruin.

She had to wait for her moment and make it seem like a natural shift. Tear their host's attention between Fiadh, the Rìgh, and her own story. Away from Annis.

"Are you not one of the Baobhan Sìth?" Fiadh asked. "How do you know who I am?"

The Raven sneered. Without the hood cloaking her expressions there was no sign she had kept her fabled gift of hiding her true intent, her voice continuing to betray her clear contempt for being questioned.

"Of course I know who you are," she said, her careful poise beginning to fade as she leant back into her chair. "I've known since you stepped foot on my rock. 'The Last Crow of Tur Eumor' they called you, wielding the cursed blade of Caerdrich. The fell blade, the final remnant of Eirian, the unassailable, I think I called him. A silly name, but he did so preen himself with it."

Her hand flicked lazily, as if the memory of her treachery was as banal a tale to discuss as one's morning meal.

"The very idea you could have hidden yourself from my eyes, that I would not have immediately known who you are, is an insult."

Her eyes blazed, and Fiadh saw in them an emotion that she had not seen before. Not pride, not spite or contempt, but pure unadulterated rage.

"I know what you are, revenant," she continued, both hands curling into fists. "I know you died in the seas below the Tur. I know the blade bound your soul to your corpse, that you can no more rid yourself of their chill touch than you can turn away from this petty quest that has led you to my hall. I, too, searched for a path to remain in this world and not be doomed to fade away as its denizens do. I found my answer digging up the secrets of our past. You simply threw yourself into the sea bound to an inanimate shadow of a god who had no choice but to raise you from death if they were ever to see land again. Your route was, I admit, the faster one. But what happens if I simply strip them away from you, cast them back into the sea to be forgotten, where they belong? You would fade faster than the leaves upon Samhuinn."

"So what?" Fiadh snapped. "Should I have turned my back on all we were taught, everything we pledged to the Ríagh ..."

"Do not say her name here!" the Raven interrupted, rising from her seat, both hands upon the table, the fingers arched as if to claw the stone from its surface. "Do not pretend you are on some honourable quest to serve out some final mission passed down into your hands alone. Do not judge me for turning my back when you have done the same!"

She flung herself back into her seat, her cloak drifting down upon its arms and back until she seemed to lounge in a sea of red.

"We were the same, you and I," her words drifted, her insistence replaced with a lethargy, her emotions turning so rapidly it was difficult to keep up. "Remnants of an Order long departed, of gods that forged us then abandoned us to flee their responsibilities. You do not remember, you are too young to know how mighty we were, how proudly we fought to protect our place in the world. Then *she* left."

"Did you ever wonder where she went?" she asked, though Fiadh knew she did not wish for an answer. "How long our Order wandered not knowing its purpose nor the will of the weave, long before that final gathering?"

"Why did you come back?" Fiadh asked, curling her hand around the handle of a knife on the table while the Raven's gaze drifted across the distant stars. "Why send the ships to Tur Eumor if you believed us so lost and aimless?"

A frown pulled on the Raven's lips, the creases barely hinting at her age even as the weight of years seemed to intone her every word. She continued her tale, barely acknowledging that it had been prompted by Fiadh's questioning.

"While once we Sciathán Dubh sought to protect the long threads of fate," she said. "Those who claimed to inherit her purpose were twisted by the temptations of that accursed blade upon your shoulders, enraptured by the shadow's obsession with punishing all of those who had abandoned them to their fate. They became hunters, mercenaries dedicated only to cutting out the remaining fragments of the past who dared to fight back against the end of our time on this earth. They arrived at the beck and call of weak, ignorant men to butcher the spirits and creatures who kept the magic of our world.

"No wonder they never taught you of the true nature of the Baobhan Sìth. Those of us who turned our backs after the fall and refused to be a part of their new purpose beneath a new master. Instead, they hunted my sisters wherever they hid, forcing them to find any means of survival. Forcing me to hide those of us I could save."

"Did you never wonder why all the portents of protecting the weave came down to this?" she asked, though her distant gaze continued to display her lack of interest in an answer. "All that knowledge, all that time learning the wonders that came before you, all dedicated to nothing more worthy than extermination. They would have snuffed out the light, erased everything we had built. So, I acted before they did, I learned from how my sisters learned, from the powers they used to pull on the weak souls of these mortal men and feed on their adoration. I did what was needed. That is my motivation; to seize the opportunity I was gifted from the ruins of what was stripped away."

Fiadh drew the knife back slowly, dropping her hand below the table just as the Raven's eyes snapped back to hers.

"You?" the Raven said, practically spitting the words. "You squandered it."

She stood, raising her hand once more, and the Rìgh rose from his seat and drifted over the table towards her, his every muscle taut as he fought against the magics which bound him. She lowered him to the pool, placing him on his knees before her seat.

"Revenge is such a trivial motivation," she said, her gaze now on the man turning crimson with his futile efforts of resistance. "I posed no continued threat to you. If you had fled the Tur, you could have vanished, faded away, built yourself a new life somewhere far from here. You could have found a new family and purpose. You could have surrendered, knelt when you saw the battle was lost, and walked into the arms of a new order on this isle.

"Instead, you took up the very thing that doomed all around you, throwing your life away to become a tool of their obsession, bound to a being that will gladly throw you away as soon as your corpse is of no further value, just as the blackbird would have done."

Fiadh felt them, now, not so silently, hearing their tale being retold by another. The ice-cold hand of the past began to creep across her shoulders, grasping at her skull, running down her arms and into the small blade she gripped below the table's rim.

"You forgot your kind, Crow, but I did not," the Raven continued, circling the Rìgh and running a dark fingertip along his chin. "You threw away a chance to rebuild in a new era, so I picked up the scraps left behind. You were young, still untainted by Eirian's stain. You could have been the pillar upon which I built a new order for this time of mortal kind, but instead you let yourself be consumed by the past and the rage of a blade that knows nothing but death. Leaving me to find such inferior servants as this."

She cupped the Rìgh's jaw and turned his face towards her, as the veins stuck out from his neck, his eyes quivering in their sockets behind his straining features.

"All I have done," she said, her eyes fixed on the Rìgh's own, hand still as the redness began to drain from his skin, the muscles beginning to ease in his shoulder, "is to ensure the High Chalice found that scrap of the weave I took from the weavers, granting the secrets of trapping the weavers of time to another, ensuring the god-fearing Rìgh of Ghav Rhien would not meddle any longer. I did a deal with the rulers of the sea to hide my isle and trapped the few who could undo the spell beneath the iron where Cuthac had left his mask. I made certain I would not be disturbed, that the Order of the Sciathán Dubh could be remade, and its purpose restored as it should have been, free of the blade's influence. All this I have achieved, and you have blindly stumbled across the land undoing it all. Your promise has been washed away in the shadow of the vengeful quest of another you never once stopped to question. Our Order was pledged to curiosity, to uncovering the knowledge we could pass down through the ages. Your lack of inquisition of the intent of one you hold so close is an embarrassment to our legacy."

"You ..." Fiadh said, the realisation hitting her like a rock. "You were the whispering one. This whole time, you were the voice from behind the veil."

The Raven smirked and did not deign to respond to Fiadh's moment of revelation. Even as the Rìgh's resistance began to melt in the hand of the Raven, Fiadh felt Caerdrich's own will begin to burrow into her mind, her vision narrowing to the Raven's neck. Not yet. Not quite. She needed to know more.

"Where is the blackbird?" Fiadh asked, careful not to try again to say the name of her goddess.

"She is as good as dead." Caitlin almost spat out words, her hand twisting to wrap tightly around the Rìgh's throat beneath eyes that now viewed her in near reverence. "You brought me the last key needed to finally bury her for good. Do you know how hard it is to kill a god? Well, Caerdrich does, I am sure, as you dangle from their blade like a puppet. If I cannot be rid of that blade, then they will be put to use to finish what I started. I will finally bury her beneath the heart of the Seann Àite."

There! That was it, what she needed, a final stone turned that might give her purpose beyond this hall. The Rìaghan still lived, and she knew where she could be found.

"But it is too late now," the Raven said, her attention still on the Rìgh whose resistance was crumbling in her hands. "You have made it clear that you pose a threat to me and mine, that self-interest is not sufficient motivation to prevent you becoming a threat again, too lost are you to the designs of that black blade."

"Such a waste." She gripped the Rìgh's hair, tilting his head back to reveal his relaxed neck to her. "What did you even come here for? What do you hope to achieve? To kill me in the source of my own power?"

"You don't think I can?" Fiadh asked, the darkness now gathering over her vision, cloaking everything but the target of the knife clenched in her fingers.

"I do not."

Fiadh moved faster than her body could possibly have imagined, the ice raising her seat to propel her onto the table and towards the Raven, forming beneath her feet to turn her flight into a fall directly towards her target, both hands clenched around the knife plunging down from over her head.

The Raven's head snapped towards her and, with one arm outstretched, she caught Fiadh in mid-flight by her throat. Her other hand caught Fiadh's own and with a twist flicked the knife through Fiadh's ruined palm to splash harmlessly into the pool below.

There was a clatter as the raiders broke free of their restraints and began to scatter around from the table, but it was over in a moment.

The Raven released Fiadh's hand, and with a wave they were still once more. She held the Crow aloft, still, dangling like a toy from her grip, Caitlin's expression one of bemusement.

Fiadh did the only thing she could think to do. She twisted her face and bit down hard into the palm that held her. Her struggle was rewarded with a hiss, and the world span as she was tossed across the hall and bounced to a bruised halt in the pool.

"A bite?" What began with a growl became a laugh as the Raven stared at her hand, then at Fiadh, and then back once more. "Who would have thought? We had even more in common than I could have known, you and I!"

The sound that followed made the water lurch, striking Fiadh so hard that the stars danced in her vision, every sensation swallowed by the bellow of the Horn of the Deeps. The sound echoed, though it had no walls to leap from, and it gradually faded until all was still once more. The Raven stood over her, her eyes fixed on where Annis had stood from his seat, the horn now fixed in his paralysed hand just inches from the mouth that had sounded it.

The Raven's expression twisted from bemusement into mirth.

"A horn?" She laughed; the sound as pleasant as wind chimes to conceal the spite of her words. "What a sorry descent from the hallowed halls of Tur Eumor to trading in rumours and superstition. What huntsman or wandering fool told you the secret to my heart was a horn, pray tell? Did they believe I had the ears of a bat? So sensitive to leave me numb and powerless before its onslaught."

"Really," she waved a hand dismissively, looking down her nose to where she'd tossed Fiadh into the water. "It is pathetic. It is time, I think, we finally bring this sorry story to a close."

The rumble began quietly at first, the faintest ripples emanating from every object in the pool. Caitlin's eyes widened as it grew stronger, the water dancing, her long-dead guardians beginning to draw their weapons and pull in closer.

Then it rose to a roar and the entire space shifted beneath them as if it had been punched by the fist of a true god. Fiadh was thrown across the floor, the sky and waters spinning before her cloak was caught in a wave and she was dragged under, her lungs immediately filling with the burning, frigid waters before she had a chance to take a breath.

The wave left her behind, leaving her to gasp and choke, holding herself up with a single arm above the dark surface, a surface that no longer reflected the bright light of stars.

Gone were the blue and indigo hues of the sky above that had lit the space, replaced now by the flickering amber glow of the few lanterns not extinguished by the wave. The yawning cavern was marked by jutting pillars of stone. They were not carved by human hand, but pyramids of congealed rock that had formed over aeons alone in the dark.

The Raven stood at the centre of it all, alone in the dank pool that filled the floor of the cave with her eyes fixed on the circular doorway across from her and the water that now ran down its surface. A door marked by the traces of the claws that had dug their way through so many years ago.

"What did you do?" she whispered, the contempt fading from her voice, the sound drifting, robbed of the weight of her illusion.

Whatever she said next was drowned by the scream of blades being dragged from their scabbards across the room. Before Fiadh even knew what she was doing, her own broken hand was raised towards the hilt of Caerdrich, ready to draw the fell blade into the light.

But it was stopped by a hand fixed like a vice around her wrist. She turned her head to see the Rìgh of Ghav Rhien towering over her, his other hand clenched into a fist. Below those craggy brows and the loose, damp fronds of hair that lay across his face, his eyes gleamed balefully towards her.

They glowed crimson, lit by the curse of the Baobhan Sìth.

Fiadh's struggles to release herself were in vain, and even the icy touch of Caerdrich themself could not free them, the lord's hand turning blue and then black as the water on its surface bristled into frozen peaks. Desperate, Fiadh pulled a knife from beneath her cloak and plunged it with all her strength into the man's thigh.

He did not even twitch.

She heard the splash of someone approaching and saw out of the corner of her eye the Raven wading through the now knee-deep waters. Her voice, no longer smoothed by her pervasive magical influence, now escaped as barely more than a hiss.

"What are you going to do?" she said, drawing nearer to stand beside her newly glamoured servant. "Pull the fallen champion free once more, to butcher and to maim as they have always done, sacrifice all those around you to their hunger? Would you sacrifice so many for nothing more than your revenge? Look at them, see their faces, know what you might do."

Fiadh looked past her, to where combat had broken out between the raiders and the Raven's long-deceased guard. Whatever spells had animated them had survived the waters pouring in to seal the sìd's entrance. The scene was far from desperate, and she watched Annis cut down one of the black-cloaked corpses, repeatedly hacking away at its limbs even as they attempted to recover from having their legs cut out from beneath them. Behind him Rian shouted to warn of another's approach, his own knife in hand.

A knife Fiadh recognised as one of her own. How long had she been so unaware of her surroundings? So unable to track even her own belongings? Had it been the single-mindedness of her pursuit, or the injuries she had suffered along the way?

As Annis' fist crashed through the skull of another assailant she saw wide-eyed hope in the boy's face. Fiadh couldn't remember the last time she'd seen that look, or had she simply stopped looking for it?

She was knocked from her trance as the hand that gripped her jerked back and she was pulled back into the water. Struggling to keep her footing and her head above ground, she caught glimpses of the Rìgh attempting to pull a man off him, one repeatedly plunging a short blade into his side. She recognised him. One of Ahar's men, Ciaran perhaps?

Another joined them, only to be hurled to the ground by the Rìgh's spare hand as he attempted to wade in close enough to swing. But Ciaran was behind him, shielded from the Rìgh's blows by his own bulk as one hand remained fixed around Fiadh's own, dragging her back and forth as he attempted to free himself of his nimbler assailant.

Gasping for air, Fiadh saw the Raven retreating back, her black cloaks forming in around her.

Then Ciaran landed a blow that plunged straight through the Rìgh's wrist, his fingers went limp, and she was freed.

Fiadh kicked free and splashed out of range, glancing about to try and capture how the clash was proceeding. One of the raiders was down, impaled by a collection of spears that had driven him into the waters. Annis seemed to have rallied a group and was advancing through the reanimated warriors in her direction. Ciaran and his companion were more than capable of handling the now one-armed Rìgh's attacks.

Perhaps this was it. Perhaps it all came down to those few who had come here, and the Raven would meet her fate at the hands of the very same peoples she had used to destroy the Sciathán Dubh. Perhaps, after all this time, she had nothing left. No machinations, no illusions, no final plan to beat back half a dozen raiders led by the single wounded Crow she had left to kill.

You forget, this is not your story.

The voice crashed through her thoughts anew, wiping them away and replacing them with their own. She felt the rage expanding in her chest, her relief overwhelmed by a growing craving to be freed.

She looked down to find her broken hand already upon the hilt of that dark blade, their scabbard hanging freely from her shoulder.

She did not hear the Raven speak, she did not hear anything, even as the dark cloaks that had been at Caitlin's side rushed towards her in a desperate bid to stop what was to come, to bind her before she could release that frozen fury. But it was too late, the water was too deep, and the remaining fingers of her hand had already wrapped around the black leather.

The ghostly light spilled free between the cross guard and sheath, the light of Cleddyf Llachar, the bright blade, the ghostly pale frost of Caerdrich, the ghost of the final fortress of the old gods. The light spoke to her. It wrapped its brilliant beauty around her mind and filled her with strength like she had never known before. All her pain was washed away, all her doubts and concerns drowned in the light. Fiadh's grip tightened hard on the hilt of Caerdrich. She felt their yearning, their delight, and she pulled.

The room darkened as the light was drawn to the blade, its corners bathed in shadow where the torchlight had once illuminated them, the strands of pale flame streaming through the air from the torches as the black metal emerged from their sheath.

Time slowed as she drew them forth. It wasn't light alone that Caerdrich drank. They fed on everything, every drop of life and warmth deep in this buried place. Their thoughts filled her senses, flooding her mind with broiling anger. The intensity flowed through her, her muscles tensing and teeth gritting, her heart hammering as if it sought to burst free of her chest. That rage was everything, it filled her sight and drowned out her hearing with its thunder.

Her moon-touched eye saw everything. She could see the fear begin to dawn in the raiders as their emotions raced beneath the surfaces of faces unable to register each one in time. So, they settled on the one emotion that would overwhelm all others who experienced the thirst of Caerdrich.

Dread.

The knowledge of what was to come long before it came for them. Knowing that they could not react fast enough to stop it, nor even to flee from it. Knowing that a blade that could drink from light and life itself would not be sated by merely one of them. Caerdrich's spirit began to rise from the blade, their black form gathering like smoke from their metal and from Fiadh herself, billowing above her shoulders into the vague shape of the monstrous creature they had been. Arms extended and dragged across the water, its surface freezing from the points of their claws. Great antlers reared up from the head of a slavering wolf whose eyes were bright stars shining out from the black. Pride, hunger, strength.

Everything the god had once been now distilled into the ghostly shadow that reared above her. The great warrior of the gods was gone, killed upon the mountain where they were found. Only the monster remained. The butcher, the murderer, the seething hatred of one whose only love was torn from them so long ago that they had forgotten who had taken them. This was the weapon the gods had unleashed on those who had challenged their rule, and now it was released, unchained, with no guidance other than that hunger for ruin.

Fiadh bathed in the fear she witnessed, wallowed in it, delight mingling with the anger.

The air about her froze, crystallising on all it touched, from the empty cups to the eyelashes of the raiders as their eyes stared at her in horror. They barely moved as the blade swept towards them, the air shattering into shards along her path as if reality itself was collapsing before their fury.

The first three erupted into streaks of red that rained down around her, the blade sweeping through them as easily as the air itself. She moved like the waves of a storm, skimming the ice-coated waters, Caerdrich rose up in her hands and crashed down to sunder chainmail and bone, blood spraying into a red mist spun in streaks through the air. She was coated in it, drenched in crimson as the blade rose and fell, their light piercing the frozen mist that filled the cavern where around its edge lay the crumpled bodies of all those who stood against them.

She towered over the Raven, ringed by those figures in black, her crimson hair streaming out in the wind whipped up by the blade's thunderous passage, a single hand raised against Fiadh and Caerdrich. Caitlin's mouth spoke words she could not and would not hear, a final attempt to weave the magics that had served her all these long years.

Caerdrich struck the Raven's hand like a hammer on glass. It disintegrated, and the last thing Fiadh saw of her was the shock of her own blood lashed across her features before they too were buried in the path of the blade. The black cloaks folded, collapsing into the water in an instant.

She came to rest on the pinnacle of a frozen wave, its surface stained in the red remnants of Caitlin. The blade sang, and it hungered. Fiadh turned upon her new frozen dais and took in the devastation before her, and the two that remained at the door of the chamber, having fled her passage before the others met their blade.

"It is done," she gasped, at last, shivering with the strength that coursed through her.

I will never be done, the voice thundered, the force of their will overwhelming her.

I am not your tool, Caerdrich raged, *to strike down only those you see fit, to collect only your revenge. I will take the world that was taken from me, and you shall be the bearer of my wrath.*

She raised the blade again, both hands locking around their grip, feeling the maw of Caerdrich's spirit looming over her, claws gripping her tight. She watched as Annis placed a hand on Rian's chest, guiding the boy to crouch behind him.

Begin.

She leapt across the space, the air before her shattering beneath the force of her passage, the claws of Caerdrich extended, their blade raised overhead.

Annis raised his axe and behind him and Rian's eyes filled with fear.

Those hazel eyes. She saw the eyes of the child left to die beneath the temple of the Three Willows so long ago, that had looked so similar. The fear that had been left frozen on their features, a victim of manipulations they could not possibly have understood. She saw Orlaith, walking alone in the dark, the terror of being lost in a place far from any home she had known. She remembered the face of Eònan, his haunted stare into the fires which he had lit for his kin, forever tormented by the lives he had sacrificed for power.

Everything slowed to a halt in the moment she fell from the frozen air, Caerdrich plunging from above her towards those who had been with her for so long.

I will not take the life of a child, she thought. I am not a butcher.

But you are, came the reply.

New images flashed, priests of the High Chalice dead at her feet, the people of the village she left doomed to die at their hands, Eònan drowned in the waters below his hall, the merchant of Tur Pailt screaming as his eyes were taken from him, the dead scattered within the hall of Ghav Rhien, the bodies she had staggered past to enter this final resting place, the flames licking about the walls of Tur Eumor as she tumbled from its cliffs.

The Raven, in her final moment, so small at the last, her brows furrowed in determination before rising in the realisation of the death descending upon her.

She remembered a voice warning her of what was to come.

Only death follows it.

Fiadh saw the boy hiding in Annis' shadow and she watched as Annis' face set in his own grim determination. There was no fear in his features, nothing to betray that he doubted what was approaching. But she saw the hint of sorrow tugging at his lips as he wrapped both hands around his axe's hilt.

Was that sorrow for her, or for Rian? She would never know.

But she was more prepared to see him lose one than the other.

She pulled on the strength Caerdrich had gifted her, drawing on the rage and funnelling it into her arms. Tearing one from the grip of the blade she reached down and pulled the darkness free of the other.

Her arm shattered, the cracks of her hand leaping up the length of the limb and tearing it asunder. The blade let loose a roar as it fell, tumbling away from her grasp even as she crashed into the water, breaking through the ice into the depths below.

She floated there for a moment, feeling the strength seep out of her into her frigid surroundings, seeing nothing but the pillars of light where Caerdrich's glow pierced the broken surface of the ice. It felt ... strange to be so far from them. An emptiness within her with nothing else to fill it, no drive or purpose to propel her forward.

Hands gripped her torso to drag her back out and onto the ice's surface. Fiadh felt like she should be gasping for air, but, as the wisps of strength began to fade from her, so too did the urge to breathe again.

Annis and Rian were busying themselves around her, but with what she did not know, nor did she care. It was peaceful, knowing she was at the end, knowing that the final page of her story was turning, and it was, finally, her choice to turn it.

Darkness swam at the sides of her vision, coaxing her eyes to close. But no, not yet, she still had to ensure what she had learned was not lost. Her remaining hand felt around in the dark until it found the cloth of Annis' britches, tugging on them until his face loomed over her.

"Annis," she whispered, pulling on the last wisps of energy to speak. "I need one final thing from you, please."

"Not now lass," he muttered, hand clasped around her own. "After ..."

"Ist," she said, she did not have time to delay. "The Rìaghan isn't dead. I need you to remember that. I need you to go to the ruins of the Three Willows, to the altar of Cernos on the hills behind it ..."

"Fiadh ..."

"Ist!" she insisted, though with the force of the command she felt the feeling drift from her remaining limbs. "Listen, I need you to find its keeper, tell them you have something for Orlaith, the last of her kind, that the Rìaghan is alive. She must know, Annis, she has to know that there's a chance to bring her back. Know you do not owe me; you have done everything you could have done. I leave only this final hope with you."

He did not speak, his eyes sternly fixed on her own, the world around them fading into the dark.

"Do you understand?" she breathed, her final breath escaping with the words.

He nodded and spoke. "She's gone lass, it's over, ye're free."

She tried to smile at that, one last time.

***

"Fuck," Annis muttered, as the moonlight faded from Fiadh's eye and it fell away from him, gazing out at nothing from her blood-soaked visage. Those eyes, which had always shone so eerily bright even in the night, finally lay dark, as if a hand had reached in and snuffed out the light. The hand wrapped in his own fell limp, and he slowly lay her head upon the stone.

Annis coughed against the tightness in his throat, and he let her hand slip down to her side.

"Huv ye worked it oot, lad?" he yelled over to Rian, who was sloshing back and forth through the water in front of the doorway out, where the water seeping through its cracks had slowed to a trickle.

"No yet!" he shouted back, glancing back and forth between the runes etched in its surface. "It's different frae the ither side, no all ae it matches up."

Annis sighed and stood, looking out into the cavern in front of him. Almost its entire floor was now covered in a sheet of ice, a sole white pillar beginning to emerge from it from where the sword had fallen. Here and there it was splashed with red, shining brightly in the pale light that still emanated from the blade. The air was thick with it, every ounce of moisture falling as soft snow, so much of it stained crimson by Fiadh's passage.

Some of the fallen still lay in pieces on its surface. Others had been cut down before the ice reached them and only a desperate hand or half of a face jutted out from beneath the surface. The black cloaks, where they had collapsed, looked like stains on the white expanse, the bones of the long deceased jutting from beneath the cloth.

The sound of ice cracking broke the silence, as the pillar that housed Caerdrich split along its length and the darkness that had spread from it and towered over Fiadh in her rampage began to spill out from its confines.

Annis cursed again, and snatched up his axe from the stone, watching as the darkness began to take shape.

Caerdrich was gathering themselves into a new form, free from the scabbard and their wielder. The darkness swept across the ice and began to pull from the dead, drawing together limbs and torsos into a horrifying amalgamation of flesh. The remnants of the beings that had come to this hall alive were contorted into an unnatural form, as if something larger had forced itself into the space of something small. It hunched, smoke as black as pitch rising from its exposed flesh, the skin of the dead wreathed in it as if to form a great cloak drawn about them.

Its feet made a stumbling, echoing step forward, then another, as a single face broke free of the smoke, darkness pouring from its slack jaw. A half-dozen blades were seized in its hands as the pale blade of Caerdrich themself shimmered in the ice beyond it.

One more step, and Annis watched it turn towards the Crow lying dead only feet away from him. He remembered a voice, a reminder he sorely needed.

Everything can die, Annis.

"Eirian, is it?" he growled, as he stepped forward into its path. "Ye cannae huv her, ye auld, deid, bastart."

They charged him with blades slashing the air haphazardly, feet sliding and stumbling across the ice. He moved forward to put distance between them and Fiadh's resting place, ducking below a wild swing and burying his own blade in its side. He tore it free and brought it down on one of the flailing limbs, letting it spin free as the darkness spilled from the opening.

Another swing ducked and he planted a foot against its side and shoved it back, stumbling. Pulling back, he watched as frost clung to his boot, running up towards his britches.

"We've got tae go!" he heard Rian shout from behind him, still splashing through the waters at the door.

"Ah made a promise, lad," Annis shouted over his shoulder. "You focus oan gettin it open."

"She's deid, Annis," came his reply.

"Ah ken she's fuckin deid," Annis said, as much to himself as to Rian. "She's been deid the hail fuckin time, but like fuck am Ah gonnae let this bastart mak her a puppet ony longer!"

The creature thrashed and a roar echoed across the space, the ice splintering beneath them. Annis took a step back and was nearly bowled over as it careened at him, coming to a halt only as his blade carved through two legs jutting out beneath it and sending it crashing to the floor.

Two more leveraged their way to the ground and it rose, using the blades to claw its way forward across the ice, the face at its front turning towards him just in time for the axe to strike home once more. The blades flailed, one catching his shoulder, and he immediately felt a numb chill begin to spread from the cut.

He parried another swing, but he was losing space and energy, his breaths coming in sharp bursts between dodging the blades and slicing back the limbs that bore them. But there were too many, and with every step he felt the chances of dodging another begin to fall away from his favour.

"Got it!" Rian said, the sound like music to his ears.

"Now lad!" he bellowed, turning and dashing towards Fiadh, hearing the dark beast behind him stumble and scramble to follow. Four steps returned him to her side, dropping the axe and scooping her over one shoulder and dashing for the door where Rian's knife plunged into the rock.

The door ground open, letting the remnants of the torrent pour through, dragging at Annis' feet. He snatched up Rian as the boy slipped and look set to be washed beneath the ice, clutching him close as the waters splashed up and instantly froze at the touch of Caerdrich.

The waves swept up and crashed against the creature the blade had formed, thrown up in giant sheets of ice that wrapped around it and filled the space between them. One hand around Rian, the other around Fiadh, Annis kicked against the stone and shifted his shoulders higher into the space above the water, desperately trying to pull free and into the room beyond.

At his waist Rian reached back and gripped the edge of the doorway, both of them pulling up and out of the path of the water as it continued to cascade down into the path of the beast. The ice piled ever higher, as it cracked before the roar of rage that echoed from within.

One last push and they were free, turning the corner into the space beneath the village, the last of the water held in the space pouring through and freezing on contact with that which it followed. Annis helped push Rian higher to one of the standing stones above the surface before dragging himself free and holding Fiadh's limp form as high as he could as the ice grasped hold of his legs.

The ice rushed through behind them, coating the runes that ran around the entrance of the cavern beyond. Then, just like that, it was over. The water had stopped, the scream of the blade silenced as the wall of stone rolled back into place across the door and barred the ice within. Annis carefully lowered Fiadh to his chest as Rian hopped down from his stone refuge.

"Now, lad," Annis gasped, chest heaving as he finally released his breath. "Time fur us tae get aff this godsforsaken rock."

***

Annis balanced the final stone carefully upon the others, sitting back on his haunches to take in the small cairn they had raised. Many of the crew had taken part, each picking up a piece from the ruins around them to lay down upon one another. Ahar had insisted, claiming it was good luck to say farewell to a departed fey properly.

This would be the only marker for where he had buried Fiadh, digging as deep as he could before the rocks would not move any further. It wouldn't survive the storms that struck the cliffs over winter, and maybe that was for the best.

This time, at least, he hoped she could rest undisturbed.

He sniffed and scratched at the stubble at the back of his head, not quite ready to leave. He didn't really know what she would have thought of it all; she hadn't really been one for sentimentality.

With his elbows resting on his knees, he glanced around at the broken walls and overgrown remnants of old structures and scattered bones. Tur Eumor. She'd mentioned the name so often but never once suggested a return here. After all this time it was still difficult to tell how much of her journey was driven by what she wanted, and what had been only the instructions of the dead god upon her shoulders.

Ahar had known where the ruins lay, of course. Enough tales were told aboard the ships of the abandoned ruin haunted by ancient ghosts. Tales told about this alcove high in the cliffs, littered with the toppled remnants of stone arches and murals of tales he did not know and script he could not read. He wondered where Caerdrich may have been held, where the first sails of the Raven's fleet may have been sighted.

Rian may well have been wondering the same as he wandered back from where he had been exploring the maze of corridors and tunnels burrowing into the rock beyond. Seeing Annis still there, he walked to him and stood at his side, sharing the moment before the cairn.

"Dae ye want tae write her name?" he said at last. "Ah can teach ye how."

Annis snorted. His own name he could manage just fine; it had never occurred to him he might need another's.

"No," he said, standing and groaning at the ache that had settled into his legs from being crouched down for so long. "The bastarts micht recognise it an dig her up. She wid hate that; better tae let her lie."

He turned and began to set off back to the long slope that wound its way down to the bay below, to where Ahar's ship had landed. In the distance, part way down the trail, he could see where Svana and Hengist had settled in to keep watch over the harbour. Neither had made the journey to the top.

As they reached the edge of the fort, beneath the towering gate that formed the sole remaining structure upright on the spur, their boots crunched through broken gravel still littered with the rusted remains of spear and arrowheads.

"Wis it worth it, dae ye think?" Rian asked, picking his way down the slope ahead.

Annis considered that for a moment. How long she had lasted after her death, how long she had fought to reach the isle and what lay within. It had to be worth something, in the end. Maybe she could tell him herself, some day.

"Aye, Ah huv tae," he said. "An Ah mean tae mak sure ae it. Huv ye heard ae the Three Willows, lad? Near the fort at Dun Caraich. Ah think Ah'd like tae go see it."

"Ah huvnae!" Rian couldn't keep the excitement from his voice at the promise of a new adventure, and more tales to be told. "Is it a wild place? Did she tell ye aboot it?"

"Aye, a little, she told me there's much mair tae be found there. Mebbe ye can travel wi me," Annis said, matter-of-factly, deliberately framing it more as a musing than a question.

"Oh Ah would!" The boy practically leapt. "Mebbe Ahar kens aboot it too, mebbe we cuid even tell him some stories when we're back."

"Aye well, *you* ask him, ye're his charge, maybe he'll consider it," Annis barely had time to finish before Rian broke into a run down the slope in his hurry to return to the ship and tell everyone aboard about his new destination. For the first time in a while, Annis smiled.

He paused on the path and took in the view over the glistening waters, wincing as he stretched his chest and let the sun warm him through his tunic. He looked back up to the crag, one last time. Crouched there, in the archway they had left behind, sat a fox, dark eyes fixed on his own.

They stood still there for a time. Finally, Annis felt compelled to give the creature a small nod of acknowledgement. Satisfied, perhaps, it rose from its spot and padded gently away.

THE END

ACKNOWLEDGEMENTS

The last few years have been an adventure – one that has genuinely been one of the best experiences of my life, and it simply would not have been that without the contributions of so many people who helped me along the way. So, some thank yous are needed:

First and foremost, to my family. To my Dad for introducing me to the world of Fantasy as a child, reading Raymond E. Feist's *Magician* to me for the first time; to my brother, whose similar love for the dark and otherworldly helped inspire me; to my Mum for never ever faltering in encouraging me to do what I love.

To my wife, Jude, who I've built a life and home with over the past seven years, without whom I could never have felt the love and safety that has made putting myself out there so easy.

To the team who have put in the time to turn my rough drafts into what you'll read here today – Gillian, Margaret, April, Mara, Syd, Morag, and Matt. Every one of you helped build the book I can be proud of. Especially Matt's running commentary – editing simply would not have been the same without it!

To the readers who had faith in me from the very start.

To the Edinburgh SFF community and Cymera Festival for being my home in the genre.

To Feist, Tolkein, Gemmell, Brooks, Pratchett, McCaffrey, Le Guin, Martin, Sophos and Sapkowski, who built the worlds that inspired me to build my own.

To Scotland, my new home, whose people, landscape and languages are the foundations that the Seann Àite is built on.

To Fahtee, the writing companion I'll miss dearly.

LANGUAGE NOTES AND GLOSSARY

Scots

Scots is a member of the West Germanic family of languages, a descendent of the larger, Indo-European group of languages spoken dominantly in the continent of Europe. It comes from the same route as English, sharing Old English as the common ancestor. The two languages split around the 800s, CE, similar to the divide between Danish and Norwegian, and Scots has been considered distinct from English since the 14th century CE. Scots, and its numerous dialects, are most associated with the Lowlands of Scotland, although it is also spoken widely throughout the Highlands and Islands, alongside Scottish Gaelic, in the North-east, and in the Northern Isles.

Scots dialects often share accents and vocabularies, but these can vary considerably depending on where you are. Most of the Scots across south and central Scotland is mutually understandable, but dialects such as Shetlandic, Ulster Scots and Doric are very different from one another and less accessible to those who do not speak Scots.

In the six stories in *Call of the Black Wing*, a dialect of Scots is spoken by the Àrdish who live in the South of the Seann Àite. This language spoken by the Àrdish is loosely based on the Scots dialects of Stirlingshire in central Scotland, and Galloway in the south-west of Scotland.

Most Scottish people you meet will speak at least some Scots in their day-to-day lives. Words like 'aye', 'wee', and 'bonnie', for example, are internationally recognisable, and have been given an international audience by writers like Len Pennie, whose 'Scots Word of the Day' became a viral hit on social media in the summer of 2020.

Those interested in further exploring Scots can find excellent resources online. Organisations like The Scots Language Centre, Dictionaries of the Scots Language, The National Library of Scotland, and The Scottish Book Trust, have excellent reference tools and signposting to Scots-language writers, books, events, projects and competitions. You can also follow the current Scots Scriever, the Creative Scotland-appointed ambassador of the Scots language, online.

Aboot: about
Ae: of
Aff: off
Affa: awfully; very
Afore: before
Ah: I
Ain: own
Airm: arm
Alang: along
Anither: another
Arenae: aren't
Auld: old
Aw: all; everything
Awa: Away
Aye: yes; then; always
Bairn(s): child (children)
Bi: by
Bide: stay
Bluidy: bloody
Breeks: trousers; underwear
Brocht: brought
Cannae: can't
Cauld: cold

Caw(s): call(s)
Cawed: called
Clootie: cloven hooved
Craw: crow
Cuid/cuidnae: could/couldn't
Daein: doing
Deevil: devil
Dinnae: don't
Drookit: soaked; drenched
Drooned: drowned
Efter: after
Faither: father; priest
Faw: fall
Feart: scared
Fin: find
Frae: from
Fur: for
Gan: going; go
Gie: give
Git: get
Groond: ground
Guid: good
Hail: whole

Hame: home
Haud: hold
Hauf: half
Heid: head
Hoolet: owl
Hoose: house
Hud: had
Hus: has
Huv/huvin: have/having
Huvnae: haven't
Intae: into
Jist: just
Ken: know
Kent: knew
Laird: Lord
Lass: girl; young woman
Lea: leave
Lik: like
Ma: my
Mair: more
Maitter: matter
Mak: make
Mebbe: maybe
Micht: might
Mither: mother
Mony: many
Nae: no
Naebody: nobody
Nicht(mare): night(mare)
No: not
Nocht: nothing
Noo: now
O: of
Oan: On
Ony: any
Onyhow: anyhow
Oor: our
Oorselves: ourselves
Oot: out
Ower: over
Pairt: part
Pish: pee
Pit/pittin: put/putting
Rammy: tussle; fight
Richt: right
Sae: so
Sair: sore
Snaw(s): snow(s)
Soond: sound
Soor: sour
Sooth: south
Staun: stand
Steid: land; foundation; base
Stertit: started
Tae: to
Tak: take
Taucht: taught
Telt: told
Thaim: them
Thegither: together
Thocht: thought
Ti: until
Toon: town
Twa: two
Wee: small

Weel: well
Werenae: weren't
Whaur(ever): where(ever)
Whit: what
Wi: with
Wid: would
Wis: was
Wisnae: wasn't

Withoot: without
Wull/wullnae: will/won't
Ye: you
Yer: your
Yersel: yourself
Yin: one
Yince: once
Yon: those; that

Scottish Gaelic

Scottish Gaelic, or Scots Gaelic as it is otherwise known, is a Celtic language that is considered indigenous to Scotland. It is a Q-Celtic, or Goidelic language, and is related to Irish, spoken across the island of Ireland, and the Manx language from the Isle of Man. It is considered to have been introduced to Scotland from Ireland in the 5th century, CE. Other Celtic languages include Welsh, Breton and Cornish.

Although now considered a language connected to the Highlands and Islands, it was once spoken widely across the whole of Scotland. It has suffered a steady decline in its spoken numbers since the early modern period, which was significantly accelerated by the language being identified as a marker of political dissent and constitutional rebellion, resulting in it being banned by the Crown in 1616, and further suppressed after the failed Jacobite rebellion of 1745.

Scotland's most recent census of 2021 states that just over 1% of Scotland's population, or roughly 60,000 people, can speak Scottish Gaelic today. It remains popular with language learners from among the descendants of the Scottish diaspora who emigrated to Canada, North America, Australia and New Zealand.

Those interested in further exploring Scottish Gaelic can find excellent information from: Bord na Gaidhlig – The Gaelic Language Board; Comunn na Gaidhlig – Scotland's Gaelic

Development Agency; Am Bhaile – a major learning and research resource; An Comunn Gaidhealach – Organisers of the Royal National Mod

You'll also be able to track down useful resources and signposting from The National Library of Scotland, Creative Scotland, The Scottish Book Trust and The Scottish Poetry Library.

Learn Scottish Gaelic

I began my journey learning Scottish Gaelic through Duolingo. It's a great service that really makes picking up a new language easy! If you're up for the challenge you can join almost half a million others taking their first steps learning the language:

https://www.duolingo.com/course/gd/en/Learn-Scottish%20Gaelic

Below is a phonetic guide to the pronunciation of some of the key words from the Scottish Gaelic-speaking culture of the Daoine culture. Some terms originate from other Celtic nations, including Ireland and Wales:

Baobhan Sìth: *Boo-van she*
Caerdrich: *Cy-er-drich* (ch as in loch)
Caoimhe: *Kwee-va*
Cànan: *Caa-nen*
Caoineag: *Khoo-nyak*
Daingead: *Dan-gid*
Daoine: *Doy-nee*
Dìleas: *Jee-las*
Domhnall: *Doe-nal*
Eònan: *Yo-nan*
Fiadh: *Fee-ah*
Fionn: *Fin*

Orlaith: *Or-la*
Ríagan: *Ree-gan*
Rìgh: *Ree*
Sciathán Dubh: *Skee-hawn Doo*
Seanadh: *Cher-nah*
Seann Àite: *Shawn Aa-che*
Sìth: *She*

A translation of some of the terms and creatures included throughout the stories, some of which appear as descriptors at the beginning of the book, in the World of Seann Àite:

Aodann Òir: Gold face.
Caoineag: A weeping banshee, a spirit.
Ceasg: A mermaid or sea goddess.
Ceud mìle fàilte: A hundred thousand welcomes, a greeting.
Cirein-cròin: Large sea monster that feasts on whales.
Eilean Fitheach: Raven Island.
Fáidh bhean: Prophetess or prophet woman.
Fèinne: Warrior-hunter band.
Filidhean: Poet or bard.
Geas: A spell, a debt.
Glaistig: Part human part beast fey.
Ist: Hush or Shhh.
M'eudail: My darling or my treasure.
Samhuinn: All Souls Hallowtide, festival of the coming of winter.
Sciathán Dubh: Black Wing.
Seanadh: A synod or gathering.
Sgian/Sgeanan: Knife/Knives.
Taibhse Ùine: Ghost of time.

ABOUT THE AUTHOR

Tristan Gray was a latecomer to Scotland, moving north from Jersey in 2014.

After years of searching to find the real spark behind his writing, Scotland unlocked it. The rugged landscape and dark history, which also inspired the works of George R. R. Martin, David Gemmell and Elizabeth May, gave new meaning to the fantasy tales of his childhood.

Now, with a new connection to an adopted home driving his work, and inspiration stretching from conventional novels, to graphic novels and games, Tristan is writing tales worthy of the inspiration by the land around him.

NOTES